SEVEN STORIES THAT SHOULD BE MOVIES!

Written By

DAVID GERROLD

"Now what? Are we at war?"

"We gotta do something about all the extras he's eating...central casting is getting suspicious...."

"Ask him, if you don't believe me," my weird brother whispered. "He's kidnapping us."

For the first few hours after the Los Angeles freeway system hardened, most people believed the problem was temporary and that traffic would eventually start flowing again.

"You said I could die painfully...or very painfully."
"No, I said you could take a long time to die—and die very painfully."
"I cooperated with you—"
"Yes, you did. That's why you get to take the long time to die—and very painfully. Very very painfully. Because that was what you chose."

After all these many years, and facing the end of my time on this Earth, I will finally record the true circumstances surrounding the death of Sherlock Holmes.

I am well aware that some may voice the opinion that by writing this account I am dishonoring the memory of my dearest friend, but if I do not make my best effort to relate the facts of what I observed and experienced, then I would be dishonoring myself...

All this and more await you inside...

For Cary Kozlov
with love

CONTENTS

CONTENTS

INTRODUCTION

My first few years on this planet were a time before television. If you wanted to see a picture that moved, you went to a movie theater, so movies were always a special event. Movies were magic. Movies took you away on marvelous adventures. I spent my childhood and my adolescence in large dark rooms, entranced and enchanted.

I took the Stagecoach to Lordsburg. The tornado whisked me off to Oz. I sailed 20,000 Leagues Under The Sea with Captain Nemo. I journeyed to the Forbidden Planet. I watched Kong climb the Empire State Building. I shuddered when Dr. Frankenstein called the lightning down to animate his creation. I lost sleep when The Body Snatchers invaded Santa Mira. I traveled with Sinbad on his Seventh Voyage. I went to Tara and dug for carrots. I stayed out of the water on Amity Island. I didn't get any sleep at the Bates Motel. I sang *La Marseillaise* in Casablanca. I laughed with Buster Keaton as he chased *The General.*

I fell in love with the mechanics of the movies as well—Technicolor and 3D, Cinerama and Cinemascope, six-channel THX sound and high-frame-rate IMAX laser projection—the movies overwhelmed the senses with technology at the service of imagination.

Oh, and I also read a lot. When I couldn't go to the movies, I dived into books. Those were a different kind of adventure. I had to create my own mental movie screen.

Somewhere in there, I wanted more. There were stories I wanted to see, adventures I wanted to have, but no one else was creating them, so I had to.

I began to write.

Today, all these decades later, I'm still writing. I'm still creating my own worlds and exploring them.

When I write I see the movie in front of me. I see the people, I hear their voices, I see the landscapes behind them, it's all there. I see the challenges and obstacles they face, the frustrations and the triumphs.

The story becomes my own private movie, and I sail on a voyage of borrowed emotions. As I assault the keyboard, it becomes real, it becomes an experience—ultimately an experience that can be shared.

Here is an assortment of tales that came alive on my mental movie screen. They were vivid in the writing—and based on reader reactions, they were vivid in the reading. I think they'd make wonderful movies someday, but until then, they can be marvelous movies of the mind.

Make some popcorn and enjoy.

—David Gerrold
Somewhere between the Atlantic Ocean and Hollywood, 2024

Love will find a way.

BUBBLE AND SQUEAK

Written by DAVID GERROLD & CTEIN

Hu Son ran.

He ran for the joy of it, for the exhilaration—for that moment of hitting the wall and breaking through into the zone, that personal nirvana of physical delight. What others called "runner's high." A sensation like flight—Hu's feet didn't pound the ground, they tapped it as he soared through the early morning air.

A bright blue cloudless sky foretold a beautiful day. A sky so clear and deep you could fall into it and never come back. Later, the day would heat up, glowing with a summery yellow haze, but right now—at this special moment—the beachfront basked in its own perfect promise.

Hu usually started early, when Venice Beach was mostly deserted, all sand and palm trees and stone benches, all the store fronts sleeping behind steel shutters. It was the best time to run. Hu liked the crisp air of dawn, the solitude of the moment, the feeling that the day was still clean, still waiting to be invented—before the owners could ruin it with their displays of tacky, tasteless, and vulgar kitsch.

Some of the cafes were open early though, and by the time Hu reached the Santa Monica pier, run its length and then headed back toward home, the morning air was flavored with the smells of a dozen different kinds of breakfast, the spices of all the various cuisines that flourished here.

Heading home, Hu passed other morning joggers. This was a favorite track. Nods were exchanged, or not—some of the runners were lost in hidden music, others in their personal reveries. He recognized most, he'd been running this track for more than a year. He was probably regarded as a regular by now.

The final leg now. He trotted past the last of the brash touristy areas.

Later this strand would teem with summer crowds, exploring the brash souvenir stands, the ranks of T-shirts printed with single entendres, the displays of dreadful art, all the different fortune tellers and street performers, but right now, this community was still lazily awakening, coming back to life at its own pace. There were still the occasional shapeless lumps on the stone benches—the homeless, wrapped up against the chill of the night, waiting for the heat of the day to revive them. Even in July, the morning air still had a bite, with a salty flavor from the grumbling sea.

Hu turned and jogged up the narrow way that pretended to be a street, a block and a half, slowing down only in the last few meters. He hated to stop, hated to drop back into that other pace of life—the faster more frenetic life, where you weren't allowed to run, you had to walk, walk, walk everywhere.

He glanced at his wristband, looking to see where his numbers were today. Not bad. Not his personal best, but good enough. "Probably still stuck on the plateau," he muttered. "Gonna have to push to get off. Just not today."

Hu pushed through the back gate and started peeling off his T-shirt. He liked the feeling of the cold morning air cooling the sweat off his skin. He took a moment to slow down, to let himself ease down into this world, then finally stepped through the door and called affectionately, "Honey, I'm homo—" then headed straight for the shower.

Hu Son didn't just appreciate hot water, he loved the luxury of it. In eighteen months, he'd have his master's degree in cultural anthropology, and after that, he'd go for his doctorate, but already his studies had given him a clear sense of how lucky he was to be living in an age where clean water was taken for granted—and hot water available on demand.

Hu rarely lingered in the shower. Even at this remove, he could still hear his mother banging on the door, shouting, "Leave some for the rest of us!" Old habits endured. Today, however—today was special. So he took his time, soaping up and rinsing, three times over. He closed his eyes, paced his breathing, and allowed himself to sink into his personal contract with himself.

"I am powerful," he whispered. "I am vulnerable," he continued. And smiling, he concluded, "And I am loving." He repeated it a few times, a personal mantra, until it was no longer a declaration, only his renewed experience of himself. And then, one more phrase. "Especially today!"

Opening his eyes, Hu nearly shouted that last. "Because today, I am getting married!"

An electric screech interrupted him—alarm sirens outside. It sounded like the whole city was howling. Like any other Angeleno, anyone who'd lived in the city more than six months, Hu ignored it. It was meaningless noise. Everything was noise, from the daily growl of motorcycles and Asian "rice-rockets" to the nightly screams of drunks and junkies.

Hu turned off the water, and heard James calling from the kitchen. "Hu, you need to get in here!" Something was wrong, James only called him Hu when he was upset. He grabbed a fresh towel and wrapped it around himself. A second towel for his hair and he headed toward the kitchen where James was standing, leaning with his back against the counter, a mug of tea in his hand—but focusing intensely on a small television on the end of the kitchen table. Without looking up, James held out the usual mug of tea for Hu.

Hu took it and pecked his fiancé on the cheek. "What's up, Bubble? What are all the sirens for? Some kind of test? " He didn't wait for an answer, he took his first sip. Chai.... "Ahh." He glanced toward the television. The president was talking.

"Now what? Are we at war?"

"It's Hawaii," said James.

"We're at war with Hawaii?"

"There's been a quake—"

Hu's buoyant mood evaporated. "Oh no. How bad?"

"Both Honolulu and Hilo were hit by tsunamis. Really big—the biggest ever." James turned to Hu. "When did your folks fly out?"

"They didn't. Dad needed an extra day. So they're flying out this evening, they'll catch up with us tomorrow at the hotel."

"No, they won't. And we won't be there either. Honolulu airport is gone."

"Wait. What?" At first, Hu didn't understand. How could an airport be gone? Then he realized what James was telling him. "That's not possible. A whole airport—?"

"And half the city—"

"Oh, shit," Hu said, his mug of tea suddenly forgotten in his hand. "That's—just bad."

On the TV, the president was still talking, a row of grim-faced people stood behind him. Or maybe it was a repeat. The scroll-bar across the bottom of the screen was filled with incomprehensible words. They moved too fast for him to make sense of them. And outside, the sirens still screamed.

"Shit!" said Hu. "All I wanted was one little honeymoon—" He became aware of the sirens again. "And what's all that noise about—? We're not— Shit! What's going on?"

James put down his coffee. He turned to Hu. He took Hu's mug from him. "Squeak. Sweetheart—" His expression was grim. "It's not just Hawaii. It's the whole California coast. The tsunami is headed for us now. We've got maybe three hours before it hits—"

"A tsunami? Here—?"

"A tsunami. Here. A mega-tsunami. Just like the movie, only bigger—"

"But that was only a movie—" Hu stopped in mid-sentence, remembering that movie, that scene.

James Liddle had been SCUBA diving since his teens. After college, he'd set up his own small company, specializing in SCUBA services to local studios. "Underwater? Let it be a Liddle thing. Call us!" Because of his skill, his professionalism, his dependability, and his charming good looks, he was on speed dial for several stunt coordinators.

More than once, James had been called in to teach various film and television actors how to dive safely—or at least look like they knew how to dive safely. More than once, he'd doubled for actors who were too valuable to the studios to be allowed to do their own diving, but he couldn't say who. Most of the bigger shoots involved non-disclosure agreements.

Hu's family had moved from Hong Kong to Vancouver when he was eight, where his father opened a consulting service/business school, where he taught westerners how to do business in China and occasionally set up deals himself.

When Hu was twelve, an aunt he'd never met died of cancer, so his mother came south to Los Angeles to manage her brother's large unruly family, she brought Hu with. As the new kid, as the Chinese kid, and also as the smallest and the smartest in his class, Hu was a target for bullies of all sizes—so his uncle enrolled him into a series of physical activities to build up not only his body, not only his ability to defend himself, but also his self-esteem. Eventually Hu studied karate, judo, Tae Kwan Do, and modern dance. By the time he was nineteen, Hu was earning extra money doing stunts in occasional action films. Though he never doubled for any of the major actors, he was often somewhere in the background—and in one particular picture, a comedy, he'd been featured as one of the dancing ninjas.

James and Hu had met at Culver Studios. A massive team of stunt doubles had been assembled for a disaster picture, another overblown disaster picture, a fantasy of multiple simultaneous disasters—hurricanes, tornadoes, earthquakes, volcanoes, tidal waves, and the return of disco. Everyone knew the picture was going to be awful, it was assumed (though never spoken aloud) that nobody upstairs knew how bad it was—either that, or it was actually intended from the beginning to be a flop, a tax write-off, or perhaps even some bizarre kind of money-laundering. Who knew? The only people who understood Hollywood financing were alchemists, and few of them were ever allowed out of their dungeon laboratories into the light of day.

But on the ground, the money was good. A lot of people had a profitable summer working on the film. As with any big effort, there were sexual relationships, babies started, babies stopped, babies born, and of course, a few divorces and emotional breakdowns, plus a number of life-long feuds begun and exercised, some in private, others in public.

James had worked for seven weeks on various underwater sequences. Hu had come aboard in the last week as a stunt-player, running from the onrushing water. The first few days, there was no actual water. All that was to be added later by a team of talented CGI artists in Hong Kong or New Delhi. Anyone whose name came before the credits would be taking home seven figures and points on the gross, but domestic jobs were shipped overseas in cost-cutting acts of dubious economy. But there was still work to be done locally.

They had to shoot one key scene on a stretch of Wilshire Blvd—from Rodeo Drive to the Beverly Wilshire Hotel—and they had exactly seven minutes out of every thirty when the Beverly Hills Police Department would block off traffic for the director to capture his carefully orchestrated panic, a frenzied evacuation from unseen waves.

Hu's job was to be part of the crowd, running down the street, running through the cars, until he finally hit a specific mark, where he would fall to the ground as if he was being swept under the killing wave—except one of the assistant directors liked his look and gave him a different role, he'd get to be a featured kill.

The camera would start at a high angle, looking up the row of stopped cars, with the distant wave roaring toward the foreground. Hu would come running toward the camera, running between the line of vehicles. The camera would lower, promising a closeup, but just as Hu would arrive at that spot, a panicky driver—another stunt player—would open his driver-side door and Hu would slam into it—and then the wave would inundate them both. The unseen side of the car door was carefully padded, so Hu could hit it hard without injuring himself.

The director liked the shot so much that he decided to add a follow up bit, giving Hu two additional days of work. Finished with the devastation of Wilshire Blvd., the film moved to a Hollywood backlot for specific closeups of death and destruction.

For these shots, the director needed real water, not virtual, and the production relocated to the Paramount lot, the site of the city's second-largest outdoor tank—the Blue Sky Tank, so called because its towering back wall, could be painted to represent any kind of sky, stormy to cloudless, that a director might need. Although the Falls Lake tank at Universal was noticeably larger, it was also more expensive to fill, filter, and heat.

The filmmakers needed a variety of shots with Asian men and women as background players. This was so their Chinese co-financers could edit a somewhat different version of the film for the Asian markets. The Chinese version would include several characters and subplots not in the American version. The joke had initially been whispered in the front office, but of course it eventually filtered down to the production crew as well—the picture would do well on that side of the Pacific, because Asian audiences like to see white people die. But to be fair, a few Chinese extras had to go down too.

Hu didn't care, he was just happy to work. Because of his marvelously startled expression when he'd slammed into the car door, the American director wanted to follow up by showing Hu struggling for a while in real waves before finally (fake) drowning. So Hu spent a hot August morning in the tank, pretending to die—"On this next take, could you look a little more terrified, please?" Dutifully, Hu struggled, gasped, and waved his arms for help that would never come, until finally, disappearing obediently beneath the surface of the foaming water.

The tank was barely four feet at the center, the waves were machine-produced and the foam was a specific detergent. Floating across the entire surface of the water was an assortment of Styrofoam flotsam, representing the debris stirred up by the tsunami. The shot didn't seem very dangerous—at least that's what Hu believed until he was caught unprepared by a sudden sideways push of prop debris, hard enough to punch the air out of his lungs and leave him gasping for air, involuntarily sucking in a mouthful of water, coughing, and choking desperately as he flailed.

James was one of the safety coordinators. He'd dived into the water, swam under the crapberg, grabbed Hu, and pulled him off to the side of the tank, hanging him on the sloping surface and staying with him until he regained his breath. Neither noticed when the director shouted, "Cut! That's the best one yet, we'll use that one! All right, let's get the camera in the water for the dead body shot—"

The director hadn't noticed what had happened, but one of the assistant directors had seen and on James' direct recommendation, quietly added an additional stunt-fee to Hu's paycheck. No one said anything to the film's director—a man notorious for arguing with stunt players about the cost of each gag. He had a bad reputation in the stunt players' community.

After that, James kept an eye on Hu. In the last shot of the morning, Hu had to pretend to be dead, floating face down in the water while a camera crew in dive gear photographed him from beneath. James had been there to coach the camera crew, showing them how to keep their bubbles out of the shot. And that was when Hu, not knowing James' name, had jokingly called him the bubble-wrangler.

Later on, at lunch, they sat opposite each other—the group shared a table under a large craft-service tent that dominated the parking lot next to the commissary.

Hu had a smile. James had a grumpy charm—it was enough.

The two began that long careful dance of curiosity that would eventually, though not immediately, lead to James' little house in Venice Beach. Hu had gotten his nickname—Squeak—from the sound his running shoes made on James' tile floor.

It began as a physical thing, but eventually grew into a relationship. Bed-buddies became roommates. Roommates became lovers. And lovers became—

One strange stormy night, while the two of them were lying side-by-side, staring at the ceiling and listening to the rain, the usually taciturn James had said, "What do you think—"

"About what?"

"About *us*, about stuff—"

Hu was still learning how to listen to James, but this time he heard more than the words. He heard the intention.

"I think…" he began. He rolled onto his side to face James. "I think yes."

"Yes?"

"Yes, you big bubble-wrangler. Yes, I will marry you."

"Oh," said James. "I was going to ask you if we should get a cat."

"Huh—?"

James grinned. "But getting married—that's a good idea too." He pulled Hu close, and kissed him intensely.

The rest was details.

After a few weeks of dithering about plans and schedules, and how much neither of them wanted the gaudy circus of an actual wedding ceremony they decided to just go down to City Hall, do the deed, and then fly to Hawaii for a week. Hu's parents, now together again, were initially more concerned about Hu marrying a Caucasian than a man—but finally decided to show their acceptance by joining them on the island.

The plane tickets were sitting on the kitchen table—and the president's voice was still droning on—now repeating the original broadcast. Outside, the sirens abruptly fell silent. "I suppose—" said Hu, staring at the travel folder, "I suppose—we can get a refund."

And then, it hit him.

The grim expression on James' face said it all.

"Shit! We're going to lose the house, aren't we? Jimmy—?"

"We're gonna lose everything. Everything we can't carry on our backs."

There were only three people in the world who had ever called James Liddle "Jimmy."

The first had been his mother, right up until the day he came out to her. From that moment on, to express her disappointment, he was "James." The second had been Nate Lem, his arrogant overweight fraternity brother—he'd called him "Liddle Jimmy" once too often and gotten a bloody nose for it. After that, he didn't call James anything at all, he left the room whenever James entered.

The third was Hu Son. When he said "Jimmy" it was either affectionate—or important.

James said, "They don't know how big it's going to be, but we've only got three hours to get out of here." He took a breath, his mind racing. "Let's not panic. Let's take a moment and think. It's all about the prep. We gotta get all our cash, all our IDs, all our cards. Um, I have a go-bag, you'll have to pack one. We'll need bottled water and protein bars and—and whatever else is important. Tablets, laptops. All our legal paperwork, especially the insurance stuff—"

Hu Son stood frozen for a moment, his heart racing. "You're serious—oh my god, you are. Oh, god, Jimmy—"

James grabbed him, held him close. "It's okay, it's okay,—we're going to be okay. Let's just take it one step at a time. First step, think—what's important? What are we going to need? What can we leave behind. What do we absolutely need—?"

Hu said, "Um—I don't know. Um—" He looked around the kitchen, mentally sorting through everything, his favorite mug, the pictures on the wall, the beautifully sculpted merman figurine they'd bought on a trip to New Orleans. None of that really mattered. He realized he was naked. He headed toward the room they had christened as "the badroom"—the place where it was good to be bad.

"Um, clothes. I'll grab clothes—"

"Not the big suitcase," James called after him. The one they had packed last night for Hawaii. "Only what can fit in the carry-on. Jeans, hoodies, T-shirts, underwear, socks—"

Hu was already pulling things out of drawers. "Toothbrushes, deodorant, first-aid kit—"

"Right, good." James realized he was still holding a mug of hot tea. He took one last swallow, poured the rest into the sink, and opened the dishwasher to put the mug on the rack. It didn't matter now, did it? But he put the mug on the rack anyway.

"Okay, Jimmy-boy," he said, talking aloud to himself. "What else? The camera, for sure. Eight thousand dollars for an underwater camera rig—I'm not leaving that behind. And the memory cards and batteries. Oh—" He turned to the shelf, grabbed a nearly full box of Zip-Loc plastic bags and followed Hu into the badroom. "Here. Triple bag everything that isn't waterproof."

"You think—?"

"I think we're going to plan for the worst, hope for the best, and prepare for anything. We'll stuff it into dry bags at the office." While Hu pulled on shorts and shirt, James continued sorting through drawers, throwing stuff onto the bed. "Fuck—"

"What?"

"The motorcycle is in the shop—"

"No prob. We'll take the van—"

James had gone to the nightstand. He grabbed a large folding knife from the bottom drawer, and the travel-safe, then the travel bag from the closet shelf. He shook his head. "Bad idea."

"Huh?" Hu stopped, shirt halfway down over his head. His voice came muffled.

"Squeak, you didn't grow up in this city."

"Yes, I did—"

"Not as a driver. We are not gonna be traffic today—"

Hu finished pulling his shirt down. "Then, how—?"

"My SCUBA gear is at the office. I can't leave that behind—" James tossed the travel-safe into the carry-on. He shoved the knife into the pocket of his jeans. "I don't know how bad it's going to be, but I'm thinking there's gonna be a big need for divers after this thing hits. I don't know, but I'll need to be prepared. We can bike to the office, grab whatever gear, and from there, we can head inland. Are you ready—?"

"Half a minute—" Hu stopped, looked around. "Last minute check—"

"I don't want to scare you, but we need to get moving."

Hu debated with himself, finally lost the argument, grabbed his running shoes and shoved them into the carry-on. "I paid too much for these shoes. They're coming." He stopped, looked uncertainly to James. "You think it's gonna be that bad—"

James' looked grim. "You know all those safety courses I had to take, the fire and rescue courses, the Red Cross courses, lifeguard, all the paramedic stuff?"

"Yeah. You did that for the licenses, so you'd be more valuable to the studios—"

"It was part of the job. Stunt safety. Water safety. Everything." He gave the badroom one last check of his own, still talking. "We had to learn about disasters, all kinds, and prepping for survival too. That's why I keep a go-bag under the bed, and why I'm always nagging you to keep one too." He stopped, he took a breath. "I got to see the pictures from the Christmas Tsunami and Fukushima as well, the ones they didn't show on TV. I never told you—but it was...ugly. So we are walking out of here right now and we are heading for the highest ground we can get to the fastest way we can. Is that it? You got everything?" James moved to close the carry-on—

Hu stopped him long enough to toss in two more items, a fist-sized bronze Buddha that he grabbed from the top of the dresser, a wooden cross with a naked Jesus pulled from the wall—and one more, a small resin replica of Mickey Mouse in red robe and blue sorcerer's hat. "Gotta take the household gods, Bubble. Bad luck to leave 'em."

The television was no longer replaying the President. Now, the Mayor of Los Angeles, backed up by a phalanx of City Councilmen and Police, and confronted by a forest of microphones, stood behind a podium, trying to look calm as he laid out the first attempts at emergency evacuation plans. His voice was shaking.

James and Hu stopped long enough to listen, long enough to realize that whatever the Mayor was saying, none of it was going to help them. "Wait," asked James, "Have you eaten? Grab those boxes of protein bars. Eat two of them now. And the water bottles, drink one now. Don't scarf, don't guzzle, bring it along. Come on, let's go."

They almost made it to the door, James with the knapsack holding his expensive new underwater camera, and his go-bag in his left hand—Hu with a knapsack holding water and travel-rations, his carry-on in his right hand.

Hu stopped abruptly. "No! Wait!"

"Now what?"

Hu dropped the carry-on, ran back to the bedroom, came out a moment later, carrying a small black box. "I almost forgot the rings! The wedding rings!" He held the jewelry box high for James to see, then shoved it into his pocket. "Hell or high water, we're getting married."

"Probably high water, but yeah. Hell or high water."

"Promise?"

"Promise. Now let's go—"

James pulled the plastic tarp off the bikes and unlocked them. Despite the high wooden fence around the tiny yard, he still didn't trust the neighborhood's population of permanent transients.

"I'm gonna miss this place," Hu said.

James didn't answer. He just shook his head and led them out to the bike path. They took a moment to pull on their helmets and double-check the bungee cords around their bags, holding them firmly to the racks on the back of the bikes.

"You ready?"

"No. But let's go anyway."

It wasn't a long ride to the office. The beachfront had gone curiously empty—few of the stores were open, several looked abandoned. There were still people here, but not the usual slurry of ambling shoppers and tourists. They saw a few speed skaters with backpacks, several people puffing and pulling oversized wheeled luggage, a scramble of surfers running for their van, and more bicyclists than usual. Most had backpacks and other luggage strapped to their bikes and handlebars. But everyone was moving with purpose. Most were walking fast, trotting, a few were even running. It wasn't a panic—not yet, but the clock was running.

James' company, their company now—Liddle Things—was set in a small white building, three blocks up from the beach. James didn't rent to casual tourists, too much risk, so there was little need to be on the beachfront where rents were noticeably higher. He unlocked the heavy front door, they wheeled their bikes inside and locked the door behind them. James went behind the desk and unlocked the back room where he kept the tanks and masks, the diving rigs, tool belts, and assorted other paraphernalia.

"Shit!" he said, looking around, taking stock, realizing how little he could save. He blew out his cheeks. "We're gonna lose it all, Squeak. More than fifty thousand dollars invested in this stuff—all gone."

Hu wasn't sure if he should say anything. He recognized the mood—the same growling darkness that always came over James when dealing with money, especially a shortage of it. "The insurance—?"

"Won't cover the half of it—" James shook his head. "No—there's just no way to save, no fucking way." He sighed in resignation. "All right, let's get the bike trailers. You take the new one, it's lighter. You attach, I'll do triage." He began pulling things off the wall and out of lockers.

Hu knew the drill. The bike trailers were convenient ways for cyclists to carry surfboards, SCUBA gear, camping gear, or even a few bags of groceries. They attached easily. He and James used them a lot, for almost any trip less than three miles. Hu didn't mind driving, he could listen to his music, but James hated getting behind the wheel, because he found urban traffic frustrating—the poor behavior of other drivers made even the shortest outing feel like a death-defying exercise.

James talked as he worked, annotating every decision with a justification. "I'm gonna want my wet suit and my new dive computer—$1500 that thing cost, it does everything but make coffee, and I still haven't had a chance to use it. I'm gonna need it if there's rescue work. You grab those spare tanks and put them on your trailer. And the camping bag. I'm afraid we're gonna need it. I'll take the main tanks and the portable compressor. I might have to wear the rig. Hmm, harness, backplate, maybe I should wear a couple tanks too? What else? A pro-grade mask—no the one with the dual lamps, fins, tool belt—I can hang the belt on the handlebars, anything that isn't waterproof goes into the dry bags, we can put those in our knapsacks, everything else in the travel case, that'll go on the trailer. Oh, and grab those new headlamps too—"

Hu laughed. "We're gonna look like a couple of underwater bag ladies—and you with the SCUBA gear on your back—"

"Not gonna leave it—"

"Jimmy—? Isn't it all too much to carry? All this weight?"

"If it is, then we've both wasted a fortune at the gym. And all that damn healthy eating." James paused, got serious. "Squeak, this is my career. Just like your new expensive laptop. I need this."

"You don't have to convince me, Bubble. Give me whatever you need me to carry. We'll do it."

They finished quickly. Less than fifteen minutes.

"Is that it?"

"It's gonna have to be." James looked to his partner, his tone abruptly thoughtful. "We'll take the bikeway—that'll be the fastest. The only traffic will be other cyclists. But only to 26th street, or Bundy if we can, then we'll turn north. I think if we can get to Sunset, we can go up one of the canyons to Mulholland, maybe take it to Topanga, get down into the valley that way—"

"And from there?"

"I dunno. Who do we know in the valley with a guest house? Or a backyard big enough for the tent?"

"Whatsisname—that writer who's always calling you?"

"Mr. Source Material? Maybe. What about your cousin?"

"Maybe. If you're willing to put up with my uncle—"

"Yeah, there's that."

"Maybe if we can get to Pasadena, there's Chris and Mark—"

"Melinda has a guest house—"

"So does—never mind. We have options. First thing, let's get out of here." James pointed to the bikes. "Okay, safety check on the bikes. Is everything secure?"

Three minutes to double-check all the tie-downs and bungee cords, and they were ready to leave, but at the door, they paused. James put his hand on Hu's arm. "Okay, Squeak, we've got two and a half hours. We can do this. Ten miles an hour, easy-peasy. We could get all the way to Union Station if we had to. All we have to do is pace ourselves. The idiots are going to ride like crazy and exhaust themselves before they even get to the 405. Just keep thinking of Mike Sloan's teddy bear—"

"Huh?"

"Don't you remember? Sloan's teddy wins the race—"

"Oof. Remind me again why I agreed to marry you?"

"Because I'm the daddy, that's why." James grinned.

"Except when it's my turn."

They pushed the bikes outside, first Hu, then James behind him. Hu started to plug in his headphones, but James stopped him. "You don't want to do that—"

"Shouldn't we listen to the news—?"

"Aren't you scared enough already?"

"Oh." Hu shoved the earphones back into his knapsack, glanced at his wristband, looked west toward the beach. Beyond a lonely palm tree, the horizon looked peaceful and bright. Hard to believe a disaster was rising somewhere beyond. "It's gonna be hot today," he said. "Especially inland."

"Yeah," James agreed, behind him. "Gonna need the extra water."

Hu turned back to him. "All right. I'm ready."

With the trailer attached, his bike was loaded heavier than he expected. He had to take a running start to catch up to James, but they were on their way, heading east.

It wasn't far to the bikeway, less than a mile, but they weren't the only ones who'd had this idea. The bikeway wasn't crowded, not at first, but the farther they rode, the more cyclists joined them—a steady stream of riders peddling inland with a grim determination. Every few minutes, a light-rail train passed them, howling east on elevated tracks that paralleled the bikeway. Despite himself, Hu looked up—the railcars were already crowded. James had guessed right.

"Sloan's teddy," called James. "Just like one of your marathons."

"Ha ha," said Hu. He focused on his pace, using the same steady counting exercise he used when he ran in the morning. Occasionally, other cyclists passed them at a furious pace, almost panicky. Not wise—but their choice.

Two miles in and the bikeway was filled. Most of the traffic was other cyclists in professional gear, helmets and backpacks, but sometimes just ordinary people on bicycles—sometimes whole families pedaling in a group. Most were wearing knapsacks, or had cases strapped to the back of their bikes or hanging from their handlebars. A few, like James and Hu, had well-loaded bike trailers.

Occasionally people passed them, a few speed-skaters, and motorized skateboards as well. Once a couple of assholes on motorcycles came roaring past. Hu stood up on his pedals to look ahead. If the bikeway kept filling up, kept getting more and more crowded, those motorcyclists weren't going to have much of an advantage.

By the time they reached 26th street, traffic on the bikeway had slowed to a sluggish crawl—and east of the avenue, there were so many cyclists ahead of them, riding was impossible. People had to dismount and walk their bikes. A few groaned in annoyance, a couple others shouted angrily, some muttered to themselves, but most just kept pushing along. Hu and James dismounted and walked their loaded bikes side-by-side.

More frustrated riders piled up behind them, but no fights had broken out. There was still plenty of time. Most people were helping each other. One woman was holding another's bike while the first one changed her baby's diaper. Elsewhere, a professional-looking rider had stopped to patch a flat tire for a crying teenage girl. Another was helping an uncertain middle-aged man put a loose chain back on his bicycle's gears.

It wasn't a panic, not yet. It was still an exodus. Not disorderly, but it wasn't moving fast enough. At this pace…James looked to Hu, shook his head, leaned over and whispered, "Time for an alternate route."

It took them nearly ten minutes to work their way to the next opportunity to exit the bikeway, Cloverfield Avenue. They weren't the only ones abandoning the narrow route. Some of the cyclists were turning south, most were turning north.

James and Hu went north. Just on the other side of Colorado Blvd., there was a good-sized parking lot. The lot was already emptying of cars, the last few people driving away frantically. James pointed and Hu followed.

They pulled themselves out of the steady stream of people remounting their bikes. Hu pulled out the first water bottle, took two swallows and passed it to James, who did the same, then passed it back. A familiar ritual. Having done that, they both pulled out their phones. Hu checked The Weather Channel—the temperature was already above 80 and still rising. Okay, not unexpected.

James went to Google Maps, then he tapped for Waze. Both were bad news. Red lines showing heavy traffic everywhere, some routes already painted with stretches of black Absolute gridlock was beginning. But at least the bikes were moving here—in the bike lanes and on the sidewalks, and even between the long rows of cars. The automobile lanes were barely inching forward.

"It's crowding up faster than I expected. Apparently people are taking this thing serious. All right, we'll head north here—" James started to push his bike forward again.

Hu said, "Wait."

"What?"

"I've got a text."

"Forget it—"

"It's from Karen—" A series of messages rolled up the screen. Hu looked to James. "She's at work. She needs someone to pick up Pearl."

"Can't she do it?"

"She's doing triage in the E.R. She couldn't get out, even if she wanted to. The streets there are gridlocked."

"Pearl can't get a ride?"

"The neighbor who promised left without her." Hu read the next text. "What an asshole. Apparently, her cats were more important."

"There's no one else."

Hu kept scrolling through Karen's frantic notes, his expression darkening. "Doesn't look like it. Karen says it's desperate. Pearl is trapped. She can't get an Uber or a Lyft, Ride-Share is down, Access isn't picking up. The Fire Department is moving all their equipment eastward. She tried calling for an ambulance, but—" Hu lowered his phone. "James, we can't leave her there. We gotta get her."

James made a razzberry of disgust. "Fuck. The problem is...that damn wheelchair."

"Can we pull her—?"

"I'm thinking—" A heartbeat. "The wheelchair is light enough—it's Pearl. She's not exactly a spring potato. Fuck."

"James—"

"I know, I know—" He puffed his cheeks, blew out his breath, exasperated. "Yeah, we have to try. Uh...all right, lemme think." He went to scratch his head, fingers fumbling across his helmet instead. "Fastest way there—"

James made a decision. "Okay. Forget Sunset. Forget the mountains. We'll go up to Santa Monica, it's the next one after Broadway. Then..." His voice tailed off as he plotted a route. He turned to Hu. "It's a long slog. If Pearl can get herself down to the street, we'll figure something out. We might have to lose one of the trailers, I dunno, I'll do the math in my head while we ride."

"Can we make it in time?"

James looked at his watch. "Yeah, I think so."

"Can we get her to high ground? Can we get us to high ground—?"

"Straight north up Fairfax would take us to Laurel Canyon. Might be high enough. I don't know. That's not a great route, but...fuck, I don't know." James shook his head. "Worse comes to worse, I don't know, we might be far enough inland. Even a ten story building might be tall enough. Maybe. I don't know. This is fucked. Let's just do it. Come on, we've been through worse—"

"No we haven't," said Hu. "*This* is the worst." But he was already tapping a message into his phone. "We're on our way." He sent it to both Karen and Pearl, shoved his phone back into his pocket and grabbed his handlebars. "Okay, let's go."

James and Hu pedaled east on Santa Monica Blvd., weaving their way through a slow-moving mass of cars and people. But at least it was moving. Both sides of the avenue were headed inland. There was no westbound traffic. It helped—a little.

It was a business district here, but none of the stores were open. There were a few broken windows, but not many. People were determinedly walking east, most of them turning north at suitable intersections. Some of the cyclists were walking their bikes because there wasn't enough room to ride. James and Hu had dismounted as well and were now walking their bikes side-by-side.

The exodus was serious now. Even the motorcyclists were having trouble maneuvering through the impatient lines of automobiles. It was turning into a crush. The inevitable speed-skaters darted everywhere, sometimes nearly colliding with unwary pedestrians. Occasionally, they saw an ambulatory bundle of rags doggedly pushing an overloaded shopping cart. Even the homeless were leaving. And once, a pair of hipsters rode by on hoverboards.

A woman behind them started complaining loudly—making pointed remarks about their overloaded bikes and bike trailers. James muttered a curse under his breath, but shook his head and kept pushing forward. Hu looked over to him. "Are you okay?"

"I will be. Are you?"

"I'm … not complaining," said Hu. He had a thought. "I'm wondering. Do you think maybe Pearl's building might be tall enough? If we could get her to the roof—"

James went silent, thinking about it. Finally, "I wouldn't want to risk it, would you? It's an old building, wood frame, it might not survive the impact. It's not just the water, it's all the crap being pushed by the water. It'll hit like a horizontal avalanche. And even if the building survives the impact, she could be stuck up there for days before anyone could get to her. And the damn wheelchair is another problem. So, no."

"It was just a thought. I was worried about the time."

James looked at his watch. "We're okay." He pointed. "We're almost to the freeway. Once we get to the other side, it should be easier going. Well, could be. We'll burn that bridge when we get to it." James pushed his bike ahead, effectively ending the conversation.

The 405 freeway divides the LA Basin. It separates the western and southern communities from the rest of the megalopolis, as it winds south, vaguely paralleling the coast. Parts are elevated highway, parts are sunken, but all of it is a ten-laned barrier to traffic trying to move to and from the coast. The inadequate and infrequent underpasses and bridges that cross the 405, its on- and off-ramps, are bottlenecks that can backup traffic for blocks even on a good day.

This was not a good day. Gridlock spread outward from every crowded access ramp and crossover. In a few hours the entire length of freeway—from the Sepulveda pass all the way to the Mexican border would be gone. But right now it was a major obstacle.

Where Santa Monica Blvd. crossed under the 405, several LAPD motorcycle officers were calmly working to unravel the chaos at the underpass. Surrounded by frantic and desperate drivers, they were doing their best. They were scheduled to withdraw at least twenty minutes before impact—if they could get out. That wasn't certain anymore.

At the mayor's desperate orders, both sides of all major surface streets were now mandated for eastbound and northbound vehicles, especially through the underpasses and across the bridges. Both sides of the 110 and the 405 were now handling northbound traffic.

It wasn't enough.

Police and news helicopters circled overhead. Other choppers, all kinds, were shuttling east and west, their own small contributions to the evacuation. The apocalypse was being televised. Further south, at LAX, every plane that could get off the ground was heading inland, some with passengers sitting in the aisles.

James and Hu came to a stop on the sidewalk just past the Nu-Art theater—an ancient movie house that had survived for more than nine decades. For most of its history, it had been a cinematic sanctuary, un-spooling an assortment of independent films, obscure foreign dramas, various cult classics, assorted Hollywood treasures, a variety of otherwise forgotten and questionable efforts, occasional themed festivals, and the inevitable midnight screenings of crowd-pleasers like The Rocky Horror Picture Show and other film-fads of the moment. In a few hours, it would be closed forever.

James pointed ahead—the underpass was gridlocked. The officers had blocked off the northbound onramps with their motorcycles, and were now directing traffic to use the southbound offramp instead, their only remaining access to a northbound escape, but even that was moving slowly. Too slowly. Even with cars crawling along the shoulders of the freeway, the 405 just couldn't accept any more traffic.

Los Angeles had not been designed for an evacuation—not on this scale. No city had ever been designed for such a massive torrent of people, an exodus of unprecedented size, a titanic crush of desperate humanity.

And yet, somehow, it moved.

Not fast enough. Not nearly fast enough. But it moved.

Some of these people would survive—if they could just get over the hill into the San Fernando Valley, or even halfway up the Sepulveda pass. There was time.

Except—

—except for the angry shouting.

Which was why James had stopped.

An old green van, a decrepit-looking Ford Windstar, hastily overloaded, had collided with a silver Lexus, a fairly new model. Both vehicles were in the middle of the road, blocking three separate lanes. A frightened woman sat in the passenger seat of the Lexus.

Two desperate drivers had left their vehicles to confront each other—neither had given way, both had tried to force their way forward, only to demonstrate that specific law of physics that two objects cannot occupy the same space—so now they were screaming at each other in near-incoherent rage.

A crowd of other drivers surrounded them, also screaming, demanding that they move their fender-crunched vehicles out of the way. Snippets of conversation echoed off the underpass walls—

"Get your fucking cars out of the way—"

"Not until I get this asshole's insurance—"

"It's your goddamn fault, I want your insurance—"

"There's no time for that, you assholes—"

"Will both you idiots move your goddamn cars—"

"Daddy, I wanna go home—"

"The police are right there—"

"Good! They can arrest this jerk—"

"Just please move it to the side, so the rest of us can get by—"

"Move it where?! We're boxed in by the rest of you—"

"I don't back up for assholes—"

"It's okay, I do—"

"I'm not moving till he gives me his insurance information—"

"We don't have time for that, and your piece of shit Ford isn't worth it anyway. You're just trying to hold me up, and I won't stand for it—"

"That's just the attitude I'd expect from a spoiled brat manbaby—"

"Guys, please! This isn't helping anyone—"

"Daddy, I gotta pee—"

"If you won't move it, I will—"

"Touch my car and you'll regret it—"

"Why don't the police do something—"

"Okay, enough is enough. You're gonna move this shit outta the way now—"

That last was a burly member of the sasquatch family—red-faced, long-haired, scruffy-beard, flannel shirt, and the kind of expression that usually stopped all conversation.

"You gonna make me—?"

"Officer, over here! Please!" That was a woman shouting.

Two of the officers were busy trying to stop impatient drivers from backing up onto the south-bound onramp, intending to join the north-bound exodus that way. Two more were struggling to keep the evacuation orderly—one had to dodge sideways as an impatient driver forced his way around the sluggish line of cars ahead of him. They had more immediate priorities than the argument in the underpass. But the back-up of cars was growing, and so was the angry crowd.

From his position, at the ramp, one of the officers waved furiously at the drivers of the two vehicles, urging them to get back into their vehicles and move, but the two men were too angry, each so focused on winning this argument they couldn't see past their own rage. It looked like violence was inevitable.

"Can we get past that?" asked Hu.

"I don't know," said James. "I'm wondering if we should try to go around it." He pulled out his phone to study the map again. Where was the next closest underpass? Half a block north. Ohio Avenue.

The immediate problem would be just getting across the street. Santa Monica Blvd. was gridlocked. The closest cross street was Sawtelle, just on the other side of the Nu-Art theatre. Maybe they could thread their way around the stalled cars—

A sudden shift in sound, a scream of incoherent rage, both James and Hu whirled to see—

Sasquatch was now waving an aluminum baseball bat. "You gonna move it—?" This was followed by a well-aimed blow. The right-front headlight of the Lexus shattered in the impact. "You gonna move it now—?"

"What the fuck are you doing—?"

"Giving you a reason to move it—"

"Fuck you! You're gonna pay for that—"

"Let's make it two—" Another swing of the bat, it bounced off the left headlight. A second swing shattered it. "And three—" The windshield shattered next. The woman inside flinched and tried to scramble across the seat.

"Stop it, goddammit! Stop it!"

"Move it and I will!"

The driver of the Lexus scrambled into the car, but instead of starting the engine, he came out waving a—

"Gun! He's got a gun—!" The crowd scattered. The panic rippled outward. At its spreading edges, people ran or ducked, hiding behind the most convenient cars.

And just as quickly, three of the police positioned themselves, flattened across the hoods of several stalled vehicles, guns drawn, and pointed, held steady in both hands, red laser dots wavering on the Lexus driver. The lead officer shouted, his voice electrically amplified—"Drop it! Drop the gun! Now!"

Confused, the Lexus driver turned, staring from one officer to the next. "But he... he smashed my car." He waved the gun around, as if to point it, but Sasquatch had conveniently disappeared.

"Drop the fucking gun! Now, goddammit!" Not exactly standard LAPD procedure, but the pressures of the situation were getting out of hand.

"I just want to get out of here!" the Lexus driver wailed.

"Drop the gun and move your car!"

"No, no, no!" The man insisted. "I didn't do anything! He hit me! He has to move!" Sensing that he was blocked in, he turned around and around, pointing the gun from one driver to the next. "Everybody get out of my way! Let me out of here—" He looked desperate, he was shredding into incoherency—

"Last warning! Drop the gun. Drop it. Now."

"Please! Just let me out of here—"

"Oh fuck," said James, quietly. "They're gonna shoot him."

Hu put his hand on James' shoulder and pushed. The two of them flattened to the sidewalk together, their bikes falling beside them.

Three quick gunshots, followed by a beat of silence—and then the screaming started. "Oh my god, my god!" And: "You didn't have to do that—!" Followed by orders from the cops. "You, move that Lexus. Move it now! You, back up! You, follow him!"

But there was no organization. There were too many voices. There was too much screaming, and too many people pulling in too many directions at once—

And a couple more gunshots, coming from another direction—

James half rose up to look, then quickly lowered himself back to the sidewalk. Once, a long time ago, he's seen a riot start. It was ugly.

This was worse.

James looked to Hu. "Let's go back."

Tentatively, they levered themselves back to their feet, both a little shaken. Hu touched James' arm and pointed. The building behind them had a fresh hole in one of its windows.

James smiled weakly, nodded, pointed west.

Hu hesitated. "Shouldn't we see if anyone needs help?"

"Pearl needs us more. Let's get out of here."

Hu hesitated, uncertain.

James touched his elbow and said quietly, "Triage."

Hu didn't like the thought. But James was right. He followed.

Somehow, despite the narrow sidewalk, despite the people around them, they got their bikes turned around and headed a half block west to Sawtelle.

They weren't the only ones. Drivers who had gotten out of their cars to see what the blockage was at the underpass were now climbing back into their vehicles and turning north onto Sawtelle. James and Hu threaded their way across the intersection and remounted. There was just enough room on the sidewalk to pedal north.

It wasn't far to Ohio Ave, a block and a half. But when they reached the intersection and looked right, they came to a stop, both at the same time.

This underpass was blocked even worse. It was narrower and too many cars were trying to get through it. The avenue was backed up with cars arriving from the west, but adding to the gridlock, traffic from Sawtelle was also trying to merge into the sluggish flow.

"Can we get through there?" asked Hu.

James considered it. There was a cluster of motorcyclists blocking the sidewalk that went through the underpass. It didn't look like they were getting through. Something blocking them on the other side, maybe—?

"No," said James. "Too narrow." That was the most convenient excuse, but he was still thinking about the violence they'd just escaped. This was another potential disaster—another riot looking for a place to happen. He pointed north instead. "Let's see if we can get across. We'll take Wilshire." There weren't any other options.

They pushed their bikes forward. Most of the going was single-file, but there was still room to make it through. Despite their urgency, most of the drivers here were leaving almost enough space for the two cyclists to navigate carefully across the intersection. Their bike trailers bumped a few fenders where they had to push between the lanes, but aside from one red-faced future stroke victim who shouted at them for blocking his nonexistent way forward, most drivers pretended to ignore them.

And then they were on Sawtelle again, pedaling into the Veterans Administration Healthcare Center. Where Sawtelle dead-ended inside the campus, before a cluster of shining white buildings, there was a concrete path cutting directly north, and it was wide enough for them to pedal. They weren't the only cyclists with this idea, a few others raced past them. But James and Hu stopped to walk their bikes because of the foot traffic—the old men in bathrobes and pajamas and shapeless sagging trousers.

In the rising heat of the July day, these ancient men trudged steadily north. They were clusters of fragile age, old but determined. Most of them were using canes or struggling with walkers, a few pushed others in wheel chairs, a few were coming with their IV stands, but all of them were heading slowly and deliberately toward Wilshire. They smelled of old age and soap.

These were the leftovers, the forgotten warriors, the heroes of yesterday—the abandoned ones, abandoned one more time. No one had remembered they were here. There was no evacuation plan for them. The buses had never arrived, they'd been commandeered for the schoolchildren and for anyone else who could scramble aboard.

Maybe, when they reached the boulevard, someone would give them a ride. Or maybe they would just end up as a few more bodies in the long line of hopeful old men gathering along the side of the road, more zombies for the frightened drivers to ignore.

James and Hu passed them as quickly as they could—they tried hard not to meet their eyes, tried hard not to see their frail bodies and watery expressions. But one of the men stopped James with an outstretched hand. "You go. You go on, get out of here. Go and live. Find someone to love and live a glorious life." Another added, "But tell them about us. Tell them to remember. Please—" And a third, "Tell them how we were forgotten, betrayed, abandoned—" And a fourth, "And tell them to go fuck themselves too—"

Both James and Hu nodded and promised. "We will, we will."

They nodded and said yes to everything, they shook the trembling hands of those who reached out to them—and then they pushed on, a hard lump in their throats. They wanted to do more, but what could they do?

And then one of the old men called, "Jimmy, is that you?" Hearing his name, James stopped. Force of habit. He turned and looked.

A frail spectre, dragging an IV stand, came wobbling, hobbling across the grass. "Jimmy, it's grampa."

No, it wasn't. All of James' grandparents had passed a decade earlier. But still, he was startled enough to stop and stare.

Another old soldier came shuffling up. "It's all right, pay him no mind. He's—he doesn't know who anyone is anymore. "

But grampa had grabbed Jimmy's arm. "I knew you'd come," he said. "I told them, I told them you would come to see me—"

The other man shook his head. "Jimmy died. A long time ago. But he doesn't believe it. Or he forgets."

James said, "Hu, hold my bike." He dismounted, put his arms around the self-appointed grampa. "I love you, grampa. I'm sorry I waited so long to come and see you. I missed you so much. I have to go now. Your friends will take care of you. But I have to go. They need me at the... at the station, okay?"

The old man didn't want to let go. His frail hands trembled as he tried to hang onto his long-lost grandson, but Jimmy pulled away anyway, and finally grampa said, "Okay, Jimmy. Okay. You be a good boy now. You tell your ma you saw me, okay?"

"Okay, grampa." Jimmy gave the old man a quick hug, then pulled away just as quickly. He took hold of his bike again—

James mounted and they pedaled on.

"That was... that was a good thing you did."

"Triage," said James. "Goddammit."

Hu didn't answer.

They traveled past the line of old men, castoffs in a younger world, all of them struggling in the rising heat. As they turned right to go up the ramp to Wilshire boulevard, even more old and frail men were gathering in a crowd. Some of them were weeping. Others were stepping into the traffic lanes, knocking on the windows of slow-moving vehicles. Others stood silently on the sidewalk, sunken in despair, gaunt and resigned in the heat of the day. Two looked like they were unconscious on the sidewalk. Here and there, car doors were opened for them—but not enough.

It was a nightmare.

They pushed past. Most of the old men ignored them. They were just two more bodies in the passing parade of people who couldn't or wouldn't help them.

A couple of the old men were shouting obscenities—mostly at the cars, but a few directed their streams of abuse at James and Hu. One hollered at Hu, "That's right, you dirty Jap, run away, run away—or we'll get you again like we did at Pearl Harbor—"

"I'm Chinese," said Hu, but the old man didn't care, or didn't hear. Hu followed James, they pushed on.

There were officers working the underpass here too, but without the same frustration and confusion that they had seen a mile further south at Santa Monica Blvd. The officers here were also directing traffic up onto the southbound lanes of the 405, pointing cars up the offramp, shouting and waving them forward, even demanding they use that side of the highway as an additional northbound escape. Some drivers looked reluctant, this felt *wrong*, but they followed the officers' directions and headed up the offramp anyway

The traffic inched along slowly, jerking spasmodically, filling every spare foot of space—but it moved—only a little at a time, but it *moved* with a single-minded purpose. If these vehicles could get far enough north, far enough up the Sepulveda pass, these drivers would likely survive.

James and Hu lowered their heads and pushed themselves forward as quickly as they could. They blinded themselves to the naked desperation and pushed east, somehow getting through the traffic at the ramps and into the cooling shadow of the underpass. They didn't linger, the place smelled of fumes. Finally, they were out to the other side and across Sepulveda.. They threaded their way through the cars on this side.

When they came to the giant Federal building on the south side of the boulevard, a massive white monolith Hu looked to James, an unspoken question in his glance. They looked to the crowds gathering at the structure, surrounding its entrances, including another legion of old men. James shook his head, an unspoken reply. Bad idea. Not gonna be enough room for everyone... and still too close to the shoreline.

They pushed on.

A long row of tall buildings lay ahead of them, not quite skyscrapers in the modern sense, but tall enough to be imposing—tall enough to look like safety. Already, the foot traffic was getting thick, businessmen, residents, students from the UCLA campus, a mile north—the buildings were filling up. The top floors would be crowded.

When James and Hu finally got to the intersection of Westwood and Wilshire Blvds, they hit a new obstacle—a huge gaping hole in the ground that was the excavation for the Westwood terminus of the Purple Line, the latest extension to the Los Angeles subway system.

If it had been completed, if the tracks had been laid and energized, the city could have evacuated another half-million people. But today, it was a gaping promise. Unfinished. Empty. And shortly to be flooded, inundated, and scraped away by a bulldozer of debris—

James stopped himself.

Don't go there. Just don't.

He checked Google Maps, nodded, pointed to the right. "We'll take the side streets."

A block south, along Wellworth Avenue, they could easily pedal east again. It was a residential area, mostly one or two-story houses. Traffic was thick here, but not impossible—just a steady stream of cars, pushing slowly east. James and Hu kept to the sidewalks, there weren't many other riders here and they made the best progress since leaving Venice.

James glanced at his watch. They were behind schedule, but there was still time. They were going to make it.

If there were no more shootings.

They followed the side streets —Wellworth, Warner, Ashton, Holmby—past the worst of the jams, and then they were back on Wilshire. It cut easily through the golf courses, but it was an uphill slog and the bikes and trailers were heavily loaded.

Halfway up the hill, Hu called for a stop. He opened a fresh water bottle, drank half of it, and passed it to James, who finished it… and tossed the bottle over the fence onto the green. "Always wanted to do that."

"Jimmy—?"

"Yeah?"

"It's awfully hot."

"Yeah—" But he knew that wasn't what Hu meant. Their shirts were sweat-stained, they were both damp with the effort of pedaling with the extra weight. The uphill part was just an excuse to stop.

"The bike-trailers," said Hu. "The tanks—"

"I know—"

"They're holding us back—"

James fell silent. He took a deep breath, then another, tried to compose himself. Hu was frustrated. And when Hu was frustrated, then

James got frustrated, because he had to talk Hu down. But this was different.

"I think we can make it."

"I don't think I can."

"We have to try." James pointed. "This part is all uphill. Once we get to the top, it'll be an easy ride down the other side."

Hu looked past James, up toward the crest. It really wasn't that far. He knew he could make it—but it wasn't the top of the hill he was worried about. It was the rest of the distance, to Pearl's house and then to safety. He felt overwhelmed, almost to the point of tears.

"Jimmy, you know I'd never ask you to—"

James leaned his bike against the fence, went quickly back to Hu. "Squeak, I know, you wouldn't ask unless there was no other way. And it's the same for me. I wouldn't ask you if I could see any other way. But I don't think we can leave any of this behind." He stopped himself. "Wait—"

Beside them, the traffic chugged slowly past. James ignored the curious stares of several small children leaning out the open windows of a passing SUV.

"Okay, look," James said. "Let's put only our must-haves into our backpacks, okay? All our paperwork, money, phones, your computer, all the stuff we can't leave behind. The stuff in the dry bags, right? And then let's see how much farther we can get with the rest. Is that okay?"

Hu nodded reluctantly. It was a concession. Not the one he wanted, but he had to trust James—James was the better planner. He started thinking what he could repack. It wasn't much. He'd already put the most important things in his knapsack. Some of the weight was water bottles. He felt damp and sweaty all over. For a moment, he dreamt of the long luxurious shower he could take when they got back home.

Then he realized he would never see that shower again. Abruptly he realized he had to pee.

Hu looked around, they were at least a mile from anything that might serve as a rest stop—the hell with it—he turned to the chain-link fence, lifted up the left side of his shorts and let loose a personal torrent, splashing at the fence. James joined him, yanked down his own shorts, and for a moment, their two streams arced toward the silent green of the golf course.

Hu giggled.

"What?"

"Don't cross the streams—"

"You see too many movies."

"You watch 'em with me."

"Hey!" a distant voice called. "Stop that!"

They looked through the fence. Three middle-aged men in bright-colored shirts and pants were playing golf, totally oblivious to the evacuation. One of them was waving his golf club angrily at them.

"Didn't you hear the news?" James called. "There's a tsunami coming in."

"Don't you believe it," one of them called back. "Just another drill."

"Fake news," muttered the second.

The third said, "I'd rather die golfing than running—"

"Have it your way," said James, zipping up his pants, and suddenly doubting. What if they were right—?

No. They were wrong, he wished he could believe them, but they were wrong—and in a couple hours, they'd find out how wrong. He wondered if they'd make it to the 18th hole in time, shook his head in disbelief, turned back to Hu. "Idiots."

Hu smiled weakly. "Suddenly, I don't feel so stupid."

"Yeah. Let's get out of here."

Refreshed by their rest, rehydrated by the water, they made it to the crest of the hill, then half-coasted, half-pedaled down the other side.

They continued east on Wilshire Blvd., past the Beverly Hilton Hotel to where it criss-crossed Santa Monica Blvd. Navigating the wide diagonal intersection with Santa Monica wasn't as hard as James feared. Traffic was inching along here, but there was still room to thread the bikes between the ranks of cars.

Wilshire was a straight line east from there, a gilded belt around the waist of Beverly Hills, lined with elegant palm trees. Much of the traffic here was turning north at every opportunity, aiming for Benedict Canyon, Coldwater Canyon, any higher ground at all. A lesser but steady stream of vehicles pushed eastward and inland. At an average speed of ten miles per hour, there was still a chance for most of them to survive.

Overhead, the sky was filled with more helicopters than either James or Hu had ever seen. Police, news, rescue, fire, military, and private services as well. Some were monitoring, others were evacuating.

Here, the sidewalks were wide enough, they had room to ride—they werean incongruous sight pedaling through the most elegant district in Los Angeles. Elegant—and doomed. All the surrounding communities that kept these businesses thriving would be gone in less than two hours.

As James and Hu pedaled steadily east, they heard a steady drone of chattering voices leaking from the radios of the vehicles they passed, bits of audio flotsam that refused to assemble into any kind of coherent narrative.

Here, the pedestrian traffic was lighter. There were other cyclists on the road and on the sidewalk, but not a lot. Motorcycles growled between the rows of cars. Three people on Segways rolled past them. And surprisingly—for this neighborhood anyway—they even saw a pair of homeless women, determinedly pushing their overloaded shopping carts eastward. There were buses too, all kinds, packed and overloaded, some with people even riding on the roofs, something Hu had never expected to see in America.

If anyone had expected last-minute desperate looting of Wilshire Blvd.'s elegant storefronts, they would have been disappointed. Even those who might have been tempted were seeing survival as a much more useful priority.

The day was growing hotter, and this far inland, the hot yellow sun was shaded by a smoggy brown haze—a rising cloud of dust, stirred up by a million vehicles.

For some reason, James was reminded of a scene from Disney's *Fantasia*. The "Rite of Spring" segment. All those thirsty dinosaurs, plodding slowly east across an orange desert, toward a sanctuary that didn't exist, eventually dropping to the dirt and dying, leaving only their whitened bones as evidence they had ever existed. He wondered what future archaeologists would be digging up here, a thousand, ten thousand years in some unimaginable future.

"James?"

"Huh?"

"Are you all right?"

"Uh, yeah. I'm fine."

"It's time to stop. Drink some more water."

James shook his head to clear it. He rolled to a stop. Hu was right.

But they'd made it down the hill, past the golf course, past the Hilton, past the intersection, even past the Beverly Wilshire Hotel. What was that—two miles? Three? Whatever. He was starting to feel the exertion—not tired, not exhausted, but definitely, his muscles were tightening. He hoped Hu wouldn't mention the trailers again. He might be tempted to give in.

But Hu said nothing. He passed James a water bottle. James had to resist the temptation to gulp it all down. Instead, he sipped carefully, once, twice, a third time. "Where are we?" he asked, looking around.

"We just passed Robertson. We've still got another couple miles." Hu burrowed into his pack. "Do you want a protein bar?"

James nodded, held out his hand. He unwrapped the little granola brick and hesitated with the wrapper—then he realized how little difference it would make if he found a trash can here in Beverly Hills or not and let it fall to the sidewalk. He chewed and swallowed slowly.

Hu grabbed a water bottle and a protein bar for himself as well. "Do you think the tsunami is going to get this far?"

James didn't answer immediately. He chewed thoughtfully. "Well…if this wave is as big as the president said, a hundred feet high, it'll certainly get as far as the 405, but how much farther, I dunno, that's a lot of water. If it was less, then the 405 would be a pretty good breakwater—except around LAX, of course. The airport's just gonna disappear. But—" James frowned, picturing the geographical layout of the basin in his head. "But I don't think the 405 will stop it. Might slow it down a bit, but a lot of water is still going to get over it, under it, through it." He took another bite, still thinking. "Y'know, those underpasses are bottlenecks, they're going to generate a lot of pressure, all that water trying to force through. Anything directly east of any of them is probably gonna take a hit, and if the pressure is strong enough, the overpasses will certainly blow off. So yeah—it's gonna get this far. A hundred feet—it's just too much water."

Hu looked west, toward the beach, as if he could already see the onrushing catastrophe. He looked at his watch. "How far east do we have to get?"

James shrugged. "It's not just one wave. It could be several waves. You haven't seen the footage I've seen, from Sumatra and Fukushima. It's not what you think. It's not like a wave at the seashore, just bigger. It's like the whole ocean rises up in a flash flood that comes in for… I don't know, an hour? Maybe more? All that water pushing in behind. It has to go someplace, the path of least resistance."

"It's gonna hit hard, really hard. It's gonna knock loose, knock down, knock out everything it hits, pushing it all forward, like a horizontal avalanche. Everything loose, cars, boats, buses, everything that breaks free, trees and billboards and lamp posts, everything that collapses, houses, stores, buildings. All that water, it's going to drive that in like the front end of a bulldozer. "

"It's gonna be bad. Real bad. Maybe those golfers had the right idea. Do what you love doing, right up to the end." He took another bite and waited for Hu's response.

Hu looked nervously to his watch, then back to James. "We're not gonna make it, are we? I mean, with Pearl. Where she is, she's awfully far from any hills—and we're running out of time."

"I know—" James said. He took another thoughtful bite, chewed for a moment, then spoke with his mouth half full. "But I've been thinking. There's that big black building, less than two blocks from Pearl's house. It's what?—ten stories high. We can get there, easy-peasy. The top two floors should be high enough."

"What about the bulldozer—?"

"There's a big building just to the west of it that should catch the brunt of the wave and most of the crap it's pushing."

"It'll be crowded—"

"Probably. But it's our best hope." James took another drink of water. Despite the grim conversation, he was still concentrating on energy and hydration. "Squeak. There has never been a mess like this before. It's gonna be—well, a challenge."

"We're gonna be on our own for a bit, won't we?"

"Yeah," said James sourly. "It's gonna be an adventure all right." He looked to the street, at the desperate stream of cars filling the boulevard. A terrible thought was finally becoming real.

"That bad, huh?" Hu asked.

"Worse than that," James said. "Worse than anyone can imagine. Hate to say it, but a lot of people are gonna die—"

And even as he said the words, he realized just how impossible an idea it was. He couldn't comprehend that all this—the cars, the buildings, the people, everything—was about to be wiped away. And yet, he couldn't deny it any longer. The magnitude of this thing—James couldn't speak it, but he realized that somehow he was still hoping that this was somehow all just a colossal mistake, a false alarm, and that maybe somehow—

He finished the last bite of his protein bar, took a last swallow of water and tossed the empty bottle at a darkened storefront. It bounced harmlessly to the street.

"—But not us. Not today. Come on, let's go."

Two blocks west of La Cienega, James and Hu turned right on South Stanley Drive. Halfway down the second block stood a white two-story building. Once, it had once been a private residence, but now it was subdivided into three Tetris-shaped apartments, with a handicapped access ramp cutting through what had once been a lush front lawn.

At the bottom of the ramp, underneath the inevitable palm tree, Pearl sat waiting in a lightweight folding wheelchair. She had a carpet bag on her lap and she held the leash of a large, sloppy-looking beast that might have had some pit-bull in its parentage, but probably dumpster dog as well. She waved happily when she saw "the boys," James and Hu. They pedaled to a stop in front of her. Several cars passed them in the street, drivers looking for alternate routes.

James looked unhappily at the dog.

"Oh, don't mind Fluffy—he's just a big friendly goofball."

"Fluffy?" Hu raised an eyebrow.

"That's what we call him. His real name is—never mind. He's Joey's dog, but Joey's off in Bakersfield or somewhere, so we keep Fluffy when he's traveling. Mrs. Petersen hates it, but she's afraid to complain or we'll tell the city about her cats."

"Some people—"

"Tell me. She went screaming out of here with a dozen cat carriers the moment the president said tsunami. But the old bitch wouldn't take us. Didn't want to be in the same car with Fluffy. Selfish old bitch. And I just couldn't leave Fluffy behind. He's family."

James sighed. "I admire your gumption, Pearl, but sometimes—"

Pearl's expression changed then. "Honey, where's your car?"

"We didn't bring it," said Hu. He waved his hand to include the bicycles and the trailers. "This was faster."

"Are we in trouble—?" Pearl asked.

"I don't think so—" James pointed. The top of the LFP building was visible even from here. "We'll go up there. It's high enough. If the wave is only a hundred feet high when it hits the shore, by the time it gets this far inland, it'll have lost most of its power—"

"James! What are you talking about?" Pearl half-rose out of her chair. "Not a hundred feet! Three hundred!"

Both James and Hu stopped in mid-word. "What—?"

"*Three hundred feet!* It's what the guy on the internet is saying! The one in Hawaii—the one who measured it!"

"Oh, fuck—" That was Hu.

James didn't say anything. His expression went ashen. When he finally did speak, it was almost automatic. "No, no, it can't be, the president—"

"Honey, that sumbitch is just plain wrong. Or stupid. The guy on the Internet is an actual geologist. He's the director of the Volcano Lab. Now, who ya gonna believe? The politician or the scientist?"

Hu touched James' arm. "What are we going to do?"

James ignored it, he leaned in, grabbed Pearl's arms, stared into her face, and almost shouted, "Are you certain? There are a lot of cranks on the Internet."

She met his stare, unflinching. "James, honey—what do I do for a living? I do research, remember? For the studios. For that stupid movie where you two met. I didn't just google him. I did the whole data-dive. This isn't bullshit. He's for real. *Three hundred feet.*"

James released her, whirled away, furious. "Fuck," he said. "Fuck, fuck, fuck, fuckity-fuck, fuck, fuck." He turned to Hu. "Remember that map I hung in the office? The one that showed the effects of global warming—what the coast line would look like if all the ice caps melted and the sea level rose two hundred and sixty feet?"

Hu nodded. "Yeah. Everything up to Boyle Heights would be underwater."

"Yeah. Well, if this guys's right, this is gonna be worse."

Hu said, "Okay, okay, okay—but we're not dead yet. I've got an idea."

"It's too late—"

"No, it isn't. Hu pointed east. "The subway! The La Cienega station. It's across the street from the tower. Remember how excited Pearl got when it opened? If we can get onto a train, we can get all the way downtown in ten minutes, fifteen."

"And then what? We're still in the disaster zone."

"We'll do what you said. We'll figure something out." Hu rubbed his chin. "I dunno, maybe the Gold line out to Pasadena. Maybe Chris and Mark can put us up. They're always having those big sprawling house parties. If not—I dunno. Maybe Amtrak to my cousin in New Mexico? If we have to pitch the tent in some park, we can do that. But let's go."

"Oh, hell—if I'd known you boys didn't know, I'd have wheeled myself over—" Pearl's face crumpled. "Oh, boys, I'm so sorry. I'm so stupid, you could have gotten up into the hills by now—"

"Stop it, Pearl." That was James. "You're family. Shut up and let us rescue you!"

Just out of her field of vision, Hu tapped his watch meaningfully.

"Right," said James, as if the matter was finally settled. "So let's get out of here. Um—" He fumbled with one of the ropes on his bike trailer. "Here, tie this to—um, loop it around yourself—and we'll pull you."

In reply, Pearl handed him Fluffy's leash. "Here. Tie this around your handlebars. The monster-dog will help pull."

"Really?"

"Really. Let him lead. Don't worry, people will get out of his way. Real fast."

"We're gonna be a whole circus parade," said James, but he took the leash.

Fluffy led the way. He pulled pulled his own weight, and half of Pearl's too—up the side streets back to Wilshire, a block east and the subway station was directly ahead. The station had only been open a few months, a promise for the future, but this would be its last day of operation. Even if the system survived, there would be nothing left above ground for anyone to come to.

James was right, they did look like a parade. But Pearl was right too. People saw them coming, saw Fluffy grunting and slobbering in the lead, and they moved fast to get out of the way.

They had to wait a few minutes to cross the street. James kept glancing at his watch. Hu put his hand on James' arm. "It's okay. We're gonna make it. We will."

"Cutting it close, too close," James muttered.

"Sloan's teddy..."

"Sloan looks terrible in a teddy," James said, then added. "Halloween. Before your time."

"Oh. Dear."

"Let's go. Light or no light—" They pushed their way into the street. The huge garbage truck waiting to turn north had left enough room for them to squeeze through. The next driver, a frightened-looking woman, had opened her car door and was standing in the street, still clutching the handle, looking confused and desperate. "There's not enough time, is there?"

"Come with us. The subway's still running—"

"The subway?" Her confusion increased. "Los Angeles has a sub-way—?"

Hu pointed past her. "It's right there—"

The woman grabbed her purse and hurried after them. A few others followed, a black woman dragging two small children, a portly man with his arms full of file folders, the driver of the garbage truck as well.

The elevator to the lower level wasn't working and even if it had been, neither James nor Hu wanted to risk getting stuck in it. The station's turnstiles were frozen open for the evacuation.

The escalators weren't working either, but there was a wide staircase and most of the travelers with baggage were hurrying down it. Hu wait-ed with the bikes while James maneuvered Pearl's chair down the stairs, Pearl held Fluffy's leash, his stub of a tail wagged in excitement, he was having a great time. He looked around the platform eagerly—all these great new playmates—but even the nearest people were keeping a careful distance.

James came trotting back up the stairs and he and Hu began working the bikes and the trailers down. A couple of people grumbled at them as they passed—but they were dragging their own bags down the steps, so James and Hu ignored the comments.

The bottom level was crowded, but not packed, not insane, not pan-icky. Most of the people who had thought to escape by subway had al-ready gone. These were stragglers, people who had finally abandoned their vehicles. Many were carrying backpacks or dragging suitcases on rollers.

The overhead signs were promising trains arriving at this terminus every four minutes. Hu pointed. "See, we'll have time."

James started to say something, thought better of it, and shut up instead. He scanned the faces of the crowd, looking for signs of despera-tion or panic. He could still hear the screams and the gun shots from the Santa Monica underpass.

At Union Station, the Red Line and Purple Line trains were arriving so fast, one after the other, that sometimes as many as three trains would have to wait in the tunnel while the first in line unloaded. As fast as each train unloaded, it was sent out again.

The outbound Red Line trains went directly to the Hollywood and Highland station, picking up passengers there and taking them out to the North Hollywood station on Lankershim Blvd. The area surrounding the Universal City station had already reached overload capacity. Inbound, all the trains were staggered to pick up passengers from the most overloaded stations. As soon as any train was packed to capacity, it went straight to Union Station. It was a frustrating experience for those waiting on the platforms, watching the densely packed trains screech by without stopping, but every available train was running and most people were able to board a train in less than twenty minutes.

The Purple Line trains were on a similar schedule, with most going directly to the Wilshire/La Cienega station, picking up passengers from the most desperate locations first.

Several trains were running direct shuttle service to the Seventh Street station, the terminus of both the Expo Line and the Blue Line from Long Beach. While many evacuees assumed they would be relatively safe this far inland, most were taking advantage of the train service departing from Union Station.

At Union Station, every available train—both passenger and freight—was loaded to capacity. Most were heading north through Glendale and Burbank, all the way to the Burbank airport, where a tent city was being set up on the top level of the parking structure. Others were heading west with stops in the San Fernando Valley and Simi Valley. Ventura County was an uncertain risk. Although parts of it were sheltered by the Santa Monica mountains, there wasn't a convenient train service. Other trains headed north to Santa Clarita, or as far east as Ontario. The closest returned for another trip as soon as they were unloaded.

Additional relocations would be necessary after the initial evacuation. Las Vegas, Phoenix, Tucson, Salt Lake City, Albuquerque, and other cities were already making plans to receive refugees. But the initial goal was to get as many people as possible out of the disaster zone as fast as possible.

In the last half-hour before impact, police and fire rescue would withdraw their personnel and any vehicles still not evacuated. When further evacuation operations became too risky, the subway trains would also be removed to their safest locations.

The last train from Union Station was being held for emergency workers. As soon as the tsunami reached San Clemente Island, a five-minute alarm would sound and the train would pull out before the onrushing water overwhelmed the coastline. It would not wait for stragglers,

That was the plan anyway.

Just one little glitch.

Roy Jeffers.

He did not look like a hero. He did not intend to be a hero.

He was a skinny little bastard (accident of birth), stuck behind thick glasses and a scowl. He was also a stubborn son of a bitch. He had issues with authority, and the surest way to get him to do anything was to tell him, "No, you can't."

Roy Jeffers had another bad habit as well. He was a rescuer.

He had a long history of opening his house in south-central Los Angeles to anyone needing a place to crash—cousins, friends, stray dogs, the occasional feral cat, and once in a while, even a girl friend. (And once, as an experiment, a boy friend.)

At the moment, however, he was single, about to be made homeless by the tsunami, and genuinely resentful that the evacuation was going to take a horrendous toll on those who could least afford it, his entire demographic. People of Color was the current euphemism. Among friends, he'd occasionally rant, "First we were Colored People. Then we were Negro, then we were Black, then African-American. Now we're People of Color. Progress my black ass!" But he didn't have a lot of friends, so it wasn't a rant that many had heard.

Adding to his annoyance was his realization that as a driver for the Purple Line, he was servicing many of the wealthier neighborhoods along Wilshire Blvd., where if he had been working the Blue Line, he would have been rescuing his own neighbors. Even the knowledge that the Crenshaw connection directly served part of his community did not alleviate his smoldering anger.

But—

The knowledge that the Crenshaw connection directly served part of his community had somehow transformed his annoyance into a specific commitment. He wasn't going to abandon anybody and he didn't care what color they were. He was going to do the job anyway.

So when he unloaded at Union Station and his supervisor, Molly Cantway waved to him and said, "Okay, that's it, Roy. Take your train out to the service yard," Roy Jeffers said no.

"There are still people out there. My people—" he insisted. "*Our* people."

Cantway shook her head. "Roy, I am not sending any more trains out. There's no time."

"Then let's not waste it arguing," Roy said. "I'm going."

"You do and I'll fire you."

"Ain't gonna be no job after today anyway—"

Jeffers pushed the control lever forward. His train rolled west into the tube. Cantway didn't know whether to be annoyed at the inevitable loss of a Purple Line train—or admire Jeffers' for his stupidity.

On the other hand, there probably wasn't going to be much of a subway system after this. After Hurricane Sandy, parts of the New York system were down for five years. This was going to be worse than that. Maybe Los Aneles would never have a subway again.

Cantway watched as the last car of Jeffers' train disappeared into the dark tunnel. If that damn fool was able to outrun the incoming flood, he'd be a hero. If not—well, he'd get a nice obituary. And maybe even a funeral, if they ever recovered a body.

Somebody called for her attention and she turned back to the more immediate problem—getting the last of these people upstairs and onto a train out of the city.

And very shortly, herself as well.

She crossed herself and went back to work.

Across the LA basin, the subway platforms were still filling up. More and more people were realizing that an eastbound train might be their only remaining hope of escape.

Hu and James, Pearl and Fluffy joined the stream of future refugees coming down the stairs, others hurried down the frozen escalator. As the crowd became ever more dense, people jostled for position, all wanting to make sure they'd board the next train.

Most kept checking the overhead arrival signs, but even before the sign flashed, "Arriving now," they could feel the breeze of its approach, as it forced the air from the tunnel ahead of it, then a distant howl echoing out of the tube, a glimmer of light that ballooned into a glare, and finally the train came screeching into the station.

As soon as the doors slid open, the crowd pushed in.

Hu held the bikes and James pushed Pearl forward. Fluffy grumbled at the people pushing past him. Abruptly, a female police officer blocked their way. She was short, all muscle, and she wore don't-fuck-with-me expression. Her name tag identified her as Officer Reese.

"You can't take that dog on the train," she said.

Almost immediately Pearl began wailing loudly. James recognized the performance, he'd seen it before, an award-worthy rendition of Frightened Old Crippled Lady. It usually worked. "Oh no, no," cried Pearl, clutching her heart. "I can't leave him. He's my service dog. He doesn't bite. He's big and friendly. I don't know what I'd do without him!" She was loud, very loud, and people already aboard the train, or still trying to board, turned to look. Pearl was playing to the court of public opinion.

Reese was immovable. "Sorry, ma'am. That animal looks dangerous. We can't take any chances—"

James started to object. "You want to leave him here to die?"

But Pearl spoke first. "No, no, James, we must obey the officer. Officer—" She peered forward. "—Officer Reese." She shifted her performance from Frightened-Old-Lady to Frightened-Old-And-Confused-Lady. She held up the end of the leash, offering it to the officer. "Officer Reese, will you hold him till we get back?" Pearl patted the dog's head. "Here, Slobberchops, go with the nice lady."

Fluffy's posture changed dramatically. He was suddenly alert, suddenly eager—he curled back his upper lip, revealing enough teeth for a piano keyboard. He grunted and drooled and pulled at the leash as if someone had just announced fresh peasant for dinner.

Officer Reese put her hand on the hilt of her gun.

"No, no, don't do that! He's just being friendly. Honest. He just wants to play."

Officer Reese must have been painfully aware that all eyes were on her. And the clock was ticking. Fluffy grumpled impatiently. Reese blinked—and took a step back and aside. "Oh, the hell with it. Just keep a tight leash on him."

As James pushed Pearl into the already jammed subway car, those nearest squeezed back to make room, especially room for Fluffy. James bent to her ear and whispered, "Slobberchops?"

Pearl whispered back. "That's his real name. When you say it, he gets ready to play. That was his smile. Works every time."

"Nice." James let go of the wheelchair, turned back to Hu. "Come on—"

Hu gestured. The bikes? "There's no room—"

"Leave them. Grab your case. Come on—"

"You sure, James—?"

"Just do it!"

Hu let go of the bikes, grabbed his most important bag, and started to board, but Officer Reese stepped in ahead of him, into the last available space, blocking his way. "Sorry. This one's full."

James started to object. "But he's my—"

She half-turned, "You got the dog, don't push your luck. There's one more train coming, he can get on that one."

James made a decision. He leaned quickly down to Pearl. "Give 'em hell, sweetheart." Then, "If he stays, I stay." He pushed past Reese and stepped off the train.

As the subway doors closed, Officer Reese glared at them both. James didn't care. He grabbed Hu. "Wedding or not, you're my husband and I'm not going anywhere without you." Then he kissed Hu passionately.

Which surprised them both—because James had never kissed Hu in public anywhere before.

They weren't alone on the subway platform. There were at least thirty or forty others, the last few stragglers. Several of them were screaming at the departing train they'd been unable to board A couple had even been pushed out as the doors closed in front of them.

"You selfish bastards!" Somebody else yelled, "That was the last train." Followed by, "Come on, upstairs. The roof of the—"

His words were drowned out, running for the stairs. There was still time to get to the roof of the tallest nearby buildings. It might be enough. But if Pearl was right—and Pearl was rarely wrong—it probably wouldn't be.

James looked to Hu. "You want to follow them?"

"She said there was one more train coming."

"Do you believe her?"

"She wasn't Miss Congeniality, was she?"

"More like, I dunno, Miss Convenience Store." James looked to the stairs, looked down the track, looked to the stairs again.

Hu said, "Are we fucked?"

James didn't need to consider the question. The answer was obvious. "Well… yes. Probably."

Hu looked at his watch. "The water is probably pulling away from the shore by now."

"Uh, no," James said. "It's not gonna work like that. Not this one."

That's what they were explaining while you were in the shower. A big part of the island fell into the sea, it pushed an equivalent volume of water outward. The first thing that hits is the wave. Afterward, more waves. Like the whole Pacific is sloshing."

"Should we wait here? Or...?"

Before James could answer, a Korean woman came dragging a little girl, five or six, maybe seven, running down the stairs. "She was out playing, I couldn't find her! Are we too late? Are the trains still running—?"

And as if in answer, they both felt a rising breeze.

"One more," Hu said to the woman. "The last one."

"Oh, thank God, thank God."

Down the tunnel, the distant light became an onrushing glare. The train's horn howled like an electric banshee. It came screeching into the station, the doors sliding open almost immediately.

James and Hu let the woman rush past them, the little girl almost flying like a rag doll, then they pushed their bikes into the subway car. The bikes and the attached trailers filled the space at the end of the car designed for bikes and wheelchairs and luggage on wheels. As soon as the doors slid closed and the train lurched into motion, James looked to Hu and smiled. For the first time today, since walking out of their small house in Venice Beach, James allowed himself the smallest bit of confidence. Finally, they were on their way. If they could beat the onrushing wave to Union Station, maybe.

Would there be a train waiting there? Maybe. Maybe. Otherwise...

Without stopping, the subway could get downtown in seven minutes, probably less. If they stopped for passengers, if there were people still waiting at each station, and there probably would be, then you'd have to add a minute for each station, maybe even two or three for braking, loading, accelerating again—okay, so figure maybe fifteen minutes at worst.

James wasn't certain about the speed of the onrushing water, somewhere between ten or twenty miles per hour, but that was an ordinary tsunami. A mega-tsunami? That was a whole different kettle of physics, but he had to believe they had a chance.

Union Station was sixteen miles inland from Santa Monica. The waters should be slowing that far inland, but—again, the physics on this were unknown. Okay, doing the math in his head, fifteen minutes to get downtown, maybe there's another ten or fifteen minutes margin at Union Station. If Pearl was right, there would be that one last train for evacuees and emergency workers. They'd probably have to abandon the bikes and take only what they could carry. James studied what they'd brought, already sorting it in his head.

The train stopped at the Fairfax station, there was a larger crowd here, everyone who couldn't fit into the previous train. But there was room. At least a dozen more people pushed into the car. James and Hu pulled themselves back against one side. The woman and her little girl stood across from them, the little girl staring curiously at their bicycles. The doors closed and the train lurched forward, quickly gaining speed and rushing eastward toward La Brea.

"What's that?" The little girl asked, pointing at the air tank on James' bike-trailer.

"It's my rocket-pack," said James. "For when I'm being rocket-man. Like in the song. Do you know the song?"

"No it isn't," the girl said. "It's an air tank. And you're being silly."

"Well, if you knew it was an air tank, why did you ask?" James pointed at her, as if catching her in a game of tag. She giggled and buried her face in her mother's side.

"What's your name, sweetheart?"

That was enough. She stopped hiding and turned back. It was all a game. "Julia. What's yours?"

"I'm James." And then, for no reason he could understand, maybe because he just didn't care anymore, he added, "And this is my boy friend. We're going to get married. His name is Hu."

Julia looked at Hu curiously. "Who?" she asked. "Like Doctor Who?"

"No," Hu said. "Just Hu. Like boo-hoo without the boo."

"Oh, okay." And then she said, "Could I be your flower girl? I did it for my cousin's wedding."

That's when Julia's mother put her hand on the little girl's shoulder, pulled her back. "That's enough, Julia. Don't bother those men."

Something about the way the woman said "those men"—James sensed her disapproval. Her expression had hardened.

"It's okay, ma'am. Just being friendly. We're all in this together." But he turned away anyway. Maybe another time, another place, he might have said something more. But not here, not now. There was still the problem of this time and this place.

Hu put his hand on James' arm. "What's the matter?"

"Nothing—"

"You should tell that to your face."

"I was just…doing the math in my head."

"Are we all right?"

"Should be."

Hu knew James too well. He recognized the lie. But he said nothing. Neither of them said anything until they reached the La Brea station.

This platform wasn't as crowded as the platforms had been at Fairfax and La Cienega stations. Fewer people here believed they were in danger. Maybe they were right. Or maybe they'd believed that they would find safety on their roofs.

The train was momentarily delayed in pulling out—there was a last minute rush, someone up ahead was holding a door and calling something to the motorman. The reason was quickly apparent. Nearly a dozen people, including several police officers, came charging down the stairs and across the platform—they pushed into the forward cars.

As the train pulled out again, Hu looked to his watch. "The wave, the first one. It just hit." He held up his phone for James to see. "No wi-fi down here, but I downloaded the sim while we were getting Pearl to the subway."

James studied the screen, a blue stain spreading inland. "You think it's accurate?"

"It's the one all the links pointed to. It's that scientist in Hawaii. It's supposed to be the most accurate geographic model. If his timeline is correct, our house is gone, the Third Street Mall—" Hu looked at the map. "Everything up to Bundy. Do you think the 405 might slow it down?"

James shook his head. "Not a chance, not if the wave is as high as that guy said."

"Well, Pearl said he passed the sniff test. And she is the research queen." Hu frowned at his phone. "I wish we had wi-fi down here."

"I don't."

"We could see what the news choppers are broadcasting—"

"I don't need to see it." James said. "I don't want those pictures in my head. Do you? Give me your phone—"

"Huh?"

"Give me your phone."

Hu handed it over. "Why?"

James didn't bother to answer. He pulled out his own phone and shoved both into a water-tight bag, then slipped it into his backpack.

"Really?"

"Just a precaution."

"Uh-uh. You're thinking of something."

James lowered his voice. "When the wave hits, if it reaches the Purple Line before we're in the safe zone, that water's gonna go down into the stations and flood the tunnel. We may not be safe down here."

"How long till it catches up with us?"

James stopped. He hadn't considered the question. He'd been so focused on just getting to Pearl, just getting her to the subway, just getting everyone aboard a train, just outrunning the wave front—he hadn't thought much beyond that. He frowned in thought, trying to decide what he could say—and whether or not he should say it.

"James. Answer me. Can this train outrun it?"

James didn't reply immediately. He took a deep breath. Finally, he reached across and put his hand on Hu's arm, sliding all the way up to his partner's shoulder. "We're making good time, Squeak. A mile a minute. We're moving faster than the wave front—"

Hu reached over and put his hand on James's. Quietly he said, "I looked at the video—the simulation. It looks like the water comes in awfully fast. 50 miles an hour, maybe even faster—"

James thought hard. Finally, he admitted, " It's plumbing. It's physics. It's everything. It's the depth of the water, how much volume on the surface, how big the tunnel is, and how much pressure—" He trailed off, trying to visualize the problem.

"If there's a hundred feet of water above us—" He was thinking aloud now. "I don't dive usually that deep. A hundred feet, maybe a hundred thirty, that's pretty much the limit. At a hundred feet, that's 3 atmospheres, 4 counting the weight of the air above the water, 44 PSI—pounds per square inch. That's a lot of pressure. If there's that much water, it'll be coming in fast, over the streets and through the tunnel. And if the water's higher, there'll be even more pressure. It'll move even faster." Seeing the look on Hu's face, James stopped himself.

"We're gonna get hosed, aren't we?" Hu said. He kept his voice soft, trying not to attract the attention of the other passengers.

James realized his mistake then. He tried to cover quickly. "Only if it hits, only if it hits—" It wasn't enough.

Hu closed his eyes against the mental picture, against the rising turmoil of emotions that were suddenly flooding up inside him, fear and anger and something unidentifiable. His expression collapsed and suddenly, he was sobbing. "I'm sorry, Bubble."

"What for—?"

"For...everything. For the subway. It was a stupid idea—"

"No, sweetheart, no. It was a good idea. A really good idea. You'll see. We'll be okay."

But Hu refused to be reassured. The moment was reawakening his panic—that same panic he'd felt that day in the tank at Paramount. And this time, there wouldn't be anybody who could save either of them.

James slid his hand up Hu's shoulder, putting his palm on the back of Hu's neck—their own private gesture of reassurance. He pulled him into a hug and whispered, "Hell or high water, Squeak. I promise."

Hu pulled back, just enough to smile at him.

The train screeched and rocketed through the dark tunnel, but James and Hu didn't notice, didn't care. They had retreated into a private space between their shining eyes, their own special world of connection.

After a moment, Hu pulled away, recovering enough to reach into the pocket of his jeans. He pulled out the small velvet-covered box, opened it, withdrew the larger ring and slid it onto James' finger. "This is not the way I wanted to do it, this is awful, but...I take thee, James D. Liddle as my awfully wedded husband, forever and ever, and for all the days of my life."

James took the box from Hu, took the second ring and likewise slid it onto Hu's finger. "I take thee, Hu Son, to be my husband, to be my lawfully bedded husband, forever and ever, and for all the days of my life."

They looked into each other's eyes again, trying to make the moment last forever. Finally James leaned forward and gently kissed Hu. He wanted to kiss him more passionately, but it wasn't necessary, not here—not with so many strangers watching. He hadn't realized they had attracted an audience. Several people applauded and cheered, but not the uncertain Korean woman still clutching the little girl close to her.

There were tears forming in Hu's eyes. He said, "This is the real one, Bubble, but I still want a ceremony." He whispered, "After all, we've already got a flower girl. I mean, if her mother will let her."

It was too much, all too much. James finally laughed. "We're about to lose the house, the car, the motorcycle, our business—we still don't know if we're going to survive—" He couldn't help himself, the words came fumbling out. "—And here we are, this is the happiest day of my life."

"It's certainly going to be one to remember—"

And that's when the subway train lurched.

The train lurched as if it had gone over a speed bump. Someone gasped, someone else screamed. Then the train roared on, faster than before.

"What was that—?" Hu had to raise his voice to be heard.

James shook his head. "Dunno. Felt like a power-glitch to me."

"Do you think they're shutting down the grid?"

"Makes sense they would—"

"But not the subway—"

"We're still rolling—"

Hu opened his mouth, not quite a yawn, something else. "James—?"

"What?"

"My ears just popped."

"Yeah." James forced his own yawn as well. "Mine too."

"What would—?" But Hu already knew the answer.

"Air pressure," said James. "The water is definitely in the tunnel. It's coming in fast, compressing the air—"

"It's gonna hit us, isn't it—"

James didn't answer. He looked down to the rear end of the car, but there was no view out the back. Even if there had been, there were too many people in the way. He turned around to his bike, pulled his dive-belt off the trailer, made sure his knife was in its sheath. He pulled Hu to his side. "Face your bike, now. If you have to, throw yourself over the tank. Hide it from view."

"What? Why—?" And then understanding. "Oh." And then, "Oh, shit—"

"Yeah," James finished buckling his divebelt around his waist. "It's gonna get ugly."

"James—"

"There's nothing we can do—"

Hu grabbed his arm. "We can do something. We've got two regulators on each rig. We can save Julia and her mom."

James wanted to argue, but Hu was right. He stepped over to the Korean woman, looked directly into her terrified eyes. "Come stand next to us. Both of you. Please." He reached out and touched her elbow. It was enough. Still clutching her daughter, she moved closer to the bikes.

"Listen to me," said James. He lowered his voice, almost to a whisper. "I'm a SCUBA professional. The wave is coming, it's going to flood this car. When the water hits, it's going to get panicky in here, but each of the tanks has two mouthpieces and there's enough air here for four people, Hu and myself—and both of you. You'll be okay if you do what I say. Here's what you need to know. Are you listening, Julia?"

The little girl nodded, her eyes wide.

"Okay, when it's time, Hu's going to give you a mouthpiece. We don't have a mask for you, so you're gonna want to close your eyes and just concentrate on breathing as slowly as you can. Take really long, really slow, breaths, in and out, only through the mouthpiece, really slow—okay?"

Julia nodded solemnly.

"Now, remember, I want you to keep your eyes closed and just concentrate on breathing—" Julia looked confused. James leaned down and whispered in her ear, "Okay, here's how to do it. You count a hundred breaths to yourself, because that's how long it takes. And if the water still hasn't gone down, then you start over and count to a hundred again. You might have to do that more than once, but that's how Hu and I are gonna do it—" He straightened and turned to the mother. "Did you get all that? You and I will share the other tank—"

The woman started to say something, an objection—?

James held up his hand. "Don't say anything. Just stand here. Turn away from anyone else. Both of you. Keep your backs to them. And—"

The subway lurched again. This time, the car bumped as if something had struck it from behind. Someone at the other end of the car screamed, several people screamed, both men and women—

Something lifted the rear of the car off the tracks, tilting them forward. Outside there were sparks—the train was slowing, there was no more power to the wheels—and then there was light outside, flickering light—the subway train was careening into the Wilshire/Western station and angry brown water flooded up onto the platform from the tracks. More water poured down the stairways and escalators, battering the walls and the train with debris, all of it rising rapidly and rocking the car with its force. The air smelled suddenly *wet*.

The other passengers, mostly men began shouting and pushing

scrambling at and over each other. Muddy water was already flooding into the car from Underneath. Men were shouting, several were trying to force open the doors, trying to escape. Others were demanding they stop, terrified because the darkness outside the train was already rising past the windows—

And then someone finally pushed the doors open and the flood— cold, salty, and gritty—came roaring in, pummeling and pounding, an inescapable torrent. People screamed and floundered, pushing at each other, climbing over each other, trampling anyone smaller, fighting their way through the current, desperate to get up the station stairs toward the air they imagined was waiting for them.

And then the last of the lights went out.

Green emergency lights flickered on, self-powered, but they weren't enough. And they didn't last. They were extinguished one by one by the rising muddy water.

James and Hu were already pulling the bungee cords off the bikes, off the tanks. They fumbled in the gloom, depending on experience and muscle-memory.

Hu pushed the first regulator at Julia, the water was up to her chest. She grabbed the mouthpiece with both hands, pushed it into her mouth. James had already pulled Julia's mother to the other bike—yanking the whole rig off the bike trailer, he shoved a regulator toward the terrified woman, then helped her get it into her mouth as the water rose to her neck. He looked to Hu, who gave him a quick thumbs-up, pushing his own regulator into his mouth.

Hu rummaged in his case, triumphantly pulled out two headlamps, and pulled one over his head. Right, James thought, we're going to need those! His own facemask had a headlamp built in, but he felt around in his case for the other lamps. He slipped one of them over Julia's mother's head, started to hand her the second one for Julia—

"Please, sir—me too, please—"

James grabbed his face mask and pulled it down over his eyes just as the water came rising up over his chin. He turned and saw a frightened young teen, a black boy in a red T-shirt. The boy bobbed up desperately, his hand out for help. "Please—"

"We'll have to share—"

"Okay, yes, okay—"

James held his mouthpiece to the boy, they were bumping up against the top of car. "Long slow breaths, okay. Two, three breaths—into the mouthpiece, both in and out. Then it's my turn. Okay?"

"Okay." The boy took the mouthpiece just as the water forced the last of the air out of the subway car. James put the last headlamp on him. It switched on automatically when the water hit it. Then he turned to his left, looking to make sure Hu was all right.

He wasn't.

There was a struggle going on. James couldn't see far in the murky water, but one thing was clear. Someone was fighting Hu for the regulator. Someone else was trying to get to Julia. She was curled up in a ball, holding her regulator tightly in both hands.

James kicked off, directly head-butting into Julia's attacker, pushing him backward toward the open subway door. Outside the rushing water surged past the train, filling the station and pushing into the next bore. James head-butted the man again, forcing him into one side of the open door. The current grabbed him, yanked him away and he went flailing into the turbulence, disappearing into the dark and muddy gloom. James had to grab a pole to keep from being pulled after him. Desperately, he grabbed the overhead bar and worked his way back to Hu.

Hu's eyes were wide, his mouth bubbling open. The stranger had gotten the regulator away from him. Hu was grabbing futilely for it—it was his drowning nightmare all over again, but there was no James at his side.

The stranger was holding Hu at arm's length, while sucking greedily for air. Hu saw the man pulling away into darkness—until one arm came reaching around the stranger's chest and another hand sliced across his throat, releasing a cloud of red-brown darkness, expanding outward like inky smoke. The man stiffened, choked, gasped, struggled, and thrashed away in the dark, pummeled by the rushing water, but still held by the regulator tube.

James came around from behind the thrashing man, pulled the regulator from his mouth and as the body turned away into darkness, he pushed the regulator into his own mouth, grabbing a quick suck of air for himself—rule number one, take care of yourself first—but he was already swimming back to Hu. He met Hu's terrified eyes, then passed the regulator over, watching to make sure that Hu had it safely back in his mouth. James held firmly onto Hu, watching to see if all his careful training was paying off. Hu was scared, but somehow he remembered what to do. He choked past his panic—James watched to make sure that Hu was finally breathing again, breathing slowly and deliberately, before he gestured for the regulator. He'd waited almost too long—his own lungs were feeling tight.

Hu passed the regulator back to James, who took three hasty breaths, then turned headed back to his own tank. He had to take a moment to steady himself. This was all happening too fast. He was still feeling his own adrenaline-panic as he swam back to the teenager, still holding his knife—

He had vision—of a sort. The new headlamps he'd grabbed back at the office had switched on automatically when the water hit them. Each had a pair of matching LED arrays, so he could see where Hu and the Julia were by the illusion of bright eyes in the darkness. Paired fingers of light probed at the gloom, illuminating almost nothing.

The black boy and the Korean woman were equally visible, another small circle of brightness. James swam back to the teenager, still holding his knife, and turned the boy to face him. The water was cold and it was pounding at them, shoving them this way and that. The boy could barely focus in the dark, he didn't have a facemask, but he saw the lamps on James' mask and he could see enough to recognize the man who'd saved him. He gave James a thumbs-up and passed the mouthpiece over—

James was glad. One murder was already one murder too many. He knew that Hu had seen it, but he couldn't tell what Hu was thinking, how he was reacting. Probably he was still trying to calm himself. James hoped that both Julia and her mother had kept their eyes closed as instructed. This was going to be a long afternoon.

Now it was James' turn to manage his breathing—and his fear. If he didn't manage himself, he couldn't manage anyone. He took three long breaths, then passed the mouthpiece back to the boy. Then, finally, he remembered to slide his knife back into its sheath.

The thrashing of the water was lessening. They were still being pummeled by surges of uneven pressure, why was that? Something up the tunnel must be blocking the flow of water, alternately blocking and opening. James imagined a giant pink heart valve, but it was probably a humongus piece of debris being pushed back and forth by the torrent. If it could settle, if it could block the worst of the flow, then maybe—but no, they shouldn't depend on it.

He had to convince himself that they could do this. He wasn't sure for how long. It depended on how much water they had above them, on how much pressure they could stand, on how long their air would hold out, and on how long they could last in the cold. Maybe the incoming coastal waters were warm enough they wouldn't be plunged into hypothermia. Maybe, just maybe, they had enough air to hold out for an hour, but probably less because they were sharing? He had to figure this out—

Then he remembered. His $1500 dive computer. He'd packed it, hadn't he? For a moment, he felt embarrassed, but then he realized, he'd hadn't had a chance to use it, so it wasn't part of his muscle-memory. What bag was it in?

He went back to the boy, shared his three breaths, steadied his breathing, and visualized the morning. He usually talked to himself when he worked. Saying things out loud imprinted them in his memory. Ah, there—

He passed the regulator back, went straight to the case he'd almost left behind, and it was right where he remembered, right where he'd said when he packed it. It would have been easy to find anyway. It had switched itself on when the water hit it—its display was bright, even in this darkness, and now it was beeping an alarm. He slid it onto his left wrist and tried to focus on the dials.

The numbers flickered with confusing speed. The device kept beeping contradictory warnings. James was an expert in with sport diving. At a hundred feet deep, a diver would use his air four times faster, but right now the dive computer was telling him that his current rate of air consumption might be ten times faster, might be twenty, might be five—the numbers kept changing, up and down, too fast to make any sense. They were either five hundred feet underwater or fifty. It was the fluctuating pressure of the water still pounding through the tunnel. The damn thing couldn't calibrate.

James tried to visualize what was happening. How much water? Too much and they wouldn't be able to stay down for long. If they needed to decompress, then the longer they spent under pressure, the longer decompression would take, and if they had limited air that would be a problem. They'd have to start up as soon as the flow of water ebbed. But how long could they wait for the current to slow? He had to balance time at this depth against time needed to ascend.

The tsunami was still pushing inland, what were the physics of that?

Here in the tunnel, the rushing water was still battering at the car and stirring debris throughout the station. And all the things that should never have been debris—

Unless and until things equalized, they could be stuck here. How long until the water stopped flooding eastward? How long till it settled? How long till it started receding back into the sea? And how fast would it retreat? When would the next wave arrive? James had no idea.

He wondered if Pearl's train had made it safely to Union Station. Maybe. Probably. It had been packed full, so it wouldn't have made any stops. They would have gained a few minutes. And maybe ith this train blocking part of the tunnel, maybe the flow would have been less, and maybe Pearl's train could have made it all the way downtown—?

And maybe that was all wishful thinking.

And maybe, despite everything they weren't going to make it after all.

The churning slowed.

It didn't stop, but it slowed.

And they were still alive.

How did he know that?

Because they were still alive.

It didn't make sense.

They hadn't outrun the tsunami.

And they were under how many feet of water—

And yet…here they were, still alive, still breathing.

Still alive.

The water was brown and murky where the headlamp beams pierced it for a few feet it looked like as much mud (and who knew what else) as water. If they hadn't had the headlamps…

Maybe that was what had attracted the attackers, maybe they saw the light as a beacon. He wasn't sure. It had all happened too fast, the subway car had flooded so quickly. James was wearing a professional-grade mask, it had extra-bright lamps, but down here, the advantage was minimal. He had only a small tunnel of vision, a gloom just a bit lighter than the darker gloom surrounding. He hung in place, thoughts trying to race, circling in confusion. He was a frozen moment of awareness in a shadowy underwater coffin.

He looked to the others. Julia was holding onto the regulator with both hands, her eyes were closed. She was fine, almost relaxed. Her mother too, though not as calm—she understood how precarious their situation was. Hu was floating close to Julia, watching her carefully. And the teenager—he was watching James as warily as a feral cat. He must have seen what James had done. James took his three breaths, then turned to look toward the raised end of the car. There were dark shapes floating in the water, he didn't look long, he didn't want to see them clearly. He already knew and his gut churned.

He turned his attention to the dials on the tanks. They had air—just not enough. Nowhere near as much as he had hoped. The chaos, the exertion, they were sucking air faster than he had planned. And the pressure, more pressure meant each lungful sucked in more air. He had to assume they were under at least a hundred feet of water.

But how deep were they, really? How much water was pressing down on them?

It didn't matter. They were in trouble. They had to move.

James wanted to stay nice and safe. Underwater was always nice and safe—if you knew what you were doing. But if you knew what you were doing, then you'd also know, you can't stay underwater. It's not just how much air—it's the *other* reason. At any serious pressure, they'd get wonky.

James knew what it felt like. It's a little like being drunk or stoned—except it isn't. It's the rapture of the deep. And if you succumb to it, you become a statistic of the deep. No, you have to focus. You have to concentrate on every single task. Each specific task, one careful moment after the next.

James focused. He took his next three breaths and passed the mouthpiece back to the boy. Options. He had to consider the options. They weren't good. But they were options. That was more than most people had—especially the ones now floating limp in the darkness. There were so many of them, and they couldn't escape them, could they? They were a silent gauntlet, guarding any exit.

In the chaos of the moment, James hadn't considered the panic, the terror, of those caught in the water, unable to escape, those last few desperate moments of grasping for possibility, gasping for air, choking on their own last screams of denial and rage.

James knew what it was like to drown. It had been one of the worst parts of his training. He'd never understood the necessity of the exercise—being pushed into that near-death moment—at least, not until afterward when he'd been painfully pulled out of the tank, choking and gasping and coughing up water, not until the medic checked his heart and listened to his lungs and nodded to the trainer. Not until the trainer had looked him straight in the eyes and said, "Now do you understand what you'll be dealing with when you try to rescue a drowning man?"

And James had somehow managed to get the words out, "Was that fucking necessary?"

"I hope to fucking God it never is. But if it saves one life—yours—then, yeah." The trainer added, "Given a choice, I'd rather lose the idiot. His funeral I don't have to go to."

James had made up his mind, there and then, never to repeat the experience. Not voluntarily. And definitely not involuntarily!

That had a lot to do with his relationship with Hu, as well. That first day, in the tank at Paramount, he'd been watching this beautiful young man with multiple overlays of awareness. At first, he'd thought him just a gangling teenager, then he realized not only was Hu older than he looked, but also how inexperienced he himself was at gauging ages, especially the ages of Asian men. He just didn't have enough history.

For a moment, he'd wondered if Hu were...what's a good word? Accessible? An interesting question, not one he usually considered, and not one he intended to pursue here. It was only a passing thought, quickly pushed aside by the necessities of the job.

Once in the tank, once the plastic and Styrofoam flotsam had been added, once the wind machines had been turned on and the mechanically produced waves had started churning, it became obvious—to James at least—that Hu did not have a lot of experience with this particular kind of stunt work. And even though plastic and Styrofoam looks and feels lightweight—if enough of it piles up against you, or on top of you, it can rapidly become an impenetrable mass. You can drown just as easily as if it were the real thing.

So James had watched Hu. He watched all the people in the water, but he watched Hu especially—because the beautiful young man wasn't watching out for himself, not the way a more experienced stunt player would have.

James hadn't waited for anyone to call "cut!" The rule was simple. Don't worry about ruining the shot. Get out of the way of the bus. Dodge the falling rocks. Don't get bitten by the mechanical dinosaur head. Don't. Get. Injured. Especially don't get killed. That costs money. It shuts the production down for two or three days. And it pisses off producers.

Rule Number One: Getting killed can ruin your whole day.

So James had dived into the tank, swum under the prop flotsam, grabbed Hu, and pulled him off to the side. He hadn't been thinking of anything more than just getting the poor dumb schmuck out of danger. It wasn't until later, over lunch, that he'd realized what an amazing smile shone on Hu Son's face.

And even then, he hesitated. He'd been burned enough in the relationship fire. He wasn't that eager to put his hand back into the flames—or any other part of his anatomy. But one thing led to another anyway—and now he had a ring on his finger.

It was an unfamiliar sensation. Hu's life was the other half of his now. His responsibility. And not just Hu. Three other lives were depending on his expertise.

So. Options. They could head up the nearest stairwell, head for the surface. Except, where was the surface? Right now, Wilshire was under water. James didn't know exactly how much, but it had to be a lot of fast-moving water. 10 mph, 20 mph, it didn't matter. It would be like stepping into a hurricane, except they'd be weightless with no footing. The waters would carry them away like balloons in a storm.

Wait for the waters to subside? That would work. If they subsided fast enough, before the five of them ran out of air or succumbed to cold. That was another problem. The temperature of the water. It was cold—not cold enough to produce hypothermia in an adult, not right away, but Julia's smaller body put her at increased risk. And perhaps the skinny teenager as well. They had to get above the water.

The subway car lurched, distracting James. Not quite unseen, the drifting bodies lurched too.

James took an extra deep breath, then passed the mouthpiece back to the young man. He swam deeper into the car to investigate. His headlamp gave him some sense of the mess—one of the subway doors was jammed open—by a body. His internal conversation was deafening. *Please, God, no children. No children, please—*

God did not comply.

His beam illuminated an infant, blanket still unraveling around its lifeless body.

Oh, fuck, fuck, fuck—fuck you, God—

James retreated, his mind already postulating what must have happened. A mother rushing home from work, finding the baby-sitter gone, grabbing the baby, rushing for the subway, but somehow getting to the station just a few minutes too late, getting on the last car, hoping to escape. Dying in cold dark terror.

He bumped into a floating cat carrier, a furry body within, the handle still gripped by an elderly woman, her white hair floating around her head like a cloud.

Another body, this one in a dark uniform, the garbage truck driver? James didn't want to know. It was too much. He was starting to feel the horror—and painful pressure in his chest.

The subway lurched again—and all the separate bodies echoed the movement, a synchronized ballet, all the different dancers bumping sideways to the same unheard music. The moment passed and they resumed their slow deliberate gavotte. No longer panicked, in death they had become patient observers, the staring jetsam of disaster, their faces now relaxed and lifeless, they hung almost motionless, a silent jury—their fatal judgment dark and unspoken.

The dive computer was certain now, it beeped in alarm—they were too deep. They had to start ascending now. And as quickly as possible. Too much water, too little air—the bends would be inevitable.

James swam back to the others, back to the air tanks, still struggling with the math of their survival. He couldn't sort it out, it was the pressure, the paralyzing effects of it. His thoughts wandered in a drunken haze—and if he was having trouble, then the others were probably faring worse.

He had to focus. He hadn't expected to do this, not this soon, but there wasn't any alternative. He had to switch the tanks now, before he got fuzzier.

Switching tanks underwater wasn't hard. He'd done it before, but he hadn't done it a lot, so—after the necessary three breaths—he took his time to make sure he was doing it right. He had to focus carefully on each part of the process. As soon as the connections were secure, as soon as the pressure gauges were good, he relaxed a little. Hu and Julia had a little more time. He'd switch their tanks in fifteen minutes, maybe ten.

What had he been thinking about? He concentrated—oh yeah, options. Can't swim for the surface, can't wait for the waters to subside. Could they get higher?

Maybe! The Wiltern—wasn't there something? He tried to remember. There was a subway entrance in the building, wasn't there? Part of some expansion project? A pedestrian tunnel under the street, from the lobby to the platform. That would get them up a couple floors—that is, if the building was still there and if it was tall enough to stick out of the water, then maybe they could get to one of the upper floors before they ran out of air. So many ifs—

But, the numbers didn't leave any room for negotiation nor delays. They were too deep and they had too many bodies breathing too little air. But maybe—

Everything was maybe. James shared another three breaths, passed the mouthpiece back, then fumbled in his bag of gear until he found what he was looking for—a plastic panel and a grease pencil on a leash. Another three breaths of air, then he wrote frantically. "Get out now. Tunnel to Wiltern."

He didn't have time to write more. He wouldn't have anyway. But when the waters started to recede, when worst of the flood finally started to flow back to the sea, he worried that the pressure in the station would also reverse and the subway train would be sucked back into the tunnel, where no escape would be possible. He wasn't sure about the physics, his mind wasn't focusing that far, but he couldn't chance it.

Three breaths, then he held the panel in the teen's headlamp beam. The boy's eyes were wide, bright in the gloom, he gave a thumbs-up response. James maneuvered himself over to Hu, held up the sign. Hu gave a thumbs-up too, then reached for the panel. He touched the Julia's shoulder. She opened her eyes and then squinted them almost shut—this muck hurt! Hu tapped her shoulder again, holding the sign in front of her, his lights pointed at it. She nodded. She was tired, she was scared, but she was determined. James admired her spirit. She gave him hope.

James took the sign back, turned back to his own tank for another three breaths, then to hold the sign for Julia's mother to see. She was too frightened to respond with anything more than a half-nod of acknowledgment.

Another three breaths.

Stay focused, James told himself. One thing at a time.

Another tough decision. They were going to have to leave the bikes behind—and everything they'd so carefully packed. Abandoned. For a moment, he considered the impossible—could they carry any of this? None of them were wearing weight-belts, they had a buoyancy problem, they were all bobbing toward the roof of the subway car, the bikes might serve as ballast, and keep them from rising too fast—

No, it was too much to ask, too much effort. Not enough air. But at least, he and Hu had already transferred their most important belongings to their backpacks, they could take that much at least.

Three more breaths. He waved to Hu, caught his attention, and pointed to his backpack. Hu nodded. He gave a double thumbs up and checked his straps. At least they could save what they could wear.

James turned back to the bikes and pulled the air tanks off the trailers, the ones they were using, and the last set of spares. Another three breaths and he gave the signal. He was in a small circle of light, fingers of illumination surrounded him. He gave a thumbs-up signal and the entire group began to move—Hu and Juilia, the teen and Julia's mother.

They worked their way to the jammed-open door of the subway and somehow he managed to push the bodies out of the way. Two? Three? He wasn't sure and it didn't matter. The doors stayed open, one small piece of good luck.

Three more breaths.

The subway car was tilted. A wedge of debris had been thrust under its rear wheels, raising at a lopsided angle—it leaned away from the platform, its upper frame jammed against the outer wall of the tunnel. The end of the car was more than a foot above the platform, wheels caught on the edge of it. Their door at the front of the car was almost a foot above the platform, and angled upward. Without the water, it would have been a hard leap. Here, this deep, under this much pressure, gravity was almost irrelevant. If anything, they were going to have a hard time staying down.

Three more breaths.

James swam to Julia's mom, patted her on the shoulder reassuringly, gave her a thumbs-up, then to the boy to reassure him as well—three more breaths—and then back to look at the pressure gauge on Hu's tank.

Two and a half adults had drained his own tank, but Hu's tank, with only one and a half bodies draining it, still had a useful margin. James gestured to Hu, pointing at the mouthpiece. Hu understood, he passed it over, sharing his air.

James took four breaths, a luxury, but a necessary one, then passed the mouthpiece back. James went through the door first. Hu brought up the rear. He had learned from James, they'd spent time together underwater. Be slow. Be methodical. Keep the beginners between you. Do one thing only, then the next. There's no rush. Impatience kills. Panic kills. Count to three. Or four.

Once out the door, they bobbed upward, bumping into the ceiling. Hu shared his air with James again. He looked worried, but James refused to acknowledge it. He'd already made up his mind. They were going to live. They hadn't come this far to die.

Another few breaths from Hu's tank and James swam away for a quick reconnaissance of the flooded station. He had to find the pedestrian tunnel.

There were bodies here. Too many, most of them floating up toward the ceiling, bobbing there like dreadful balloons. He tried not to think about them, but some of them turned toward him as he passed, he couldn't ignore their faces.

And fish, there were fish here too! Not a lot, and nothing James could identify, but some struggled feebly in the muddy currents. They wouldn't survive.

It gave him pause. Maybe later he would think about it. Maybe later someone would be able to explain how they got there. Maybe there'd be "later." Too many maybes.

At the front of the train, where it had shuddered to a stop, James pulled himself down to look into the first car. His headlights found the motorman's booth, the driver still behind the controls, his face an angry expression of disbelief and rage. James' beams illuminated the badge on his chest. It said "Jeffers."

You stupid schmuck, thought James. *Stupid, stupid, stupid. You should have just run for home, we could have made it. But no! You had to stop, didn't you. One more station, one more heroic pickup. Instead of saving a few, you killed us all.*

That last thought startled James. He hadn't realized it, but he'd been identifying with the dead. Down among the dead men, he had no choice. Despite his conviction, he still had no certainty.

It didn't matter what he thought. He kept going. He pushed a little further into the gloom, now exploring along the walls—no, nothing here, nothing here, nothing here. The darkness refused to give up its secrets. The tunnel had to be in the other direction.

Feeling the pressure rising in his lungs, James headed back to Hu and sucked eagerly, much too eagerly, at the regulator. He had to take a minute to recalibrate himself. Slowly, dammit, slowly.

This time he headed around the escalator, feeling along the walls—but carefully. If he bobbed up that diagonal shaft he might not be able to get back—but there it was. The pedestrian tunnel, a darker dark in the dark. Maybe it was his brain playing tricks with his eyes, the way he could "see" the furniture at home when he got up in the middle of the night to pee. And maybe it was a hallucination from nitrogen narcosis. Too many maybes. But no—a little closer and he was sure. It was the tunnel. He turned around, and just as carefully, he worked his way back to the others.

Three more breaths.

Time to switch out the tank that Hu and Julia were using. It didn't take long, but he had to concentrate, had to be careful. He had to focus.

When he finished, all the headlights were pointed at him. He existed as an oasis of light in a dark universe. He passed his mouthpiece back to the boy and pointed. Time to go.

Everybody but Julia had to carry a tank. They had the two they were still breathing from—and the last two spares.

As a group, they moved, all five of them—James and Hu, Julia and her mother, and the unnamed black teen. It was a tough swim, they bounced along the roof of the station, James herding them carefully away from the escalator shaft. Their headlights weaving in the dark.

They made their way slowly toward the promise of escape.

James didn't know what was at the end of the tunnel. He hoped it wasn't blocked by debris. Or worse—

There were bodies floating in the pedestrian tunnel. Their headlamps revealed a gauntlet of bobbing shapes. James tried not to think about the panic that must have happened in here, the water flooding in so fast, it would have been like trying to swim up a waterfall. Dark shapes bobbed everywhere. And the floor of the tunnel was littered with everything they'd tried to carry with them.

They paused several times for James to suck air. This was not what he had expected. Or hoped for. They had to push their way through a nightmare, faces coming out of the dark—all too close. It was a bumping gauntlet of horror, a gallery of silent accusations, each body turning in its own final orbit. James tried not to look, tried not to illuminate them, but he had no choice. They were passing through a tunnel of horror—a silent community, patiently waiting for James and the others to join them.

Three more breaths—

And at last, the end. Another set of steps. They half-swam, half bobbed up the diagonal shaft. At the top—only darkness. James made them wait. He took three breaths and entered first, turning around slowly, looking to see if it was safe.

He could barely make out any details. It was still way too dark in here. But they were definitely in the foyer of the Wiltern tower, the part that had been carved out for a pedestrian entrance to the subway. That much he could recognize, but he was otherwise unfamiliar with the building. The lobby ceiling was high. He didn't want to get caught up there with no weight-belt to bring him down. There was a railing here, he held onto it against the eddies of current. He could feel himself being pushed this way and that—not a lot, but enough to make him uncomfortable. Outside, the water must still be moving, but he couldn't tell which way. The gloom was that complete.

James swam back into the tunnel. He took breaths from Hu, then from the boy. He didn't want to be selfish, but he didn't want to lose himself to the rapture either. He steadied his breathing and aimed his light around the group. He wasn't familiar with the layout of the building. This was the lobby of the theater. He grabbed his grease pencil and scrawled on the plastic slate. "Stairwell?"

Hu shrugged. He didn't know either.

But Julia's mother reached out and grabbed his arm. She pointed outward and then toward the left. Over there—

But they couldn't just swim over. The problem was buoyancy. They needed to get across the lobby without rising so high they couldn't get to the door.

James looked back into the tunnel. A weird though—

Three more breaths.

He swam back into the pedestrian tunnel, searching. The bottom was littered with the abandoned belongings of the dead. James was looking for suitcases—the canvas ones with one handle on top and another on the side. Whoever these poor fools had been, they weren't smart enough to leave their lives behind. James tested several of the cases for weight, then pulled the two heaviest back to the end.

Three more breaths.

Hu understood immediately. He'd take one suitcase, holding it by the top handle. James would take the other. Julia's mom and the teen would hold on to the side handles. Hu would hold Julia's hand. They should be able to make it.

Three more breaths—and James gave the thumbs-up signal.

As a group, they moved, a curious underwater tableau, a cluster of bobbing lights that revealed air tanks and baggage and faces tight against any further horrors in the dark. The Korean woman kept pointing and gesturing. James kept checking back to her, but in the darkness, it was impossible to know if they were actually heading in the right direction. He had to stop for breath again—and even a second time, until he realized they were paralleling a wall. But he wasn't sure if it was the outer wall of the lobby or the one they had been swimming toward. He didn't know this building, but maybe the lobby wasn't rectangular.

Left or right? James had to guess. He could make out vague shapes in the distance, but those could have been hallucinations. He took three breaths from the teen, then make a decision—the fire stairwell would be against an outer wall of the lobby. Okay, he'd lead them to the left and hope it wasn't a dead-end.

It wasn't. Left was right. He realized with a start that he shouldn't be thinking word games now. That was dangerous.

But they were at the door. It had a wide emergency bar, the kind that pushed to open. For a moment, James felt fear. Without leverage, how could he push it?

Hu was already there, he batted the door with the heavy case he was holding. It bumped open enough for James to wedge his shoulder in. He pushed it further open, revealing only darkness.

James let go of the case he was dragging and entered the stairwell. He grabbed a railing and turned around slowly, looking to see if it was safe. Above, far above, did something glimmer? The surface?

It looked doable.

He gestured, a slow-motion wave.

Hu and the others pushed their way in. James shared three breaths and considered their circumstance. The stairwell was a silent column of dark water, but it was clearer water. They could actually see something. Their headlight beams penetrated for several yards. There wasn't a lot of debris here, and nowhere near as much mud and murk. The water must have filtered in instead of flooding, rising at its own rate.

James looked back. Hu had dropped his case to push the door closed.

His own abandoned suitcase—the teen boy was pulling at its zipper, curious to see what was inside. James swam over and touched the boy's shoulder. The boy looked to him and he waggled his finger no. We're not grave-robbers. Out of the water, the boy's gesture would have been a puzzled shrug, but he let go of the zipper anyway.

Here inside the stairwell, with the fire door closed behind them, they should be safe from any rough currents. Even better, if all the fire doors above were closed, then this column of water would be a convenient chimney. They could ascend at their safest rate. Maybe... If the building hadn't been weakened, if it didn't collapse around them.

The dive computer was still beeping in annoyance. It said the water's surface was less than 100 feet above them. It wanted to know how much air they had—but James couldn't tell it, he didn't know.

The surface might be reachable. If their air held out. If hypothermia didn't get them first.

If a second wave didn't arrive and destroy everything the first wave had already weakened.

James calculated in his head, it was still hard to focus down here, but the math wasn't impossible. One floor every five minutes. Maybe two—? No, they didn't have enough air. They had to get as high as they could as fast as they could. They might manage an extra ten or twenty minutes of decompression nearer the surface. Maybe they could make it.

He took his three breaths, passed the regulator back, and pointed upward.

The light at the end of the tunnel was still a hundred feet above them, and it was still invisible.

It is not a good idea to laugh underwater.

You could drown.

But as James did the math in his head, as he computed the safest rate of ascent through the stairwell measured against his estimate of the amount of air they had left, he ended up reminding himself—

Sloan's teddy....

For a few dangerous seconds, he splurted bubbles. The more he tried to stop himself from laughing, the funnier it got. Hu looked at him, curious, then worried. James finally somehow managed to control himself. He held up a hand, he grabbed his board and wrote on it. "I'm fine. I'll tell you later."

Three breaths and he pointed upward. A single flight of stairs. Then another. Thirty feet. Sloan's teddy indeed.

Five minutes max, then they bobbed up a flight of stairs Except the dive computer on his wrist beeped to let him know that they were still ascending anyway, even as they waited. The waters were receding and somewhere, the chimney must be leaking. Not good. If it leaked too fast and too much. If they "ascended" too rapidly, they were in serious trouble.

James had had the bends. Twice. Once was bad planning, once was stupidity—not his, the diver he'd had to rescue—but either way, it was not something he wanted to do a third time. Rashes, joint pain, headaches, even paralysis. But the bends are survivable—most of the time. Symptoms of decompression sickness can show up in the first hour, almost certainly in the first six hours, and if not in the first 24 hours, then probably not at all.

But if it was a choice between the bends and death?

Another joke occurred to him. "Death? Good choice. But first, Oompah!" He had to suppress a giggle. And then he wondered, what the fuck? Am I getting giddy? Nitrogen narcosis was playing at the edge of his brain.

Three breaths from Hu, then three breaths from the boy. He was going to have to start watching himself. All these people were depending on him. It was time. He pointed. Up the next flight of stairs. And the next. And the next.

The higher they rose, the brighter the stairwell, the brighter the promise above. The water here wasn't as murky as it was below, but now there was debris floating in their way—a lot of paper, and a large rubber trash can, someone's jacket, and when James looked up, he thought he saw a body caught under a railing.

He checked his goddamn beeping dive computer and frowned. There was nothing he could do. Maybe they should wait an extra two minutes here? He took three breaths from Hu, three from the boy, gestured for them to wait and swam halfway up to look.

Yes, a body. A woman, stocky, possibly in her fifties, hard to tell. Her hair floated like a cloud around her head, but her dress had floated up revealing thick legs and pale underpants, they had become translucent, revealing her nakedness before his light—one last embarrassment. The tsunami had not only taken her life, it had taken her dignity as well.

James came back down again, grabbed another six breaths, then gestured for the others to follow him—but he waved his hand down past his eyes to show Julia and her mother to close theirs. Up the stairwell and James tried to push the woman's body into a corner while the others rose past. Her name badge identified her as Mrs. Hayes. She was entitled to this much consideration—he didn't want the others to see her shame. Poor Mrs. Hayes.

Another flight up, another rubber trash can. And here was the cause of the decreasing pressure. The fire door was jammed open by another body, this one a janitor in a dark uniform. James could feel the current here—the water was being sucked away. Outside the broken tower, the current must have become too strong to resist. James felt himself being pulled—it was strong enough to be a challenge.

He pulled on the fire door, pushing it open enough for the poor man's body to be sucked through and away. He let go and the current pushed the door shut again, cutting off the water's escape.

He was surprised that he'd been able to pull the door open at all. The force of the water was less than he'd expected. This was both good news and bad news.

They were closer to the surface—but they were also more at risk of decompression sickness. He swam back down to the others. Three breaths from Hu, three breaths from the boy, and three more breaths from Hu. They were going to have to wait here ten minutes at least. Maybe more.

And they were already on their last tanks. He didn't remember when they had switched over, but apparently he had done so at some point up the chimney of the stairwell. Maybe at the bottom, before they started up? Not a good sign that he didn't remember. He studied the dials on the last two tanks.

Good—

—Just not good enough.

He floated on his back so he could peer upward through the gap between the stairs. There was light up there, brighter than before. He watched his bubbles rise up through his headlamp beam toward it.

He did the numbers in his head. The math was not negotiable. The bends were no longer a risk, no longer a possibility. Now they were simply inevitable. The only question was how to manage the ascent to make them survivable.

They had maybe twenty minutes of air left in the tanks, maybe thirty. They had at least fifty feet still to ascend. That is, if the dive computer was correct. James sorted through his memories—his research, his training, and the experiences of other divers.

His instinct was to ascend slowly and safely. That was what his training demanded. But the math said no—not gonna make it. The alternative was to rise to a point maybe ten or fifteen feet just below the surface and wait there. At that depth, their air would last much longer, giving them more time to decompress before it ran out. From there, they could safely ascend the last short distance to the surface.

James would have preferred to stick with the advice of the nagging, beeping dive computer, but that wasn't his best option. The water was still receding, draining out of the building around them. Even if they waited here, they were still ascending—or rather, the surface was descending to meet them.

And in addition to everything else, he was starting to feel the cold as a painful presence. He was starting to shiver. That was okay. If he stopped shivering, that would be very not okay. It would mean his body was shutting down. He wasn't worried about that, he knew his tolerances. But what about the others?

He was reaching that point where he really wanted to get out of the water—he wanted to get out *now*. And if he was feeling this way, then it was probably a lot worse for the others. He turned his headlamps toward Julia and her mom, who was holding Julia close to her body, trying to share warmth. In this water, it was a futile effort.

James took his three breaths. He looked across at Hu, who looked back at him hopefully.

It was enough.

Fuck it. We are not going to die today.

He swam from one to the other, Julia, her mom, the boy, and finally Hu, checking once again to make sure that each was all right. Later on, perhaps, he might be able to marvel at their endurance—but right now, they had no choice. Either they hung on, or they became like all those others they had passed below. Like poor Mrs. Hayes.

More breaths. And another flight of stairs. Another and another.

The surface was a lot closer than he realized. The stairwell must be leaking somewhere. Had they closed the door at the bottom? He didn't remember. Or maybe the fire doors weren't all that water-tight. Or maybe there was enough structural damage that the whole building was as secure as a screen door.

The good news, the afternoon light flickered brightly above. He could see rippling light through the water's surface now, a promise of survival, and even though he still swam in a dirty murky world, filled with little floating things, the walls of the stairwell were no longer hidden behind a fog of gloom. But he wasn't ready to feel confident. Not yet. Overconfidence is just another way to die.

They had to wait here as long as possible. James took his three breaths and studied the dive computer. It had finally given up and stopped beeping, but it still insisted that the surface of the water was steadily descending to meet them.

A large rubber trash can drifted by. Was this the fourth or fifth? Why so many? Something else to wonder about. He began to imagine the episode of Nova that would examine these events.

Three breaths. Three breaths. Three more breaths.

He checked the gauges again. He studied the dive computer, blinking. It didn't make sense. No, it made sense. *He* wasn't making sense. It didn't matter what the gauges said, they were running out of air. There was no more time.

Not today. We didn't come all this way to die here.

James fumbled for the plastic slate, felt along the leash for the grease pen, wrote on it frantically. "Drop tanks. Go up. My signal." He turned to the others, holding the slate so that each of them could see the words. He took three quick breaths, then pointed up. Waving his arm in a broad "Let's go, now!" motion.

He didn't have to push them. They were eager to go. They each took a last long suck of air, then dropped the regulators and scrambled up. Hu grabbed Julia by the waist and they half-swam, half-walked up the last flight of stairs. James pushed Julia's mom and the black boy after them. He followed, the pressure in his lungs growing. He should have taken a last breath himself.

He looked back. The tanks were tumbling away. bouncing in slow-motion irretrievably down the stairwell, a lost opportunity. He pushed himself upward. He couldn't see. His vision was blurry, closing in, he needed one more breath, he couldn't hold it—

The top of the stairwell was open to the sky. The walls were broken here. A twisted doorframe remained where a fire door had been. James struggled to reach for it, he felt himself sinking back—

—and a pair of hands reached down and yanked him roughly out of the water.

A confusion of words, an unfamiliar voice, "Are there any more—?"

"No, no. Just the five of us—" That was Hu. His voice sounded strange, garbled by water. Someone else was choking, a small high voice. Julia?

He couldn't see. Everything was a glare. He was on his back, gasping, choking, coughing up water—how had that happened? His last strangled ascent? Everything here was blue, incongruously bright. Two faces abruptly blocked his view, dark silhouettes, he didn't know them. Where had they come from?

"Don't try to talk. Just concentrate on breathing, okay?"

There were hands all over him, pulling away the last of the rig on his back, pulling his mask away, loosening his shirt. Someone had their head to his chest, trying to listen to his heartbeat. James coughed, choked up more water, and the person pulled away. His lungs hurt badly.

"Hu—?" he called. "Hu?"

"I'm here. I'm okay." A hasty answer.

James concentrated on breathing now. A deep breath. Another. Stop to cough, spit up, cough, then breathe again.

Three deep breaths. Three more. Three more. Don't hyperventilate. Hold your breath a moment and appreciate that you can.

He was almost back when he suddenly remembered an old movie, a favorite. He called out, "Are we dead, mon?"

Hu called back, falsetto. "I'm not dead yet, I'm not."

James laughed. He laughed until he coughed and choked up even more water. His throat hurt, but he laughed anyway. He rolled over on his side and looked across at Hu. His husband was half up on his knees, also laughing.

James flailed, helplessly, trying to sit up. Hands grabbed him from behind, someone helped him to a sitting position. James looked around. They were on a wide empty floor, slightly tilted, very broken. But his vision was still blurry, partly from the glare of the day, partly from the painful tears filling his eyes, an involuntary reaction to the overwhelming dazzle. The whole world looked overexposed, the people here were silhouettes, vague shapes in the glare. Maybe a dozen, he wasn't sure.

Hu scooted over to him, looked at him carefully, then scooted around to sit beside him. He bumped him affectionately with his shoulder. James looked at Hu, a weak grin on his face. Hu looked tired. But alive. Even smiling.

After a moment of silent acceptance, a moment of just surviving, James looked around at their rescuers. "Who are you people? How did you get up here? How did you get through?"

"We should ask you the same question," said one of the men. "I'm Scott Copeland. Who are you?"

"James Liddle. And that's Hu Son. And the little girl is Julia. I don't know her mother's name. Are they all right?"

"They will be, yes. Sophie's looking after them. And the teenager too. Looks like you had a rough ride."

James nodded. "The subway. The last train. Didn't make it."

"Yeah, we heard—" The man pointed. "We've been following the news. The cellphone towers are down, but Jack's Walkman has FM. Three trains were lost."

"Three—?"

"Yeah. Real bad scene at Union Station."

James didn't say anything then, didn't want to say what he was thinking, didn't want to make the fear real. He realized he was weak. Exhausted. He looked around. They were on a sloping tile surface. The stairwell was a square opening with a few broken steps rising out of the water. "Is this the top floor?"

"No. This was the tenth floor. The top three floors were ripped away." Copeland's expression went grim. "That's where most of the people went. I suppose it seemed like a good idea. It was wall-to-wall crowded. Probably exceeded the structural limits. But, see, the top floors of a building are never the strongest. The lower floors are built to hold the weight of the floors above."

"You're a builder—?"

"Architect. I know this building. It's a good one. Well, it was. We started on the seventh floor, that's where our offices were. When the water started rising, we moved up to the eighth, eventually the ninth. Had to stop there. The people above wouldn't let us keep going, said there was no more room." Copeland sighed and shrugged—a gesture of both sadness and grim irony.

"We'd been shredding old blueprints. We had thirty or forty bins of paper we still hadn't emptied. When the water broke the windows and started rising inside the building, we emptied all the biggest trash cans, turned them upside down and stuck our heads in to breathe. It was a gamble, but it worked. Each bin had enough air to last ten minutes, twenty if we were careful. And we had, I dunno, thirty bins. I saved my people. Most of them."

"But you lost a couple…" James glanced toward the broken stairwell, wondering if the bloated cadaver of poor Mrs. Hayes might suddenly bob up in the surface of the trapped water.

Copeland followed his glance. "Yeah. We had some panic. It was pretty bad. We did everything we could." Copeland was reluctant to explain. "What about you? Down in the subway—?"

James remembered the man who'd tried to take Hu's regulator. He could still see the man's startled expression, the sudden horrified realization that he was dying—dying twice, once by drowning, once by knife—and the crushing certainty that this was truly death. James shook his head, he didn't want to talk about it.

Copeland recognized the expression. "Yeah. Bad day all around." He straightened. "Let me see if there's any water left." He disappeared from James' field of view.

James concentrated on his breathing for a while. Open air. There was a delicious luxury. How had he ever taken breathing for granted? Finally, he looked around, searching for Julia and her mother. Spotting then, he crawled over on his hands and knees. He still didn't feel like standing. Julia was clutching her mother, her face buried in her mother's side, her shoulders rising and falling as if she was sobbing.

"Are you okay?"

"I prayed to God, and he sent you to save us."

"Well, I don't know about God, but—"

"No, it was God—"

"Okay. It was God. I'm just glad that you and Julia made it. You must have been scared."

"No. I knew that God sent you. So I wasn't scared. I just kept praying and thanking God for sending you to us."

"Ahh. Well, I guess it worked."

"Yes. And God will bless you for what you did."

"Not gonna argue that—I can use all the blessings I can get. I'm just glad you both made it." James patted her shoulder, patted Julia's shoulder, but the little girl didn't look up. James had seen this behavior before, Julia was going to have nightmares. She was going to have some serious post-traumatic-stress. And she was going to need some serious therapy. Oh, hell—they all would.

He turned away, crawled back to Hu. The unnamed black boy was sitting next to him, sucking at a bottle of water. He passed the water bottle to Hu, the two of them had been talking, sharing, debriefing each other.

Hu looked to James. "This is Jesse. He's a student at LACC."

James held out his hand. "I'm James. I'm glad you made it."

"So am I, man! That was intense! I am never riding that subway again!"

"I don't think anybody will," James agreed.

Jesse waved his arm, indicating the world around them. "How long we gonna be up here, you know?"

James hadn't even considered the question. He put one hand against a fragment of wall. He raised himself half-up onto his knees—

The hot July sun blazed above. The landscape rippled and foamed below. Everything was too bright. It took a moment for James' vision to clear, for his eyes to focus all the way to the horizon. And then it took another moment for him to make sense of what he was seeing—all the devastation that surrounded them.

James levered himself to his feet, holding onto the spur of the broken wall. He turned slowly, slowly, shaking his head, saying only, "Fuck. Oh, fuck. Oh, fuck." And then, even more sadly, "Oh, fuck."

They were alone in the middle of a vast brown sea. The water was receding—slowly. But more water was still trying to push in—uneven ripples of the reverberating shockwaves. Everywhere, the water foamed and surged, churning the debris. Things tumbled in the water, all kinds of things, broken signs, buses, cars, trees, the inevitable palm fronds, pieces of buildings, roofs and walls—and bodies. Too many bodies.

The sea of desolation extended north, all the way to the Hollywood hills. A few buildings stuck their tops out of the water—but not many. To the west and the south, the view was much the same. There was a rise in the southern distance. Baldwin Hills was now Baldwin Island, probably nothing more than a naked lump. The ferocious power of the waves would have scraped everything away.

The rest was mud.

James saw the past as if it were still the present. The riot at the Santa Monica underpass, the old men at the VA Health center, the carefree golfers, and all the people in all the cars they'd passed, the little boy staring from a car window on Wilshire Blvd...

How many of them had escaped and how many more had been caught in the overwhelming wrath of the tsunami? It was all unknowable, all washed away too quickly to comprehend.

James tried to imagine—something, anything—a future.

He couldn't.

It would take months just to catalog the devastation. The scale of this thing—there was nothing left. Nothing to rebuild. The city was gone.

"Fuck," said James.

It was going to be a long uncomfortable afternoon.

Hu pulled him back down, pulled him next to him. "You okay?"

"No."

Hu didn't respond to that. He waited a bit before saying anything else.

Finally, "You kept your promise."

"I did?"

"You said we weren't going to die today."

"The day's not over."

"Shut up." Hu said it gently, affectionately. He took James' left hand and held it up to admire the gold band on the third finger. He traced it with his own fingers. "But I will say this." He paused.

"What?"

"This is the worst honeymoon I've ever been on—"

"Oh, really? How many others have you had—?

"This is the first."

"Then it's also the *best* honeymoon you've ever been on."

"Yeah, I guess so." Hu leaned his head on James' shoulder. They were silent for a while. Just being together.

"Hey—" said Jesse, interrupting their silence.

"Yeah?"

"You guys are fags, aren't you?"

James hadn't heard that word in years. He was more surprised than offended. "Yeah, I am. I'm not so sure about my husband though. Is that a problem?"

Jesse pointed to James' discarded facemask, as if looking for the lost regulator. "Yeah, man—! I had your—your thing in my mouth. Yuck—" He got up and moved away.

Hu and James looked at each other. Both started laughing.

"What an ungrateful little prick," Hu said. "Why did you save him, anyway?"

James shrugged. "It seemed like a good idea at the time."

Swarms of helicopters filled the air over the seething brown water that used to be Los Angeles. They were clattering dragonflies, darting here and there, exploring, recording, reporting. The afternoon was bright, but ugly.

Some of the newer buildings, the ones designed to resist a massive earthquake, had survived. They stuck up out of the water like broken stumps.

Where there had been neighborhoods, there was now only mud and water and debris, occasionally patterned by the gridwork of streets that had survived. Mostly the terrain below was a vast sea of desolation. What remained of the 405 was a scar. The Federal building looked like a fractured tooth. The Veterans' Health Care Center was gone, only a broken steel outline remained to mark its location.

Nevertheless, the choppers swarmed, relentlessly searching—and occasionally, improbably, also triumphantly rescuing. Here and there, despite impossible odds, some people had survived the onslaught of the tsunami. Soon or eventually, whenever they could get to safety, they would have the opportunity to tell their stories to the hungry cameras. Every survival was an improbable adventure—a delusion of luck and prayer, sometimes even a bit of good judgment and courage.

Several Air Force communications planes circled patiently overhead, coordinating the fleets of choppers. The Army, the Navy, the Air Force, the Coast Guard, and several civilian companies were patrolling, each in their assigned area. All other air traffic was forbidden. Even the news choppers were under military guidance now. The Goodyear and Fuji blimps as well.

Three Navy choppers were assigned to an area formerly known as Little Korea. There were few landmarks left on the ground, they had to depend on GPS mapping to locate themselves.

"There—" said the co-pilot. "Two O'clock."

"What am I looking for?"

"Over there. It's a light, hard to see in the glare—"

The chopper pilot brought the machine around. "That green stump sticking out of the water—?"

"Yeah? See that flicker?"

"I see it." As they approached, the pilot said, "Holy shit. That used to be the Wiltern!"

"You recognize it?"

"My grandmother used to live in this area." He added, "Actually, it's the Pellissier building, but everyone calls it the Wiltern."

They came in lower for a closer view. The tsunami had ripped the top off the building. But it had left enough for several stories to remain sticking up out of the water. Open floor space was visible, enough for several people to gather. One was waving a light of some kind.

The co-pilot called to the divers in the back of the machine. "We've got survivors. More than a dozen."

"Any injuries?"

"Maybe. Some of them are down."

"We'll take the worst. Blue Team can pick up the rest."

"Copy that."

The chopper came in low and the people on the top of the building stood up to wave at them. One of them was aiming the headlamps of a diver's mask. He switched it off as the aircraft approached.

The heli hovered over the building, stirring up the waves in great rippling circles. Four lines dropped from the machine. Two figures in wetsuits came down two of the lines, two rescue stretchers came down the others.

"Who's the worst injured?" asked Seal Team Commander Wright.

The survivors looked around, uncertain, but a young Chinese man pointed. "Take the little girl. She's got hypothermia and maybe the bends."

"The bends?"

"Long story," said the man next to him. "And her mom too."

The other Seal was already pulling the rescue stretchers over to Julia and her mother. "Anyone else with the bends?" asked Wright.

The Chinese man pointed to an African-American teenager, held his own hand up, then pointed to the man next to himself, who tried to wave them away. "I'm okay—" But his hand trembled.

"Bullshit, you are." Commander Wright peered from one to the other. He spoke to his microphone. "Gonna need two more stretchers. No, make it three." He turned to the other survivors. "We've got another bird coming in behind us. We'll have you all out of here as quickly as we can." Back to the microphone. "We'll need water and blankets. And maybe some protein."

The first two stretchers lifted away, one after the other, Julia and her mother wrapped in heating blankets. Three more stretchers, all tied together, hanging in a cluster, came down another line—and another Seal Team member as well.

When they came for James, dragging a rescue stretcher with them, he shook his head. "No," he said, pointing. "Hu Son first."

"What?" asked Wright?"

"He's on second," said James. But they were already wrapping him, lifting him into the stretcher, fastening the Velcro straps.

As they secured Hu into his own rescue stretcher, he looked over to James a bemused expression on his face. "I can't believe you just said that."

James said, "It's been a long day—" and passed out.

Wright signaled the chopper, the first stretcher with James lifted away. A moment later, Hu followed. Then Jesse. Wright followed them up, leaving two Seals behind with the remaining survivors. Even as they clattered away, the second chopper was moving in for the pickup.

"Where we taking them?" Wright asked.

"Wait a minute—" Co-pilot called back. He was talking to someone on one of the communication planes. "Getty isn't taking anymore. And Dodger Stadium is full. The parking lot is tent city now." Abruptly, he paused, listening. "Okay, Copy that." To the pilot, he said. "Griffith Observatory."

Pilot nodded. The co-pilot turned back Wright. "Did you hear that? Griffith Observatory. They've got an aid station there—and they're running shuttles down into Burbank. They want to shorten our turnaround time." Turning back to the pilot, he added, "They're bringing a fuel truck up too."

Pilot nodded, his only acknowledgment.

The Hollywood Hills were directly ahead. But below them, muddy water still churned across the flooded city.

The center of Los Angeles was gone —and so was its heart.

Griffith Observatory stands on one of the highest hills on the northern edge of the basin. It overlooks the entire city. It is a familiar landmark for both tourists and filmmakers.

Today, its wide lawn and parking lot served as a rescue station, a place for helicopters to bring survivors and refuel, a place for ambulances and buses to take survivors down the northern side of the hills to Burbank and North Hollywood, and other places safely beyond the reach of the churning ocean.

James and Hu stood at a western railing, one of the better viewing positions, and looked out over what was now called The Bay of LA. Or Bayla for short. On the hills to their right, the Hollywood sign survived untouched. It still declared the fabled town, but of Hollywood there was nothing left. Only a sea of mud. Already a smell of wet decay was rising from below. Despite the lingering heat of the day, they were both wrapped in blankets.

They held hands, but neither had anything to say. Despite their mutual joint pains, their headaches, and their blotchy patches of red skin, they had not been considered at severe risk. They'd been given oxygen, it had helped, but Julia's condition was much more serious, so was her mother's, so they were taken for immediate treatment. James and Hu would have to wait awhile for further attention. If at all.

"Triage," someone had explained, not understanding why Hu and James had exchanged a look.

But it was obvious now. Sooner or later, everybody is triage.

They both hurt all over. Hu had thought to dump the contents of their medicine cabinet into his backpack. They had Ibuprofen and it helped—a little. Just not enough. They were going to have to walk this off and wait it out.

The wide lawns in front of the observatory were filled with tents, tables, and bustling emergency workers. The parking lot in front of that was filled with more tents and more crowds of people. The only open area was a space set aside for helicopters to land and take off. A fuel truck waited nearby. Several television vans were parked on the grass.

A Red Cross tent had been set up where people could get coffee and donuts and even some packaged meals, but despite their growing hunger, neither James nor Hu felt like eating. They were still too uncomfortable.

A young black woman came up to them, carrying a tablet. Her badge identified her as some kind of city official, James couldn't read it. He was still having trouble seeing clearly.

"Have you been logged in?" she asked, holding up the tablet.

James shook his head.

"We're trying to assemble a roster of survivors. You were in the Wiltern building?"

"No. We were in the subway. We came up the fire stairs of the Wiltern building—"

She looked puzzled. "How did you do that?"

"SCUBA," said James. He was still holding his facemask. He held it up as if that was the only explanation he needed.

"Um, okay," she said, not quite sure what he meant, but it didn't matter anyway. "Your names?"

"James Liddle. Hu Son."

The young woman was wearing a headset, she repeated their answers to her headset, checking that the tablet properly translated her speech to text.

"Address?"

"Nowhere now," said James.

"Venice Beach," said Hu. He told her their address, but it was meaningless now.

The woman asked a few more questions: Email addresses, cellphone numbers, Social Security numbers, birth dates, and preferred gender identification. Finally, "We're going to try to find you a place to stay. I can't promise that you'll be together—"

James held up Hu's hand in his own. "He's my husband. We stay together."

She didn't blink. She referred to her tablet. Apparently it was connected to some master database somewhere. She looked up. "Do you have any documentation?"

James held up his left hand, showing the ring. "Is this good enough?"

"Um, I'm sorry. No. We've had people trying to lie to us."

"Does it matter?"

"Yes, it does." She looked annoyed. "The relief benefits are different for married couples—"

Hu interrupted. He was already fumbling in his backpack, pulling out a dry bag. "Does a marriage license count?" He had a sheaf of papers, all safe inside three concentric Zip-Lok bags. He sorted through the papers, passed one over.

She took it, looked at it, shook her head, and passed it back. "It's not signed—"

"We were supposed to get married today. We would have been on our way to—to our honeymoon."

James said, "Is there a judge up here? Or a minister? Someone who can sign this?"

"Uh—" She looked confused. "Let me check." She walked away, already pulling her phone out of her pocket.

Hu said, "Well, that's—"

"— fucked." finished James.

It was all too much.

James turned away, leaned on the stone railing, not wanting to look at anyone or anything anymore. But there it was—the muddy sea of Bayla and its broken towers. He tried hard not to give in to his rage. But—it was all too much. Everything was gone. Everything. He had nothing. No words. No feeling. He was numb.

He had the clothes on his back, whatever was still attached to his tool belt, a diving watch that had stopped, an expensive dive computer he never wanted to see again, a half-empty backpack, and for some reason, he was still holding onto his facemask, afraid to be let it go, even up here.

And Hu.

He still had Hu.

But … he had nothing else. Nothing left to give. Nothing for Hu. Nothing for anyone. He was empty. Scraped raw. Numb.

He had finally hit bottom.

Hu stood next to him, silent. He put his hand on James' shoulder, but James didn't react, didn't even acknowledge the touch. Finally, Hu reached out to take the facemask from him, but James pulled it back.

"Jimmy—? Talk to me. Please?"

James didn't respond. He looked at the mask—as if seeing it for the first time, an ugly reminder of everything he would never see again. It was a useless appendage. He might as well throw it away and have nothing left at all. Without thinking, he lifted his arm, poised to throw it over the edge of the railing and down to the rough hillside below.

But Hu grabbed his wrist and stopped him—

"Jimmy, no—"

As if startled awake, James looked to Hu. "What—?"

Hu took the mask, turned it around and held it up to show something to James. "Did you know your camera was on?"

"It's automatic," James said. He took the facemask from Hu. A pair of fisheye lenses were mounted above the glass, one on each side of the two headlamps—they were designed for capturing virtual-reality 3D video.

James frowned at the readout on the left side of mask. "Hmp," he said. "Looks like it recorded everything from the moment the water hit—"

"Really?"

"I'd have to pull the card, but yeah—"

Hu cut him off. "Jimmy, maybe we could sell that footage to someone? Some news channel? Or maybe even Nova? Someone? It might be worth something—"

James shook his head. "I doubt it. Everybody will have footage. Every survivor with a phone. And probably a few thousand amateur drones as well. There's going to be more video than anybody will have time to review."

"But nobody has underwater footage of the subway—"

James stopped in mid-sentence. Hu was right. He started to agree, then stopped abruptly. "No. We can't."

"Huh? Why not?"

James put his hand to his belt, touched his knife.

Hu's eyes followed. "Oh," he said, realizing what James meant.

"Squeak—I killed a man—"

"It was self-defense—"

"No. It wasn't. It was deliberate—"

"We could talk to a lawyer—"

"Christine retired, remember the party—"

"She could recommend someone. Maybe Suzanne? Or Cindy?"

James didn't answer immediately. "Yeah, maybe. But—"

"But—?"

"But—that's not the point."

"What is?"

"I killed a man, Hu. That's murder. I committed a murder—"

"Jimmy—"

"And I did it without thinking. I did it so easy—"

"You didn't have a choice. You did it to save me—"

"—and I'd do it again. In a heartbeat. But—"

Hu understood it—James was in pain. A lot of pain, and most of it wasn't physical. Hu wanted to say something, but he didn't know what. "Bubble—?"

"I don't know who he was. I don't want to know. What if he had a family? People waiting for him? Oh, God. What if they recover his body someday. They'll see his throat. And someone will figure it out—"

"Jimmy! Stop it. Look out there. Look at that mess—nobody's going to recover anything."

"Squeak, you stop it! I know what I did! I have to live with it."

Hu put his hand on James' arm. "Bubble—listen to me. What we went through—it was horrible. It was all my worst fears, everything, all at once—but I made it because you were there—you. Just like the first time."

James started to protest, but Hu grabbed him by both shoulders and poured out the rest of his words in a frantic rush. "Out of all the millions of people who died today—God knows how many, but we survived, you and I—and Julia and her mother, and that little prick, Jesse too. We survived because survival is what you do. It's who you are."

"Who I am—?" James couldn't stand it. "I know who I am now. I don't want to be who I am—I couldn't save him! I had to—had to—"

"No, listen! Listen to me—as much as I hate to say this, because it's so fucking cruel and selfish to even think this way, but it's still true anyway—that man was already dead when he boarded the subway. Every single one of them. We all were. We just didn't know it. And if you and I had left the bike trailers behind, if we'd abandoned the tanks when we thought they were too heavy, we'd be dead too. All five of us. And your last thoughts would have been rage at yourself for listening to my whining—this is better! Isn't it?"

But James was adamant in his pain. "I know what you're trying to do, Squeak. And I love you for it. But—I know what I did—and it hurts me so much inside to know that I did it—that I'm even capable of it. This hurts like you can't imagine—"

"Excuse me, guys—?" An interruption. A voice from behind them. They turned to see Seal Team Commander Wright. He was holding Jesse by the upper arm. "You the guys from the subway?"

"Yeah?"

Wright let go of Jesse, but not before saying to him. "Stay." Then he held out his hand to James. "I heard what you did down there, heard it from the kid. It must have been rough, but I wanted you to know, it's one of the best things I've heard today. I mean, you done good." Wright shook James' hand, then Hu's. He nodded back toward the chopper. "We're refueling, going back out in thirty, but I wanted to make sure you were good. And uh, the kid here has something to say to you too." He poked Jesse. "Go ahead, mister."

Jesse looked embarrassed. He swallowed hard and looked at his feet. When he looked up, his eyes were wet. "I'm sorry for what I said. I don't know why I said it. It just fell out. But I wouldn't have made it if it wasn't for you guys. So ... um, I guess, I want to say thank you, I owe you my life, and I hope you'll forgive me for being such a dick."

Hu's smile came easier than James'. He said, "It's okay."

"No, it's not. I mean, why'd you do it? You didn't have to. I mean, I saw what you did to that other guy and—"

James interrupted quickly, "You said please."

"Huh? That's it?"

"Yeah, that was it."

"Whoa," said Jesse. "Whoa."

"Yeah, whoa."

Jesse looked confused. "I don't get it."

James smiled sourly. "Neither do I, kid. Neither do I."

Wright had watched the whole exchange. He spoke up now. "There's nothing to get. You did what was in front of you." To Jesse, he said, "He gave you a second chance. Now you gotta make the most of it. Make a difference." He pushed the teen gently.

Jesse held out his hand. James took it, shook it. So did Hu.

"We're good then?"

James and Hu nodded. Wright seemed satisfied. He lifted his hand in a salute of respect and headed back to his chopper.

Jesse stood there, still looking embarrassed, shifting from one foot to the other. Finally, he gave a nervous smile. "I'm gonna go get in line for the phone. Okay? Gotta call my gramma and let her know I made it. I hope you guys land on your feet." And then he was gone too.

"Well," said Hu. "That was something."

"Yeah," agreed James. "He said please."

But he was still in a funk so deep it was no longer blue, it had gone to indigo. He turned back to the railing and stared across at the Hollywood sign without really seeing it.

"Excuse me—?" Another interruption.

This time it was a man in a clerical collar. He looked like some casting director's idea of the perfect priest—but one who is falsely accused of molesting little boys until exonerated in the third act denouement. "Are you the ones looking for a minister? I'm Father Feigenberg—"

"*Father* Feigenberg? Really? You're kidding me."

"I get that a lot, yes. Someone said you needed a priest." He looked at them with puzzled curiosity. "Do you want me to pray with you?"

James and Hu looked at each other, then back to Father Feigenberg. Hu spoke first. "We need you to make us legal. We want you to say some nice words and then sign this—" He passed over the marriage license.

Father Feigenberg looked at their marriage license, looked from one to the other, back to the license, then back to the two of them again. "Um, I'm afraid I can't—my faith doesn't recognize same-sex unions."

"Oh, hell!" said James, frustrated. It was just too much. He said it loud enough that a few nearby people turned around to look. James turned angrily to the railing, glowered out at the landscape of mud and desolation and everything buried under it—then, just as abruptly, he whirled back. "Father? Will you hear my confession?"

Hu's eyes widened. "I didn't know you were Catholic—"

"Recovering," admitted James. "Father—?"

Father Feigenberg nodded. He led James a short distance away, to the best privacy they could find—a quiet space behind a pedestal with a bronze bust of James Dean. It had been installed as a commemoration of the famous observatory scenes in Rebel Without A Cause.

Hu watched from a distance as both James and the priest knelt together. First James crossed himself, then bent his head to whisper to Father Feigenberg's ear. He took a long time, and halfway through, the priest reached over to put his hand on James' shoulder, a gesture of solidarity and comfort. James kept talking—and then a little after that, he started weeping. Father Feigenberg pulled him close and let him cry into his shoulder.

Finally, James pulled back and Father Feigenberg made the sign of the cross over him, and said some words in Latin, some words that James so desperately needed to hear. His whole body relaxed. And even from a distance, Hu could see that James' pain had been lessened. Not released, not yet—but lessened. It was a start.

Finally, after a few more minutes, Father Feigenberg led James back to Hu—the two shared a look.

"Are you all right?"

"A little better. Yeah."

Feigenberg looked from one to the other. He hadn't met many same-sex couples, a side-effect of his particular calling. But he felt there was something else he needed to say before this moment could be considered complete.

"The two of you—" He looked from James to Hu and back again. "You didn't get here by accident. You got here because...yes, I know it sounds presumptuous, and you don't have to believe me, but I'm certain that the two of you are here because you're supposed to be here. Together."

That last word from Father Feigenberg surprised both James and Hu. It wasn't the word so much as the man saying it.

Hu managed to speak first. "Thank you."

Feigenberg nodded an acknowledgment. "So how long have you two been together?"

"Three years."

Feigenberg was impressed. "Mm-hm. That's a commitment, isn't it?"

"Commitment, hell," said James. "It's a privilege." He put his arm around Hu's shoulder and pulled him close. "He's the one."

"Yep," agreed Hu, smiling. "Today was gonna be the day." He held up his hand to show his ring.

James held up his hand to show a matching ring. "We made a promise. Hell or high water, we're saying our vows today. It was high water. Really high water. So we said 'em. In the subway. Just before the water hit."

Hu said, "It was really romantic. And terrifying too. I spent the whole day afraid I was going to lose him—"

Feigenberg nodded gently. It seemed a polite acknowledgment, but then he said, "Listen to me. As a priest ordained in the Catholic church, I cannot formally bless your union in the eyes of God. But...as a legally established authority in the state of California, empowered to recognize the union of two consenting adults—" He paused to clear his throat. "—I now pronounce you...married. Congratulations. Mazel Tov. Now, let me sign your document." He held out his hand for the marriage license.

And now it was Hu's turn to cry—but this time for joy.

A different kind of urban fantasy.

THE THING IN THE BACK YARD

That Pesky Dan Goodman is not a bad person. He has a good heart. He's well-intentioned. And I just might kill him anyway. Every time he wanders through my life, the unintended consequences are always disastrous.

Always.

I ran into him at Bob's Big Boy in Toluca Lake. It's a local landmark. Weekends, the parking lot is filled with classic cars and the wait time for a table is an hour. It's a coffee shop decorated with as much history and ambience as Los Angeles is capable of—plaques and photos dating all the way back to 1936. The food ranges in quality from meh to meh-plus. Be grateful it won't kill you. But this is one of the few places that still knows how to make the classic Big Boy double-deck hamburger, of which all other double-deck hamburgers (including the Big Mac) are mere imitations.

For me, the Big Boy hamburger is comfort food, because Bob's is where my dad used to take me on special occasions. We called it "Big Bob's." So it's where I take my son when we need a special night. I don't always order the Big Boy anymore, because now it falls into the category of one of those things that you eat until you hate yourself. The food coma hits before you can get to the parking lot.

Never mind. This time, I had an afternoon meeting in Burbank. I was feeling a bit peckish—that's a strange word to me, an English term, I don't really get it, but never mind, I've always wanted to use it in a sentence and now that I've done so, I can die happy. It'll never happen again.

I was hungry and I stopped in for a salad. I like their blue cheese dressing. Or is it bleu cheese? However you spell it, it's only good when it's fresh.

And that's when and where and why That Pesky Dan Goodman found me. But then, he always finds me in restaurants. This is why I carry antacids with me. And too often, the meeting ends with me picking up the check for both of us. I think he has a tracking device in my wallet.

He plopped himself down opposite. "May I join you?"

"You just did." I looked square across at him. "And no, you may not nominate me for the presidency of the Los Angeles Science Fantasy Society or the Board of Directors of any other organization. And whatever else you're going to ask, the answer is already no. So don't bother asking."

He said, "Okay." And maybe I was going to be lucky. Maybe the conversation was over. But he waved at the waiter. "I'll have an iced tea, please."

Back to me. "You look annoyed about something."

"Yeah, a little—"

I was annoyed—annoyed at having my private time interrupted. I politely closed my laptop, I'd finish proofreading the manuscript later. But I was too courteous to say that I was annoyed at the intrusion. That was my first mistake.

"Can I help?"

And this is how the Goodman trap is sprung—with some innocent remark that leads into what looks like a harmless conversation. And I, not watching where I'm going, step right into the bear trap hidden beneath the pine needles.

"We've been having a burglary problem. We think we know who it is, but we can't prove it."

"How are they getting in?"

"The alley in back. They're coming over the wall. Three meter high cinder block affair, but there's a telephone pole at one corner, so all someone has to do is climb it."

"I'm sorry to hear that. I hope you didn't lose anything important."

"We had a PlayStation stolen. Some CDs and DVDs. Those are replaceable. But they took my Z1U."

"Ouch. What's a Z1U?"

"Six years ago, it was one of the best professional-level HD video cameras you could buy. Five kilobucks. It's still a great camera. Or would be if I still had it. Now I've got a box of tapes that I have no way to transfer to the hard drive. It'll cost another two or three thousand dollars to pick up a used or refurbished one."

"You said you know who it is. Can't you get it back?"

"We can't prove it. We think it's one of my son's friends. Ex-friends. Someone the dog knows."

"Dogzilla?"

"Yeah. She only bites strangers. She bit one guy who tried to sneak in our back gate while we were cleaning out the garage. A week later, he had the gall to come to my front door with his doctor's bill—until I showed him the video surveillance. He was definitely on my property."

"So you've got a dog, you've got video, and you've still got stuff disappearing?"

"Yeah."

"You need an on-site security force."

"I wish—"

There. That was the sound of the steel jaws of the trap snapping shut, but I was too busy stuffing salad into my face to hear the clank.

"Hmm," said Goodman. That should have been my second warning. The way he said, "Hmm."

"What?"

"Nothing," he said. "Just a weird idea."

"Not garden gnomes," I said.

"No. Not garden gnomes. They're very territorial. And if you have cats or small dogs, they don't get along. Especially if the dog pees on one." He sipped at his iced tea. "And while they're great for rodent control, unless you bring in an armed squadron they're lousy at security." Another sip. "And then there's the noise problem. They drink too much and they like to party all night long. That's if you have only male gnomes. If you bring in a few female gnomes, the party usually gets quiet sometime after midnight. Although...on a quiet night, you can still hear a lot of grunting and moaning."

"You're speaking from experience?"

"I live in Burbank. You know all those bungalow units they built in the twenties and thirties? Where all the little old ladies live now? They think gnomes are cute. That's what they get when they're not allowed to have more than three cats. They put out gnomes."

"Oh, yeah."

"One year, the gnomes and the lawn flamingos next door got into a terrible fight—" He shook his head. "The SWAT team had to come in and impound them all. No one was injured, but it could have been a lot worse."

"There's probably a story in that."

"Disney already owns it. Scheduled for summer after next. Working title is *Gnome on the Range*. But that might change. Anyway—" He paused while the waiter refilled his tea. "—let's talk about your problem."

"Right. No gnomes."

"Do you have a running stream on your property? A koi pond? A pool? With a waterfall?"

"I've got a pool. No waterfall. Why?"

"Fairies. They like water, even one of those little Zen waterfalls would be enough. You could bring in a few fairies."

"And what good would that do? It'd be like having sociopathic dragonflies with ADHD."

"More like cosplay hummingbirds, but yes, fairies can be problematic. On the other hand, if they like you, your flowers bloom, the birds don't eat the fruit off your trees, stuff like that. They bring you a lot of good luck. Little things mostly. They get along with some cats and dogs, but it depends on the animal. It also depends on the person. If they don't like you, you bump your shins a lot, bees sting you, and it's a bad idea to go barefoot. Unless you're looking for Legos."

"Sounds like a high-maintenance relationship. That's not me. I raised a teenager, remember? That put me eight years behind schedule. And still counting."

That Pesky Dan Goodman grinned. "You knew the job was dangerous when you took it."

"No, I didn't. They don't put warning labels on children. And nobody says don't do it. 'It'll be fun,' they say. 'You'll be good at it,' they say. 'Your life won't be complete without children.' Hah! Ask a parent and they'll tell you—'You go to strangle them in their crib and they're so cute when they're sleeping, you think, well maybe just one more day.' Hah! And then they turn into teenagers. The whole thing was my mother's revenge. 'I can hardly wait till you have kids of your own—' It's like living with a chronic disease."

"But you love your kid—"

"Of course, I do. He's a Martian, but he's *my* Martian. And he's all the good luck I need. So I don't want fairies, thank you."

"No. You need something bigger."

"Uhh, no thanks. Do you know how much it costs to feed Dogzilla? What are you suggesting?" I should have shut my mouth after the second sentence. I should have gnawed off my leg and hopped away on the other. I should have paid the bill and run for the exit.

"There's more to the ecosystem than fairies and gnomes, you know."

"My neighborhood isn't zoned for dragons," I said. "Not even fire-lizards."

"No, I was thinking of something more…more down-to-earth."

"More down-to-earth? I'm not sure I like the sound of that. What are you suggesting? Zombies? Ghouls? No thanks. I had a vampire for a roommate once. Not fun. Not fun at all."

"Really…?"

"Long story. Some other time." I added, "Day sleeper."

"Of course. Anyway, I have this friend. A young guy, just starting out in life. His name is Emmett-Murray."

"Is he a redhead?"

"Very funny. No. He's half-troll. On his mother's side."

"Huh?"

"I said, he's half-troll—"

"I heard you. It's still sinking in. What was his father?"

"Human, he says."

"Hard to believe. Have you ever seen a female troll?"

"Don't be judgmental. It takes all kinds."

"Pesky. Look at me. I'm not as stupid as I look. You might want to Google how trolls mate. I have. That's why I don't write horror stories. There's nothing that can scare me anymore." I looked across at him. "Have you met the father?"

"He's deceased."

"Ah. Never mind. You just explained it."

Peskydang waved it off. "Anyway, Emmett-Murray needs a place to stay."

"Not in my house."

"No. Your back yard. You have a pool, a garden. You have a lawn. You have a lot of space there. And Emmett-Murray doesn't take up much room. He's only about yay-high." Pesky held a hand at waist-level. "He's a little guy, practically a munchkin."

"Yeah? Have you ever seen a munchkin eat?"

"Don't be racist."

"I'm not. I'm just—Never mind. I can't win that argument."

"Let me bring him by. You'll meet him."

"No, really. I don't see how—"

Pesky held up a hand to stop me. "Just meet him. Trust me on this."

"Last time I trusted you, I nearly got my passport revoked—"

"Clerical error. You did get it straightened out, didn't you?"

"Only because my sister is on first-name terms with our congress-man."

"Well, there, you see? No harm, no foul."

"I don't think you're getting my point."

"Sure I am. You need security. Emmett-Murray needs a quiet little corner. You won't even know he's there."

"No, I really don't think this is a good idea—"

"It's a *great* idea, I'll bring him by Saturday. No obligation. Just meet him, he's a sweetheart. You'll love him."

"Pesky—"

"Oops. Look at the time. Gotta run. See you this weekend. Trust me, this is a win-win for everybody."

"I've heard that before, too—"

But he had already slid out of the booth. Leaving me with the check. Again.

And that's how I ended up with a troll—a half-troll—living in my back yard.

To be fair, Emmett-Murray was a cute little guy. He looked a bit like a munchkin, a bit like a gnome, but mostly like a Mini-Me Sasquatch. He stood waist-high, barely a smidge over a meter tall. And he had the kind of cabbage-patch grumpy-face that made him almost adorable. He was *cute.*

And I'm a sucker for cute.

They arrived after sunset. Peskydang thought it best to be discreet, so I let them in through the back gate, the one that opens onto the alley. Pesky made introductions. Emmett-Murray didn't offer to shake hands. He'd already learned how fragile human bones could be. He just held up a paw in a high-five gesture. I gave it a friendly slap.

"Thank you," he said, "for letting me stay with you." He spoke with an endearing froggy-gravelly voice.

"Um, that hasn't been decided yet—"

"I promise I'll take care of your gopher problem. And I won't eat your dog."

"Uh, thanks. That's reassuring."

"I can dig a hole over there, behind the tree, for my poop."

Pesky interrupted, holding up a large orange box. "I think he'd rather you use these hazmat bags."

"Oh, okay. I can do that."

"See?" said Pesky. "No problem at all."

Emmett-Murray puffed up his chest. "I can growl ferociously at anyone trying to come over your fence. How's this?" He opened his mouth as wide as he could—kind of like one of those kitchen trash cans where you step on the pedal and the whole top flips open—and let loose with a sound somewhere between an air-raid siren and a grizzly bear on the receiving end of unlubricated and unwelcome anal intercourse.

The transformer on the power pole exploded in a shower of sparks. And all of the avocados blasted sideways off the tree, ripe or not, splattering across the yard and the wall and the side of the garage. Several splashed into the pool where the water was already roiling in uneasy waves. Dogzilla, who had been cautiously sniffing from a distance, yelped and ran, disappearing with a crash through the doggy door into the house, probably ending up cowering in the far corner under the bed.

"Um, look, guys. I don't think this is such a good idea—"

"Oh, the dog will get used to him. Emmett-Murray likes dogs."

"That's what I'm afraid of—"

"Oh, no. I won't eat your dog. I already promised."

"Yes, that's very reassuring. Pesky, can I have a word with you, please?" I led him aside to a place I hoped was out of earshot. I glanced back. Emmett-Murray was sniffing the corner of yard. "Pesky, I know you have a big heart. I don't. I need my privacy."

"Only for a few days, a week at most. Two. Until we can find something more permanent for him."

"How about your place?"

"I'm only allowed a cat. Maybe two if they're clean. You know that."

"I really can't do this—"

"Only for a little while. You'll never know he's here. He'll dig himself into the ground and look like just another boulder in your rock garden."

"Right. A big shaggy boulder."

"But think about it. Your burglar will come over the fence, Emmie will open his mouth, he'll let loose one of those roars, and that'll be the last you'll ever have to worry about theft—"

We were interrupted by sirens. Three cruisers, a fire engine, and an ambulance. Two minutes. Impressive. The cops came carefully through the back gate, guns drawn, shouting. "Police!" and "Freeze!" A chopper moved into position, circling overhead, its finger of light prowling across the yard.

Officer McBride recognized me immediately. "You good?"

"False alarm," I replied.

McBride shouted back over his shoulder, "Clear!"

"Can I lower my hands?"

He nodded and holstered his gun. The other cops holstered theirs, but slower.

"How's the boy?" McBride asked.

"Keeping his nose clean."

"Good. Glad to hear he survived his teens. You, too. Some doubt there for a while."

"Yep," I agreed.

Abruptly, the chopper's beam found the darkest corner of the yard and stayed there, revealing Emmett-Murray—illuminating him in stark relief as he pawed quietly at the ground. The cops froze. All six of them. Their hands went back to their guns. McBride spoke first. "Is that—? What is that?"

"It's a half-troll. On his mother's side."

"Is it yours?"

"Uh, no. He's just visiting."

"But he's on your property. And it looks like he's digging a burrow."

"Oh, um—"

Another officer stepped up. I recognized her face, didn't remember her name. I had to glance at her name-badge. Benson. She didn't look friendly.

"Do you have a license for that troll?"

"He's not mine."

"He's in your yard."

"Okay, fine. Do you want to take him away?"

Officer Benson glanced around to the other officers. To the firemen. To the paramedics crowding in beside them. They all shook their heads. She looked back to me. "All right...." She took a breath. She went to McBride and the two of them whispered together for a few moments.

Finally, she returned. "We're not going to do anything tonight. We'll give you some time to sort this out, but we'll be back in 30 days. If he's not licensed by then—"

"You'll take him then?"

"—you'll be subject to civil penalties and fines."

"He's not mine."

"He's in your yard."

"Not by my choice." I looked around. Pesky was nowhere to be seen. Houdini could not have effected a better escape.

"You realize we're going to have to report this."

"I know."

She handed me her card. "I have to give you my number. It's policy. I hope you don't need to use it. I really do not want to come back."

By the time the police finally left, Emmett-Murray had dug himself a nice little burrow. He was almost invisible. And I was emotionally exhausted. Okay, maybe a few days. I could earn some karma points. I'd track down Pesky tomorrow and have him find another placement for Emmett-Murray, but for the moment not even the cops were coming into my back yard.

I had to admit, there was a certain sense of security in that.

And what with one thing and another, I couldn't find That Pesky Dan Goodman even if I laid out a trail of hundred dollar bills and jelly doughnuts. His phone message said he was off on another retreat—a very appropriate word in this case.

So I told myself I'd been through worse and reminded myself of my mantra for difficult situations. Grit (my teeth) and bear it.

There were adjustments to be made, of course.

I didn't warn our regular pool man in time. The new pool guy charged an extra $50 a month.

Dogzilla refused to go in the back yard again. That meant she had to be taken out front to pee. And that meant I had to interrupt my schedule several times a day to make sure she could go. On a leash. Because "Come back now" and "Go inside" were no longer in her vocabulary. And she spent a lot of time curled up in her blanket. Whimpering.

And now, there were some very odd smells coming from the back yard, like someone barbecuing a skunk, or a Volkswagen. On those days, we closed all the windows and turned the fans to high. It helped. A little.

One week passed, then another. Pesky remained unreachable. But he'd told the truth about one thing. Little Emmett-Murray kept mostly to himself. Except for the strange smells and the weird howling noises at three in the morning and the occasional unexplained seismic thump and the weird mound growing in the corner where he burrowed and the dead patches of grass around it, we never would have known he was there.

I live on a dead-end street for the quiet. And most of my neighbors are fairly calm people—especially since the six wannabe terrorists in the house to the north grew up and moved away.

On the other side of the alley behind my back wall, there's a two story office building. The windows of the dentist's office provide a pretty clear view down into my yard, so I do my skinny-dipping at night. I can float on my back and watch the stars—although there are nowhere near as many visible anymore due to light pollution.

I hadn't seen little Emmett-Murray since he'd burrowed in. I assumed he was still hibernating or whatever it was he was doing when he was curled up like a rock. But no, he wasn't hibernating.

After a deep underwater lap, starting at the shallow end and heading diagonally across the length of the pool, I breached at the far side, grabbing a serious breath—and screamed in surprise at the unexpected thing that was standing there.

Little Emmett was not so little anymore. He was a huge dark lump, a hulking blob. I fell back into the water, shrieking and floundering, came up choking and gasping, grabbed for the deck, and coughed out a couple of soup bowls of chlorine and phlegm.

"Are you all right?" he gravelled.

"Uh, yeah. I'm fine. I will be. Thanks for asking. You just startled me."

From my vantage point, treading water in the deep end, Little Emmett looked to be chest-high now. He'd lost a lot of his baby fur, leaving behind a patchy mass of uneven hair and oily skin. He looked like an orangutan with mange. Only not as attractive. His posture was ominous and his features were solidifying into a disturbing frown. Almost a glare.

I felt suddenly uneasy. I kicked away from the side, turned over, and swam quickly back to the shallow end. I could feel his eyes on me the whole distance. I grabbed my towel, wrapped it around me quickly, and dripped all the way to the back door of the house and into the kitchen. "That was weird," I said to no one. "Just weird."

I grabbed my phone, dialed with shaking hands, but Pesky was still in retreat. Not a retreat, more of a rout. His message started with that annoying *doo-dah-dee* disconnect tone to discourage automatic-dialers, then went to a deep radio-announcer voice saying, "Thank you for calling. All of our operators are busy right now. Your call is important to us and will be answered in the order received. Click-buzzzzzzz." Ha-ha. Very cute. And as useful as a bronze tribble.

By the time Pesky got back from wherever he was retreating to, three weeks had passed and Little Emmett was almost as tall as I was. Pesky came by, looked at him, and nodded approvingly. "Ahh, yes. I get it. He's thriving."

"Thriving?"

"Of course. You should understand. When a child, or any young mammal, is placed in an emotionally sterile environment, they don't grow as fast as they would if they were being nurtured by an appropriate caregiver. It's called 'failure to thrive.'"

"So you're saying I'm a good parent for a troll?"

"Half-troll. On his mother's side. And yes."

"I've had nothing to do with him. I ignore him. In fact, I resent him. I resent the fact that he's here." I turned to Emmett-Murray. "Don't take it personally. It's not about you. It's about the loss of my privacy." Back to That Pesky Dan Goodman. "I resent that you plopped him into my back yard, *against my wishes*, and then disappeared for a month—"

"Three weeks and two days. And yes, resenting him was exactly what he needed. In his previous placement, they were cuddling him. You don't cuddle trolls."

"They're not exactly cuddle toys, you know."

"The more you resented him in your back yard, the bigger he grew. Now you have a *real* security system."

"I didn't want him here in the first place."

"You needed him. He needed you. It's a perfect match. Stop complaining. That could be dangerous. Trolls are subject to gigantism."

"So you want me to love him—?"

"If you don't want him to outgrow your yard, yes, that would be a good idea. You should be happy. Your collection of Mickey Mouse Fantasia figurines is safer than ever."

"That's not the issue—"

"Well, it should be. You had a problem. I found you a solution. Now you can stop worrying about burglars. You should be thanking me.

You're an ungrateful ass."

"Yes, I am. I want him out of here. The dog is terrified to go out. She's peeing in the house. And the neighbors are complaining. And in a week, the police will be back with citations and warrants and subpoenas and god knows what else. You said this placement was only temporary until you found something more permanent for him."

"Okay, okay!" Pesky backed away, holding up his hands as if to ward me off. "Just don't piss him off." Behind me, I could feel the subsonic rumble of Emmett-Murray growling.

"What about pissing me off? Look!" I pointed around the yard. "He leaves footprints five centimeters deep already."

Pesky frowned. "What is that in inches?"

"Two. Two inches deep."

"I wish you hadn't gone metric—"

"Liberia, Myanmar, and the United States are the only three countries that haven't. I'm learning how to think international." I caught my breath. "And I wish you'd stop changing the subject. Look at my yard. He's cracked the pool decking in three places. His burrow is turning into a small mountain. And he's uprooted what's left of the avocado tree. This is—this is—this is just—" I threw my hands in the air in a gesture of helplessness. "I admit it, I've run out of words."

"I get it," said Pesky. "You're frustrated—"

"Frustrated? Is that what you think this is?"

"Glrgh—"

Slowly, I removed my hands from Pesky's throat. "I want him out of here. I want him out of here now. I want my life and my privacy back. I never asked for him. I never asked for this—" I waved my hand around at the war zone that used to be my back yard. "This was all because you don't understand the word *no!*"

"All right, I'll see what I can do—"

"No. You'll do it. Tonight—"

"Tomorrow at the latest. Do you know how hard it is to place a troll—"

"Half-troll," I corrected. "On his mother's side. And I want him out of here."

Pesky looked past my shoulder. "Did you hear that, Emmett-Murray?"

"But I don't want to leave," he whined. Like a garbage disposal eating marbles. "I like it here."

"I can see that," Pesky said. "But I'll bet I can find you a place where people hate you even more."

"I don't know," grumbled Emmett-Murray. He pointed at me. "This one treats me right. The way I want to be treated."

"Oh, crap. I give up. What do I have to do? Burn the house down?"

"I wouldn't advise it," Pesky started to say—but Emmett-Murray interrupted quickly, clapping his huge hands in delight, booming like a Kodo drummer. "Would you? Would you? I like fires. Big fires. The bigger the better."

"No, no no no no no no. Out of the question. Don't even think about it. Don't even think about thinking about it. Pesky, get him out of here!"

Pesky looked helpless. "I'll have to rent a truck—"

"I'll help you pay for it!" I stalked back to the house, grumbling and swearing in every language I knew, including several dialects of Pascal, Java, C++, and Assembler.

Grabbed the laptop and started Googling. Eviction. Ejectment. Pest control. Troll removal. Exterminators—

The problem was that despite my being the property owner, I had limited legal rights. There's this thing about squatters. They're like vampires. If you invite them in, you're doomed. With trolls, it's even worse because trolls are considered an endangered species. So you're not allowed to interfere with their existence in any way, shape, manner, or form.

And while I hadn't exactly invited Emmett-Murray in—Pesky had mostly abandoned him here—there was an implied contract in existence. Security services in exchange for a place to burrow. According to some of the horror stories on the Web, a good lawyer could establish that Emmett-Murray had more right to stay on my land than I did. As long as he deterred intruders, he was fulfilling his obligation.

Essentially, this: if a troll doesn't want to leave, there's not much you can do about it. And the more you nurture a troll—the more you resent him—the more he thrives, the bigger he gets. You can go out on the patio and stand and stare and hate him intensely and watch him grow five centimeters per hour.

The police came by on the thirtieth day. Pesky still hadn't found a truck rental that would haul a troll for less than three thousand dollars, and another thousand in mandatory insurance—and at the rate Emmett-Murray was growing, we had to find something soon or even an eighteen-wheeler cattle-hauler wasn't going to be big enough. Officer Benson knocked on the front door, McBride stood politely behind her. She had a clipboard with a thick sheaf of papers.

She started off with "maintaining a public nuisance" and ended up with "failure to remove hazardous waste material." She added complaints from the neighbors and then worked her way through a long litany of legal horrors, including damage to the local sewage system and other utilities, various zoning abuses, endangering the neighborhood, failure to secure appropriate licenses and permits, failure to neuter—Oh, yeah? You try it! Be my guest!—failure to abide by state animal control regulations, violations of the Endangered Species Act, and various federal statutes, regulations, and restrictions, all warranting further investigation by the Environmental Protection Agency.

"Sign here, please." She pushed the clipboard and a pen toward me. "Your signature acknowledges that you have been served and that you understand the consequences of failure to comply."

"I've been trying to comply—" I stopped myself. "Look, I acknowledge that what I have in my back yard is a suburban horror story, okay? I'm afraid to leave my house because he says he likes fires. I called my lawyer. She hung up on me. I can't find another lawyer. They just laugh and say, 'Whoa. You *do* have a problem.' So what do you suggest? What can I *do?* I mean, aside from just abandoning the house and fleeing out of state—"

"That won't help. You can be extradited." She sighed. "I'm not unsympathetic but you let him burrow in. The responsibility is yours."

"I didn't *let* him. He was abandoned here. Doesn't the state have some agency or something? Some way to remove him? I mean, this can't be the first time a troll has settled in somewhere he's not welcome."

She shuffled her papers. "According to this, he's only a half-troll—"

"On his mother's side, I know."

"—and that complicates things. Is he covered by the laws of the reservation? Or is he covered by human laws? It depends on his tribe, whether or not they want to take responsibility. Usually, they don't. It depends on his parentage and his DNA. It depends on a lot of things. The legal processes could drag on for years. The law is still trying to sort these issues out and until we get a Supreme Court ruling, nobody can say for sure."

I sagged. Beaten.

Officer Benson wasn't without feelings. She saw how close to despair I was. She looked to McBride. He nodded. She turned back to me.

"Look," she said. "I'm not supposed to say this. This is off the record, okay?"

"Okay."

"But if you can get him to leave on his own, all this paperwork" —she held up the thick sheaf of forms— "all of this would magically disappear. Because nobody really wants to pursue this. Because pursuing it would mean some agency or other would have to take responsibility. And nobody wants to go there. So, if you can figure out a solution to this problem, if you can get him to leave on his own, you're pretty much off the hook." Then she added, "Just don't file a missing-troll report. Please? Because nobody's going to go looking for him. I can guarantee that."

I took a deep breath. I even made an effort to straighten and meet her gaze. "Thank you. Thank you for that."

"But you gotta do it quickly." Again, she held up the clipboard. "Once this stuff starts working its way through the system—it'll be death by a thousand paper cuts. Dipped in battery acid."

"Okay, yes. Thank you."

As soon as they left, I tried calling Pesky—

Doo-dah-dee! "Thank you for calling. All of our operators are busy right now—"

The thing I hate about cell phones is that you cannot slam them down into the cradle when you are frustrated. You can slam them down onto the countertop, but that just shatters the screen. It's (you should pardon the pun) counter-productive.

By now, little Emmett-Murray was three meters tall. His hair, what was left of it, was coarse and patchy—and curly. He looked like he was covered with a bad case of pubic hair. His expression had hardened into a permanent glower. Most of the time, he was a large lump burrowed into the earth—the cinder block wall separating my yard from the next was leaning precariously outward and would probably topple into the neighbor's patio in a day or three—but occasionally Emmett-Murray could be seen wandering restlessly around the yard, frowning and rumbling and squinty-glaring at the ground.

It wasn't like he was searching for something. It was more like he was pacing out his territory. From time to time, he would stop and stare at the cinder block wall, as if he could stare right through it, as if he wanted to knock it down, as if he wanted to own the neighbors' yards too.

Back to the laptop—to Google troll behaviors.

Oh, crap.

I did not sleep that night. I didn't even try going to bed. I just paced around the house—the human version of Emmett-Murray's restless circuit.

"I'm smart," I told myself. "I'm smarter than the average troll. I should be able to solve this. This isn't the worst thing that ever happened in my life—" I had to stop for a moment and consider that sentence. No, it wasn't the worst thing I'd ever experienced. Not even in the top five. "And I'm still standing. So I should be able to handle this. I'm smart enough, right? Right? I just have to outthink the situation."

See, that's the thing about writing. On paper, the pauses don't show. In real life, it's a never-ending series of long pauses. It's a maze of twisty little passages, with dead ends, locked doors, and pitfalls. Not to mention the occasional concealed tiger-pit with punji sticks at the bottom. You keep banging your head, your whole body, into barriers of all kinds—floors, ceilings, brick walls, until either they or you break open and you find something that looks like a solution. Writers are people who believe there is always a solution. (Successful writers, anyway. Unsuccessful ones never find one, so they never finish. Among other reasons.)

The point is, the reality of a situation is never as malleable as the description of it.

Okay, start with the obvious. Deal with it head-on.

I went out into the back yard. It looked gloomier than ever—twilight even though it was only afternoon. Do trolls have so much antigravitas that even photons avoid them? Emmett-Murray was standing motionless before the cinder block wall that separated the back yard from the alley, staring at it, frowning, rumbling to himself. I could feel the vibrations of the ground through the soles of my boots. I now had to wear heavy boots to go out into the back yard.

"Don't like wall," Emmett-Murray said. "Blocks my view." He looked a lot bulkier than he had just two or three days before. Pesky would have said he was filling out nicely.

"I need the wall," I said. "Please don't knock it down."

"It's in the way." He assembled his sentence slowly.

That was the other thing—the bigger a troll gets, the more he hardens. His brain processes get slower. His language abilities deteriorate.

"Umm, Emmett?"

He swiveled his huge head around to look down at me, his expression frozen in ferocity. "Yah?"

"Look, I know I did you a big favor, letting you stay here. But I need—um, I'm going to—I need to do some remodeling now. So I have to ask you to leave. Please. You'll have to find some other place to stay."

He ignored me. He looked at what was left of my house behind me. The roof over the patio had collapsed sometime during the night and the kitchen wall now sagged as if it was melting. "House blocks my view too."

"Did you hear me? I'm asking you to leave. Please."

He looked down at me again, an expression both implacable and challenging. Ugly. "I like it here."

"Emmett, you can't stay."

"Yes, I can." He frowned in thought. "You can't...make me go. I have...rights. We made a deal. I have to keep my word."

"I didn't make any deal. Pesky did—"

"Still counts. I have...a job."

My neck was starting to hurt from looking up at him. "But I have rights too, Emmett. I'm the property owner. And you can't stay here without my permission."

He shook his head. "I like it here." He turned away, as if that was his final word on the subject.

"Emmett—?"

"Go away now, you. No more talk." He stared at the back wall again. "Ugly, very ugly."

Okay...

So that wasn't going to work.

I headed back into the house. I had to go around the side to get to the front, because the back door wouldn't open anymore—because the kitchen wall was leaning sideways and the door was jammed in its frame.

I made myself a cup of tea.

While the tea was cooling, I fixed myself a rum and Coke. Malibu coconut rum and a twist of lime. You put the lime in the coconut, you drink it all up. It's called a Hairy Nilsson. If you use diet Coke, it's a half-Nilsson.

The tea remained forgotten in the microwave.

I stood there in my kitchen, in the dark, leaning against the now-crumbling marble counter, brooding, thinking, pondering, considering, rationalizing, hating—

That was the problem. The more I hated him, the more he thrived.

I should stop hating him.

Right.

I should go out, give him a big effusive hug, pinch his cheeks and tell him he has a *shana punim* and gush like a fanboy at a *Star Trek* convention. If I did that every day, how long would it take for him to grow disgusted?

No. It wouldn't work. He'd know it was an act. He'd just get taller. How big do trolls grow anyway? Some researchers claimed that trolls could grow as tall as five to eight meters. The Norwegians said the ancestral beasts were even bigger.

The noise of the back wall coming down startled me out of my reverie.

"It was in the way," Emmett-Murray explained. "It blocked my view. Of the alley." He thought for a moment, scratching himself in various places. "I will stack the blocks for you. So you can use them again."

"Thank you," I mumbled. And staggered back around to the front of the house and inside.

I was not insured for a troll infestation. And trolls were not considered an act of god either. Hell, no. It didn't matter. The insurance company had already sent me a notice of cancellation anyway. As soon as the damage started spreading to the neighbors' lots, the lawsuits would be inevitable.

Maybe I could get my lot rezoned as a troll-ranch? No, that wouldn't work. A pig-farmer would be more popular in this neighborhood—and the last one had left seventy-four years ago.

Flashes from the back yard caught my attention. I peered out the window in the broken back door. A carload of teenagers was just easing past the hole in the wall. Two of them were leaning out and snapping pictures with their cell phones.

"I should charge them for that—" I started to say.

And stopped cold.

Halloween was only two weeks away—

And this neighborhood took Halloween seriously. There were at least half a dozen haunted houses advertised all over the valley. And the agricultural college had a corn maze and hayrides and other harvest-themed events. There were at least a dozen costume stores within walking distance—one in every strip mall, it seemed.

Maybe—

Almost—

Ideas do not leap fully formed from my skull like Athena bursting from the forehead of Zeus. (If only...)

But I always know when I'm on to something. The internal fireworks start going off like cosmic popcorn. In this case, it was the Fourth of July. There were too many possibilities. I had to sit down and list them all, crossing off the ones that were too much work as well as the ones that would probably not be cost-effective.

Flyers. Internet postings. Facebook. Possibly a couple of videos on YouTube—maybe they'd go viral. I didn't need a lot, just enough to establish the right narrative. Obvious in retrospect. I should have realized it from the beginning.

First thing, I needed a good photograph. Not too hard to obtain. I could shoot out through the window of the back door. Emmett-Murray was silhouetted standing in the rubble of the cinder block wall, backlit by the security lights on the building across the alley. A great angle, brooding and mysterious. I just hoped he wasn't thinking about how the building blocked his view of the boulevard.

Next, a little tinkering in Photoshop. Bring up the contrast, adjust the colors—turn the orange of the argon lamp into a futuristic glow for the background, then darken the hulking off-center shape in the foreground with blackened indigo. Then the title across the top in dripping crimson. The Lonely Troll! It came out looking like a movie poster.

Now, the text, in white below.

"Feared and hated! Trapped in a hostile world. Unloved and unwanted. Lost in an uncaring city! All he ever wanted was a hug, a simple moment of kindness! Just a little bit of love!

"Come and visit the Lonely Troll. Show him he's not alone any more. Show him that there are still people in the world who can open their hearts to those who are different. Bring your children. Reawaken the heart of the troll!"

And then, below that: "FREE TO THE PUBLIC! HALLOWEEN WEEK ONLY! Starting a half-hour after sunset! Donations gratefully accepted. All proceeds will go to the creation and maintenance of a permanent loving home for this poor misunderstood beast." Then a map directing people to come up the alley.

I uploaded the flyer to my website, to Facebook, to Twitter, to Tumblr, and even Grindr. What the hell. I invited people to share it everywhere.

Then I went onto the website of the local print shop and ordered five hundred matching flyers. I'd paper the neighborhood.

I also ordered a couple arrow-shaped banners to put up, one on each side of the hole in the wall. "The Lonely Troll!"

Plus several large signs that said: "Have your picture taken with The Lonely Troll! Only $25!"

And then a couple more signs that said: "Hugs! $100! At your own risk. Please ask permission before hugging the Lonely Troll."

I could pick those up tomorrow, while taping up flyers. No. I had a better idea. I'd pay the neighborhood kids to post the flyers everywhere. And they could hand them out at the mall and at the college too. That would work. If we ran out of flyers, I'd order another five hundred. And five hundred more after that.

Finally, the hugest banner of all. "All You Need Is Love!"

And one last thing. Music. I'd load the stereo system with a selection of Disney songs—"Hakuna Matata", "A Spoonful Of Sugar", "Can You Feel The Love Tonight", "You've Got A Friend In Me," and of course, "It's A Small World." I'd crank up the speakers to eleven.

And then, one thing after that—I went digging for the card Officer Benson had given me. She answered on the second ring. "Is he gone?"

"Not yet. But..." I took a breath. "I just wanted to let you know that there will probably be some increased traffic in the alley behind my house, starting tomorrow night. We might need a police presence to, um, monitor the situation—"

"Now what?"

"I'm holding a fund-raiser for Emmett-Murray. To help him find a loving home. Oh, hell, any home, loving or not. Just as long as it's far far away."

"Do you have a permit?" she asked.

"Haven't even considered it," I answered.

"You could be cited."

"Do you really want to shut this down? And have him stuck here?"

Silence.

"I see your point. Have a good time. I'll let the rest of the division know."

It worked.

Every night, the crowds cheered as Emmett-Murray emerged from his burrow. Emmett-Murray's expression went from hateful to sullen to confused to fearful. The crowd interpreted it as loneliness. I enrolled a couple of friends to help me with logistics and we moved through the crowd every ten or fifteen minutes collecting donations in huge Mason jars. I couldn't believe how eager people were to stuff fives and tens and even twenties into the jars.

On the second night, people started throwing flowers and bouquets. Little children ran to hug his legs. Teenage girls lined up to kiss him on the cheek. Grown men studied him warily, then grinned reluctantly and waved.

People waited patiently in long lines for family pictures. Little children wanted to be photographed sitting on his shoulders, grown-ups wanted to perch on his knee. Emmett-Murray rumbled in distress. He lowered his head sadly. He looked to me for explanation, obviously unhappy, moving himself back and forth in slow confusion. "This is all for you, Emmett-Murray! You've transformed the neighborhood. This is your party! It's to honor you and show you how much you're loved!"

By the third night, I was even believing it myself. I didn't have time to count the money, I just dumped it into a huge black trash bag and stuffed it under my bed.

On the fourth evening, as the silent firestorm of sunset faded from the west, the largest crowd of all had gathered. They waited impatiently, filling the alley in both directions. Several police cars, a fire engine, an ambulance, and a few fully suited members of the SWAT team were also in attendance, but the crowd was peaceful. I recognized a few faces. People were coming back every night now. Many were carrying homemade "We love you!" signs as well as flowers and even stuffed animals.

But Emmett-Murray did not come out of his burrow.

After a bit, the crowd started chanting. And singing. "We love you, Emmett! Oh yes we do! We love you, Emmett. Please don't be blue!" It was wonderful.

I got down on my hands and knees and crawled as deep into the burrow as my nose would allow. The stink was incredible. My eyes were watering so hard, I could barely see. "Emmett, you have to come out now."

"I don't wanna."

"I know, but you gotta."

"No."

"Pesky will be very unhappy. So will I."

"Good."

Oops. Wrong thing to say. Try a different tactic—

"Emmett, listen to me. It's very important that you come out now and see all the people."

"No. I said no."

"If you don't, they'll just start singing louder. They won't go away. They'll be here all night."

"All night?"

"Yes. All night. Until dawn. They came to see you and they won't leave until you come out."

"If I come out, they'll go away?"

"Not right away, but yes, they will. They just want to see you."

"No. They'll want to hug me too."

"We'll tell them no hugs tonight, okay?"

"No hugs? You promise?"

"No hugs. I promise. Just some pictures. And songs. And maybe some flowers too."

"You promise they'll go away?"

"I promise. But you'll have to come out and see them. Fifteen minutes. And then I'll tell them you're very tired. Okay?"

"Fifteen minutes, that's all."

"I promise."

"I don't wanna."

"I know. But they won't go away until you do."

Long stinky silence. The singing outside grew louder.

"Okay. As soon as they stop singing."

"Okay, but if you don't come out, they'll start singing "It's A Small World" again."

Emmett-Murray didn't answer.

I backed out of the burrow, brushed off as much of the dirt as I could, then held up my hands to silence the crowd. "He's coming. He is. But he's asked for quiet. No singing, please. Okay?"

The crowd quieted down expectantly.

We waited. And waited. And waited.

I walked to the burrow and called down. "Emmett? Emmett-Murray?"

A deep unhappy rumble, but the ground began shuddering and I knew he was crawling up the tunnel to the surface.

When he finally emerged, the crowd couldn't help themselves. They cheered loudly! Hundreds of flashes sparkled from every direction, blinding me, blinding Emmett. He held up a huge paw in front of his eyes and flinched. It was like being onstage with the Beatles. The shrieking was pretty intense as well.

It was wonderful. I kept Emmett-Murray in front of the crowd for an hour and a half before I let him crawl back down into his burrow. My helpers and I circulated through the crowd and filled three huge trash bags with eager donations. I stuffed them under the bed with the rest.

On the fifth night, Emmett-Murray was gone.

He didn't leave a forwarding address.

The burrow was cold and empty.

Reluctantly, I pulled down the banners and the posters. As the crowd gathered, I stood on a ladder and held up my hands for silence. "Emmett-Murray has gone. I can't really speak for him, but I know he was deeply affected by all your love and affection. It was overwhelming—but it was also very stressful. All the lights and noise and attention. As you know, trolls are very private and very sensitive. They don't deal well with crowds. As much as Emmett-Murray appreciated your attention, your flowers and signs and stuffed animals and songs, it was also very embarrassing for him, so he's moved on to a quieter place. Speaking for myself, we're enormously grateful for all the donations, of course. We're going to use some of it to rebuild this wall as a shrine to Emmett-Murray, and whatever other repairs have to be made in the neighborhood, and the rest, whatever's left over, we'll pass on to the local troll reservation. I'm sure Emmett would approve. I'll circulate among you one last time…"

All totaled up, we had over seventeen thousand dollars in donations, enough to repair most of the damage to the back yard.

We filled in the burrow—the contractor had to bring in several truckloads of dirt and gravel, we had no idea where most of the dirt had disappeared to, had Emmett-Murray just eaten it? That would have explained some of the mystery of his bulk. We laid a concrete deck over the top.

I was able to get a reasonable price for repairing the back wall and the patio. The kitchen wall and door had to be completely rebuilt as well. After the last bill was paid, I sent the remaining two hundred and fifty dollars to the Federal Agency for Troll Affairs.

I won't say that things are completely back to normal. Dogzilla still won't go into the back yard to pee. But my therapist says that if I stay on the medication, the nightmares will eventually subside. I'm down to only one or two a week now.

The good news? That Pesky Dan Goodman is still respecting the restraining order.

And Officers Benson and McBride invited me to their wedding.

From time to time, curious people stop by and ask if I've heard anything about Emmett-Murray or why he left. "No, sorry, I can't say."

But if I'm having a good day, I say, "Ask not for whom the troll bailed…"

The grim future of reality television.

DEATH GAME

There were a lot of articles about how it started, where the idea came from, but elimination contests weren't new. That's how we pick presidents. But yeah, there were all those seasons of *Survivor*, and all the copycat shows, and there was a Japanese game show that started with thousands of contestants, and then there was that Korean movie, and all of them made big bucks, so this particular iteration was inevitable. All those others were metaphors. This was real.

The tough part was making it legal. The producers originally wanted to go to one of those libertarian enclaves, you know, off on some remote island that nobody had ever bothered to claim, but the overhead on that didn't work, it wasn't cost-effective.

So the whole thing just floated around for a few years, like a thought experiment, not really possible—not until South Dakota legalized assisted suicide, and then everything started falling into place. It's no secret that somebody spread some big bucks around the state buying a lot of support. And the law was so loosely drawn that nobody knew how to interpret it, so most of the legal challenges didn't get very far, because the courts needed to see how it would all play out. Anyway, the game was on.

The moral questions? Those arguments are never gonna end—and I'm the wrong person to have an opinion. Obviously.

Okay, so the actual experience? That's what you want to hear. That's what everybody wants to know. It isn't like there haven't been a dozen documentaries and movies and God knows how many articles and books—but Jack and I, our story is the one everybody wants to know.

Jack and I had been together for three years. He was smart and funny and he knew things, weird things, so he was interesting. He always had some odd fact to share. But he was obsessive too, always looking for that extra angle, so the game was perfect for him. And me? I came from a—

well, let's just say I didn't have a great family. So I was afraid of losing him. Afraid of being alone. Some people called me Jack's enabler, but that wasn't the relationship. We kinda completed each other. We were better together than apart.

Did you ever see any of those articles, the psychological studies, about the kind of people who joined the game? Really interesting stuff. Thrill seekers—that was obvious, but also a lot of desperate people. And disbelievers too, people who thought it was all some kind of stunt, and no, I didn't feel sorry for them when they found out that the game was played for real. And yeah, the suicidal ones, the ones who were ready to die— and just wanted one last chance to feel alive. A lot of different stories there. The ones who did interviews, we saw them. We saw them in the room too. Some of them were courageous. Some...well, it's all on video. You can see for yourself.

But you want to know about me and Jack, right? How we got into it. I didn't want to do it, but Jack didn't want to play alone. He had to have someone to share it with. At first it was roller coasters, the bigger the better, and a couple of them were more than frightening, they were unsafe—actually dangerous. That was when it started. Jack got addicted to the thrill of danger. And the thing about addiction, you have to increase the dose every time just to experience the same thrill. So after roller coasters, we went skydiving, and then spelunking and scuba, and whatever else had some kind of risk. A NASCAR ride-along. The vomit comet. If we could have afforded it, we'd have bought a tourist ride to orbit.

It was exhilarating. But it was also exhausting. I was working up the courage to tell him no more. Yeah, the after-sex was great, but did you notice I have a slight limp? I broke my leg the third time we went skydiving and I was in a cast for ten weeks, so maybe that put me off the next big adventure.

But then he said the next one could make us rich and that was my mistake, I listened to him because I wasn't ready to argue. The second mistake was saying, "Okay, I'll think about it," which is my way of saying no, because I wasn't going to think about it at all. But Jack took that as a yes and signed us up for the game without telling me.

I thought I was only going with him for moral support, I didn't find out that I was a contestant until we got there, and Jack told me that he had paid a thousand dollars for each of us to play. If I didn't play, we'd forfeit the thousand. "Come on, buddy, it's only one round."

"Not one round," I said. "As many rounds as it takes to earn back the thousand. That's what, five rounds?"

"Um, six."

"Six. Right."

"Do the math. What are the odds? A thousand to one, eight hundred to one, six hundred to one. It'll be fun and we can make some money."

I did the math. If all the contestants and the alternates, the hundred or so on the waiting list, had paid a thousand dollars each, then the production company already had a million dollars in the bank. Add to that the advertising revenue, and they were making at least twenty-five million per hour of broadcast, maybe that much again on the streaming services. And how many millions of subscribers paying five bucks an episode? Multiply that by ten or twelve episodes and you're getting close to a billion gross. Gross is right.

And on the front end? Every contestant gets a hundred dollars for playing the first round, so the show was spending only a hundred thousand there, and maybe another five hundred thousand in production costs, not a lot when you think about it, so the show was bringing in some serious money, just not the contestants. Not yet. You had to be in it to win it—and once it got serious, well no. I think they miscalculated the dropout rate. I don't think they meant for it to go on for as many rounds as it did. But I don't think they cared. By the time they got to the sixth or seventh round they were bringing in over a hundred million per hour.

According to the publicity, the first thousand contestants included an equal number of men and women, and some non-binary too. The demographic representation was based on the projected audience. For the first round, they also had several hundred alternates standing by, also demographically selected.

The producers had presorted all the applicants, but they sorted us again when we showed up—probably by who would look good on camera. They selected several people out, they didn't explain why, and replaced them with alternates. They got their entrance fee returned. Anyone who didn't play got their money back.

Jack and I were chosen early, I don't think that was ever in doubt, so now we were committed. We showed up at the assigned location, nervous, giddy, anxious, uncertain. And yes, scared. All the contestants and alternates were gathered in the same place, a repurposed warehouse.

When they checked us in, they took away our phones and locked them in metal boxes, so we couldn't be tracked. Then they put us on buses with the windows blacked out. Even the driver's section was blocked off so we couldn't see out the front either. Some of us speculated, others sat in silence while we drove around the city. It was a long drive with lots of turns so we couldn't figure out where we were headed—until finally we pulled into a huge indoor stadium that had been redressed for the game. When they let us out, most of us just stopped and stared.

I don't have to describe it, you've seen the pictures, It was big, but the pictures don't give you the real sense of it. I can tell you that it smelled clean. Antiseptic. Like it had been scrubbed by a hazmat team. Not unpleasant, but seriously sanitary.

The floor was marked out in grids, ten of them, each grid divided into ten rows of ten squares—each square was ten by ten feet. a hundred separate spaces. A thousand contestants. Empty, it looked like a geometrical diagram of uncurved space.

Each square had a chair and a stand with a folder on it. A dozen drones circled above us, whispering through the air, recording everything. A dais stood at one side of the space, the nominal front. Large screens all around displaying the views from the drones.

We were directed to move to any empty chair in any of the grids and sit down with our hands in our laps. Do not touch anything. Do not open the folder. I wondered if the behavior of the drones might be a clue to which chair not to sit in, but if there was a pattern, I couldn't figure it out.

Jack and I found seats next to each other. We weren't the first, but we weren't the last either. People were still filling in as more and more buses arrived. I think that's when the reality of it began to sink in. This was actually happening. Other people were realizing it too. A few refused to get off the bus. One woman got off the bus, but refused to take a seat. Another man had a panic attack and his wife had to walk him out. Of course, once you left, you were out of the game. The empty spaces were given to the alternates, again based on demographics.

Finally, all the spaces were filled, everyone was seated. The alternates were seated behind a curtain near the buses. We were ready to begin.

At exactly 7pm, the screens lit up and a garish fanfare announced the entrance of Randy-The-Host. He was that inevitable friendly face from all those game shows and reverse mortgage ads and irritable bowel commercials. You couldn't get away from him. I guess they picked him because they thought he would be reassuring, but Jack and I both thought he was ghastly. Even more so, because he was trying so hard to project seriousness now. Randy-The-Host stepped up onto the dais, looking both serious and cordial. He welcomed us and thanked us for accepting the challenge. We were about to begin a great adventure. He spoke as if we were all friends. Except, you know, friends don't play these kinds of games, do they?

Then he introduced the producers, and they introduced the logistics team who explained the security and secrecy measures necessary to make sure the game was fair. The placement of the capsules was entirely random. The giant screens lit up to show why.

Three hours before the game started, nine hundred and ninety-nine capsules were put into a transparent spherical container. One more capsule, identical to the rest, was added. The container was then sealed and rotated for five minutes. When it finally stopped, it deposited the capsules, one at a time, into small black boxes, displaying the count as it did—exactly a thousand. They filled a long low table.

Then ten identical bots lined up at the table. Each bot took only a hundred of the little boxes, each bot displayed its own count as it worked. Then, when all were loaded, each bot went to its own specific ten-by-ten grid. They moved with mechanical precision. They rolled up and down the rows, stopping at each stand to set out the necessities of the game: a folder, a pen, a small package of tissues, a bottle of water, and finally a little black box. The bots all finished within seconds of each other. They each rolled to the forward left corner of their respective grids to wait patiently. They would stay there as guards to make sure that no one could approach their grid or tamper with the contents of the stands.

The entire process was displayed on all the giant screens—multiple angles, close-ups, aerial shots, time-lapse. everything. There was no way anyone could know the location of thousandth capsule. The entire process was automated and random. No human agent could have affected the result.

When the videos finally concluded, the lawyers took the stage, three of them, they looked like robots themselves, all black-suited, blank-faced, and dispassionate. Jack whispered to me, "Larry, Moe, and Curly." I whispered back, "Dewey, Cheatem, and Howe."

Dewey, Cheatem, and Howe took turns explaining the legality of the game. Then they took turns explaining the rules. There were a lot of them. No watches, no phones, no mechanical or electronic devices of any kind. No alcohol, no drugs, no leaving to pee or poop. No side chatter. Remain in your seat for the entire round, unless otherwise instructed. Remain silent unless you are given permission to speak.

And then there was this:

"Every time you complete a round, your winnings will be put into escrow. You will then have one week to sign up for the next round. If you do not commit to continue during that sign up time, your participation will end. All players will receive their accumulated winnings after the final round of the game.

"If it is your intention to continue to the next round in the game, you must abide by the following rules. You will not give interviews, you will not attempt any publishing or performance contracts, you will make no arrangements of any kind with any outside agency until the game has completed.

"We will give you an opportunity at the beginning of each round to leave the game with your accumulated winnings. That will be the only opportunity within the round. You will not leave the round until the host says, 'You may now leave the round.'

"Failure to abide by these rules will be an automatic disqualification and the forfeiture of all accumulated winnings. Forfeited winnings will be divided among the remaining contestants, so it will be to your benefit to be rigorous about the way you participate.

"No questions, no negotiations, no excuses, and no refunds. These are the rules of the game. The rules are absolute."

Of course, we knew all this. It had been in all the applications, all the waivers, all the contracts—all the assorted documents necessary to free the producers from liability. We'd had to sign and thumbprint and notarize all of it—several times. Nobody was going to sue for misrepresentation. This was airtight.

The lawyers took their time reviewing all of this—but it wasn't just to remind the players what we'd committed to, it was for the home audience too. They had to know this wasn't a stunt. Dewey, Cheatem, and Howe presented all this information with the same joyous excitement of an old sock drawer.

When they had said everything they needed to say, they gave us some time to consider our commitment. "The game will officially begin when every contestant has agreed to the rules. If you agree to the rules, remain in your seat. If you do not agree to the rules, you may leave now. Get up and proceed to the marked exit. Your entry fee will be refunded and an alternate will take your place."

Three people got up and left. They were quickly escorted out. Three alternates were directed to their separate seats. I looked to Jack. He shook his head. Okay, we were in.

"Does anyone else want to leave?" Dewey, or maybe it was Cheatem or Howe, asked the question again. Two more people left.

Finally, when the question was asked and no one got up to leave, Cheatem said, "If you are staying, then you are agreeing to the rules. The game starts now. The rules start now."

I looked to Jack. He grinned. I knew that grin. The after-sex would be delicious. Okay. One round. A thousand to one.

Now, Randy-The-Host returned. He told us to open the folders in front of us and read the documents inside. "Do not sign anything until you are told to." He explained, the session wouldn't resume until everyone had read it and every question had been answered. It wasn't the standard assisted suicide waiver. Several key clauses had been amended, but they were all legal. A panel of three judges had approved the language.

There weren't any questions. Most of them had already been asked and answered at the orientation. And people were getting impatient to move on. When there were no more hands raised, we were told to fill out the forms. They walked us through it, step by step. Name. Address. Phone. Email. Then sign in all three spaces where we acknowledged that we understood the contract, that we agreed to its terms, and that we had joined the game under our own free will. I gave Jack a look on that, but I signed anyway.

There was also a beneficiary agreement. If you did not survive the round, your heirs would get a hundred thousand dollars. Plus your winnings. Even the winnings from the round you didn't win. To make it even more attractive, each round the beneficiary payout would go up another fifty thousand dollars. I put down Jack's name. He put down mine, he held up the form to show me. Fair enough. He'd signed me up for this.

Then the folders were gathered by the staff—they all wore identical jumpsuits and they were all deliberately dispassionate.

The folders were stacked on a table in front of the dais and the staff went through them quickly, opening each one and sliding the forms into a scanner. The scanner blinked green after each page. Until one time it blinked red.

Apparently each folder was linked to a specific grid location, because the staffers quickly conferred and two of them went to a square where a burly man sat with his arms crossed. They spoke to him quietly. He wasn't that far from me, so I caught the word "disqualified" and that he would have to leave. He didn't like that. He cursed the staffers, but he got up anyway and stormed out. An alternate came in, carrying her own folder. She handed it to one of the staffers and sat down in the man's place. Her folder was added to the rest and the scanner blinked green.

So far, very methodical, very serious, right?

Randy-The-Host came back now. He smiled that godawful smile. "All right, let's play. Let's start by finding out a little bit about you. Who wants to share why they're playing?" A lot of hands went up. Not mine. Not Jack's either.

You can look at the shares. They're all online. Not just the ones that were in the hour-long episode, all of them. Some of them are funny and some of them are sad, a couple are just silly, I don't think those people were really taking the game serious, not yet.

By the time everybody had had a chance to share, we'd been sitting for two hours. Finally, Randy-The-Host asked if we were ready. Did anybody else want to leave and get their entry fee back? Last chance?

Three people got up and left. Three alternates replaced them.

"Right," said Randy-The-Host. "Let me remind you again, the rules are now in effect. If you do not follow the instructions to the letter, you will be disqualified. If you are disqualified your entry fee will not be refunded. That part is over. We are now playing for keeps. Are you ready? Right. We will now begin." He looked around the room, as if to underline his words. "Now, listen carefully. Do not do anything, do not touch anything until I tell you. First, I will give you all the instructions, then I will tell you to begin. No, I am not taking questions."

He paused a moment, looked at the vast sea of expectant faces, as if searching for agreement, then continued, "When I say 'begin,' but not until then, you may open the bottle of water. You may take a small drink. Take only a small drink, do not drink it all. You will then replace the bottle on the table and wait for the next instruction. When you are ready to proceed, raise your hand."

Overhead, the drones circled, watching. A few others began raising their hands. I looked to Jack. I raised my hand. Jack raised his. Around the stadium the giant screens showed a landscape of upraised hands.

Finally, Randy-The-Host gave us permission. "You may now open the bottle and take a small drink. Begin."

We drank. We put the bottles back. Then we waited. Finally, Randy-The-Host said, "When you are ready to proceed, raise your hand."

I kept my hands in my lap. I was annoyed at the authoritarian way this game was proceeding. They were turning us into machines. They were training us to act in unison. They were training us not to think, but to wait. Finally, I raised my hand. I was one of the last.

Randy-The-Host said, "You may now pick up the box in front of you and examine it. Do not open it. Begin." The display screens switched to show a scattering of close-ups. The box was small, it had a dark grim surface. It felt heavy in my hand,

"Hold the box over your head, so we can see that everybody has one." The drones swept across the room, they circled and dodged. The overhead displays were a confusion of boxes, hands, faces.

"All right, you all know the odds. You've seen the articles, the videos, all the different analyses on how to play the game. You now have five minutes to trade your box for any other box in the room. Begin."

Some people traded with their neighbors, others shook their heads and held their boxes close. A few stood up and crossed the room to trade with someone as far away as they could get.

Jack and I traded our boxes too. I don't remember when he'd suggested it, but I'd shrugged and agreed. One of the actuarial analyses suggested this was a good strategy, but I figured the odds remained the same no matter what.

When the trading period ended, Randy-The-Host held up his hand and waited for silence. Somewhere in there, he had stopped being the friendly presence of daytime television and had become something else, something more sinister, something a little ghoulish perhaps. Maybe that's why they'd hired him.

"All right. Listen carefully to the next instructions. In a minute, you will each open your box and look inside. Do not do anything else. Just look. Inside, there will be a single white capsule. Do not touch it. Only look at it. Study it. Consider what it means. No, I am not taking questions, put your hand down. When I say begin, you may open your box.

Begin."

He waited for a moment, while we all opened our boxes. "Let me remind you that nobody in this room or out of it could possibly know which box holds the final capsule. You all have the same opportunity. You all have the same odds. From this point on, there will be no talking, no trading, and no more opportunities to leave."

I was getting impatient. I think a lot of other people were getting impatient too, but it was all part of the show—building up the suspense.

"You may now pick up the capsule. Hold it in the palm of your hand. Look at it and consider why you are here."

The pill wasn't large, and it didn't look dangerous. I glanced over to Jack. He was staring intensely at the pill and I began to realize that maybe, just maybe, he was hoping that he was holding The Pill. Why was he so desperate to die? Everything we had done together—did he not realize how much I needed him?

And why had I gone along with all of his risk-filled adventures? Did I need him that much? What if he was right, what if he got his wish, and I was single again? Did he need death more than me? And why had I followed him here? What did I want?

I don't know how long they let us look at those innocent-looking little white capsules, but it was too long—I was sweating and feeling chills and very much afraid of what might happen next. A thousand to one. No, a thousand to two. Five hundred to one. Still....

"I will give you a signal," Randy-The-Host said. "When I say begin, and not until then, you will put the capsule into your mouth. You will take a drink of water and swallow it. Anyone who does not follow instructions will be disqualified. You will not get your entrance fee refunded." He paused, waiting, extending the enormity of the moment. Faces, hands, pills. The screens showed a sea of emotion, strange waves of expectancy.

And then Randy-The-Host said, "All right. This is it. On my signal. Three...two...one.... Begin."

I did. Jack did. We all did. In unison. The giant screens what the drones were seeing. We were a machine, functioning in perfect synchronization. A suicide cult.

Nothing happened. Not for a long moment.

And then giggles of relief.

Until —

The drones circled, the screens focused. The center screen showed a young woman, rigid, her eyes rolling up into her head as she slipped down out of her seat. She thrashed for a few seconds, then she was still.

"We have a winner," said Randy-The-Host.

The room went silent. Stunned.

And then, gasps, sobs, even a couple of shrieks. Someone shouted, "No, this isn't right. This was supposed to be—"

"It is what it is," said Randy-The-Host. "Nobody lied to you. You came here to beat the odds. Nine hundred and ninety-nine of you did that. Congratulations. This part of Round One is now complete. You may acknowledge yourselves."

A few people applauded. Then a few more. Then the whole room. It was bizarre. A young woman had died and the rest of us were laughing and applauding that we had beaten the odds. Her name was Rose and she and her fiancé had entered the game to get enough money for a big wedding.

Jack and I went home and weirdly we did not have sex. We just crawled into bed and he held onto me for the longest time without saying anything. Perhaps he was finally realizing the reality of death. Or perhaps he was trying to convince me that we had to go onto the next round.

Now that everyone knew it was serious, a lot of people had to be having second thoughts. By morning the online discussions were ferocious. Most of the game's official forums and most of the un-allied social media sites had comment threads in the tens of thousands.

Some people were arguing that the whole thing was a stunt and that everybody had gotten sugar pills. Despite the horrifically publicized shock of the woman's fiancé, the online disbelievers were adamant that the dead woman was really an actress and everything would be revealed at the end of the game.

Well, maybe—Jack and I wouldn't rule it out. But we had to take it serious. And most of the other contestants did too. A lot of the chatter was recorded and shared with the worldwide audience. The comment threads were ugly with speculations about the contestants. That was why Jack and I said nothing where we might be heard. We weren't going to be picked over by carrion-feeders.

The following week, only eight hundred and seventy-two people returned for the second round. There were only nine grids of chairs now, and the last one was smaller. The survival prize was upped to two hundred and fifty dollars. Nobody left at the opportunity. Even though I wanted to quit, Jack pointed out that we were still eighteen hundred dollars behind and the odds were still in our favor. Jack would not consider quitting until we had recouped our two thousand and perhaps a little more.

We boarded the buses at a different place every week. This was a deliberate ploy to avoid crowds of onlookers as well as demonstrators and protestors—and maybe even the risk of violence. Contestants were told the location only an hour before.

The step-by-step procedures were same. Every week, as if we had never heard any of it before, the lawyers repeated their long dull presentations. Every week, we signed a new set of waivers and release forms. Some people shared what they were feeling. Fear. Excitement. Uncertainty. No surprises there. Then we were given an opportunity to quit. Sometimes people did. Sometimes not. Eventually, we opened our water bottles and traded our pills and swallowed. An old man named Joseph died.

The third week, six hundred and twelve people showed up and there were only six grids of a hundred chairs, one had an extra twelve. The survival prize was five hundred. At the end of it, we had won a total of seventeen hundred dollars between us. Only three hundred more to break even.

This time, it was the quiet lady who never spoke to anyone, it was her turn to "win." I never got her name.

Four hundred and ninety-one people showed up for week four. And only five squares of chairs. The reward was a thousand dollars for staying in. By now, it was obvious, we were all crazy to continue. The commentariat buzzed with noise and judgments. But Jack was obsessed with getting our money back, I couldn't talk to him, I followed in silence. The odds were tightening, but even though we'd be ahead seventeen hundred that wasn't the goal anymore. Not for Jack.

We traded our pills and swallowed. This time it was Zach who died. He was a med student hoping to pay off some of his loans. He was playing for the big prizes. Sorry, Zach. But his beneficiaries could now pay off those loans with two hundred and fifty thousand dollars in death benefits.

The worldwide audience was now over a hundred million and most of the people who had gotten this far were getting all kinds of interview requests—news channels, lifestyle outlets, journalists, bloggers, vloggers, influencers, anyone who thought they had an angle—but contestants weren't allowed to participate in any unauthorized publicity of any kind. Not until the game was over. No interviews, no book deals, no TV appearances, nothing. It would be instant disqualification with no payout at all.

Contestants were allowed, even encouraged, to participate in a private forum. Contestants only. No one else. Jack and I skimmed the threads and decided not to participate. We lurked. We observed. We read what the others were thinking and feeling and saying, but we weren't going to comment. We didn't know who was monitoring what was posted and what they might be doing with that information, so we chose to keep our heads down. "In it to win it," Jack said. "Nothing else."

There was also a public forum, where contestants could share their thoughts, explain their feelings, justify their participation—and reveal who they really were. There was no comment thread on that forum, but there were a lot of other forums where the uninvolved public could offer their criticisms and judgments and speculations—and even their feelings about who they thought should survive. But there were some who were deliberately vicious—rooting for the deaths of contestants they hated.

Based on those posts, based on the relative popularity of various contestants, the Las Vegas odds-makers were now taking bets. Because we had not participated on any forums, Jack and I had mostly escaped notice. We were not on the betting boards. Not yet.

Jack did point out one thing—the remarks posted on both the private and public forums showed that the surviving contestants were becoming a community. Little support groups were forming. People were talking about how long they intended to stay. Others were computing their own odds based on that information. Jack and I weren't the only ones with spreadsheets.

I was ready to quit. I'd had enough. But Jack wouldn't hear it. We argued the odds against the risks for a long time, but he was unshakable. Finally, I went into the bathroom, took a long hot bath, and tried not to think about what it might feel like.

Twenty-five hundred dollars if you survived the fifth week. Nowhere near enough to justify the risk, but three hundred and sixty-eight contestants showed up anyway. Three and a half grids. Three people got up from the half grid and left at the opportunity.

We traded our pills in silence. I was trembling, but Jack looked more alive than ever. After Teresa died, he talked all the way home, babbling about numbers and odds and what the big prices might be worth—not just the game, but all the paid interviews afterward as well. My hands were cold and sweaty. We'd certainly had our two thousand dollars worth of excitement and we could now walk away with sixty-seven hundred dollars between us and call it a win. But no. As whenever I tried to approach the subject, Jack gave me the look—the one that meant, "I don't want to have that conversation."

I thought about sleeping on the couch, but we had a rule— nobody goes to bed angry. Instead, I put my hands on his shoulders and looked him in the eyes. I said, "Jack, you're scaring me. This whole thing is scaring me. People are dying."

He didn't answer. Maybe he was thinking about it. Maybe he wasn't. Maybe he was so focused he couldn't think. "I hear you," he said. "Yes, it is scary. That's the point." That wasn't an answer. It wasn't even the start of a conversation. Maybe one more round, maybe a little more cash, maybe then—?

And then we'd have the conversation again. We would have that conversation every round, it didn't matter. We were going all the way. Because that was Jack.

Week six, the game was down to two hundred and twenty-three contestants, and there were only two squares of chairs now, and the survivors would each take home five thousand dollars. The amount was pro-rated. The more people who quit, the larger the pot would get. One of the public commentators said it was the producers' way of dangling bigger and bigger pieces of cheese for all of the rats in the race.

Our combined winnings would put us more than sixteen thousand dollars ahead. I wanted to quit. I could justify it. This was getting dangerous. The odds were shrinking, we were dancing on the edge—

Jack wouldn't hear it. It wasn't about the money, he said. It had never been about the money. It was the danger. It made him feel alive in a way that nothing else could—not even our lovemaking. I walked away from that conversation wondering if we would survive—not just the game, but our marriage.

The worldwide audience was now more than two hundred million and we were both getting fan mail, though not as much as most of the others, the ones who were more visible.

Jack and I traded pills. Then Richard, the architect, offered me his pill box. He was sitting in front of me. He turned around in his chair and held it out. He had an infectious grin. So even though Jack and I had an agreement, I figured it didn't matter. I traded pills with him.

Richard died badly. Later, they determined he had several specific antidotes in his bloodstream. He had doped himself before showing up. But it didn't work, because the capsules had multiple active agents. Whatever they were, that was a secret too. So some of the antidotes worked—and some didn't. They didn't protect him enough. So the pill didn't kill him quickly. Instead, it tortured him. He screamed, he vomited, blood flowed from his eyes and nose. He thrashed in his chair, knocking it backward when he fell to the floor. He rolled back and forth, gasping desperately for breaths he couldn't take because his throat had swollen shut. He ended up at Jack's feet, sprawled on his back staring in frozen horror at the circling drones above. And he stank. All the blood, the vomit, the urine—all the shit. If anyone still thought this was all a hoax, that the dead people were actors, Richard proved them wrong.

Jack stared at him, looked to me, looked down at the empty box in his hand, rehearsing the trades in his head. His eyes went wide. And for a moment, I thought, yes, maybe, this is it—we can stop.

But no.

Jack was exultant. When we got home, he grabbed me and danced me around the living room. "That was incredible. We dodged the bullet. The odds are on our side now. Think about it. Nobody gets the pill twice."

"Yeah, because they die the first time."

He ignored me. "The next round will be worth ten thousand dollars. We're finally getting to the real money. Only a hundred to one, maybe a little more, depending on how many people commit. We can do it."

"Jack, this is insane. Richard is dead. If we hadn't traded, I would have died. If you hadn't traded with me, you would have died. I can't do this anymore."

He took me by the shoulders. His eyes were shining. "Listen to me. We can't quit now. Ten thousand dollars! Each."

"And after that? Another round? For twenty-five thousand dollars? And then the one after that? Because it's the big money? Jack, all we're proving is how cheap we value our lives. Well, I'm worth more than that. And so are you." I put a finger across his lips to keep him from talking. "Please listen to me. What happens if you're wrong about the odds.

What happens if one of us dies, then what?"

"It's not gonna happen."

"Yeah, that's what Richard thought. And how he's dead. He was a nice guy. We could have been friends if we weren't all in the game. Jack, I'm serious. It's time to get out."

Jack shook his head. "I hear you, I do. But we've come so far. Surely we can go a little farther. Run the spreadsheet. Put in the new numbers, look at the odds. We can do this."

"You keep saying that we'll talk, but then we don't. Tell me for real, how far do you plan on going? When do we quit? Really?"

"Okay," he said. "I want to go for the twenty-five thousand dollar round. Between the two of us, we could make enough for a down payment on a house. And if we go for the round after that—"

"And if one of us dies, there's what? Half a million? For a down payment on a house the other lives in in alone."

"We have a week to think about it."

"You're not listening."

"I am listening," he insisted.

"Okay, you're listening. But you're not hearing."

Jack stepped over to me. He put his arms around me and pulled me close. "I'm hearing you, sweetheart. I need you to hear me too. We need—I need to do this. And I need you to do this with me."

"But why?"

"Because I need to."

"I don't understand—"

"Neither do I," he said. "I just know I need to do this."

We circled the subject without ever finding the center. Jack couldn't say why he needed this and I couldn't say why I needed him to stop. We exhausted ourselves. Finally, I said, "Do you want to lose me?"

He shook his head—not denial, not rejection, just that thing he did while thinking about something unpleasant. "No. Of course not. But let's just see what happens next round, okay? Please?"

I was tired. I wanted to go to bed. "Okay. Yes. Fine."

The sex was mechanical. Vaguely unsatisfactory. Like his body was there, but he wasn't. We rolled apart without talking.

Week Seven. A ten thousand dollar payout. Four hundred thousand to the beneficiaries of the winner. This was absurd, but one hundred and twenty-six contestants showed up. Including Jack and myself. We were down to one square of chairs. Twelve rows of ten and six at the back.

Four quit at the opportunity. We didn't. I didn't know what I was feeling. I almost refused to trade pill boxes with him, but at the last moment relented. We both survived. Miss Daniels did not. We didn't know her, except by sight. I never understood why she was in the game. Maybe she thought she was doing the right thing, but she left three children motherless. They'd been cheering her from the sidelines. I couldn't imagine how they felt. The cameras zeroed in on their terrified reactions. The prying eyes of vultures.

The producers were allowing a live audience to sit in the stands now, only a limited number, but enough. Social media called them death eaters. But Jack and I were thirteen thousand dollars richer. So who were the real death eaters?

We hadn't been the only couple in the game. There were three other married couples and two that had been planning to get married. Everybody's biographies were posted on the website and the Las Vegas odds makers were now betting on who would drop out and when. After Rose's death, two of the other couples didn't come back. Only two others made it to week five and one of them dropped out right after. There was only one other couple in the game now. The odds-makers were figuring that in their calculations too. Would both drop out together?

The eighth round would be worth twenty-five thousand dollars to every survivor. The death benefits continued to rise as well. Four hundred and fifty thousand now. It hardly seemed worth it. But the money was blinding everyone. Even Jack. He was intense. He took me by the shoulders. "Want to buy a house? We're getting close. We'll have enough for a down payment?"

"I don't want a house. I want you. I want us to take our winnings and get out."

He looked like I'd slapped him. His expression hardened. "I want you to trust me. I want you to be my partner in this."

The more I argued for quitting, the more he needed to continue. He had to prove something to me. To our relationship.

So I stopped arguing.

It didn't matter. The damage was done. Jack was going all the way. I knew that now.

And I was going with him.

I had to admit it—not to Jack, never to Jack, but to myself. I was becoming addicted, that's the right word, addicted to the adrenaline rush—that moment of joyous relief when someone else died. Not me.

Seventy-seven contestants in the eighth round. Seven rows of ten chairs. Twenty-five thousand dollars to the winners. Two left. No one died. The fatal pill was under an empty chair. Somewhere, Melanie was thanking her fear.

We returned a week later to replay the round. One person left. Anna died, leaving Frank widowed. Now we were the only couple in the game. At home, I said, "They were playing the same odds we were. It wasn't seventy-four to one. It was thirty-seven to one against them. Against us."

Jack said. "You're right." But it didn't change anything.

We didn't stop. Jack committed to round nine without telling me.

The ninth round was worth fifty thousand dollars. Our combined total from this and all the previous rounds would be a hundred and eighty-six thousand, seven hundred dollars. It would be more money than either of us had ever had in our lives. The number gleamed with its own perverse attraction.

We had a fan club now. People were rooting for us. The Vegas odds-makers gave all the contestants the same chance of survival, it didn't matter, people were betting on their favorites and after Richard died, Jack and I started climbing in the ranks. We were bouncing around in the top ten. I didn't understand that. I never thought that either of us were charismatic, but there we were. Jack said it was because we were mysterious. Because we weren't participating in either the private or the public forums, nobody knew who we were, that made us strange, enigmatic, alien—whatever.

But maybe that was why some of the other contestants were starting to hate us. We saw their remarks in the private forum, the sideways snark, the nasty speculations, and even the occasional personal attack. They blamed us for giving the fatal pill to Richard.

Sixty-six people showed up for the ninth round. Seven rows of nine chairs and three more at the back. No one left. The odds were thirty-two to one against us. For the first time, Jack looked a little uncertain. Had we gone too far? A hundred and eighty-six thousand dollars didn't seem like enough anymore. Not when it was measured against the risk.

The huge stadium, beautifully redressed for the game, had once felt crowded and busy. Now, it felt empty and cavernous. And yet, somehow, it still felt claustrophobic. We went through the opening rituals like robots. Where once they were boring, now they were ominous. There was an unspoken sense of doom in the air. The staff must have felt it too. They looked grim and unhappy. Even Randy-The-Host seemed a little less Randy. I had begun to hate him. I don't think I was alone in that feeling. The room seemed to get visibly tense whenever he stepped up onto the dais. Two people left at the opportunity. I envied them. I sat with my hands in my lap, my head down. We signed the forms. We sipped at our water. We traded our boxes.

And Eddie died. We didn't applaud. We just went home.

We didn't talk. Jack and I showered together and then went to bed. We had intense wordless sex. And this time, I was on top.

The tenth round was worth a hundred thousand dollars each. The worldwide audience was more than five hundred million viewers. Gross income for the game was nearly a billion dollars. Ten million dollars to buy a thirty-second commercial, ten commercials an hour. Another hundred million dollars every round. A great investment—for the producers. Just not for the nine people who had died for it.

Some in the media asked how long the game could go on. The producers replied that the game would continue as long as there were contestants, but after the next round all continuing players would be sequestered in a secret location.

Jack didn't sign up immediately. He thought about it for two days. When he finally logged on to sign us up, he found that I already had. He looked at me, his expression unreadable.

"You started this," I said. "You're the one who's going to have to stop it."

"We were supposed to talk about this."

"When did that start, Jack? How many times did you sign us up without talking to me? From the very beginning, you never talked to me."

"I don't like it."

"Yeah, now you know how I felt. You want to quit? We can quit now. We can walk away at the opportunity. Is that what you want?"

"No."

"Then let's play. And neither of us signs up for anything anymore unless we both agree to it."

He nodded.

Forty-two people showed up for the tenth round. A much smaller grid of chairs. Six by seven. It felt weird.

The odds were one in twenty-one that either Jack or myself would be going home alone. But this time, it was Frances who died. Frances was an unlikable woman, always going on about this and that and the other thing. For someone who talked about manners a lot, she didn't seem to have any. She was uncourteous and judgmental. I wasn't going to miss her.

And the rules of the game got even tighter.

We were removed to a nearby hotel. We weren't supposed to know which one, but it wasn't too hard to figure out, not after we looked out the window. We could see the sports arena and the convention center and downtown. We had our phones and our laptops, we could reach out to the world, but we were cautioned not to discuss the game with any outside contacts, or even with other players. That would be grounds for disqualification.

We could still read the chatter on the private forum. But even that discussion had evolved, no longer the same community—now it had become a cluster of angry cliques, little groups of people actively hoping for others to die. Jack and I were at the top of the list. Jack and I took turns stopping each other from diving in to respond. We had to see those people as irrelevant, so irrelevant that they were not worth us investing our energy. Just the same....

Meals were brought to us in our room. If other players were dropping out, we couldn't know.

For two days, Jack and I didn't talk about the game. We didn't have to. It was in the room with us, it was in our heads, it was our constant waking nightmare, and it was the reason neither of us could sleep. It was the reason we couldn't talk. We didn't know what to say. Sometimes we just held each other tight.

Where once the odds had been in our favor that was no longer the case. We were staring at the black wall of oblivion. If we wanted to quit, all we had to do was pack our suitcases and leave the hotel. We could walk away with our winnings. Nobody would question our decision. But once we got on the bus, no. Quitting then was disqualification. Forfeiture.

We didn't know how many other people might still be playing. We guessed maybe twenty or thirty. Maybe less. This close to the end there was no rational reason for anyone to stay—except none of us were rational anymore. Rational people wouldn't have signed up for this game.

The eleventh round would be played for a half million dollars. But it didn't feel like enough.

If we won...

If we won, we'd have more than one point three million dollars and some loose change, another eight-six thousand. We could pay cash for a house. We could travel. We could, if we managed our investments carefully, even retire. And if one of us lost, the survivor would still have that, plus another six hundred thousand as the beneficiary. One point three for the two of us or one point nine for one of us. It was an interesting dilemma. Losing would actually put more money in one of our accounts. I didn't have to say anything, I knew Jack was looking at the same numbers.

But at this point, it didn't seem like much anymore. In fact, it had never been enough. But all of us—not just Jack and myself—all of us hadn't been playing for the money. Whatever it was, it hadn't been the money.

The other contestants had to be thinking about their own choices too. The numbers spoke too loudly. Anyone who walks away now collects four hundred and forty-four thousand dollars—and their life. But then again, anyone who'd come this far would have to be thinking about what came next. A million dollars. It was tempting. It felt like it was shouting, "Come on, boys. One more time."

All right, figure maybe ten of them walk away. That would leave thirty people in the next round. Thirty-two counting us. The odds would be fifteen to one. Dangerous, but not impossible. The risk to reward ratio was... almost acceptable.

Jack sat me down at the table. He looked serious. "What are you thinking?"

"The same thing you are. Do you want to stop?"

"It's just that we've come all this way."

"Is this where you say, 'Just one more round?'"

"I was thinking maybe you should say it."

I took a breath. I let it out. "Jack, we've reached a point where there's no difference between winning or losing. We can be millionaires together—or one of us could be a millionaire alone."

"The thing is—" he hesitated. "I've been stupid. We are not death-defying superheroes. We've been taking some seriously dreadful chances."

"I wish you had said that weeks ago. "Have you seen some of the things people are saying about us? Not just the other contestants. Everyone out there. It's not pretty. I don't like being hated."

"You shouldn't be reading that stuff."

"It's hard to miss. It's all over the net. You've seen it—"

"Maybe that's why we have to go on. Because they hate us."

"Even if one of us dies?"

He didn't answer immediately. He shook his head. "You know why they hate us? Because we're partners in courage. Because we're invincible." He paused and looked at me. "That doesn't make sense to you, does it?"

"It doesn't have to make sense, does it?"

He waited for me to explain.

"There's the logic of numbers," I said. "That's one kind of logic. Then there's the logic of emotions. That's a whole other kind of logic. I've been doing numbers. You've been doing passion. Numbers can't argue with passion. Never could."

"So what do you want to do?"

I took another deep breath. "One more round. Logically, it's stupid. Emotionally, it's the only thing to do."

For the eleventh round, they transported us individually, so no one would know how many others were playing until they entered the arena. First thing I did, I counted. Twenty-three players. The odds were slightly better than ten to one. It was scary. I could feel my heart pounding in my chest. I had to remind myself to breathe. I closed my eyes and counted. Five seconds inhaling. Hold it for a five count. Five seconds exhaling. Wait five before inhaling. I barely heard Randy-The-Host when he said it was time to trade. Jack called my name. I heard that and opened my eyes. Jack held out his box to me. I was afraid to take it. But we'd made a promise, a deal, a commitment—maybe even a mistake. I handed him my box and took his.

When it was time, I swallowed the capsule. And closed my eyes. Five seconds inhaling. Hold for five. Five seconds exhaling. Hold for five—I heard a noise close by. I was afraid to look. Until Jack called my name.

Leonard the asshole. Arrogant. Hostile. Deliberately nasty. And dead.

I sobbed in relief. Jack grabbed me then. I held onto him for the longest time. I couldn't let go. I buried my face in his shoulder and wept. But he was right. We were invincible. The logic of emotion.

We rode back to the hotel, stunned. We held onto each other, delirious with fear and relief and amazement bordering on hysteria. Not quite joyous, not yet, not until we recovered from whatever strange exhilaration possessed us. We were caught in a whirl-storm of feeling, a passion that hadn't yet been identified, let alone named.

The next day the news reported that the worldwide ratings had hit five hundred million, so the producers were increasing the prize money for the twelfth round. Five million. And one million in death benefits.

Those bastards. They were making it impossible to quit. The logic of the numbers swamped the logic of emotion. If we both survived, we'd have more than eleven million. If only one survived, he'd have twelve million. Plus a lot of change. An individual share of the disqualification money was now over one point four million. If my projections were accurate, that pot could reach a hundred million or more. But only if there was a single survivor. No one knew when we would reach the final round. Would it be a two-person duel? What if it was Jack and myself?

"It's insane," Jack said."

I agreed. "We keep doing this, one of us is gonna die, I know it."

"Yeah, I'm thinking the same thing."

"It all depends on how many others continue."

Jack looked to me, his expression serious. "How many do you think will quit?"

"All of them, probably. If they're smart."

"If they were smart, they wouldn't be in the game."

"Yeah, now you admit it."

Jack grunted, a sound as close to agreement as he ever came. "I'll tell you something. All those things we did together—there was never any real risk. But this thing—it's different. I just thought, okay we'll play a few rounds and we'll get out. But I got caught up in it. And now we can't get out, can we?"

I popped open my laptop and opened the spreadsheet. "We quit now, we walk away with a buck three-eighty. That's more than we ever expected to win. And nobody would fault us for that."

"On the other hand—"

I put my finger across his lips. "Don't. Just don't."

But when I removed my hand, he said, "Five million. Each."

Jack took me by the hand and led me to bed. We spent half the night talking about how we could spend that much money—and half the night speculating about which of the others might drop out. What if it turned into a game of chicken? A face-off between the last two or three contestants. Eventually we fell asleep exhausted.

In the morning, I felt fine. I had no idea why. Maybe it was because Jack and I were finally on the same page.

Jack ordered breakfast. Orange juice, tomato juice, French toast, maple syrup, poached eggs, ham, bacon, coffee. The works. By the time I was out of the shower, room service had delivered. Jack hummed "Somewhere Over The Rainbow" while he puttered around, unloading the cart, setting the table.

I popped open the extra laptop, the one that we'd paid cash for at an out-of-town pawn shop, the one that we'd wiped clean and hardened, the one where we'd installed an obsolete fork of Linux as the operating system, the one on which we'd created multiple false identities, the one that we used only to monitor some of the darker things—don't ask, just things.

Logged on with a previously unused hoax identity, created a one-time encryption protocol, then into a chain of proxies and virtual private networks. Browsing wasn't quite grounds for disqualification, but what I was browsing, I wasn't taking any chances. There is one thing I know about social media. It's as secure as a sieve. Everything leaks. Nothing is secret.

Finding information is mostly a matter of knowing how to look and where. There were private places where some of the people who'd quit and some of the ones still in the game had gathered. Interesting. Maybe the producers knew, maybe they didn't. Maybe it was smarter to just monitor it. But whatever—the comment threads were...interesting. And bizarre. Some people like to show off how much they know even when they don't know anything.

"You were right," I said, as he shoved a loaded plate in front of me. I turned the laptop to face him. "Look at that."

"Ah," he said. "They really do hate us."

"Uh-huh." I reached over and pulled up another page. "And this. The Vegas odds-makers think this will be the last round. How do they know that? You don't offer those kinds of odds unless it's a sure thing."

He nodded. "Somebody's pretty sure about the number of dropouts."

"We need to talk."

"Right," he agreed. "Right after breakfast. Eat first, then we talk."

We talked. But neither of us had anything new to say. Nothing was changed. We were in the twelfth round.

We rode in silence. We held hands the whole way. And this time, we held each other's hand as we walked into the stadium—a defiant declaration.

There was no grid, just a single row of nine chars.

Fourteen people had taken their winnings and dropped out. One point four million each. And change.

It wasn't unexpected. These were people who said they wanted to watch us die. By dropping out, they narrowed the odds against us. They'd talked about it on the forum. They'd planned this.

We took our seats in the middle of the row. Let them hate us. That made us the stars of this game. Jack and I stayed silent, it was the way we played, but we were both doing the same mental calculations. The odds were three and a half to one. If this were a Poker draw, it might be worth calling the bet, maybe even raising on a bluff. But this was not Texas Hold-em or Seven Card Stud. This was Russian Roulette. Jack looked at me and nodded. He squeezed my hand.

The other contestants arrived, one at a time. They looked grim. A couple of them frowned when they saw us. Dora, the black woman sat as far away from us as she could. The two Karens, as we called them, did the same on the other side. Leo, the bearded man took the empty seat beside the Karens. The last three, Lawrence, Moe, and Charlie, sorted themselves into the last three chairs.

Randy-The-Host took the stage. "It has been a long hard journey," he began. "Three months. We have now reached the twelfth round, perhaps even our final round, depending on what each of you choose."

That was a very odd phrasing. What did he know? We didn't have time to wonder about it. Randy-The-Host introduced the lawyers as if they were old friends—maybe to him, not to us. They gave an abbreviated summary of the rules. As always, we signed the contracts, the release forms, the waivers. And then Randy-The-Host returned. "Thank you all for participating. Congratulations for getting this far. As we have said every week, the game will continue for as long as there are competing contestants. And as we have said every week, every round will begin with an opportunity to leave the game and collect your winnings when the last round is complete. This is that opportunity now.

"If you choose to leave the game, you will stand up. You will pick up y our folder. You will take it to the staff table and turn it in. You will then proceed to the marked exit for final sign-out." He paused, looking across the row, looking at each of us with a plastic smile. "Those of you who wish to leave may leave now."

For a moment, no one moved. Then, almost in unison, the two Karens stood up, picked up their folders, and walked to the staff table. Almost immediately, Leo followed. Jack and I looked at each other. This was not good.

Dora stood up noisily. She gathered her coat and picked up her purse from the floor. She picked up her folder and followed the others.

Randy-The-Host stood silent. "Anyone else?" he asked.

Lawrence, then Charlie.

That left three of us. Jack, myself, and Moe.

"Anyone else?"

Jack and I looked at Moe. He folded his arms resentfully. His expression was somewhere between a hate stare and a threat. At the staff table, Lawrence turned around and looked at him. He gestured—get up.

Moe grumped. But he got up. He snatched his folder and followed the others.

Well, crap.

"I guess that was their plan," said Jack. "To put us face-to-face."

"They really hate us, don't they?" I said.

He nodded.

Randy-The-Host waited until the others had been escorted out. He said, "If either of you quit the game now, the other will win five million, seven hundred and thirty-four thousand. Would you like to have a conference?"

Jack got up and came over to me. He pulled me up, pulled me into a long hug and whispered into my ear, "I love you so much. I really do."

"I know. And I love you too. Okay, let's do it."

He held onto me for a while longer, then finally we both sat back down. "All right, let's play."

Randy-The-Host looked alarmed. Worried. Uncertain. "Excuse me," he said. He hurried over to the staff table and conferred quietly with the lawyers. We couldn't hear what they were saying. We saw them shaking their heads. Finally, Randy-The-Host came back.

"All right," he said. "Let's play. The opportunity to leave is over. We are now proceeding to Round Twelve." He cleared his throat uncomfortably. "Would you like to trade boxes?"

Jack and I both nodded. We traded the pill boxes, then sat down. We looked up to Randy-The-Host, waiting for the next instruction.

"You may take a drink of water."

We both did.

"You may now open your boxes. You may look inside."

I opened my box. This pill looked no different.

I looked to Jack. He had his box open too.

"You will now put the pill in your mouth. You will take a drink of water. You will swallow the pill."

The odds were not exactly against us. There were pill boxes under the other seven chairs. I didn't like those odds. And neither did Jack. Even if we both survived this round, we'd have to come back for Round Thirteen. And there would be no margin then.

Randy-The-Host said, "Begin."

I started to lift the pill, but before I could put in my mouth, Jack was on his feet screaming. "No, no, no! I won't do it! I won't. I'm out of here!" He threw the pill at Randy-The-Host. He kicked over the stand, he tossed his chair. "This is wrong, all wrong!" Then for the exit before anyone could stop him.

I put my pill back into the box and closed it. I put my hands in my lap, I lowered my head, and waited.

Randy-The-Host was conferring with the lawyers. More head-shaking, but eventually some kind of agreement.

Randy-The-Host returned. He stood before me. "Jack has been disqualified. You are the only remaining contestant."

"The game is now over." He tried to look enthusiastic. It didn't work.

"Congratulations. You have won the final round. You have won five million dollars, plus six hundred and ninety-four thousand dollars from your eleven previous wins. You have also won all the accumulated forfeitures of all of the other disqualified contestants. That total is—" He referred to a card in his hand. He swallowed hard. "Eleven million, four hundred and thirteen thousand, three hundred and fifty-seven dollars."

I put my head in my hands and cried. It was over.

Later, when I escaped the lawyers, when I escaped from the lights and cameras and shouted questions—when the limo finally delivered me home, when I finally escaped another cluster of frenzied reporters, when I got upstairs to our apartment, Jack was there—he pulled me into his arms and held me close while we both sobbed and gasped and laughed. It was a long time before either of us said anything.

"They didn't think it out," he said. "They hated us so much, they didn't realize—"

"Shh, shh," I said. "It's over. It's over. We're done."

"Did you hear the news?" he asked. "What do you think? They're going to do it again—"

I slapped his face. Not hard, but hard enough to keep him from finishing the sentence.

But I knew he wasn't going to stop thinking it.

This is the movie I really wanted to see.

KING KONG, BEHIND THE SCENES

The sound track begins with a scratchy buzz, then we see a badly framed industry leader counting down to:

Black and white, flickering, grainy, scratched, a terrible old print of one of the most exciting sequences in the original 1933 classic, KING KONG. This is a full shot of the great gate of the natives—Kong is slowly pushing it open as the natives run screaming in terror.

As the great ape comes stamping through, suddenly the music becomes a full stereophonic orchestra, color floods the image, the screen swells to a full 70mm image—and KONG, the most magnificent ape of all comes charging, roaring, bellowing into the native village to wreak havoc upon their homes—The sequence runs through its most exciting shots, and then, as it peaks—we hear a voice say, "Cut, cut, cut—"

The camera pulls back and we are looking at a backlot set. Extras, dressed as natives, mill around with bored expressions, while the director—Ernest B. Schoedsack—calls Kong aside for a conference. We see, in middle distance, the two of them discussing something in the script; Schoedsack is speaking in low tones, Kong is replying in deep, guttural grunts. Kong nods his head knowingly, Schoedsack pats the ape's arm reassuringly, and then this huge 20-foot ape shambles back onto the set and back into position while an assistant director hollers, "All right, places everybody."

Schoedsack calls, "Let's try another take. Lights, please. Camera. Action."

—and the take continues, with Kong smashing his way through the rest of the native village. We climax with Kong picking up one of the natives, popping him into his mouth and biting his head off. (This is one of the famous "missing scenes"—eventually rediscovered and restored.)

"Cut. Print. That's a take," Schoedsack calls, "Next set-up please."

We go to a wider angle on the set. We see Kong retiring to a large chair with his name on the back. He starts paging through a copy of Variety, circa 1931. An assistant director confers with Schoedsack in low tones, "We gotta do something about all the extras he's eating...central casting is getting suspicious...."

And we go to titles:

KING KONG: BEHIND THE SCENES

OPEN ON FAY WRAY, an elegant older woman, being interviewed by an offscreen reporter.

She is reminiscing about the first day she reported to work for Merian C. Cooper and Ernest B. Schoedsack.

At that time, they had just begun working on a new picture that all of Hollywood was buzzing about....

DISSOLVE TO: 1931. A young Fay Wray (dark-haired) coming on to the soundstage for the first time and being introduced to her co-star, young Kong—a hulking 20-foot ape.

"I remember Kong as being very good-natured, very eager to please, but very very naive about life in the big city. He let people take advantage of him something awful. Even though he'd been in Hollywood for two years before being discovered by Mr. Schoedsack—Mr. Schoedsack had seen him in Schwabbs eating a four foot banana split—Kong never became hard or cynical like so many other young actors whose careers are faltering, because he never lost his optimism, so he never fell for the whole 'Hollywood' thing. Even afterwards, the fame never went to his head. He was always his own quiet self—I think that's what I liked about him the most."

We see Fay Wray shaking hands with Kong, who is carrying a script under one arm. "I'm looking forward to working with you, Mr. Kong."

Kong gives one of his familiar guttural grunts in reply.

She twinkles, "And you can call me Fay—"

And we see the first beginnings of the love affair between Kong and Fay, right here in their first meeting—she can't take her eyes off of him, and he is equally entranced by her. Voice over narration continues, "If only I had known what lay in store for both of us...."

We see the dailies:

The shot is Kong battering at the gates of the wall—this is the view from his side, before he has managed to push the great doors open. The dailies are in black and white, of course, and there is the usual run of out-takes.

We see Kong leaning patiently on the door, while a slate pops into foreground. Offscreen voice calls, "Action," and he turns and knocks politely.

We hear producer and director comments over all this. "Well, you can't fault his manners."

Slate and second take. Kong knocks a little harder, but still not in character. (The audience knows what the shot should look like—they're feeling what the director is feeling now.)

Producer: "I don't think he understands the scene...."

Slate and third take. Kong finally begins to knock properly. An extra falls off the top of the wall.

Producer, "Oh, shit—"

Director grunts.

Producer, "He's awfully hard on the extras, isn't he? How many does that make?"

"Six. I think."

Slate and fourth take. We see Kong getting a little more fidgety in the background between takes. "Action," and he begins banging on the wall again. This looks like a good take, until part of the wall—the wrong part—collapses, revealing stage hands and lights behind it.

Director: "That's when we broke for lunch."

Slate and fifth take. We see director and Kong conferring softly, director acting out the motion, Kong nodding. Re-slate, Kong goes through action.

"I don't know. He just doesn't seem to have the feel for it."

"He's young—give him a chance."

"What about that little Italian kid—Dino whatsisname? The one with the rubber suit?"

"No, no, I think this will work out better in the long run. Give Kong a chance."

Slate and next take. Kong falls on his ass.

"He was getting tired there, but I think we can cut away, then cut back and use the stuff from the other side of the wall."

End of take, setting up for next one, camera still rolling—

"Hmm, I must have forgotten to call a cut."

We hear the extras jeering Kong, calling him a "big monkey." We see Kong finally getting honestly angry—and he bashes down the wall exactly as we remember him doing it from the classic film.

"Hey—!!"

Fay Wray narrating again:

"That was Kong's screen test. He wasn't a very good actor at first, it was all very new and strange to him to be in the movies, and he had a lot to learn—but Mr. Schoedsack was very patient and kind, and Kong was a fast learner. There was something about him, a raw power...that couldn't be denied. I had to dye my hair blonde for the first day of shooting, and...."

We see Kong's famous entrance scene recreated for the watching cameras—the first time the theater audience sees him as he comes crashing through the forest, parting trees and as he catches his first glimpse of Fay Wray....

"There were fourteen takes—"

We see a montage of Kong reactions—excited, stunned, happy, and so on.

"—he was very pleased when he saw me as a blonde; he thought it did wonders to bring out the color in my cheeks."

We see Kong and Fay Wray talking softly between takes, she holding a coke in one hand, he holding a barrel.

"Kong was just a big overgrown kid—the theater audience didn't realize it at the time, but he hadn't even reached his full growth. In fact, he grew another four feet while the picture was in production, which explains why he looked taller in the New York scenes.

We were in production for two years. But at the beginning, he was very shy and needed a lot of coaching. He had a tendency to overact on some of the subtle scenes, and not be big enough on the more dramatic shots."

We see Fay and Kong sharing a quiet moment together.

"Kong also had a terrific sense of humor..."

We see Fay recreating the famous scene with Robert Armstrong, where he is making the first screen tests of her aboard the ship. She is wearing a long white dress, and Armstrong is exhorting her to, "Look up, up, now you see it, it's huge, it's horrifying—"

We cut to a wider angle—and we see Kong standing off to one side, watching the take—and making grotesque faces at Fay—

"He used to try to make me break up during a shot."

In the shot, Fay starts giggling, and Kong delightedly slaps his thighs.

"He thought that was great fun. Mr. Schoedsack didn't dare bawl him out for it in front of everybody, but you could tell he was annoyed. I think Kong must have been very lonely at that time. He was always on the set—even on days when he wasn't needed, he was always there. I think he just didn't have any other place to go. And he felt at home on the soundstage. As if we were his only family. I guess I felt sorry for him, at first."

Fay finishes the take and rejoins Kong.

"Later on, I grew to see the nobler qualities of this very misunderstood actor—"

Fay narrates her first meetings with Bruce Cabot, and we see an innocent and charming boy-girl relationship developing between them; it is not serious, but the moment between them is one of those moments so easily misinterpreted—

—we see Kong entering the soundstage at an inopportune time, and abruptly seeing his co-star spooning with her "other leading man."

Kong's face darkens and he sulks off the set....

In the next take, we see Kong losing his temper and punching down a scaffolding with some natives on it—another one of the famous missing scenes—but now we know why Kong was so mad.

Narration: "We had some trouble in planning the ending of the picture. For one thing, we weren't sure where to stage it...."

We see shots of Kong holding Fay Wray atop a variety of 1933 landmarks: Radio City Music Hall...Grand Central Station...The Chrysler Building...the Statue of Liberty....

"...But none of them seemed to feel right. Finally, someone remembered that the Empire State Building was due to be finished soon, and it was going to be the tallest building in the world. Out of desperation, because we couldn't think of any place else, we decided to stage the ending of the picture there. It seemed like a good idea at the time."

We see the Empire State Building, still uncompleted, Kong climbing it slowly....

Fay Wray narrating: "One of the best kept secrets was that Kong was very much afraid of heights—but there was no other way to shoot some of the scenes for the ending, except to go to the newly completed Empire

State Building and actually shoot them there."

We see Kong and Fay Wray on the top of the Empire State Building, makeup men working on both of them, then hurriedly leaving the scene. We see a camera plane circling nearby. An Assistant Director with a radio set signals them for action, and we see a take of the "original" ending of the movie.

"Ann Darrow is on the roof of the Empire State Building, threatening to jump. Kong comes up to the top in an attempt to save her, thus proving he is not a monster at all, but really a very good guy at heart. The closing shot is the two of them watching a tranquil sunrise over 1933 New York, fadeout."

The first take isn't good, however, and while we reset for another take from the camera plane or perhaps a camera dirigible, Kong and Fay Wray talk over their difficulties.

Grunt, grunt.

"Kong, don't you see—we can't go on meeting like this."

Despondent grunt.

"All this sneaking around, hiding from other people—"

Very despondent grunt.

"—your family doesn't like me at all. And there's the religious differences. How would we raise the children? And all the social pressures—and there's another thing—"

Grunt. Grunt. I don't want to hear it.

"—it would mean the end of your career. You know how prejudiced people can be. I don't mind giving up my career, but I can't let you deprive the world of a great talent—"

Kong is very upset. Grunt,. grunt, grunt, grunt. He turns away from her.

"Oh, please—don't talk like that. You know you don't mean it."

Grunt. Grunt. I do too.

"Kong, don't you see—it's over. It's bigger than both of—well, it's too big, anyway—"

Kong rages—

In the camera plane, we see the director and cameraman. Cameraman says he's ready, the director says, "Roll 'em.

Back on the tower, Kong is still raging angrily at Fay Wray.

The A.D. calls, "Action," but Kong ignores him, ditto Fay.

"Kong," she says, "I know it's hard, but it has to be this way."

Grunt. Grunt. I can't live without you. And he turns to jump—
"No, don't—"
He turns back to her, reaching, imploring—She reaches for him—
And he loses his balance—
And falls—exactly as we remember him falling in the 1933 original.

Fay screams, horrified. The makeup men and assistant director have to hold her back to keep her from throwing herself off after him. "Oh, god, no—"

Down on the street, we see Robert Armstrong push his way through the crowd...and someone behind him says, "He fell—"

And Armstrong says, "Oh, no. It was beauty killed the beast."

Next to him, an A.D. notes, "Hey, that's a good line."

Fay Wray's voice over narration, continues: "Of course, we had to change the ending of the original picture. Kong was supposed to rescue me, now he dies in the attempt. Mr. Schoedsack used the film they had already exposed, and the wonderful Mr. O'Brien superimposed in all these biplanes, so his experiments with stop-motion animation paid off after all.

"Of course, there were all those terrible rumors that circulated for years afterward that Kong hadn't really died, that his death had been faked, and that he's been living in secret up in Benedict Canyon for all this time—the fact that no one was allowed near his body and that the funeral was very private seemed to prove those claims—but I was there, I loved Kong more than all the millions of his movie fans, I loved him more than anyone, and if he was still alive, I would certainly know it." She is very very wistful. "Even today, so many years later, I still put a wreath on his grave every year."

The angle widens and we see Fay Wray looking very very small and sad and obviously in a great deal of pain because of her memories. "I guess Robert Armstrong was right...I guess, beauty did kill the beast."

As the interview concludes, we hear a car pull up, and a door slam offscreen. Fay says, "Oh, that's my son coming home now."

We hear a familiar heavy footfall, followed by a very familiar grunt. All offscreen.

Fay says, "He's just like his father."

And we fade out.

A different kind of family adventure.
Let's go to the moon.

JUMPING OFF
THE PLANET

"Ask him, if you don't believe me," my weird brother whispered. "He's kidnapping us."

"Thpffft," I said.

"Think about it, Chigger. Why do you Dad is bringing us all this way?"

"It's a vacation, stupid."

"Up the Line? And then he's going to bring us *back*?"

I didn't answer that. Weird was 17, almost 18, and he was starting to think like a grownup—stupid. My stinky brother was only 7, almost 8, and he didn't think at all. I turned my back on both of them and stared up at the Line.

Maybe Weird was right. Dad and Mom hated each other. And Mom was always calling her lawyer, screaming about visitation and child support and how he couldn't have one if he didn't supply the other. I don't know what the lawyer said, but it never made Mom any happier. The best part about a vacation with Dad was that it was always a lot quieter. Sort of. Stinky made up for it with his whining. That was why I was sure Weird was wrong—why would Dad want Stinkenstein?

Weird and I had our stuff in backpacks. Dad lugged his in a rollaround. And Stinky had half his clothes in his own backpack and the other half in a smaller one on the electric monkey. Dad bought the monkey for him in Arizona, hoping it would keep him quiet on the trip. Wrong again. Stinky held the monkey's hand and chattered at it like they were married. It waddled beside him like an obedient child with a full diaper. I said they looked like twins, which got a protest from

Stinky, a laugh from Weird, and a dirty look from Dad.

Maybe Weird was right. We'd come a long way to Terminus dome—all the way from El Paso to Ecuador on the Super-Train. That wasn't a normal vacation for Dad. I didn't know what to think, so I leaned out over the edge of the balcony railing and gawked. Weird lifted Stinky up so he could see too.

The three cables of the Line plunged straight down from the very top of the Terminus Dome into separate holes in the floor of the station. They were as big around as buildings. Bigger. As we watched, an elevator car slid down one of the cables into a reception bay; at the same time another one popped up on the other side of the same cable.

Dad came back with our tickets then and herded us down the ramp to the boarding level. The cars were shiny blue metal with silver trim. There was a row of them, all creeping toward the Line together. The edge of the platform was a moving slidewalk, rolling at the same slow speed, so boarding the elevator car was a lot like getting on a car in an amusement park ride, only you stepped in through a triple-layered hatch. After we boarded, they slammed it shut with a scary *thunk*. Like once it was closed we couldn't get out again.

Our car was filled to capacity—not exactly crowded, but you had to watch where you were stepping. There weren't that many tourists aboard; it was mostly locals. There was a big tropical storm moving inland and a lot of the folks who lived around the base of the Line were going up to One-Hour to wait it out. They said it was the safest place to be. There were hotels and restaurants and theaters up at One-Hour, so they were probably going to make a party of it.

At last, our car was in the number one position. There was a gentle bump and then the car was locked into the launch tube. That's when I started getting scared. I wanted to ask if I could get off, but I didn't want Dad and Stinky and Weird to know how scared I was. So I just grabbed Stinky's hand tighter and said to him, "Any minute now. Don't be afraid."

He looked at me with a funny expression. "I'm not scared. It's only an elevator."

There was a chime then and everybody else who hadn't yet found a spot at the windows, came pushing in behind us to look. At first we didn't feel anything, but the cable-wall next to us started sliding down and then we rose out of the launch cradle and up through Terminus station—and my heart did one of those sudden flip-flops like it does at the top of the roller coaster when you realize you're strapped in and it doesn't matter what you want to do anymore because *this* is what you're *going* to do, *whether you want to or not.*

We were on our way.

Up.

The One-Hour platform is called that because it takes exactly one hour to get there. It's also the legal limit of the atmosphere, so anyone who visits One-Hour can say that he or she has traveled into space.

One-Hour is also one of the biggest of the platform cities. Seven stories thick, it's suspended from all three cables; it fills the space between them and extends quite a ways out beyond as well. It's a city floating in the sky. You're high enough to see the curvature of the Earth in all directions. You can see as far as Mexico to the north and Peru and Bolivia to the south. To the west, the Pacific Ocean slopes away.

Directly below us was a humongus storm—except it wasn't a storm anymore. Now it was a hurricane. It was a great whorl of white, so big it covered more than half the world below us. From up here it looked as peaceful as a swirl of whipped cream on top of a big lemon pie, but if you watched long enough, you could see the banks of clouds moving slowly around a common center. Almost a hundred klicks an hour. They were calling it Hurricane Charles. I didn't feel honored.

Then Stinky asked the important question. "Can we call Mom now? And tell her where we are?"

"I thought we were going to wait until we reached Geostationary," Dad said cautiously.

"But I wanna talk to Mom *now.*" There was something real frantic about the way he said it.

Dad looked uncomfortable. He glanced to both Weird and me as if looking for help—but Weird just said, "It might not be such a bad idea, Dad. Mom might be a little worried about us. We should let her know we're out of the storm." This made Dad even more annoyed, but he finally sagged and assented in that way he does when he's giving in to something he doesn't really want to do.

Stinky had already run to a phone booth, one of the ones with glass bottoms, so you can see all the way down. He was already punching for

Mom. "I wanna show her my monkey!" He'd put his phone-home card in the slot so there was nothing for Dad to do except step sideways out of camera range. Me, I studied the walls, the ceiling, anything but the floor, until the screen finally lit up. First it showed a map of the US, and then it zoomed down in as it tracked her location. Mom wasn't at home; she was in San Francisco. She answered almost immediately; she looked tired but happier than we'd seen her in a while. Behind her we could see somebody's apartment, and out the window, we could even see what looked like trees or bushes. In the background, I got a quick glimpse of someone—a woman, Mom's age—but I didn't see her clearly.

"Hi, Mom!"

"Bobby! Where are you calling from?" At first her expression was surprised—as if she hadn't expected to talk to any of us for a while, but then her eyes flicked down as she read the information at the bottom of her display. And her expression darkened immediately. "Put your father on!"

Dad stepped into view then. "Hello, Maggie," he said grimly.

"You're doing it, aren't you!"

"I told you I would. It's the only way to be fair."

"You son of a bitch! The court said no."

"The court said not without your agreement."

"And I said no! So that means the court says no too!"

"Maggie—" Dad was keeping his voice deliberately calm. "I will not let you abuse the children as a way of getting even with me. They are old enough now, they're entitled to make up their own minds." Douglas shot me an *I-told-you-so* look.

"I'm going to stop you, Max—I'll see you in jail, you lying pig!" Abruptly, she remembered that Weird and Stinky and I were there too. "You kids—Bobby, Charles, Douglas—why did you let him do this? You stay where you are! Don't you go *anywhere* with him. I'm calling the police." Behind her, a woman's voice was asking, "Maggie? What's going on—?" And then the screen went blank.

There was silence in the phone booth for a moment. Finally, I said, "So this wasn't such a good idea, was it, Dad?"

"Shut up, Chigger!" said Weird.

"I wanna talk to Mommy!" Stinky wailed.

I realized then that after her hello, she hadn't said a thing to any of us kids, except to order us to stay put. For some reason, that made me feel really angry at her. If she really cared about us as much as she said she did—why was she yelling at us? At least, Dad didn't yell. He just went silent.

He was silent now. He looked uncertain. Actually, he looked old. Beaten up.

"Dad?" asked Weird. "Are you all right?"

"No," he said. "Look. I need you to understand something. All three of you. Your Mom didn't want me to bring you on this trip. So I did it without her permission. Maybe it wasn't the smartest thing to do. But I have to do this. I really do." Dad dropped to his knees in front of Bobby and me and put his hands on our shoulders. "I've made a lot of promises to you kids and I haven't been able to keep all of them. Just once in my life, I wanted to do something out of this world for you. And this is it. And I wasn't going to let anybody say no."

He looked so sad and vulnerable—and for a moment, he even looked *old*—that I couldn't help myself. I flung myself into his arms. And so did Bobby. And Douglas. Not because he was right, but because he was Daddy. And he *needed* us. And suddenly it was very scary, the whole thing, and I guess *we* needed him too, and then Stinky started crying. And I have to admit, even I—

Dad pulled back and looked me in the eyes. "Are you all right?" I guess he'd felt me trembling.

"Yeah," I said. "I'm fine. I just don't like her yelling at us all the time. That's all."

"Me neither," said Stinky petulantly.

Dad looked at Weird. "Douglas?"

Weird shrugged noncommittally. "It's just Mom. That's just the way she is."

"Do you want to go back?"

"She's going to call the cops on you."

Dad sighed and nodded. "I hope she doesn't. For your sakes—" he added sadly. "Because then we could both lose custody. And you guys would end up in foster homes. And that wouldn't be good for anyone." He looked sorry he'd said it, but it was too late to take the words back. Foster home? I'd never thought of it.

Abruptly, he looked at his watch as if he had an appointment to keep. He straightened up. "So? Are we going to Geostationary? Gotta make up your minds now."

I looked to Weird. He gave me a half-and-half expression, and finally said, "Well, it'd be silly to come all this far and not go all the way."

"Yeah!" I said. Because I really did want to go, no matter what Mom said. And so did Stinky.

We were going up again.

Our cabin attendant was named Mickey and he looked so shiny and clean he could have been a robot. He had one of those perpetual smiles that wouldn't quit and he acted like he was genuinely glad to see us. He kept trying to make friends with me and Stinky and Weird as if he'd been waiting all his life for this moment.

Our cabin was up at the top of the car. This car was bigger than the one we'd caught at Terminus. It was ten levels and each level was big enough to hold ten cabins. The level we were on, there were only four cabins and they were all big. We had a wall of windows with drapes that were secured at both the top and the bottom, and a big overhead window too, so we could look straight up.

What was weird was the way everything looked. Even Weird said it was weird. Mickey just smiled and explained that this was because the inside of the car was built to rotate around its central axis, so that it could be spun like a top as we approached micro-gravity. Then the outer walls would become the floors, and all the furniture and appliances had to swivel; that's why they were built the way they were. He said they'd spin us up to one-third gee. It would feel almost normal.

There was a chime then and Mickey said, "I've got a launch station to attend to." He bounced out, leaving us in a cabin that was bigger and more comfortable than our living room back home in El Paso.

Below us, the Earth was bathed in ghostly sunlight. The storm clouds shone so cold and white and bright that it was hard to believe how ferocious the winds must have been underneath them. I was glad we were out of it. Someone said that the storm was likely to disrupt passenger traffic up the Line for as long as three days.

The last chime sounded, and the car started sliding upward. We hardly felt anything, but out the window the beanstalk started moving downward. Actually, it looked more like One-Hour was falling down the Line while we hung motionless in place. As we watched, it dropped away faster and faster until finally it disappeared into the distance. We weren't just leaving One-Hour; we were leaving the Earth behind. Our next stop was (approximately) 22,300 miles above. 35,770 klicks. Compared to that the distance from Terminus to One-Hour was insignificant.

I felt sort of *squooshy* inside. For a lot of reasons. My stomach felt as mixed up as my head. I looked to Weird and said, "Well, are you going to ask him—or not?"

Dad said, "Ask me what?"

Weird cleared his throat and managed to stumble over a whole paragraph. "Well—it's about you and us and mom. Chigger and I were talking—and well, I mean—are you kidnapping us, Dad?"

Dad didn't answer right away. He sat down, nodding his head as if he had been expecting this conversation for a while. "I guess we should talk." He sighed. "You know that your Mom and I aren't on very good terms. I'm sorry about that. I wish it were different."

"Mom always maintained that the divorce was your fault—"

"I asked for the divorce, yes, but I think you should know why. I found your mother in bed with someone else—"

"That woman we saw on the phone?" Weird asked.

Dad shrugged. "I don't know if she's the same one or not. It doesn't matter. I've had a lot of time to think about this, Douglas. I've been paying the price ever since, because I don't get to be with the three people I love most in the world—you kids."

"Yeah, Dad, we've heard this part before," I said. "Every year, when we go on vacation. You always spend the first three days trying to make up for everything. Except it can't be made up."

He nodded his agreement. "Charles, I think you're the one who's been hurt the most by all this, and I wish I knew what to do for you to make it all right. It isn't easy being the middle kid. You're always getting overlooked and taken for granted and I don't blame you for feeling the way you do—"

"Yeah, Dad, yeah," said Weird. "We've all heard that speech before too. Tell us what's going on now." I was mad at Weird for interrupting. I had thought for a moment that Dad was finally going to say something that would make a difference. But maybe not, because he just let Weird change the subject without even noticing how unfinished I still felt.

"I've been thinking about this for years," Dad said. "Leaving Earth. It's something I've always dreamt of—going out into space and never coming back. But I was never sure where I should go. There were too many possibilities, and I could only have one of them. And then one day, I realized that not choosing meant I wasn't having *any*. So I made a choice. And then I started thinking—if I leave, I'll never see you boys again. And if you hated me for not being there when you were growing up, you'd hate me all the more for abandoning you. And I just couldn't stand that thought. So—" He stopped to take a breath and to figure out how to say the next part.

Weird filled the silence. "So you decided to just grab us and take us with?"

"No." Dad shook his head. "No, that's not it at all. I do have tickets for you, but they're refundable. I'm taking you only as far as you want to go. I'm trying to give you two things here, Douglas—the trip I've always promised you, and the choice you never had before on how you want your life to turn out."

Dad turned back to me. "You said something once, Charles, that has stayed in my head like a ball-bearing bouncing around the inside of an empty steel drum. You said that it was your family too and nobody ever asked you what you wanted. Well, this is me asking you. All of you."

"Do we have to decide now?"

Dad shook his head. "No. There's time enough when we get to Geostationary. You can go back down if you want. Or you can come on out to launch point with me. From here on in, whether you come with me or not is all your own decision. But at the very least, you're going to get an out-of-this-world vacation. I asked your mom—I said I wanted you to come with me up the Line, and then I'd send you all back home again. She said no. She was sure that I was going to try to steal you. And then she threatened to go to court and I realized just how angry she was and that she was going to try to hurt me any way she could. Even if it meant hurting you too. And that's when I started thinking that if jumping off the planet was a chance for me to have a better life than is possible on Earth, well then maybe it might be a chance for you kids too. But I promise you, Douglas, I won't take you anywhere against your will. I just want to spend some time with you before I go. Is that too much to ask?"

"Why didn't you tell us this before?" I asked.

"If I had, would you have believed me? Would you have come?"

I thought about that. He was right. I wouldn't have believed him. Would I have come? That was a harder question. Not believing him, I don't know what I would have done. In reply, I shrugged.

Stinky had been silent the whole time. I wasn't sure how much of this he understood, but he'd been listening carefully and suddenly he piped up, "Aren't we going home? I wanna go home!"

Dad and Douglas and I exchanged looks. Dad scooped up Stinky and held him on his lap. "Hey, kiddo. You're going to go home real soon, if that's what you want. But Daddy's going away for a long time, and I wanted us to have some time together before I say goodbye, that's all."

"Where are you going?"

"Very far away. So far away that you can't even imagine it."

"Why?" demanded Stinky. "Don't you love us anymore?"

"I love you more than anything, sweetheart."

"Then why are you going away?"

"Because it's something I have to do."

The frustration on Bobby's face was evident. He began to cry. *"But why...?* It isn't fair!"

"I'm not sure I understand it all either, kiddo. This is just the way it is." Dad hugged Bobby close, probably because he didn't have anything else to say.

Douglas gave Dad a weird look then—one of those looks that got him his nickname. He shook his head over some personal annoyance that maybe only the two of them understood and headed for the door.

"Where are you going, Doug?"

"Nowhere. Out."

Yeah. Like where *could* he go? And then he was gone anyway.

About three hours later, Weird came back. Without a word, he went straight to the bathroom. He was in there for a long time, and when he came out again he looked weird. Weirder than usual. Even for Weird. He looked flushed and upset and scared, but he also looked excited about something—kind of like the time he got off the roller coaster and discovered he'd crapped his pants.

Sometimes Dad can be very smart. He put his book down, went over to Weird and put a hand on his shoulder. Very quietly, he asked, "Do you want to talk about it, Douglas?"

Douglas gulped and nodded. He couldn't even talk. He managed to say, "I just joined the Elevator Club."

Elevator Club—?! Huh? I wondered who the unlucky girl was.

Stinky was already demanding— "What's the Elevator Club? I wanna join too!"

I stared at Douglas in amazement—suddenly realizing my big brother had just crossed a line and even though he was still my big brother, he was finally and irrevocably a grownup too. He had the secret handshake. And Bobby and I were still children. I turned to Bobby and said very calmly, "You have to be eighteen to join. It's like a driver's license. I can't join either."

Dad gave me an appreciative glance. "Thank you, Charles," he said. He patted Douglas on the shoulder. "You want to talk privately?" Douglas nodded and Dad and he went into the bathroom and shut the door behind them. I thought I heard Douglas stifle a sob, but I couldn't be sure.

After they were gone, Stinky looked at me. "Well, what kind of a club is it—?"

"It's a secret. You have to be eighteen."

"Well, what do they do that's so secret?"

"That's the secret."

"But that's not fair!"

I shrugged. "You're finally starting to get it, Bobby. Nothing is fair. Grownups make the rules—and they make them for grownups, not for kids. And that's the way things are."

"When I'm a grownup, I'm not gonna be like that."

"Oh, yes you will. So will I."

"No, I won't—"

"Yeah, you will, and I'll tell you why; because when you're a grownup, you'll have waited all your life for your chance to make your own rules, and you aren't going to give it up when you get it. Nobody does."

"It's still not fair."

"Yeah," I said. "It sure feels that way." But all of a sudden, I could see Dad and Douglas's point of view a lot clearer than I could see Bobby's. I wondered if that grownup thing was starting to happen to me. It's that thing that Dad is always talking about. Personal responsibility. Is this what it feels like? I said a bad word.

"Umm," said Bobby. "I'm gonna tell."

"Go ahead. I don't care. Maybe I'll even tell Dad myself."

Dad and Douglas were in the bathroom for a long time, and when they came out, neither of them looked like anything had been settled—

but they were smiling, so at least I knew they were talking to each other again, and that was something.

"*Señor* Dingillian?"

Dad turned around to see who had called his name. It was a fat man, a very fat man. He looked Mexican, but he could have been from anywhere. "Yes, I thought I recognized you. I am Doctor Bolivar Hidalgo of Mexico City. I am an Associate Representative for Baja to the SuperNational Congress." He strode over and pumped Dad's hand enthusiastically, as if they were old friends.

Dad looked worried, but *Señor* Hidalgo reassured him quickly. "Oh, please, sir, have no worries. I don't think anyone else on the car is aware of your...ah, circumstance, I wouldn't fear. Here, come sit with me—no, please, I insist. You will be my guests for dinner, I will not take no for an answer." He indicated a booth in the corner.

Dad tried to beg off, but *Señor* Hidalgo insisted, and he had a firm grip on Dad's arm. *Señor* Hidalgo—"

"*Doctor* Hidalgo," he corrected. "Doctor of Political Science."

"Since when is politics a science?" Weird asked.

Hidalgo laughed. "I've often wondered the same thing myself. Here, you sit next to me, *muchacho*. Roberto, correct? No? Bobby, *si*. And you are Charles, yes? And of course, this handsome young man, so tall and skinny, must be Douglas. You have fine sons, *Señor* Dingillian."

Dad shrugged off *Señor* Doctor Hidalgo's inquiries with noncommittal answers, but I could see him mentally counting his pennies. Despite the wad of cash he was carrying, he had to be worrying about expenses. He accepted with a nod and dropped into a chair, but not before turning to the rest of us and cautioning us not to eat like pigs, we were guests.

"Don't be silly, *Señor* Dingillian. You are my guests. Order anything you like. I'm not paying for it anyway. I will charge it to, let me see..." He pawed through a fistful of credit cards. "Ah, here we are. These people owe me many favors. And I owe them nothing. They shall pay for your dinner tonight." In explanation, he added, "I have many sponsors. Politics costs money—especially when you are on the side of the poor. The rich can buy as many politicians as they want; the poor have only the leftovers and the castoffs." He laughed, as if this were funny. "Nevertheless, do let me recommend the ceviche. Or the —"

After a while, Dad finally interrupted. "Your courtesy is welcome, Dr. Hidalgo; but you barely know us. I can't help but wonder—"

"Forgive an old man his vanities—"

"You're not that old," Dad said.

"Old enough to be working on my second bottle of Tabasco," Hidalgo said. "You don't believe me? Cut me in half and count the rings. I'm old enough to have seen Lucy in first-run—"

Weird shook his head. "Now, I know you're teasing us, Dr. Hidalgo. "Lucy was born before the First American Civil War."

"Ahh, the *first* Lucy—I was thinking of the second one. And you're thinking of the Second Civil War. But yes, you're right, I'm not quite that old, but almost. Nevertheless, please accept my hospitality. I have no one else to share my table—now, let's have a look at this menu and see if they have an old-fashioned chocolate soda for Roberto here. You do like chocolate, don't you? I'm sure you do not get very much of the real thing. It's quite expensive, you know. Trust me, the chocolate sodas here are very very good."

Dad was curious about Dr. Hidalgo's intentions, and some of his impatience was starting to show, but the old man just kept chattering away about inconsequential things, refusing to let politics—or anything else—interfere with a good dinner. And it was a good dinner. There were things on the menu that I couldn't even pronounce, but the *Señor* Doctor ordered them anyway, and when the waiter put the plates in front of us, they looked and smelled delicious, and tasted even better than that. So for a while I didn't care what Dr. Hidalgo wanted. I was too busy eating. And Dad too, finally gave in to the inevitable and ordered himself a steak so thick you could have insulated a wall with it.

For dessert, the waiter rolled a big cart up to the table covered with cakes and puddings and things even Dad didn't recognize. I'd never seen so many different kinds of fruits in one place before in my life. And chocolate! Stinky's eyes went as wide as saucers, and I guess mine did too, and I think for the first time, I began to realize just how poor we really were.

I didn't know what to pick, and even Stinky and Weird were overawed too because everything looked too good to eat. Weird actually smiled at me. It made him look almost human. All three of us—four, counting Dad—just stared at all the desserts so long that Doctor Hidalgo just started pointing and ordering. "Apparently, the boys cannot make up their minds, and neither can I. So we'll have it all. Just the best. We'll start with some of those fat red strawberries in cream and definitely the fresh grapes on a bed of thick rice pudding—and a big slice of the Chocolate Death, *por favor*, we shall all share that. Bring extra forks."

"Doctor Hidalgo—" Dad began slowly, "I appreciate your generosity, almost as much as my boys do, I'm sure, but it makes me very uncomfortable—as if you're trying to get to me through my sons."

Hidalgo wiped his mouth with his napkin. "Ahh, *Señor* Dingillian, a thousand apologies. Sometimes my generosity overwhelms people. I am used to giving. Sometimes I forget that other people are not used to receiving. I meant no offense. I only wanted to share some time with you—a man so committed to his sons that he will risk his freedom for them. I think I understand your situation, sir. And I think I might be able to help you. Conversely, you might be of some use to my people too—in your situation, you are probably going to need some useful friends, *comprende?*"

Dad sighed. "Doctor Hidalgo—"

"Please, call me Bolivar. Or Bollie. We have broken bread together." He waved at the table. "A great deal of it, indeed."

"Doctor Hidalgo—" Dad tried again. "I want you to understand something. I'm *not* kidnapping my children. I'm giving them the choice that their mother tried to deny them."

"Yes, I'm certain that's what it looks like to you, and I'm not so big a fool as I seem, that I would try to argue that with you. And that is not the discussion I want to have with you anyway." Hidalgo stifled a belch, wiped his mouth again, and conveniently looked at his watch.

"Oh *Madre de Dios*, look at the time. I have a very important conference call that I must be a part of. *Mucho importante.* It starts in five minutes. I must rush. Thank you so much for your company tonight, all of you—you have been very kind to an old man. No, no, sit down, finish your desserts. Do not leave the table until all of these plates are clean—" He shook hands all around. "I shall see you again before we reach our destination, I'm sure of it. *Señor* Dingillian, we do have much to talk about, and let us connect with each other tomorrow. For breakfast, perhaps? Or lunch? Please. Your company has been most gracious. *Au revoir.*"

Douglas giggled. *"Au revoir—?"*

Dad smiled. "Perhaps he forgot he was supposed to be Spanish." He glanced at his own watch. "That certainly was a convenient departure on his part. Just when he was getting to the punch line."

"Do you think he timed it that way?" Doug asked.

"I think *Señor* Doctor Hidalgo is way too good a snake-oil salesman to leave anything to chance. Yes, I think he timed it that way."

"Snake-oil?" Stinky asked.

"It's what you buy when your snake gets squeaky," I said, wondering what it really meant. Mostly, it meant another trip to the dictionary.

"Right," said Dad, heaving himself up from the table with a satisfied grunt. "And right now, it's time to get our squeakiest snake into bed—"

When we woke up in the morning, the gravity was completely sideways. Except it wasn't gravity—it was centrifugal force. We were so high, the pull of the Earth was insignificant. While we were sleeping, they had spun the car on its vertical axis, just enough to give the feeling of one-third gravity. We all wanted to see how high we could jump, but after Stinky bumped his head, Dad told us to stop, so we did—at least while he was watching. Instead we practiced walking back and forth for a while. It felt weird to be that light.

The door we had come in by was now on the ceiling— "How're we going to get out?" wailed Stinky. Weird went to one of the side walls and opened a circular hatch. Last night it was locked, because it would have opened onto a vertical shaft; now it was a horizontal corridor so we could walk the length of the car; except Dad wanted us to stay in the cabin.

Mickey brought us breakfast. He didn't say much; he just pushed the cart into the room and laid out everything on the table and then left quietly. Dad eyed him warily. Douglas looked like he wanted to say something, then went into the bathroom until he was gone. Dad made a show of turning on the video.

Hurricane Charles was still all over the news. The winds were still too high for the cleanup and the rescue crews to go in, and there had been a lot more damage at Terminus than they'd expected. They were already calling this the hurricane of the century. They expected Line traffic to be disrupted for weeks.

While we were watching, the door chimed—it was *Señor* Doctor Hidalgo. He looked flushed and impatient. "*Señor* Dingillian, I apologize for interrupting your morning, but I must speak with you. I had hoped to see you at breakfast, but that did not happen. The attendant told me that you were keeping to your cabin—good morning, *muchachos. Buenas dias.* Please, may I come in?"

Dad let him in and offered him a seat. "Would you like some tea, coffee? Something to drink? We have a bar."

"No, no—*muchas gracias*, anyway. I appreciate the thought. But you cannot afford to feed me or give me drinks in the style to which I have become accustomed. Even *I* cannot afford the style to which I have become accustomed. Never mind that—we must talk frankly. Can you send the boys out?"

"Out where—?"

"Yes, there is that. Very well then, I shall have to speak candidly in front of your sons. May I?" He pushed Stinky's monkey out of the way and sat down on the couch. He sank down into it, although he didn't sink as far as he would have the night before. Even in micro-gravity, he was still heavy. Dad sat down in the chair opposite him. I notice he didn't sit too close.

"Please forgive my bluntness, *Señor* Dingillian. There isn't much time—the people I work for know that you are carrying something of some importance. These people would be willing to pay you very handsomely—much more than your present employers—for the package. Two times, three times as much. Plus whatever other protections you need."

Dad stood up. "Thank you for coming by, Doctor Hidalgo. I appreciate all your courtesies." He offered his hand—whether to shake Dr. Hidalgo's hand or help him out of the couch, I wasn't sure. Dr. Hidalgo took the hint and levered himself up to his feet.

"I am very sorry you feel that way—I had hoped we could negotiate."

"There's nothing to negotiate. I don't know who you're working for, and I don't much care. I'm not carrying anything. And I'm offended at your offer. I'm not the kind of person who sells property that is not his to sell."

Hidalgo sighed. "Yes, I see. Of course. In that case, I must tell you—please do not take this the wrong way, I am not threatening, but I mean this in the sincerest sense—I am seriously worried about what will happen next. Money does what it wants. Money buys whatever it has to. I am afraid that the money will try to stop you, may even try to hurt you or your sons. Please reconsider—I will be available to you, wherever you are. If there is anything that I can do to help you, I would consider it an honor and a privilege to be of service—"

Dad was standing at the door, holding it open for Dr. Hidalgo. I sort of felt sorry for him, for both of them. I'd never seen Dad looking so grim. I know it hurt him to behave rudely toward anyone.

"We have nothing else to talk about, Doctor Hidalgo. Thank you for your courtesy and your concern."

Dr. Hidalgo looked very upset, like he was going to have to go tell someone some very bad news. He shook his head and sighed and pushed himself through the hatch. Dad sealed it behind him.

"Okay, Dad," said Douglas. "If you're not carrying it, where is it hidden."

"I don't know what you're talking about, Douglas. I'm not carrying anything."

"Uh-huh. Right. And our Christmas presents weren't hidden in the closet behind your file cabinets either."

Dad looked startled. "How did you—" He shook his head, exasperated. "Never mind. Just drop the subject, okay, Douglas?"

"He threatened us, Dad."

"I'm not deaf, Douglas. And I'm not stupid."

"Neither are we, Dad. What's going on?"

Dad turned to Douglas and took both his hands in his own. "If I ask you to trust me, will you?"

Douglas gave him that sideways look he does so well—the one that translates out to, "Excuse me? Did you really just say that?"

"Douglas, please—?"

"The money for the trip, right? That's where it came from."

"I can't talk about this. And you mustn't either."

"Uh-huh. Right. It's our lives too—and we're not allowed to know. You did it to us again, you son of a bitch, didn't you?" Douglas pulled his hands free and started toward the door, but he pulled free too hard and both he and Dad bounced in different directions, which would have been funny if it hadn't been so scary at the same time.

"I'm trying to protect you—goddammit!!"

"I don't want your protection! I want the truth." And Douglas was out the door—

We were traveling upward at 1600 klicks per hour, so the car started slowing thirty minutes before we reached Geostationary. By the time Mickey came by again, we were already packed and waiting. He had a serious expression on his face.

"Station Security knows you're here. Yes, Douglas told me what's going on." Dad gave Douglas a furious look, but Mickey interrupted him. "Mr. Dingillian, even if he hadn't, I already knew. I was only waiting for Douglas to ask me for help. There are officers outside waiting to take you into custody. They can detain you until proper paperwork is filed dirtside. And they will."

Dad had that perceptive look on his face. The one he wears when he's just figured out you're lying about something. "Go on," he said.

"Do you have a colonial sponsor?"

"I had one when we started. Sierra Corp."

"Had?"

"It was withdrawn this morning. My wife's lawyer filed some kind of a claim and Sierra withdrew. Some kind of protection clause in their boilerplate."

"Actually, that's a bit of good luck," Mickey said. "I have a friend who can get you a placement. It might not be a great one, but it'll be better than most. If you want it."

I spoke up then, annoyed—"Why the hell should you care, you're just a sky-waiter." Both Mickey and Douglas glared at me.

"Charles—" Dad warned.

Douglas answered for Mickey. "The Elevator Club. It was Mickey. That's why."

"Huh—?" And then I got it—*Oh!*—I didn't know what to feel. Angry. Or jealous. Or hurt. Or curious. Or just disgusted. Mickey? I didn't know what to say—so I said something to my brother I'd never said before. At least not like this. "I'm sorry, Douglas."

He reached over and put his hand on mine. "There's nothing to be sorry about, Chigger. I've sort of known it for awhile. Now you do too." He sounded like every other grownup.

I shook his hand off, and turned back to Mickey. "I don't understand —what does a sponsor do?"

"A sponsor gets you off this car safely and legally and puts you in the custody of a major corporation. At that point, you become their investment, and your mother—your wife, sir—will have to contest your status against a battery of very expensive lawyers who are perfectly willing to tie the legal system in knots rather than let the precedent be established that their indentures can be invalidated by decisions made in dirtside courts."

"How do you know all this?" I demanded.

"I learned it at my mother's knee." He picked up my backpack and shoved it into my arms. He turned to Dad. "Your sponsor is waiting outside. Are you coming or not?"

Mickey led us down the corridor toward the aft hatch, located at the former bottom of the car. "This is the cargo access. Service goods are brought aboard and waste is removed through this hatch."

"Are we going out in a dumpster?" I asked.

"Nothing that dramatic. Watch that light. As soon as it goes green, I punch this button and that door opens. There'll be a woman standing there holding a document. As soon as your dad signs it, you'll be under the full legal protection of Partridge Colonial Enterprises."

The green light went on, and Mickey hit the button. All three doors of the hatch whooshed open and a stocky older woman carrying a big business bag stepped in. "I'm your new lawyer. Call me Olivia. You're Max Dingillian? Pleased to meet you. Sign here, here, and here. She pulled a camera out of her purse.

"You kids, up against the wall. I need your pictures." Snap, snap, snap. Dad too; one more snap. "Raise your right hand. Do you solemnly swear that the information provided in these documents is true to the best of your knowledge, so help you God? Thank you. Congratulations, you are now clients of Partridge Enterprises. Would you thumbprint this, please? Right here. And here. Thank you. You kids too please?" She folded the papers and stuffed them into her purse, then turned to Mickey, wrapped him into her big arms, and gave him a hug that I thought would crush him. "How're you doing, sweetie?"

Mickey grinned at Dad. "Mom's the best. She eats human flesh. Raw, if she's really hungry. She can strip a full grown cow to the bone in seven minutes."

Olivia directed us into the transfer pod and hit the go-panel. Nothing happened at first; then we felt like we were getting lighter and lighter. "The pod-drum has disengaged from the cabin. It's slowing down now.

As the spinning slows, we lose pseudo-gravity. Just hold on." For a moment, we were weightless, or close enough that the difference was insignificant. It kind of felt like we were falling, but not quite. After a moment that sensation went away and we weren't falling at all, we just kept feeling like it. Stinky started giggling. I felt like I was going to puke.

Something outside thumped softly and Olivia said, "We're connecting to the disk now. You'll have the feeling of weight in a second or two. Main level gives you one-half your normal weight, just a little more than the elevator car." Even as she said it, we were already sinking down to the floor.

The door popped open and we were staring at a hallway long enough that we could see how it curved up in the distance. "We're here," said Olivia. "Come on, I'll walk you through customs. Got your ID's and passports? Now, listen—you're going to be stopped by security agents. You've got to let me do the talking. Don't say *anything*. Nothing at all. They'll be recording everything." She looked to me, Douglas, and Bobby. "Look determined, okay? Like this is what you want."

"There they are—" The ugly little man saw us first and came advancing like an attack Chihuahua. He wore a wrinkled suit; it looked like he'd gotten it from his older brother and still hadn't grown into it. Two security guards came following after with bored expressions. A fourth man came running with a multi-lens vid-cam aimed at us. I said the word again.

Olivia saw them at the same time they saw us. She put on her biggest smile and said, "Howard, how nice to see you again. I understand they're getting an ambulance up here for you to chase."

"Don't be nasty, Olivia. I have a court order—" He held up an official looking document I guessed was a subpoena.

"Fold it and stuff it, Counselor. I have a Colonial Contract." She held up a paper of her own. Our contract. For a moment, the two of them faced each other like they were about to start a sword fight—only with folded documents instead of swords.

"I'm filing a complaint with Judge Griffith. You had unfair and unauthorized access."

"My clients requested that I meet them as soon as possible precisely to guarantee their rights of residence. That's all the authorization I needed.

Why don't you try another line of work, Howard? You're not very good at this."

A crowd was starting to form. Olivia turned her attention to the guards, incidentally making sure that she was facing enough toward the man with the vid-cam that he would have a good angle on her. "My clients are under the protection of Partridge Colonial Enterprises. Whatever claims any groundside agency has against any of these individuals must come through me. I will receive service of summons forthwith—" She plucked the subpoena from Howard's hand and stuffed it in her purse. "But please be aware that under the terms of the Singapore Convention, custody of my clients may not be transferred without a hearing before Judge Griffith. You may not arrest, detain, or otherwise hinder the movements of these four people. Do you understand?"

Apparently they'd heard the speech before, because they looked bored as she went through the recitation. "Right. We know the drill." One of the guys didn't look happy; but the other said, "Are you going to be at Lemrrel's party Saturday, Olivia?"

"Of course, wouldn't miss it for the world. See you there." She stuffed her papers back in her purse and started to push forward—

"Hold it, Olivia. Not so fast. There are minors involved this time!" Howard stepped in front of her. He motioned to the guy with the camera. "Get in close for this, will you?" He stepped up in front of us and said, "Which one of you is Charles?"

Olivia nodded to me and I held up my hand politely.

"Thank you, Charles." He stepped in closer. He had bad breath. "Now I want to ask you a question and I want you to think very carefully before you answer. You don't have to answer for anyone except yourself. Are you going with your father of your own free will?"

I looked to Olivia, as if to ask her if I should answer. She held up a hand to stop me from speaking. "I take exception to this, Counselor."

"Nevertheless, Counselor—" Howard said right back. "For the purposes of this case, the court has seen fit to require evidence that the children are not being held against their will." He handed her another folded paper. She unfolded it and looked through it quickly. She nodded. "Well, I'll be damned. You got one right, Howard. This is all in order." She handed the paper back. "All right, Charles, you may answer the nice man."

"What was the question again?"

"Are you going with your father of your own free will, or are you being forced? You don't have to go with him if you don't want to. That's why these agents are here. To protect you."

"Oh," I said. "I think I'd rather stay with my Dad."

Howard frowned. He looked to Stinky. "You must be Douglas—"

"No, I'm Bobby. That's Douglas."

"Ah, thank you." Howard turned to Weird. "Douglas—are you accompanying your male parent of your own free will?" Douglas didn't like being pressured, but he nodded slowly. Howard leaned in toward him. "What was that? I need you to say it aloud. For the camera."

"Yes," he said loudly. "I'm going with my father of my own free will. And you need a better mouthwash." The crowd laughed.

Howard ignored it and turned to Bobby. "And you, young man—are you going with your father too or do you want to go home to your Mommy? You know she misses you *very* much."

"Watch it, Howard—" Olivia said warningly.

"I'm going with Chigger and my monkey," Bobby said. "Wherever Chigger goes, I go."

"The monkey?" Howard looked momentarily confused—

Stinky put the monkey down on the ground. "Show this man a 'farkleberry.'" He pointed toward Howard. The monkey immediately did a funny little dance in a circle, ending up in front of Howard, where he turned his back, yanked down his pants, and made a horrendous farting noise. The crowd roared. Some of them even applauded. Olivia guffawed like a horse.

Howard was not amused. But instead of losing his temper, he turned to Olivia and waggled his finger in her face. "Judge Griffith's, first thing tomorrow morning. The child did *not* indicate a preference for the male parent. We're calling in Social Services for a Protective Custody Interview. 9:00 am. It's already on the docket."

"As you wish, Counselor," Olivia said, calmly. She pointed us toward the Customs' officer. "Pick up your monkey, Bobby. I don't want it getting any fleas from the lawyer. See you in court, Howard."

Olivia guided us into her apartment and pointed us at chairs, with a brusque, "Get comfortable." Then she headed straight for her work station. "Power up, Betsy. Momma's got work to do. First things first. Do you want Italian or bleu cheese on your salad? You kids, what do you want on your pizza? Let's get the important decisions made first—then we have a lot of paperwork to review. I'm afraid your case has just gotten a little more complicated." She surveyed all of us on our likes and dislikes for dinner, finished punching the order in, then turned back to us expectantly.

"Is there a problem?" Dad asked. He looked worried.

"Yes and no. Your ticket's one-way, isn't it?"

"Yes. Mine is. The boys' aren't."

"Good. Then there's no problem. As long as you're not coming back any time in the next seven years. Statute of limitations."

"Huh?"

"Let me look over your resumes, your insurance, your tickets, all your paperwork. The problem is I'm going to have to void our contract. Or rather, you are."

"I don't understand."

"You're going to have to fire me for unsatisfactory representation. I'm going to have to advise you against that."

"But then they'll arrest us."

"That's why you can't fire me just yet—not until you get back on the outbound elevator." She hesitated. "No, I have a better idea. Don't fire me. I'll quit. If you get on the outbound elevator, I'll have no choice but to refuse to represent you anymore. Yes, I like that. It'll prove I have some integrity, and the result will be the same. And Howard will be *really* pissed at me. Judge Griffith will have a good laugh. She doesn't like Howard anyway. But I don't know how she feels about *this* case. We'd better cover our asses with a lot of paper tonight." She patted her ample butt. "And that's going to take a *lot* of paper.

"Now, hmm. How're we going to get you out to Disk Seven? Howard will have his goons posted by now."

"What about Dr. Hidalgo?" Douglas asked. Dad had told Olivia of his offer and his threat.

"He's not a problem. Not yet. Whoever's behind him, it's going to take them some time to organize. And I really think Dr. Hidalgo would rather negotiate. That's his style—I've seen him in action. Next time around, he'll offer you ten times what you were paid. If you refuse, then we'll have to worry about your life expectancy." She pulled her chair up to the computer and started typing and talking at the same time. She frowned and slapped the side of her monitor. "Come on, Betsy—get your fat ass in gear." Apparently Betsy didn't, because Olivia swiveled in her chair to face Dad. "Y'know—it's risky, but I could put you on the outbound without a firm bid. That way I could get you out of here— wait, let me check." She swiveled back. "Betsy, how soon would Max and his children have to leave to catch the earliest possible lunar launch?"

The computer answered quietly, "The midnight car is the earliest one with open bookings. Should I make a reservation?"

"Yes. Use the Goodman account. If it's not overdrawn again. Two rooms for six people. Cancel two of the people just before boarding and sell the other four tickets to the Dingillians." To Dad, she said. "That should confuse Howard. He'll be watching for any booking for four, especially in your name." She turned back to her keyboard. "If I can get you out of here and on the way to Luna, that gives me two days to find you a placement." Abruptly, she pushed herself back from the keyboard. "I've got another idea. Betsy, get me Georgia."

Almost immediately, there was a chime and a woman's voice answered, "Olivia, how are you?"

"The pizza's on it's way, Georgia—where the hell are you?"

"Pizza? Tonight? I thought we were getting together on—" The voice stopped, then came back laughing. "Oh, that's a good one, Olivia. Very good. You almost caught me. What do you need?"

"I need you for dinner. I have some people I want you to meet."

"The Dingillians, right? Howard was just here."

"I want you to interview the kids, sweetie. This is a beautiful family. They don't need a Protective Services evaluation."

"I'd rather do this through channels, Counselor."

"Georgia, so would I—but these people have already had one bid withdrawn because of this publicity. And there aren't going to be any more bids for them until this is resolved, we both know that. This is a delaying tactic by Howard—"

"Acting on behalf of the mother—" Georgia put in.

"Nevertheless, it's a delaying tactic designed to keep my client from his freedom to emigrate."

"Downside sees it as a custody battle."

"Yes, that's true. And starside sees it as a freedom-to-emigrate issue."

"Either way," the unseen Georgia said, "it comes back to the rights of the child."

"Precisely," said Olivia. "That's why I think you should meet the children. Tonight if possible. Not in a court of law. You need to see these kids as people, not specimens."

Georgia sighed. There was a pause. Then she asked, "What's on the pizza?"

"Your favorite. Mushrooms, onions, tomatoes."

"No Martian anchovies?"

"Have you seen the price of Martian anchovies lately? Next year, when Mars gets a lot closer, we'll talk anchovies. Can you be here in fifteen?"

"The distance has nothing to do with the price. You're just a cheapskate. And I'll be there in ten. Open a bottle of Lambrusco and give it a chance to breathe."

"Yes, your honor."

"This call is adjourned." Judge Griffith clicked off with a sound like a gavel coming down.

The pizza arrived then, filling the apartment with thick tomatoey smells. I didn't know pizza could smell so good. At home, pizza is an industrial product, little squares rolling out of a machine. But this one was round and Olivia said it was hand-made. I couldn't imagine that.

Before Olivia could finish laying out plates on the table, a laughing woman in a wheel chair came rolling in. Judge Griffith. "I hereby declare this dinner officially in session," she boomed. And rolled right up to the table to put a small vase of flowers in the center. "From my own garden, Olivia. You always liked the blue roses, didn't you?"

Her chair had a built-in swivel, she wheeled around to face us. We were both staring at her open-mouthed. "You must be Charles and Bobby. Douglas? Pleased to meet you. Max Dingillian? Wish I could say the same. You've sure stirred up a fine kettle of worms. Made a lot of extra work for all of us." She looked around, blinking. "Where's Mickey?"

"Late as usual," Olivia said. "We can start without him. Come on, everybody to the table—did you kids wash your hands? No? Well, hop to it. The pizza's getting cold. More wine, Your Honor?"

"How can I have any more when I haven't had any yet?" Judge Griffith held out her glass impatiently.

"Excuse me?" Dad said, when we were finally all seated and Olivia was passing out thick slabs of fresh hot pizza. "But am I the only one who sees a possible conflict of interest here? The lawyer and the judge and the defendants all having dinner together?"

Olivia and Georgia exchanged glances. And laughed.

Georgia said, "If this were a trial, yes, there would be a conflict of interest. But you're not defendants. Not yet. Tomorrow's hearing is investigatory, not evidential. My coming here is to obtain background information on the case, at the request of your attorney. And just in case you haven't noticed—" Georgia pointed toward two of the corners of the room where vid-cams were mounted. "—your kindly old Auntie Olivia is recording everything. For her protection, and for yours. When did you start the files, dear?"

"When you rolled in, Your Honor. All of the discussions we had before you arrived are in separate files, private-coded. These recordings are being made with grade-three authentication."

Georgia turned back to Dad. "This is upside law, not downside. We do things differently up here. You may have noticed that already. We don't have time to spend a year or two on a legal matter that should be resolvable in a couple of days. Nobody benefits from that. Justice delayed is justice denied. And pizza delayed is asphalt. So eat before that piece cools off in your hand."

Dad took a bite. Thoughtfully. Then another. He looked uncomfortable and he kept looking back and forth between the two women at the table. We'd just met the both of them and suddenly our lives were in their hands. How had we stumbled into this? Was this going to turn into a bigger mess now?

Olivia noticed first. "Max," she said, almost conversationally. "Do you have community standards classes in your town? Seminars?"

"Sure, doesn't everybody?"

"What's the stated purpose?" The way she asked, there was obviously more to her question than curiosity.

"To establish stability for the entire community. The most good for the most people."

Olivia looked to Georgia. "Sounds good to me—for dirtside. How about you, Your Honor?"

Georgia shrugged and spoke around a mouthful of salad. "Yeah, sounds good for dirtside."

I was starting to get the feeling that "dirtside" was a nasty word. A rude way of talking about people who lived on the ground.

"Well, it is good," Dad said. "There are seventeen billion people on the planet. You can't have everyone running around making up their own rules and setting their own standards. The, uh—the social contract and all that. The common good requires that people have a common context."

"That sounds pretty common to me," Olivia nodded.

"Yep," agreed the Judge. "Me too."

Dad finally got it. He narrowed his eyes. "Is there something wrong with the idea of the common good?"

"Nope," Olivia said innocently. "Not if you don't mind being common."

Judge Griffith leaned forward then to explain. "Max, downside, you can talk about things being common, because for most people, that's exactly how they are. Common. Ordinary. But up here—" She waved her hand to indicate not just the room, but everything beyond it. Geostationary. The Line. The moon. "Up here—*nothing* is ordinary. *Everything is extraordinary.*

"People don't come up here looking for more of the ordinary, they come up here because they want to get away from the ordinary. That's what space represents, the last chance for the *extra*ordinary life. This is a lifeline for the human race—a way out of the trap."

Dad shook his head. "The last report I saw said that there are still three million babies being born every day, something like that. The Line would take eight months to boost that many people into space. Assuming there would even be a place for them to go. The beanstalk isn't a way out. It's a luxury."

"No, it isn't," said Olivia abruptly. "It's a lifeboat. And there weren't enough lifeboats on the *Titanic* either."

That made for a moment of uncomfortable silence, until Judge Griffith rescued the conversation. "The point is," she said, "we're trying to get as many kids into the lifeboats as possible. And world-builders. And people who know how to make a difference. We might lose the Earth, yes—but this way at least, we won't lose the game."

———————————

Mickey showed up then, looking very unhappy. Without a smile, he didn't look like the same person.

"I told you not to be late," said Olivia. "Your pizza's cold."

"I'm not hungry—" He sat down at the table and picked up a piece of pizza anyway. "I got terminated."

Olivia sat down opposite him, immediately all business. "On what grounds?"

"No grounds." He nodded in the direction of Dad. Or Douglas. "Getting involved." Mickey looked embarrassed.

Silence in the room for a moment. Olivia looked around, saw that Douglas looked particularly embarrassed, pretended she didn't notice, then looked back to Mickey as if she wanted to say a whole lot of things to him, but didn't dare.

"It's not Mickey's fault," Douglas blurted abruptly. "I asked him. He didn't ask me. And he said no the first two times I asked."

"Thank you for that, Douglas—but it still doesn't change Mickey's responsibility in the matter. How old are you, Doug?"

"I'll be eighteen next month."

"Close enough. No problem there. It's consenting adults," said Olivia.

"Line policy," countered Georgia. "They have a case. Tell me, did you do it on your own time?"

Mickey nodded.

"Well...at least they can't get him for neglecting the customers," Georgia said, then laughed at her own inadvertent joke.

Olivia turned to Mickey now. She lowered her voice. "Just tell me one thing—"

Mickey already knew the question, even before she asked it. "Yes, Mom. He *is* special."

Olivia gave Douglas a friendly smile, then turned back to Mickey. "That's all I wanted to know." She patted his knee. "Just so long as *you're* sure." She made me wish our Mom were as understanding. She started to turn back to Georgia—

"Mom," Mickey stopped her. "We've gotta talk. Things are getting really bad downside. You haven't seen the traffic we're getting. I don't know if I want to keep doing this."

Olivia looked pained. "Mickey, please—you're too valuable where you are."

"Mom, you said I could say when. Well, I think I'm finally saying when."

Georgia interrupted then. "Tell me about the traffic, Mickey. What's going on?"

"We're getting too many rich emigrants. Whole carloads. Groups. They all know each other, and they're very tight-lipped about where they're going. It's that thing Mom's always worrying about—people bailing out. Well, I think it's happening."

Georgia nodded. "We've noticed the traffic through here. We have some idea where they're headed. It's legal. And you could probably find a lot of other reasons to explain the increase—like having three new brightliners, the new catapult, the shift in immigration policies, the changes in the transportation laws—"

"Yes, but isn't it interesting that all that stuff fell into place at the same time, Aunt Georgia?"

Georgia rubbed her cheek thoughtfully. "I'm not willing to rule on it yet, Mickey. I'm still hearing evidence."

"Okay, here's a couple more for you. Last month, we had a family come up, you know what was in their luggage? Industrial memory. Nothing else. Forty bars of it. Probably three or four billion dollars worth. They had to pay a surcharge for the extra weight; they didn't even flinch at the cost. Georgia, they had enough raw memory for a small government. Or even a corporation. Whose data were they carrying offworld? And why? And *where?*"

"There's nothing illegal about transporting memory."

"No, there isn't. But on this big a scale? Doesn't it make you a little bit suspicious? What if it were bars of gold?"

"It wouldn't be worth as much—"

"That's right. And this is the fourth time this year we've had a passenger like that. At least that I know about. I'm only on one car. There are 95 other cars a day between dirtside and here. If what I've seen is one percent, then what would it mean if there were 380 more passengers like that?" Mickey spread his hands wide. "I'm just telling you what I've seen, Your Honor. You be the judge."

Georgia smiled. Obviously, it was an old joke.

Mickey turned to his mom. "You know that booking we've been talking about? I think it's time to use it."

Olivia's face clouded. She said, "We'll talk about it later."

Judge Griffith looked at her watch. "Your mother's right. That's a subject for later, Mickey. Right now, we've got a more immediate matter to attend to. The Dingillian kids." She wheeled her chair over to where Douglas and Bobby and I were sitting. "Okay, Munchkins, let's talk. Douglas, I saw Howard's tape. You're certain you want to go with your dad, right?"

Douglas frowned. "If you'd asked me last week, I'd have probably said I'd just as soon like to stay on Earth. But that was before we came up here. I dunno. Maybe Dad has the right idea. I've learned a lot in the past couple days." He looked to Dad and smiled slightly. "I think...if I have to decide tonight, then I'll stay with Dad."

"You *think*?" Georgia asked. "This is the rest of your life we're talking about."

"I know—you want certainty. Everybody always wants certainty. And you want me to say I'm sure about this—but who's ever sure of anything? Based on everything I've seen and heard, this is what looks best to me. I hope I'm not wrong."

"For a young man as confused as you are, you are very eloquent." Georgia laughed. "Listen, you're close enough to adulthood that I can separate your case out anyway. You can do whatever you want and I don't need to know why. Just be aware that the decisions you make here today are going to stick with you for a long long time." She turned to me. "Charles, let's talk."

"I want to stay with my Dad," I said.

She blinked at my certainty. "Why?"

"Because—well, I know this might not make sense to you, but my Dad lets me listen to my music. He doesn't interrupt. He *understands*."

"What about your Mom?"

"I still love her—I guess. When she's not fussing or nagging or screaming, she can be a pretty funny lady. But...she hasn't been very nice to be around for a long time. I'd like to say goodbye to her, but I'm afraid to. Last time, all she did was scream."

"Ah, I see," said Georgia. "What if you knew how much your Mom was hurting today and how much she was going to miss you and how much you were going to miss her? Would that affect your decision?"

I swallowed. Hard. I hadn't thought about it that way. Not really. Tears started to come up in my eyes. "If I do this, I'm never going to see her again, am I?"

"No, you won't."

"But if I go back to Earth, I'll never see Dad again either, will I?"

"That's right."

"So you're asking me to choose between one parent and another, aren't you? For the rest of my life."

"Yes, I am. I know it's a tough decision. But this is a lot more decision than you had last time this battle was fought, isn't it?"

"No. Last time wasn't for keeps."

"I guess not," Georgia said. "Nevertheless, this is the decision you have to make. So what's it going to be, Charles? Do you know?"

I wiped my nose, my eyes. I tried to imagine what life would be with Dad, wherever we were going. I couldn't, because I didn't know where we were going. I did know what life would be like if we went back— if *I* went back....

If I went back, I'd be going without Douglas. And maybe without Stinky too. And even though I always used to joke about wanting to be an only child—or even an orphan—now that I had the chance to decide who I wanted to live my life with, it was suddenly a much bigger decision than I'd realized. This was like running away from home. Only worse. Because we could never go back again. This was a one-time deal.

"Charles?"

"I don't want to leave my Mom," I whispered. "But I don't want to lose my Dad either. I don't know."

Georgia sighed. She turned to Olivia. "I've heard enough."

"You haven't talked to the little one."

"Do you think that's going to be any better?"

"No. I guess not."

Georgia patted me on the shoulder. "You did well, Charles. You told the truth. You made my job a little harder, but that's okay. We'll try to find a way to sort this out."

"Listen, wait—" I said. "If I could just *talk* to my Mom. Just to say goodbye. Just to tell her that...well, you know...that I love her and not to hate me, please. That would...I think that would make it all right. Maybe. 'Cause I do want to go with my Dad."

"I understand," Georgia said. She patted me on the shoulder one more time, then wheeled her way over to Olivia. "I'm not going to vacate the order. Howard has a case. At least enough for a hearing. You'd better be well-prepared tomorrow, Counselor."

Olivia stood up and pulled her chair out of the way. Georgia wheeled backward and swiveled toward the door. "Mickey, give me a hug. Nice meeting you, Douglas, Charles, Bobby—under different circumstances, I might say the same thing to you too, Max. See you in court tomorrow." She wheeled out and the room was painfully silent.

Nobody looked at me, but it was my fault. What I'd said to Georgia hadn't been good enough. I'd screwed up everything.

Olivia said a word. The word. The word that Dad keeps telling me not to use, and I keep using anyway. "All right," she said. "Let's try something else." She went back to her console, while Mickey began clearing the table. Douglas got up to help him and the two of them exchanged sad smiles.

Stinky had fallen asleep on the couch. The monkey was beside him—picking its nose, pretending to examine imaginary boogers, and then flicking them at me. Ha ha.

After a while, Dad got up and walked over to Olivia's desk. "Now what?"

She looked at him, almost startled, as if she'd forgotten we were all here. Then she snapped back to reality and said, "Okay, we go back to Plan A. We get your ass off this station as fast as we can. You'll have to fire me—sign that—and then you can hire Mickey as your agent instead. The placement will be on his license and he'll collect the fee. I'll be out of it. Here's his authorization, only don't date it until tomorrow. Otherwise, you'll be putting him in violation of the law too when you leave the station."

Dad looked to me. And Stinky. "What about the kids?"

Olivia shrugged. "They're your kids. You know them better than I. Will they be all right with it? Probably not. They're going to have a lot of anger to work out—just like before—only this time *you'll* get the brunt of it."

Dad didn't answer that. He just nodded in acceptance of the truth. Finally, he said, "I suppose I should tell you that I really appreciate what you're doing for me, but—"

"I'm not doing it for you," Olivia snapped. She looked up from her keyboard. "I'm doing it for the children."

She stood up to look Dad straight in the eye. "I hate cases like this. I hate family kidnappings. Even when they're justified. And this one isn't. This one is about you being selfish enough to think that you know better than everybody else. The fact that I agree with some of your conclusions about Earth and about what's best for your kids still doesn't mitigate the appalling selfishness of your actions. So don't assume that I like you. I don't. I just don't want to see your kids thrown back down the Line. That's the only thing you're right about. There is no future left down there." She glanced up. "Mickey? How long will it take you to pack?"

"Huh?"

"You said you wanted out. Well I've got six reservations on the midnight elevator, and Betsy is holding reservations on the next lunar shuttle. Make up your mind, right now—"

"Uh—" Mickey looked to Douglas. Douglas didn't look like Douglas anymore. He nodded shyly. Mickey turned back to his mother. "I'll go."

"Good. Then that'll settle the Dingillian placement too. I'll file it right now." She looked to Dad. "You are a lot luckier than you know. You'd better spend some serious time thanking Douglas *and* Mickey." She dropped back down onto her chair and rolled up to her keyboard. She started typing immediately, and whispering instructions to Betsy as well.

"Where are we going?" Douglas asked.

"As far as you can go." Abruptly Olivia turned to her son. "Mickey? What's the rest of it? The stuff you didn't tell Aunt Georgia? The part that panicked you so badly?"

Mickey looked very unhappy, but he stepped over to his mother and spoke quietly to her. "We had a meeting downside, yesterday morning. Elevator Security. They wanted to brief us about our responsibilities should the, uh...cable have to be shut down. Someone asked if they were thinking about it and they said that the corporation was currently examining all of its options if civil unrest should break out. The first step would be to restrict all passenger travel except to corporate passengers, which they're already doing—"

"Rats leaving the ship?"

"And their lawyers—sorry, Mom. The second step will be to restrict all travel entirely. Nothing at all will move between Terminus and One-Hour. The uh...the third step would be—more drastic."

"What's more drastic than shutting down traffic?"

"Breaking the cables at Terminus and letting the beanstalk pull itself off the planet altogether—"

"What?!!" Olivia came out of her chair so fast, it went flying backward and ricocheted off the wall. "You can't be serious—no, *they* can't be serious."

"Yes, they are, Mom." Mickey's voice was deadly quiet. "The Line has been self-sustaining for nearly a decade. There's enough farms up and down the Line, there's enough supplies stashed in the various pods—if we had to break free, we could. And apparently there are plenty people dirtside who see the Line as the perfect target. Break it in the right place and you get a wire wrapping itself around the equator of the Earth with an impact velocity of 40 kilometers per second. Nothing within 150 klicks on either side of the equator would survive. Counting passengers in transit, at any given moment there are almost 100,000 people on the beanstalk. There are six thousand permanent residents here at Geostationary alone. We've got two and a half percent of the world's wealth tied up in the Line, and the economic sphere is at least three times that large. Rather than risk that destruction of property—and the valuable shareholders who went up the Line—the corporation is prepared to pull anchor and hang free for as long as it takes, and not reestablish a ground base until Earth's governments can guarantee Line security."

"It'll never work!"

"It's already happening, Mom! They're using the hurricane as a first-stage drill. They're already moving the balance pods down the Line. They have this thing all planned out. I'm telling you, they briefed us on it—on what we would have to do in every eventuality. And the briefing officers looked scared, as if they knew more than they were saying. If we go to stage two, every elevator attendant automatically becomes a member of the Line Security force. There are stun-guns on every car now, and they're going to start stun-gun training immediately. You don't make plans that detailed and you don't brief that many people as a readiness exercise or a thought experiment. It was scary, Mom. Some of the women were in tears. The briefing officers made it sound like it was going to happen any day now and we had to be prepared."

"Why didn't you tell this to Georgia?"

"Mom! Think about it. Georgia has to know already!"

"Don't be silly—" But she stopped herself and turned to her keyboard.

"What are you doing?"

Olivia shook her head. "You don't need to know the details." She typed in a last command, then whirled to the wall behind her. She slid a panel sideways and unclipped three memory cards from their stations. She put one in her business bag, handed one to Mickey, and the third one to Dad. "Stash that in your luggage. Don't worry what it is. It's not illegal, and it's encoded. Your courier fee equals my legal fees. We're even." To Mickey, she said, "Get packed and get out of here. If I'm not at the station tonight, go without me. Can you get aboard through the cargo access?"

"If Alexei's on duty, we can board in a cargo bin—"

"Eh?" She raised her eyebrow.

"Mom, an empty cargo bin can be very useful for...you know."

"No, I don't know. And I don't want to hear any more. At least not now."

"Excuse me?" said Dad. "What's going on?" He waved his hand to indicate he meant *the whole thing*.

"Nothing, I hope," said Olivia. "And I'm too old to be taking these kinds of chances." She stopped long enough to look at Dad, "You picked a *lousy* time. You're trying to leave town in the middle of a corporate war. And this could be particularly bad for you because Security is going to lock down the entire Line. Even if we get you on a car, it's going to be tricky. It depends on how screwed up things get."

Mickey came out of the other room, carrying a silvery briefcase-purse thing over his shoulder. He looked like he was on his way to the gym or the skating rink; he was all scrubbed and shiny again. I could see why Douglas liked him so much. Even though I still didn't.

"All right," Mickey said. "You're going to have to do exactly as I say. There isn't time to explain everything. Is that all your luggage? Just those backpacks?" He made a face. "That's still too much. Take only what you would carry if you were sightseeing. If you can't put it in your pocket, don't bring it. Douglas, here, take this shopping bag. Anything that you really need, that you can't fit in your pocket and you can't replace, put it in here, so it looks like you've been souvenir-buying. Mr. Dingillian, that memory card that Mom gave you, toss it in here too. This is all the luggage you've got. Anything else you need, you'll pick up later. Doug, you'd better carry Bobby. No, leave the monkey—we'll get him a new one."

"Uh-uh, no way—" I said. "You've never seen a Stinky tantrum. *I'll* carry the monkey. I'll pretend its mine." I was already opening it up to switch off all of Stinky's programs. "Hey," I said. "Give me that memory bar. There's room in here for one more. The monkey's a perfect place to hide..." I stopped in mid-sentence and looked at Dad. He'd gone as white as a scream. "...stuff," I finished lamely. I looked to Doug. He'd gotten it too—at the exact same time. We both looked to Dad. He saw the expressions on our faces and he knew that we knew. And we knew that he knew that...

Douglas recovered first—neither Mickey nor Olivia had noticed, or if they had they were better actors than we were. They were talking about Olivia's connections; she'd be traveling separate. Doug tossed me the memory card and I shoved it into the last socket and closed up the monkey again, and we both pretended to busy ourselves with other stuff for awhile. Dad too. But for a few seconds, it was very uncomfortable.

Mickey delivered a running commentary as we walked, pointing things out as if we were nothing more than tourists. Douglas looked to Mickey curiously. Mickey smiled guilelessly. "Come on, let's get some ice cream."

Almost on cue, Stinky woke up, rubbing his eyes and looking around. "I didn't get dessert—" he started to whine.

"We know," said Mickey. "See, we're already here—this is going to be the best part of your trip. I know, the desserts you had on the elevator were good, but most of them are too rich and too sweet to be really enjoyed. You practically have to wear protective gear."

Dad spoke up then. He'd been very quiet ever since Doug and I had realized the truth about the monkey. "Excuse me—*why are we stopping for ice cream?*"

Mickey didn't answer immediately. He was studying the menu. After a minute, he said, "I think you should have the banana split. Bananas get more expensive the farther out you go. This might be your last chance to enjoy a banana split." The waiter arrived then and Mickey looked around the table. "Okay, are we all decided?"

We ate in silence. There was no sound except the clink of spoons against glasses and Stinky making bubbles at the bottom of his chocolate soda. Mickey looked up abruptly, "Ahh, Alexei—*dos vidanya.*" He pulled out a chair for the newest arrival, a tall skinny geeky-looking guy, all arms and legs. He looked like a spider. He gangled. He wore a Russian-looking turtleneck, shorts, and sandals—except for the shirt, it was pretty standard station wear. To the rest of us, Mickey said, "Alexei is a native Loonie, down here for college and muscles. How go the exercises, Alexei?"

Alexei grinned and made a muscle. There wasn't much to show, but he seemed proud of it. "I shall be a muscleman when I return home. The girls will flock around me at the beach." He grinned and laughed. I stared at him, so did Douglas and Stinky. We'd never met a *real* Loonie before.

Mickey must have seen the expressions on our faces, because he made introductions then. Alexei stood up and bowed to each of us, then offered his hand for a handshake. He shook hands with each of us, grabbing our hands in both of his own to do it. He turned to face Mickey and said casually, "So? You said you had packages?"

Mickey nodded toward us. "Four. Five if you count me."

Alexei glanced at us again, his face darkening. "I don't know, *Mikhail*. I'm not equipped for a job like this—this is a little big for me. You know the whole line is locking down?"

"I know," said Mickey.

"It's going to be expensive."

"I have information. *Big* information."

Alexei pursed his lips and frowned to himself. He was thinking it over. He steepled his fingers in front of his chin and nodded thoughtfully. "How big?"

"The biggest. It *will* affect your business." Mickey lowered his voice and said, "Listen, Alexei—Max here has pissed off one of the SuperNationals. Do you know Hidalgo? Yes, that one. He threatened Max—oh, not directly, of course—but there was no doubt about his intentions. This might very well be a matter of life and death."

Alexei glanced at Dad, with new respect. "I like you. You make powerful enemies." To Mickey, he said, "All the more reason why I shouldn't get involved in this."

Mickey stared right back. "You really want to hear what I know."

"Don't do this to me, *Mikhail*."

Mickey leaned over and whispered in Alexei's ear. Alexei's eyes widened and he pulled back to stare at Mickey. "You're crazy."

"No—*they're* crazy."

"They'd have to be—good God." Alexei put his hand over his mouth, shocked. It was like he didn't want to let himself say anything else. It took him a moment to find his voice again. "I have phone calls to make, lots of phone calls," he said. "I wish you hadn't told me—no, that's not true. I'm glad you told me. But now I'm obligated to do this stupid thing for you, aren't I?"

"That's why I told you." Mickey smiled sweetly.

"You have the soul of a viper. Your mother trained you well."

"I love you too, Alexei." Mickey glanced at his watch. "Come on. We'd better get going." Mickey slid his card through the table's reader. "Okay, we're paid. Let's go."

Alexei pulled out his phone and started calling people. Most of his calls were in Russian, he spoke in thick rabid phrases, shouting almost hysterically at whoever was on the other end. Each time as he broke the connection, he smiled at us. "You've got to talk to them in their own language: Stupid. Is not to worry. They will do what I tell them. There is too much money at stake." He looked to Mickey. "This is going to be very expensive—for everyone. Especially for me, not for you though. You are already paid. The information you have given me—I will make millions of dollars today. Already I am having some wonderful ideas. *Mikhail*, I hope there is time for them all. I am most grateful that you called me—I will name my firstborn child after you, even if he is a girl." He popped his phone open and started hollering into it again.

Still roaring into his phone, Alexei fumbled a pass card out of his shirt pocket and used it to unlock a wide hatchway; we followed him into a service bay and boarded a cargo elevator. Alexei gestured impatiently at the walls, and we all grabbed handholds—he hit the go-panel and we rose "up" toward the axis. Pseudo-gravity faded out. Dad and Doug and Mickey took turns carrying Stinky who hadn't quite fallen asleep again, but was content to just rest in the arms of whoever was carrying him. In micro-gravity, he wasn't as much of a burden, but he was still an awkward bundle.

Alexei closed his phone and looked at Mickey. "I am going to make too much money today, *Mikhail*. I will have to give you some of it or my conscience will trouble me—not too much, though. I do not have a very large conscience. You will share some of it with your new friends, *da?* That gives me another idea—later." He opened his phone again and yelled into it.

When we got to the top—we came out of the tube into a narrow service corridor, the floor here had the steepest curvature of all. The pseudo gravity was too light for real walking, so we sort of bounced forward, caroming off the walls for a bit until Alexei slowed us down and suggested we conserve our energy. He pointed to handholds spaced along the walls. "Use those. Pull yourselves along. Pretend you're swimming. I will carry the little one—" I wished he hadn't said that about swimming. I was already having trouble remembering up and down. This wasn't as much fun as it looked. Stinky thought it was fun. He wanted to try bouncing by himself, but Alexei promised him that it would be more fun to ride on his back, so he decided to try that instead. How often do you get to piggy-back ride a Loonie in free fall?

We passed a whole bunch of KEEP OUT, THIS MEANS YOU! and AUTHORIZED PERSONNEL ONLY! signs, but Alexei ignored them. Whenever we came to a locked hatch, Alexei would pull out an appropriate clearance card and pass us through. "How do you have all these cards?" Dad asked.

"What do you think I came here to study? Domestic Ecology. I am on a work-study plan. I earn my education with hands-on experience. I am three years here, I have clearances everywhere. I can go anywhere on the station. It is the perfect job for a young smuggler, *da?* Do not worry, Mr. Dingillian, I do not abuse the trust of my employers. At least, not very often. And usually only for a good cause. This is a good cause. Besides, if what *Mikhail* tells me is true, I think that my usefulness here has just ended. I am returning to Gagarin very shortly. I will visit my money."

"When?" Dad asked.

"Tonight," laughed Alexei. "On the very same elevator as you. We go out together. Ahh, here we are—"

Here was a thick hatch into a triple-sealed room—an airlock? Inside was a ladder up into a hatch in what would have been the ceiling if there were any gravity. Alexei passed Stinky into Mickey's arms and pulled himself up the ladder. At the top, he put his card into a reader and punched an entry code. He looked back down to us. "You must be very careful here. We are at the hub. The axis. The Line passes through the center of a pressurized core. As you come through, you'll see that the top is moving. Don't be afraid. Hold onto the railings, you'll be fine. I'll be right here to help. Any questions? Let's go."

Alexei tapped the go-panel and the hatch slid open. He pulled himself up through the opening and disappeared for a moment. Then his head reappeared. Hokay, Douglas, you come next please?" Douglas jumped and floated right up to the hatch, grabbing onto the handholds near the top. "That's right," Alexei coached. "Now just pull yourself through. Hokay, Charles—you come next. This is very easy, *da?*" I swallowed hard. For some reason, up and down and sideways had suddenly decided to stop being up and down and sideways and were all changing directions on me. I felt dizzy. I squeezed my eyes shut. Sometimes that helped. This time it didn't.

"Charles? Are you all right—?" That was Dad. I didn't answer.

"*Charles*—!" That was Alexei. "Open your eyes and look at me. Do it *now!*" His voice was so hard it startled me. I opened my eyes. He was holding his hand out toward me. "Look at my hand, see? Just grab my hand, hokay? I'll do the rest."

Before I could shake my head no, I felt Dad lifting me up to take Alexei's hand. Alexei grabbed my arm and pulled me gently through the hatch. "See, that wasn't so bad—here, grab this railing and hold on. Douglas, hold him, please? Thank you. Move down now, just a bit. Make room for the others." I was still uncomfortable—almost close to tears, I didn't know why—but then Douglas put his arm around my shoulder and held me close and I didn't feel quite so bad any more.

"*Mikhail*, I am ready for the little stinky one. Pass him here. That's it. Come to me, Bobby. Here, stick your head through. Look around—see? Nothing to be afraid of. The only monsters up here are your brothers. Hold onto this railing, please. *Mikhail*—? Send up Mr. Dingillian, please."

Dad came next, and Mickey followed. Alexei sealed the hatch behind him. Now, we were all clutching handholds on the inside of the steepest curve yet. Three meters away, the curved wall of the core whispered by. We could hear the air whooshing as it passed. We watched a steady progression of warning signs and arrows and numbers and access panels. There were tracks along the surface—and on our side too.

"Ahh," said Alexei. "Here it comes." *It* was a bright red platform sliding toward us on the rails. It slowed to a stop directly next to the access panel. It had handholds and equipment boxes mounted all over it. Alexei pulled us all aboard, and then pushed a green go-button. The platform began moving spinward, faster and faster, speeding up until we had matched the speed of the inner wall, opposite a panel marked **One-Gamma-Three**.

Alexei unfolded the collapsed contraption in the middle of the car. It was an extensible ladder and it went all the way across to the inner wall. "Hokay, let's go." He grabbed Stinky in a bear hug and started scrambling across like a pregnant spider. I shook off Dad's help, but not Douglas's. When we were all safely across, Mickey hit the release on the top of the ladder and it folded back down. Now the ceiling felt motionless and the floor was rolling past. Below, the car we'd ridden on began slowing down; pretty soon, it disappeared around the curve behind us.

Alexei was already opening the One-Gamma-Three panel and pulling us through. First Douglas, then me, then Mickey—they passed Stinky through—then finally Dad and Alexei. Inside the core—I levered myself around to look and nearly lost it—"*Douglas!*" I wailed. My brother caught me and held me tightly with his right arm. "It's okay, Charles. I'm right here. I'm not letting go. Just hang onto me—we'll be fine. Really."

I buried my face in Douglas's shoulder. I could sense that both Mickey and Dad were hovering close, but I didn't want to have anything to do with either of them. Only Douglas.

What I'd seen...was the largest interior space I'd ever seen—well maybe not *the* largest, maybe Terminus was larger—but definitely the *deepest.* It was like the inside of a giant pipe, filled with humongus wires, cables, tubes, conduits, vents, catwalks, ladders, platforms, machinery, and *stuff.* And it all looked *up* and *down* and *sideways* —all at the same time!

"Are you okay, son—?" That was Dad. I didn't answer. Douglas pulled away just enough look at my face. He tilted my chin upward so we were eye to eye and nose to nose. I couldn't remember the last time we'd ever been this close. Maybe we never had. "I'm not going to let anything bad happen to you, Charles. I promise."

"What's wrong with Charles?" I heard Stinky asking.

"Nothing. Please be quiet, Bobby. Charles has an upset stomach. He'll be okay in a minute. Go back to sleep." Douglas looked back to me. "Just tell me when you're ready."

I shook my head. I didn't want him to let go. I liked having his arm around me. I felt safe. I swallowed hard. "I don't want to lose you, Douglas," I whispered, so only he could hear. "Not to anybody—" I sort of nodded toward Mickey.

"You're not going to lose me. I'll always be your brother, no matter what."

"Is that a threat or a promise—?" I half-joked.

He half-smiled. "Yes." He nudged me. "Come on, the others are waiting. And we don't have a lot of time. Are you ready?"

"Yeah. Just stay close, okay?"

"*Hokay*," he said. Just like Alexei.

It was like being on the inside of a giant pipe that kept changing its orientation. But as long as I kept focused on the wall and pretended that I was swimming and it was the floor, I was okay. If I had to look away from the wall, for any reason, I pretended that everything else was *up*. It sort of worked, but I still felt dizzy.

Alexei pointed around the curve of the wall toward a cluster of pipes and a vertical platform on which there were some storage lockers. We pulled ourselves along a line of handholds, and when we got to the platform, we anchored ourselves against its railings.

"Do you see this pipe?" Alexei pounded on one of the thicker pipes next to us. "Put your ear next to it. You can hear the water rushing through it. Very useful stuff. We use it for ballast. We use it to balance the rotation of the disks. Sometimes we even turn it into oxygen to breathe and hydrogen to burn. And of course, we also use it for drinking and bathing and growing our crops.

"But—" he interrupted himself. "—these pipes are also very useful if you have to go somewhere and you don't want anyone to know that you are going or how you got there. And so, while we respect the water, sometimes we ride it too." Alexei opened one of the storage lockers. Inside was—scuba gear?!

"Huh? Are we going swimming?" Stinky asked.

"You? No," Alexei said. "Them. Yes." He pointed. We looked up—every direction was *up*—and saw four, no five, teenagers diving out of the center toward us. Three boys, two girls. They were wearing shorts and T-shirts and looked like they had fallen off a runaway picnic. They were laughing like they were diving into a party.

As they approached, they began waving and calling to us. They caught themselves easily on the platforms and ladders and railings around us and they shouted things at Alexei in Russian that made him blush with embarrassment. They passed him a backpack and a pair of canteens. They had a third canteen of their own, which they passed around among themselves, each one taking deep swallows of whatever was in it. From the way they acted, I didn't think it was water.

Alexei took the flask when it came to him and took a deep swig of his own, then he pocketed it, much to their dismay. "You have all had enough," he said. Then he bawled them out in Russian. Or gave them instructions. Or told a dirty joke. Whatever. When he finished, they all laughed and started pulling on the various pieces of diving equipment.

Alexei explained, "These are my fellow students and colleagues. The swimming equipment is part of our service. Sometimes we have to inspect the pipes from the inside. Sometimes there are air-bubbles. Sometimes we have to retrieve a broken robot or a piece of something that has caught somewhere. We do not have to do that very often. In fact...I can't ever remember having to go into the pipes at all for anything a robot couldn't handle. But, nevertheless, we have our responsibilities. We have to keep ourselves ready and able to handle any possibility, any emergency at all. So we practice and drill and keep ourselves focused on our responsibilities to the water of the community. Today—ah, today we get to put into practice what we have practiced. They shall be...the *decoys*."

"So this is how you do it," Mickey said. "I've always wondered about that."

"Wonder no longer," Alexei said. "Sooner or later, somebody was certain to figure it out anyway. No matter, I already have three other ways to move things from here to there—just not as exciting. I leave it to you to figure them out, *Mikhail*. I will bet you a day's interest that you cannot."

"I can't afford that bet," Mickey laughed.

Alexei laughed with him and clapped him on the shoulder. "You are smarter than you act. This is a good trait." To the rest of us, he said, "We have to assume you are being watched. At the very least, monitored through station security. There are those damnable little cameras everywhere. They saw us coming up the service elevator. They know that an access hatch was opened. That was why I used my *own* card. So they could monitor our progress. Very shortly, they will be monitoring the progress of five divers through the pipes—and one of them will be carrying my locator. Five divers, not six, we will keep them wondering what happened, *da?* They will meet the divers on the topside of Disk Seven. But by then, we will be somewhere else, and they will have lost us. I am too clever for my own good." To his Russian comrades, Alexei shouted,

"What is taking you so long? Do you think we have all night? Look at the time. We have less than an hour—"

"Alexei," said one of the men, a dark brooding fellow with eyebrows like furry caterpillars. "The deposits are made, *da?*"

"*Da.*"

"This is good. We have made our own reservations, we will be on the one ayem car. If what you say is true—"

"You have told no one else?"

Caterpillar-brow shook his head. "I think the word is already spreading. But no, we have told no one. Go now. Godspeed!" He glanced around. "Godspeed to all of you." Then he grabbed Alexei and the two of them exchanged kisses on each cheek, the way they do in Europe. I'd never seen men do that before, kiss each other—even friends. It sort of freaked me. I looked at Douglas and Mickey and tried to imagine them kissing. It didn't seem right, but it didn't seem as wrong anymore either. What the hell did I know?

We were going up the Line—*by hand.*

From an Earth perspective, we were going up. From the Geostationary perspective, we were going sideways—starside—outward toward Disk Seven.

From our perspective, we weren't going any direction at all. Just *forward* along a never ending pipe. There was water on the inside of the pipe; we could hear it. There were handholds running the length. We were climbing to forever. I wondered how long it would take to climb the whole Line—

"How come we can't take a maintenance car?" I asked. "Look, there are lots of tracks along these pipes. And there's a car over there."

"The maintenance cars are monitored." Mickey said. "We don't want to leave any evidence of where we started and where we got off. Most of all we don't want anyone showing up to meet us. Just keep pulling yourself along."

Alexei showed us how to do it. "Don't try to hurry," he said. "You'll tire yourself out. Slow and steady does the job. Do like I do, hand over hand, counting like this—like music—and one and two and three and four...like that. That's how to make the best time over a distance." He added, "If you did this all the time, you would know how to go faster, but I need you to conserve your strength. We have a long way to go. Almost two kilometers."

I concentrated on watching the handholds passing in front of me. I pulled myself steadily forward, left hand over right, right hand over left.

It took us more than an hour. We stopped once to pass a canteen around and catch our breaths; this canteen had water in it and a nipple over the opening; I sucked at it thirstily. Doug whispered to me, "Slow down, Chigger—don't pull a Stinky." He was right. I passed the canteen on. It was a very short rest; as soon as everybody had had a drink, we were on our way again.

At the top, or the far end, we exited the core the same way we had entered. It could have even been the same access panel; the only thing different was the number painted on it. **Seven-Gamma-Three**.

We transferred across to the rotating part of the disk without incident. It was a little bit easier for me this time, because I knew what to expect. We climbed back down into the service corridor, but instead of heading toward the elevator, Alexei led us in the opposite direction, looking for a specific hatchway. We passed several before he found the one he wanted.

"Okay, comrades," he said. "This is where you must each make a prayer to Saint Vladimir—"

"Saint Vladimir...?"

"I made him up. He is the patron saint of smugglers. I smuggled him into heaven. Now let's see if he is appropriately grateful." Alexei took out his clearance card and swiped it through the reader slot. He inhaled. He exhaled. The panel turned green and when he tapped it, the hatch popped open.

"Thank you, Saint Vladimir. I shall light candles at your altar." Alexei said to the ceiling. "As soon as I can find candles. As soon as I can build an altar." We passed through—into the top of a brightly lit shaft lined with machinery. It was deep and slot-shaped, and the walls were lined with tracks and service bays. On one side, we saw seven or eight elevator cars, each one docked and surrounded by lights and equipment and service gear. From our perspective, they looked like they were stacked sideways. None of them had the cabin spinning; all had their lights on.

"Ahh," said Alexei. "I have done good. Very good. And Saint Vladimir has done good. I was afraid I was going to have to replace him. See there? We are almost at the beginning of your journey. This way, citizens. We must not be seen."

We entered 1187 without incident. It was a lot like the car we'd ridden up in. We pulled ourselves in through the left-side hatch; it was the cargo hatch, the bottom. I wondered which way it was going to spin—clockwise or counter-clockwise? Would it make any difference?

We pushed and pulled ourselves into our suite and bounced into chairs. Mickey showed us how to latch the seat belts, and we belted ourselves down. Douglas wrapped a blanket around Stinky, who promptly curled up and fell asleep wrapped around his monkey. The monkey snored softly for a moment or two and then fell silent.

Alexei was already pulling rations out of his backpack. "I thought you might like a snack while you wait. I have cheese, sausage, bread, grapes, little tomatoes, carrots. Eat hearty. *Bon appetit.*" He bowed from the waist, difficult to do in micro-gravity. "I must return now—they will be looking for me. I must not disappoint them. Otherwise, it spoils the game. Besides, I need to collect some things. Including my alibi." He handed the backpack to Mickey. "*Mikhail*, please make sure my father gets this. If I am not able to deliver it myself. Hokay? Thank you." And with that, he was gone.

"Where's he going?"

"Back down."

"The same way?"

"He can do it in fifteen minutes. He was a finalist in last year's no-grav Olympics. It's those long arms of his. And all the practice he gets." Mickey explained, "He'll probably go back to the ice cream place or walk around the promenade for a while, whatever it takes, until he's sure that whoever is watching knows that he's not with us anymore. Then he'll disappear again. At least, that's my guess. Charles, do you want some grapes?"

"No thanks." I pushed the plate away. "All the grapes I've ever gotten have been sour."

"Yes, and you've done a fine job making sour whine." It was the first time Mickey had ever said anything rude to me. I looked at him surprised. He looked right back at me with a hardness I'd never seen before. "Don't you ever put a cork in it, kiddo? Do you know that you are *no* fun to be around?"

"So what?"

"So look around you and stop acting like a spoiled brat. Your family is coming apart—"

"It came apart a long time ago."

"Shut up, stupid. Try listening for a change. You might learn something. In case you hadn't noticed, your brother, Douglas, is having a very difficult time of this. And your dad isn't doing too well either—he hasn't spoken two words since we left my mother's. The only reason Bobby hasn't thrown a tantrum is that we slipped a sedative into his chocolate soda. We should have done the same for you. You're not doing anything to make this easier for anybody."

"Nobody's trying to make it any easier on me," I snapped back.

"Excuse me—?" Mickey pushed in close, getting right in my face. "Douglas wasn't there for you when you got free-fall panic? Your dad didn't lift you up when you needed it? Your dad hasn't been trying to reach out to you all evening? Or was I hallucinating? You're acting like a selfish dirtsider, Charles. And I don't like you very much, right now."

"So what? None of this would have happened if you hadn't—"

"Don't *go* there...." he warned.

"Mickey, please—" That was Douglas. "There's more to this than you know." He stepped/bounced over to Mickey and put his hand on his shoulder; they looked at each other and something unsaid passed between them. Mickey looked frustrated, but he nodded and backed off. Douglas turned to Dad then. "Okay, Dad," he said. "What's in the monkey?"

Dad shook his head. "I wish you hadn't found out about that."

"Yeah, well—it wasn't too hard to figure out. Is there anything else you want to tell us?"

Dad shook his head. He looked beaten, frustrated, angry, unhappy. "No, there's nothing else. I just thought—that maybe we could have some time together that wasn't a fight."

"Why would you think that?" asked Douglas. "Every time we get together, it's a fight. That's all we ever do. Why would you think this time would be different?"

Dad looked across at Doug and his expression was as straight as I'd ever seen. He spoke slowly and it was hard for him to get the words out. "I thought that because it would be...the last time we'd all be together as a family...that maybe we'd all try to make it something good to remember."

"Why should we? What do we owe you? Or mom? You've both been using us—and using us up. Between the two of you, Mom and her tirades, you and your passive-aggressive bullshit, you've turned Stinky into an incontinent little pissant, and Chigger—well, he's well on his way to becoming a sociopathic hermit with surgically attached earphones. I'm sorry, Chigger, but Mickey is right. You can be a royal pain in the ass sometimes."

He turned back to Dad. "And me—? Well, just look at me, Max. I'm your son. This is how I turned out. I have the social skills of a virus. Chigger is right, I am the geekoid from hell. We're all of us screwed up, Dad—and this...this isn't an answer. It's more of the same. It's you running away again. Only this time, you want us to run away with you. But how can we run away with you when it's *us* you're been running away from all this time?" I couldn't believe what I was hearing from Douglas. He was almost in tears. And Dad—poor stupid Dad—he just sat there and took it.

Douglas stopped, exhausted. For a moment, he just floated limp. Finally, he drifted down toward Mickey's lap. He bounced off Mickey and started to push himself up again, but Mickey pulled him back down and held him with one arm firmly around his waist. Douglas looked uncomfortable for a moment, but Mickey whispered "shhh" at him, and Douglas finally let himself relax. He leaned his head back and closed his eyes for a moment, not caring if we saw.

"Charles?" Dad looked at me. "Do you have anything you want to add?"

I thought about the opportunity. Yeah, I had a lot to say. But it wasn't necessary anymore. "No. Doug said it all."

"Is it my turn now?" Dad asked. "Do I get to say anything?"

I shrugged. "I don't care." Douglas shook his head too.

Dad took a breath. He was gathering his strength, and his words. Then he said, "I remember when you were born, Doug—when Charles was born too. And Bobby. How proud I was of each of you, how much I cherished you. I used to wake up in the morning, promising myself every day that I'd be the best dad I could for my boys. And I really did try. I really did. Now I wake up every morning wondering how I screwed up so badly. And what can I do to make it right? It always comes back to money. I don't have any. I'm a million and a quarter in debt. And no matter how hard I work, I just keep getting deeper and deeper. And nothing is fun anymore. Sometimes even taking the next breath is a chore.

"So when they offered me this chance to be a courier and get off the planet and make some money—and give my sons a second chance too—I didn't have to think about it too hard. It was a way out. I was drowning. What would you have had me do, Doug? Charles?" He took a deep breath then and added, "I don't know what's in the monkey, I don't even care, but someone is paying for this trip, so it must be something valuable and we'll deliver it and we'll be done. Then you can do whatever you want to. I'm through trying. I'm beaten."

Doug didn't say anything to that. Neither did I. There wasn't anything to say. And I was through trying to figure things out.

———————————————

We ate, we dozed, we waited. Pretty soon, the car started sliding along the track to the departure bay. We felt it thump into position, and then we heard the soft clunk of the transfer pods moving into place too. A little bit after that, the car started spinning and pseudo-gravity returned. A while after that, we heard people moving around outside in the corridors.

When he deemed it was safe, Mickey ducked out of the cabin—"I'll be back as fast as I can. I have to get your tickets validated. Otherwise, this cabin will show up as empty and they'll give it to someone else." To Douglas, he smiled. "Save my place, huh?" And then he was gone.

He was back almost immediately with an odd expression on his face. "Come with me," he said. "All of you. Quickly."

"Huh? Why?"

"Just come—" He was already picking up Stinky. I grabbed the monkey. Douglas shouldered the backpack. Dad picked up his worries and we followed Mickey out the hatch and up the corridor to the transfer pod. Mickey wouldn't answer any questions. "I'll explain later," was all he said.

The transfer pod dropped us down to the boarding level. Actually, there are two boarding levels. There's the public boarding level and the Very Important Person boarding level—Mickey took us to the VIP level.

We stepped out of the hatch into—

—I didn't see the room at first. It was about the size of a classroom or a lounge, I guess, but directly in front of us was Judge Griffith in her wheelchair and next to her, but not too close, there was Olivia, looking unhappy, and a couple other people I didn't recognize, but very official looking, and also that stupid lawyer, Howard. He still wore that stupid suit that didn't fit right, only now he looked like he'd slept in it, and he had a very smug look on his face, like he'd caught us with our pants down and our hands on our dicks. I was tempted to give him my own farkleberry.

"Ahh," said Judge Griffith. "Thank you all for joining us. Mickey, did you have any trouble?" Mickey shook his head. Douglas glared at him, but Mickey didn't meet his look, so Douglas stepped over and took Stinky out of his arms, then he moved away from Mickey, as if he didn't want to know him anymore. Mickey looked miserable.

"All right, if everybody will take their places, we can get this business handled once and for all." Judge Griffith wheeled backwards, moving out of the way. She pointed with her gavel; she held the head of it in her fist and used the handle as a pointer. The chairs and the tables of the lounge had been moved into positions like a courtroom. "Olivia, if you'll sit over there on the left. Mickey, you too. The Dingillians—thank you. Howard, I want you on the right. Court officers, here beside me. And... yes, that'll do it, thank you."

Dad whispered to Olivia, "What the hell is going on? What did you do to us?" Olivia just shook her head and pointed us toward the chairs. "I can't advise you," she whispered. "You're on your own now." Dad looked as angry as I'd ever seen him in my entire life.

Douglas laid Stinky down on a nearby couch. The rest of us sat down in chairs that were much too comfortable for a legal procedure. But Judge Griffith put those doubts to rest immediately. She wheeled up to a small table that was to serve as the bench; her clipboard was already open and propped up so she could see it. She reversed the gavel in her hand and rapped it sharply on the table. She glanced over to her assistant. "Joyce? Are we missing someone?"

The woman nodded. "Godot called. He'll be late."

Judge Griffith raised a questioning eyebrow. "I assume he has a good excuse?" She glanced at her watch. "Was the shuttle delayed?"

"The shuttle docked on time, the paperwork was delayed. Last I heard, he's waiting for customs to clear."

"Never mind, we can still take care of the preliminaries. And if he can't get here before we finish, then the hell with him. This Court is not on call." She turned forward again. "The Third District Court of The Orbital Space Authority, serving GeoSynchronous Station and Allied Domains, Judge Georgia Griffith presiding, is now in special session, this session being mandated by the attempted flight from jurisdiction of the following individuals..."

Olivia stood. "Beg pardon, your honor, but no one has actually fled jurisdiction yet—"

"Don't nit-pick, counselor. We caught them with the tickets in their hands." She looked exasperated. "Listen up, folks—I don't like working late. If I could think of a good reason to justify tossing all of you into the cooler for a week or two, I'd do it." She continued, with a dark glower in Dad's direction. "We're here because Max Dingillian and his three kids somehow ended up on the midnight elevator to Farpoint. I presume the destination was Whirlaway. Correct? This, in spite of the fact that a court hearing was ordered for nine in the ayem, tomorrow morning. So I am left with the not unreasonable assumption that you, sir, Max Dingillian, were attempting to evade the authority of this court."

She leaned forward in her chair, aiming her remarks directly to Dad. "However, the Court *chooses to ignore*—for the moment, anyway—the evidence of your attempt to evade jurisdiction. Sit down, Howard! I'll get to you in a moment!" She turned back to Dad. "At the very least, I should hold you in contempt of court, but it is not in the best interests of your children to do so, and it does not serve the goal of a speedy resolution. Let it be known, however, that the court views your conduct with extreme displeasure. Let me translate that for you: you've exhausted whatever good will you had here. Do you understand?"

Dad nodded. "I understand completely. And I thank you for your... uh, mercy, your honor."

Judge Griffith ignored Dad. She turned to Howard-In-The-Wrinkled-Suit. "All right, Howard, now you may object...." Howard started to stand up, shrugged, sank back down in his seat, spreading his hands helplessly.

"Right," Judge Griffith agreed. "Objection overruled. Thank you. The Court appreciates your efforts to help move this process forward as fast as possible." She turned to Olivia. "Counselor, you no longer represent the Dingillians, is that correct?"

"That is correct." Olivia's voice was unemotional. Detached.

"Nevertheless, you were planning to leave on the midnight elevator with them. Is that correct too?"

"Yes, your honor. That is correct."

"Do you have an interesting explanation for this?"

"Conflict of interest. My son has a relationship with Douglas Dingillian."

"*Had*," corrected Douglas. Judge Griffith gave him a curious look, but otherwise ignored his interruption.

"Did you advise the Dingillians to evade jurisdiction, Counselor?"

"Of course not. I'm an officer of the court. That would be unethical."

"Nevertheless, was it among the options you discussed—?"

Olivia nodded reluctantly. "Yes, it was."

"Well, Olivia," the Judge continued, "we have here the evidence that you booked the tickets yourself under one of your shadow accounts. So although you recused yourself from this case, you still managed to be a participant in an action that would have damaged the court's ability to function. The Court finds you in contempt and fines you..." The Judge consulted her clipboard, tapping at its surface as she looked something up. "...and fines you one thousand chocolate dollars." Olivia didn't react to that. Judge Griffith continued, "Sentence suspended in recognition of your assistance in arranging this special session."

"Thank you, your honor," Olivia said quietly.

"The same thing I said to Max Dingillian goes for you too, Counselor. Your store of good will is exhausted in this court. Remember that."

Now, Judge Griffith turned to Howard-The-Smug. "Any objections? No? Overruled anyway. Don't worry about your store of good will, Howard. The court's opinion of you remains unchanged." To the rest of us, she said, "The issue here is simple, and if we can resolve it in the next two hours,"—she glanced at her watch—"then the Dingillians, or at least Max Dingillian, depending on the ruling of this court, can continue their—*or his*—journey." By the emphasis she put on "*or his*," she made it very clear that she had not yet made up her mind whether Dad was going to go to the moon with us or *without* us.

Judge Griffith looked to her assistant. "Any word yet?"

"The last of the passengers have cleared customs. Godot is on the way up. Five minutes."

"All right," said Georgia. "Fifteen minute potty-break." She banged her gavel once, and wheeled toward the restroom, her assistant following.

Dad leaned toward Olivia. "Who's this Godot?"

"I don't know," Olivia whispered back. "That's what the Judge calls anyone she has to wait for." She added, "I'm sorry we got caught—but I don't think Georgia had any choice in the matter."

"*We*—? *You* got a suspended sentence. I'm likely to lose my kids—! There's not a lot of 'we' in that, Olivia! You turned us in, didn't you?"

"I didn't have a choice, Max." She sounded just as frustrated as Dad.

"Oh, terrific. You told us to go out on the limb—and then you sawed it off."

"I don't think you should say any more," Olivia said quietly, with a meaningful nod toward Howard-The-Brooding.

"You've put us in a really bad situation, Olivia."

"I'm sorry. I miscalculated."

"Apology noted. Now what are you going to do to help clean up this mess?"

"Nothing. I can't! I'm not your lawyer anymore, Max."

Dad shook his head in disgust. "I can't believe this. Why did I trust you?" He sank back down in his seat, not looking at Olivia anymore. She looked just as unhappy. Now all that was left was a fight between her and Mickey, and we'd be complete. Everybody would have fought with everybody. I couldn't think of anyone else we could fight with—

And then Godot arrived.

Godot was Doctor Bolivar Hidalgo. And following him into the room was...*Mom?!* And that other woman behind her.

Just about everybody came to their feet then. Douglas, Dad, me— even Stinky woke up, rubbing his eyes again. This time, crying, "Stop waking me up!"

Mom went straight to Dad, she moved across the room like a missile—and slapped him across the face. Hard. Dad was knocked back a step; he put his hand to his jaw and blinked. "It's good to see you again too, Maggie," he managed to say.

And then Stinky saw her for the first time and yelled, "Mommy!!" And flung himself into her arms like an automatic monkey. He grabbed hold so tight she almost fell backward. "Mommy, mommy!! Are you going with us?"

"I came to take you home, sweetie —"

"But I don't wanna go home! I wanna go to the moon!"

Mom gave Dad a dirty look and moved away from us, cooing softly to Stinky and patting his head. Now it was Doctor Hidalgo's turn. He waddled over and bowed to Dad. "My compliments, *Señor* Dingillian."

Dad just glowered.

Dr. Hidalgo pretended not to notice. Instead, he took Dad by the arm and made as if to lead him off to a corner. "Can we talk?"

"You can talk," Dad said, not moving. "Do I have to listen?"

"It would be better if we could talk alone...?"

"Anything you have to say to me, you can say in front of my children, Dr. Hidalgo. I'm not going to hide anything from them. It's their lives too."

Douglas and I exchanged a look. We came and stood next to Dad. The monkey climbed up onto my back and made faces over my shoulder. Doug hissed at me, "Turn it off, Charles," so I did.

We followed Dad and Doctor Hidalgo over to a corner of the lounge. Doctor Hidalgo plopped himself down onto a chair and started talking immediately. "If you think about the organizational effort involved and the money it takes to get someone onto a shuttle on such short notice, you might begin to understand just how important your package is. It's important enough that a great deal of money is going to be spent on the effort to intercept it and prevent its delivery. Are you convinced yet?"

"What I told you before still stands," Dad said.

"It affects the lives of your sons. How do they feel about it?"

"Whatever my Dad says, goes for me too," I blurted. "Right, Douglas?" I poked him.

Douglas didn't need to be poked. "We're a family, Doctor Hidalgo. We might be having problems, but that's our business, not yours. We don't sell each other out."

"Admirable. Very admirable." Doctor Hidalgo grunted his approval. "Not very smart, but still admirable. The smart man recognizes when he can't win and cuts his losses early. So..." He levered himself to his feet. I figured he must have massed two hundred kilos. He sure looked it. Even in low-grav, he was having problems getting out of a chair. "...so I guess we have nothing further to discuss. Let the games begin." He waddled back to the other side of the lounge.

Dad looked to me and Douglas like he wanted to say something. But there wasn't anything that needed saying, so he just clapped Doug on the shoulder—he was closer—and said, "Let's go."

Judge Griffith called the session back to order then, with three sharp raps of her gavel on the table. "All right, people, we've got a lot of work to do and not very much time to do it in. I've made a promise to some folks here to be finished before midnight so they can catch an elevator, and I intend to keep that promise. Would everybody please take their seats and settle themselves quickly?" Judge Griffith nodded to her assistant. "Joyce, please make a note of our new arrivals. Godot is here. Finally."

Mom and the woman who had followed her in sat down with Dr. Hidalgo on the other side of Howard-The-Malignant. She leaned over to confer with him. They shook hands quickly, so I guess this was their first face-to-face meeting. She held Stinky in her arms and he appeared to have fallen back asleep. He woke up just long enough to stick his tongue out at Howard and then he laid his head back down on Mom's shoulder again. Whatever they'd given him, I wanted a lifetime supply.

Judge Griffith was already moving along. She meant it, about finishing quickly. "Dr. Hidalgo, the Court appreciates your interest in this case; however, if it is your intention to complicate matters with extra-curricular issues, let me warn you ahead of time that the Court will take a dim view of any such matters that do not *directly* affect the issue at hand."

"Your honor," Dr. Bolivar spread his hands wide in an oily gesture. Obviously, someone's snake was squeaky. "I am here only as a friend of the court. I simply wish to see justice done."

The Judge snorted. "Bollie, you and I both know that you have no interest in anything except your own stomach. You brought the boys' mother up for reasons that have nothing to do with justice or friendship. Consider this a warning. Your friends have no authority over this—" She waved her gavel at him.

Judge Griffith turned to Mom, now. "Mrs. Dingillian—"

"Campbell. It's Campbell now. I've gone back to my maiden name, Your Honor."

"Fairly recently? Ah, yes, here it is. Thank you for the correction." She looked to Mom and said, "Ms. Campbell, I've spent the past several hours reviewing the records of your divorce and custody hearings. I wish I could say it makes for interesting reading. Unfortunately, it does not. It is a tiresome and petty matter, and I think both you and your husband have a great deal to be ashamed of. This is not a case where one side is right and the other is wrong. It is a case where both sides are wrong—and this Court has no interest in trying to determine which side is more wrong. The *only* issue here is the welfare of the children. Events have clearly demonstrated that *neither* of the parents has provided an appropriate commitment to the welfare of these children. Therefore—"

"Your Honor, I object to that—" That was Mom, leaping to her feet.

Judge Griffith sighed. She could see where this was headed. "Ms. Campbell?"

"I am *not* a bad parent, and I do put my children's welfare above everything else—"

Judge Griffith tapped her gavel gently to interrupt Mom. "Your husband came home and found you in bed with someone else. I suppose that down on Earth, you might be able to justify it in your mind that this was a generous and unselfish demonstration of commitment and dedication to your family, but this isn't Earth and *this* court is having a very hard time viewing it that way. This situation—this entire avalanche of errors in judgment—was all triggered by that first little pebble—"

"Your honor," Mom started to protest, "with all due respect—we *had* a working custody arrangement, until *he*," —she waved her hand angrily at Dad—"went and violated it! All I want is for you to return my children to me so we can go home!"

"Sit down, Ms. Campbell. That's *not* going to happen. At least not because you or anyone else demands it. You pushed your husband into this situation. It's all here in the history." She tapped her clipboard meaningfully. "You kept challenging his visitation rights every chance you got—you gave him no rational choice. That doesn't excuse what he did, but neither did you provide an environment in which your separate disagreements could be worked out rationally. This court has absolutely no interest in providing an arena for one more round of legal spouse-bashing. If you want to hurt each other, if that's the kind of post-marital relationship you both want, that's fine with me—I'm just not going to let you use my court for it."

Judge Griffith poured herself a glass of water. Her hand trembled slightly as she drank. She put the glass back on the table and looked from Mom to Dad and back again. She said, "In other words, Mr. Dingillian, Ms. Campbell, based on everything that has happened so far, this Court cannot justify awarding either one of you custody of these children. Do you understand what I am saying? The decision cannot be based on your credentials as parents. Neither of you deserves that consideration. This court is going to have to look *elsewhere* for guidance in this decision. It's time to let the children vote...."

She looked around the room as if daring anyone else to speak. No one wanted to. So she rapped her gavel sharply. "Douglas Dingillian, as you are only a month shy of your eighteenth birthday, this court sees fit to declare you an independent adult. You are hereby granted autonomy. You are no longer under the custody of either of your parents. Do you understand?"

Douglas nodded. He looked a little scared, but he nodded.

Judge Griffith continued. "You are free to return to Earth, either with or without your mother; you are free to continue your outbound odyssey, either with or without your father. However, before you make *any* decision, we still have the matter of the custody of your brothers to resolve, and the court will appreciate your input on that."

Douglas nodded again.

Now Judge Griffith turned to me. "Charles, I want you to understand, ordinarily I would not ask a thirteen-year old to make the kind of choice that I'm about to give you. But under these circumstances, I think this is the best way to do it—and I'm satisfied that you're up to the challenge. So here's the question—"

I could already see it coming. And I was already formulating my reply.

"—Do you want to go back down the beanstalk with your mother, or do you want to continue outward with your father?"

I stood up. "Neither," I said.

Judge Griffith shook her head, smiling gently. "I'm afraid that's not an option, Charles."

"Yes, it is," I said. "*I want a divorce.*"

Almost immediately, both Mom and Dad were on their feet, shouting: "Your Honor—you can't allow this!" and , "Charles, have you lost your mind?" Douglas looked surprised, though he shouldn't have been. Even Stinky was awake now. "Whatever Chigger gets, I want one too!" he yelled, screeching above the tumult. Judge Griffith banged so loudly with her gavel that the head popped off. She had to wait until her assistant, Joyce, went and got it and brought it back to her.

"Everybody settle down, dammit!" she shouted over the noise. "And *sit down*! I'll handle this." She banged a few more times until everyone sat down again, and then she turned back to me. "Charles—" she started to say gently.

I didn't let her finish. "I want a divorce," I repeated.

Judge Griffith looked very unhappy. "Charles, do you know what's involved in that kind of action?"

"Yes, actually, I do. At least as much as I could find out from reading about it."

"Somebody should hang a warning sign on you, Charles. Caution, contents will probably explode in your face." She smiled wryly, to let me know she was joking, but I could see she meant it too. "Why do you want a divorce?"

"Do I have to have a reason?"

"Not really. You and your brothers are the only ones who *didn't* promise to love, honor, and etcetera. And if that's not a promise you want to keep, you shouldn't be held in a situation where it's a requirement. But it would help if you did have a reason. Otherwise, children would be announcing right and left that they want a divorce every time they get sent to bed early."

I pointed at Mom. I pointed at Dad. "Those are my reasons."

The Judge nodded. "Those are two pretty good reasons. And considering everything else that's happened, the court would ordinarily be inclined to grant your request—but let's look over the edge of this cliff before we jump, okay, Charles?"

"Sure," I said. "Whatever. But it's not going to change my mind. I've been thinking about this for a long time."

"Charles—" Mom called across the room. "You don't have to do this. If we could just sit down and talk things out—"

"Leave him alone, Maggie! Haven't you done enough damage already!" Dad shouted across at her. "Look at the poor kid—!"

Judge Griffith rapped her gavel only once. Without even looking up: "Any more outbursts and I'll put the both of you in jail. In the same cell!" The threat worked. They both sat down again, glowering at each other. "Howard?" Howard-The-Troll looked up. "Are you still representing the interests of the mother?"

Howard looked to Mom, she nodded, and he said, "Yes, Your Honor."

"Would you like to question Charles Dingillian?"

"Uh—I haven't had time to prepare."

"Neither has anyone else here. Perhaps giving lawyers time to prepare is why justice always takes so long. Maybe in the future, in the interest of producing results, I should deny all recesses and continuances. Don't panic, Howard, it's a joke."

Howard came over and stood in front of me. "Well, you're the reason we're here, Charles. It all revolves around you. Let me ask you—do you think running away is going to solve anything?"

"Some people do."

"Do you?"

I knew what he wanted me to say. No. Running away never solves anything. But...sometimes running away buys you time to think.

He held my eyes with his. He didn't look nasty. He looked like he was trying to be friendly and it was a strain. He said, "Charles, do you think your parents have a responsibility toward you?"

"That's what they teach us at school. Don't have babies unless you're willing to make a lifelong commitment."

"Yes. I know that it hasn't worked out the way you think it should, but don't you think that your parents have your best interests at heart?"

"Yeah? So?"

"My point is, Charles, you've received a lot from your parents. You owe them something in return. Do you think this is the right way to repay it?"

And when he put it that way, something clicked. "Can I ask you something?"

"Yes, Charles—what is it?" He seemed genuinely interested.

"Well, when I was in school—I don't know if it's the same way up here—we had classes about social responsibility. My teacher taught us that everybody is part of society. We're all connected to each other lots of different ways. We all make work for each other, so we need each other for jobs. And we all make messes—like garbage and pollution and sewage and crap—so we all have to clean up after ourselves. And sometimes, like during flu season, we're all infectious. And stuff like that. And even if we like to think that we're individuals, we really all depend on each other. My teacher said it was Thoreau's ax."

"I beg your pardon?" said Howard-The-Puzzled. "Thoreau's ax?"

"Yeah. Thoreau was this guy who thought it would be a good idea to go out in the woods to Walden Pond, and commune with nature. He thought worldly goods distracted people and kept them from getting in tune with everything good."

"Yes, I know who Thoreau was. What about his ax?"

"Well, that's the point. Where did his ax come from? If he wanted to build himself a shelter, or chop a tree for firewood, or stuff like that, he needed an ax. Where does the ax come from?"

"From a...blacksmith," offered Howard.

"Uh-huh. That's why Thoreau was a dope. You can't just go off and live by yourself. You need the stuff that other people make. And they need what you make. And even if you think you're not connected to everybody else, you really are, because even if you're going out to the woods to live, where are you going to get your ax?"

"Judge Griffith is looking at her watch again, Charles. What does all this have to do with *your* situation?"

"Well...I can see what's going on. Some kind of evacuation. People who can afford it are leaving the Earth. Like guests leaving a party where they trashed the house. They're taking their money and they're going up the Line to the moon and everywhere else. Isn't that right?"

"Yes, Charles. I won't lie to you. There are people who afraid of the possibility of war and disease and economic turmoil —"

"That's my point—if you grownups can't keep your promises, if you can't keep your part of the social contract to the whole planet—if grownups are running away from the problems they made, then how can you ask a kid like me to stay behind with the mess? I don't know that running away solves any problems, but I don't see that I accomplish anything useful by staying either."

For a moment there was silence in the Court. A lot of people looked real uncomfortable. Dad. Mom. Judge Griffith. Olivia. Mickey. Howard. Dr. Hidalgo. Finally, Judge Griffith said, "I think he's pretty well nailed the lot of us to the wall."

But Howard wasn't finished. He said, "I can think of a reason to go back."

"What?"

"Because you love your Mom."

I looked over at Mom, she looked hopeful. Her eyes were shining. I looked to Dad, he looked kinda proud. I looked at Douglas, who flashed me a quick nod and a smile.

"Yeah," I said to Howard-The-Duck. "That's a good reason." Mom smiled at me—until I added, "But it's not good enough. Not anymore," and her expression collapsed into grief. I should have stopped there, but I didn't. "I love my Mom. I really do. I love my Dad too. But I don't like being in the middle anymore. Love's a good reason for lots of stuff—but not for doing something stupid. And going back to either of them is the stupidest thing I can think of."

Howard sat down, defeated.

Judge Griffith glanced at her watch and made a face. She turned sideways in her chair to face me. "Thank you, Charles. That was very nicely argued. Have you ever considered becoming a lawyer?"

"Only once. Dad threatened to strangle me in my sleep."

"And he's probably right. Never mind. Do you still want a divorce?"

"Yes, Judge Griffith. I do."

"Hmm." She frowned. "You know, I can grant it, right here and now. It's irregular, but so is this whole situation. So it wouldn't be out of line to resolve it with an unorthodox decision, particularly in light of some of the other pressures on us." She sighed, glanced at her watch again, and began to explain. "But I'll tell you honestly, I'm very reluctant to just bang the gavel and be done with it."

"Why?"

"You see, Charles, we have a problem here. You and I in particular. I can declare Douglas an adult, because he's only two months shy of his majority. And I can ask you what you want to do, because even though you're not yet old enough to be independent, you're still old enough to have a say in what happens to you. And if you want a divorce, I can put you in Douglas's custody. But I can't give the same choice to Bobby, can I? Do you think he's capable of making an informed decision? Do you think so, Douglas?"

I shook my head. So did Douglas.

"So you see the problem here. We have to make a decision about what's best for your brother, you and I and Douglas. I already know what your mother and father are going to say. They're going to fight over custody of Bobby, even more ferociously, because he's all that's left; so I need to hear what someone else thinks—someone else who knows your Mom and Dad, and nobody knows them better than you and your brother. So what do you two think I should do? Charles? Douglas?"

Douglas and I looked at each other. I searched his face for a clue, even a hint, of what he was thinking. He shook his head slightly—a signal to be careful? Or that he didn't know either.

"Well...first of all," I said slowly. "I want to go with Douglas." I looked to him for reassurance. He gave me a quick nod of okay, and I smiled tightly and blinked fast before any tears could come.

"What happens if Douglas chooses to go someplace you don't want to go?"

"I can't think of anyplace like that, Your Honor. I want to stay with my brother. We're family. We've always been together. I know how to live without my Mom and without my Dad. I've been doing that almost all my life. I don't know how to live without Douglas, and even though he can be real weird sometimes, I still want to go with him."

"You're sure about that?"

"As sure as I can be."

"Hm. Well. I see." Judge Griffith mulled that over. "I could probably do that. As I said, I can grant Douglas acting custody over you, subject to the approval of the jurisdiction you end up in; in the absence of any other contesting relatives, they'd probably confirm it. Your problem is going to be—or rather, it'll be Doug's problem—supporting yourselves. I understand that you're looking for an indenture, Douglas?"

"Yes, Ma'am."

"Mm. Be careful. Make sure you have an agent review the contract. But you should be able to get an indenture that covers Charles as well. He can take on a delayed indenture that doesn't kick in until he turns eighteen, and the two of you should be able to find a colony that can use a couple of fairly intelligent warm bodies. So it's doable, and I can sign off on it. But that still leaves the problem of your younger brother...?"

"Yeah, Stinky's a problem," I said. "But he's *our* problem. Douglas and I have spent more time taking care of him than Mom or Dad."

"Are you suggesting that you and Douglas also take custody of Bobby as well?"

When she put it that way...I had to hesitate. But Douglas didn't. He stepped forward. "Ma'am, I'm not saying it'll be easy. In fact, it'll probably be the hardest thing I've ever done. But I've been thinking hard about this—not just tonight, but for several days now. I think it'd be the best for Bobby. I think it'd be best for me and Charles too."

Judge Griffith sighed. She was doing a lot of sighing tonight. She steepled her fingers in front of her mouth and thought for a moment. "You have your tickets?"

Mickey stood up then. "I have their tickets, Your Honor. And unless they've cancelled my contract, I am the agent of record for this family. I can guarantee delivery to Luna and a 70% probability of an acceptable contract. I have three possibilities already. We have insurance in place against failure to contract, so the family will not end up a drain on the resources of any starside facility."

"Fair enough. Is it my understanding that you are also emigrating, Mickey?"

"Yes, Aunt Georgia."

"I'm going to miss you, sweetheart. Is it your intention to accompany the Dingillian family?"

"Uh—" Mickey looked to Douglas, uncertain. Douglas...hesitated, then nodded. Okay, so that fight was over. "Yes, your honor."

"Are you willing to accept co-responsibility with Douglas Dingillian?"

"Uh—yes, I'm prepared to accept co-responsibility up to and including such time as I can guarantee financial security through an appropriate colonial contract, and for as long after that as the Dingillians are willing to accept my support."

"Mickey—?" The Judge looked at him sternly. "You just met these folks—what is it? Two days, three days ago? Are you willing to take on this kind of a commitment on such short notice—especially now, after you've seen them at their worst?"

"Aunt Georgia, I admit that...there's a lot of dirtside crap going on. But I think these are good people. And they wouldn't be in half the trouble they're in if it hadn't been for me...."

"And your Mom," Judge Griffith added.

Mickey shrugged in acquiescence of the point. "The thing is, I like them in spite of themselves. I owe them. I want to do it."

Judge Griffith cleared her throat gruffly. "Well, that sort of settles that. The younger generation has come of age. All that's left for us old broads is to find a nice warm grave and get someone to throw some dirt over us. Olivia, you did a good job on this boy. He has a conscience." To the rest of us, she said, "All right, I'm now prepared to hear arguments from the parents. I assume you are both going to protest a ruling of divorce here—?"

Both Mom and Dad stood up at the same time; they both said yes. In unison. It was the first time I'd ever seen them agree on anything. They looked at each other in surprise. Dad made a waving gesture to Mom. "You go first."

Mom didn't spare any words. If there's one thing Mom can be counted on for, she always lets you know what she's thinking. "Is this the way justice up here works? Is your culture up here so morally bankrupt that you have to steal other people's children—?"

"That's the way, Mom," Douglas said. "Butter her up. Make her like you."

"Shut up, Douglas," Mom snapped at him. "I heard about your— misadventures. I can't tell you how disappointed I am."

"Yeah, me too," said Douglas. He looked meaningfully at the woman next to Mom.

"Douglas," said Judge Griffith. "It's your mother's turn. Sit down, please." To Mom, she said, "I assume you have an argument to present?"

Mom turned to Howard-The-Repugnant. "You're a lawyer! Do something!"

He shrugged, looked through his briefcase, pulled out a folded paper, and passed it to her.

"Huh? What's this?"

"My bill," he said. "The minute you walked in the door, you destroyed my case. Not being here was your best chance. As long as you were still groundside, I could make the argument that the children were being taken away without your opportunity to be present and have your side of the issue heard. It would have justified pushing the case into a Liaison Court, which handles mixed jurisdiction disputes. But now that you're here, this constitutes a fair hearing and all I can do is restate what's already in the record. So there's nothing I can do here, except enjoy the show. Please pay that within thirty days." Howard leaned back in his chair, grimly satisfied. He looked almost human.

Olivia grinned over at him. "I may have misjudged your intelligence. You finally found a way to avoid losing a case—stay out of it. And present a bill anyway. My compliments, Counselor."

"Belay that noise, Olivia." This was punctuated with a rap of the gavel. I was beginning to wish I had a gavel of my own. It was a great way to get people to pay attention. "Ms. Campbell, do you have anything else to say? Anything to justify awarding you custody, that is?"

"Your honor, I already have custody. You have the case in front of you. The El Paso District Court awarded me custody of my children.

These hearings are illegal. This is a kangaroo court. You have no authority over me or my children. I demand that you affirm the rulings of the groundside court."

"Thanks for the demonstration of how to put the tact into tactical, Ms. Campbell. But this hearing is *very* legal. I suggest you ask your attorney to explain the limits of groundside jurisdiction and the farther reaching authority of starside courts. You are certainly free to appeal this case to the World Court and I'll be disappointed in you if you don't— but once I make my ruling, it's going to be implemented immediately."

The woman next to Mom stood up. "Your Honor, may I speak?"

"Why not?" Judge Griffith sighed. "Everyone else is going to insist on having their say tonight. Your name is...?"

"Bev Sykes, Your Honor. I think you can understand that my partner is justifiably upset about this situation. She came to San Francisco for a much-needed vacation; the next thing, she's in the biggest crisis of her life—"

"It is a crisis which she helped create, Ms. Sykes. No one is innocent here. Least of all you, if I read this history right."

"The point is, Your Honor, that what you're proposing to do is overturn a stable situation—"

"I've seen absolutely no evidence of stability in this situation, Ms. Sykes."

Mom spoke up again then. "Perhaps if you'd ever had children of your own, you'd understand—"

Oops.

Judge Griffith's face darkened. "I had two daughters of my own, Ms. Campbell. They died in the Line accident of '97. That's when I got this chair. Do either of you have anything useful to add?"

Mom and the other woman whispered together for a moment, then they both shook their heads and sat down. They looked very unhappy. I almost felt sorry for them, but I wasn't going to change my mind, and I didn't think Doug was going to either.

Judge Griffith looked to Dad. "Mr. Dingillian, you had something to say?"

Dad stood up. He seemed strangely calm. "I want to apologize for my conduct in this whole affair. I made a serious error in judgment. I've hurt my children. I've made a lot of trouble for everybody. I know that."

Judge Griffith was studying her watch. "Get on with it, please."

"Your Honor, whatever you decide, I'll still be the boys' father, and Margaret will still be their mother—regardless of how you assign custody, we have the right to spend time with our children. And if our children want to spend time with us, they should have that right as well."

"The Court is already taking that into consideration," Judge Griffith said, typing something into her clipboard.

"Well, that's my argument, Your Honor. If the children end up in a location so far removed that visitation is impractical to the point of being impossible, then those visitation rights are effectively denied."

Judge Griffith raised her eyebrow. "In view of the circumstances which forced this hearing, the court finds it profoundly ironic that you should be making that argument, Mr. Dingillian."

Mom snorted. Loudly. I knew that snort.

Dad remained nonplused. "Nevertheless, Your Honor—if it was wrong for me to consider denying my wife access to her children, then it is equally wrong for the court to allow a situation to occur where visitation is impossible."

"Now that's a good point," Judge Griffith said, gesturing with the gavel. "But it seems to me that if visitation with your children is important enough to you, it's your responsibility to make sure to keep yourself near to them. The problem in this family is that both you and your wife have been attempting to make visitation impossible for each other, she by legal means, you by moving the children around. And the Court finds that behavior an intolerable state of affairs. Not because it is unfair to either of you, but because *it is unfair to the children.*

"You both claim that you are interested only in the well-being of your children, but you have both put enormous emotional burdens on them. Your children need a place to heal, a place to recover from their parents. Considering the abuses of the visitation process in this case, the Court is not inclined toward allowances for the needs of the parents. I won't rule out visitation rights, but I'm not going to make visitation rights as large a part of the final decision as it would be downside. Anything else, Mr. Dingillian?"

Dad looked beaten. He shook his head and sat down.

"All right then." Judge Griffith rapped her gavel. "Here's my ruling. It is the decision of this court that Douglas Dingillian is to be regarded in all rights and privileges as a legal adult. It is the further decision of this court that Charles Dingillian is granted a summary divorce from both of his parents and given to the care and custody of Douglas Dingillian, contingent on the co-responsibility of Mickey Partridge. Charles, this divorce is contingent on review by the legal authority of whatever jurisdiction you and your brother settle in. So choose your destination carefully."

"Yes, Your Honor."

"In the matter of Robert Dingillian, the court recognizes the long history of custody disputes in this case, and acknowledges the already established legal rights of both parents...and sets them aside. The welfare of the child always takes precedence. Because the parents of Robert Dingillian have not demonstrated, in the opinion of *this* court, sufficient commitment to the child to put their own disputes aside, the Court is left with no alternative but to remove the child from the custody of the parents and place him in the care of his elder brother, Douglas. This is also contingent on the statement of co-responsibility from Mickey Partridge, and final review by the legal authorities of your ultimate destination. Mickey, I mean it, choose *carefully*. This concludes the business of this court. And if there are no further objections, I declare this hearing adjourned—"

But before she could rap her gavel on the table, Dad stood up—"Your Honor? Point of order? Um—may I ask for clarification, please?"

Judge Griffith hesitated, the gavel poised above the table. "Go ahead."

"My sons are free to use the tickets I purchased for them, if they wish to. Is that correct?"

"Your sons are free to choose their own destination. Yes, they can use the tickets you paid for. The Court has not terminated your access, only your custodial authority."

"I understand that, I'm just trying to get clear on where the line is drawn. Am I *also* free to use the ticket I purchased for myself?"

"Yes," said the Judge. "You are."

Over on the other side of the room, I heard Mom gasp. "I can't believe this—"

Both Dad and the Judge ignored her. Dad asked, "Even if it means traveling together with my sons? Your Honor, you do understand that if my sons use their tickets to go on to Luna, we'll be sharing the same cabin...?"

"Mr. Dingillian, the Court has no objection to you traveling with your sons, if that's what they want." Something about that last part, I looked over to Douglas. He'd caught it too, but Judge Griffith was still talking to Dad, "You *are* entitled to visitation rights. But you no longer have any custodial authority over them. That's the limit of this ruling—"

"Oh, great!" said Mom. "We're right back where we started! He has no custodial rights, but he still ends up with the kids! What kind of a kangaroo court is this?" She turned to Hidalgo. "You said you could help me! This is the way you help people?!"

Hidalgo wasn't stupid. He didn't even try to calm her down. He was already pushing himself ponderously to his feet, raising his hand for attention. "Your Honor, there is one other matter left unresolved. If I may beg the Court's indulgence...?"

"Just a moment, Dr. Hidalgo." Judge Griffith turned to Mom. She finally laid her gavel down. "Ms. Campbell, please understand, you have the exact same rights—or should I say, lack of rights. If you wish to travel with your children, you may do so as well. Under the same terms as your ex-husband. If the children wish it." There it was again—

"Oh, yeah, right! With what money?! I don't have a SuperNational credit card—I can't go to the moon!"

"Somebody paid for two tickets on the express shuttle...." Judge Griffith left the second half of that thought unsaid. Mom fumed and sputtered, but the Judge was already moving on. "All right, Bolivar. You paid for two tickets to this circus—let's hear what you have to say." She glanced meaningfully at her watch.

"It is the matter of *Señor* Dingillian's financial status. If you will consult your own records, you will see that this man does not have the resources to have paid for even one ticket up the beanstalk, let alone four."

"So?"

"So if he is going to the outbeyond, the Financial Responsibility Act requires proof that he is leaving behind no significant debts."

Dad stood up. "Your Honor, there is documentation on file with the Emigration Authority to demonstrate that not only are all of my outstanding debts paid off, but that there is a fund in escrow to handle any future claims that may arise. Additionally, there is Emigration Insurance to cover any contingencies that exceed the funds in escrow."

Judge Griffith was sitting at her table with her hands folded in front of her chin again. She looked from one to the other, more amused than anything else. "Is there a point to all this?" she asked.

"With the Court's indulgence," Hidalgo said, "I would like, at this time, to present documentation that *Señor* Dingillian's trip has been financed by certain SuperNational interests, and that in return, he is functioning as a courier for them—"

"So what?" said the Judge. "We have private couriers going up and down the Line every day. Many people finance their emigration that way. There's nothing illegal about it."

"Your Honor, may I please direct your attention to Section Four of the Line Authority Transportation Act? There are a number of restrictions on private courier service. It is illegal if the item being transferred is contraband or stolen property or if the intent of private service is to avoid legal obligations, such as liens, claims, custody, or taxation. If a courier is suspected of carrying items in violation of Section Four, the Line—that's you, Your Honor—has the authority to investigate and, if appropriate, require divestment of any and all packages."

"I see you've done your homework, Bollie. As usual. So what is it that Max Dingillian is carrying that you want to get your hands on so badly that you're willing to pay for two premium class round-trip shuttle tickets?"

"Your Honor, it is not for myself that I act, it is on behalf of the—"

"I've heard the speech, Bollie. More than once. Just tell the Court what the McGuffin is."

"Your Honor, six days ago, Stellar-American Resources transferred an extremely large amount of money into an American-Lunar transfer account. The account is a pipeline that may be accessed freely both on Earth and on Luna. It is commonly used for holding funds being moved off-world. Stellar-American Resources has three transfer accounts of their own, all bonded and monitored, which they normally use for off-world access. That they are suddenly using this account to transfer an extremely large resource suggests that they are attempting to avoid transfer taxes, as well as legal scrutiny. Not even the company's own stockholders are aware of this transfer—"

"But you are?" Judge Griffith noted with mild sarcasm.

"There are people who tell me things, Your Honor. Be that as it may, however the information comes to light, there is certainly enough to be suspicious about. And it is my solemn duty to call this to your attention. My people believe that *Señor* Dingillian is carrying one of three password-checks necessary to complete the transfer of funds. The other two may have already arrived on Luna."

"Just how much money are we talking about, Bolivar?"

Hidalgo pursed his lips and looked extremely uncomfortable. "It is over three trillion dollars, Your Honor. Perhaps as much as ten. The money came out of nine thousand different accounts that my people regularly watch, and at least ninety thousand more that we have not yet found a way to monitor. For this much money to move off of Earth so abruptly—"

Judge Griffith rapped her gavel. "The money flows, Bolivar. The fact that you don't like where it goes doesn't make the river a crime. This isn't a McGuffin at all. It's the stuff that dreams are made of."

"Your Honor, I respectfully request the Court to require *Señor* Dingillian to divulge the truth about what he is carrying. If it is a legal transfer, then I shall apologize profusely for taking up his time and the Court's. But if *Señor* Dingillian is carrying a check of such enormous size, I am certain that there are law enforcement and tax agencies both groundside and starside who will want to check that no laws are being broken by such a transfer." Hidalgo folded his hands across his paunch and waited.

Judge Griffith frowned. "I understand exactly what you're trying to do, Bollie. But what you're asking is generally beyond the reach of this Court. I can ask Mr. Dingillian to reveal what he is carrying, but absent of any evidence of a crime, he isn't required to violate his own privacy. If there is no evidence of wrong-doing, I can take no action."

"I understand, Your Honor, but I believe it is in the interests of justice to compel such performance as is appropriate."

"Mm. Yes. Bollie, I know you—you always want the best justice money can buy. So be it." She turned to Dad. "What are you carrying, Max? You don't have to tell me, but if it'll get Bolivar Hidalgo off your back...."

Dad shook his head and spread his empty hands wide. "Your Honor. I am not carrying anything."

The way he said it—with an unspoken *now* attached to the end of the sentence—was enough to raise Judge Griffith's eyebrows. "Have you already delivered it?"

"I have not delivered anything, Your Honor." Again, the same unfinished tone. If you didn't know Dad, you might not catch it; but if you were smart...like Judge Griffith, you could hear that what Dad *wasn't* saying was almost as important as what he *was* saying.

Judge Griffith hesitated. I could see she'd figured it out. But of course, being a judge, she'd probably learned how to tell when people were telling the truth or not. And by now I figured she probably had some game of her own working....

"Well, then," she said. "If you're not carrying anything—this court has no further business with you."

"Your Honor!" That was Hidalgo. "Ask him who paid for his tickets and what he had to do in return!"

She appeared to be mulling it over. I glanced over at Doug, he looked to the monkey in my lap, I shrugged and looked at the ceiling. Dad looked back and forth between us, carefully blank. Despite the Judge's decision, Stinky was still asleep in Mom's lap, and I wondered if we were going to be able to get him away from her.

Judge Griffith unfolded her hands. "Dr. Hidalgo, I think you're asking me to get into an area that is beyond the scope of this session. I told you earlier that I would not get into any inquiries that did not bear directly on the custody of the Dingillian children. I'm not going fishing for you. While the matter you have raised is certainly an important one, we cannot pursue it here. If you wish, you can pursue this in another court." She started to pick up her gavel again—

Almost as soon as the Judge had begun speaking, Hidalgo had nudged Howard, who began fumbling in his briefcase. Now, as Judge Griffith finished, Howard leap to his feet. "Uh, not so fast, Your Honor, I have a warrant here—"

"And you're just serving it now?"

"I hadn't expected that it would be necessary."

"Pass it up."

Howard-The-Unkempt gave the paper to Judge Griffith's assistant, Joyce, who passed it to the Judge. She unfolded the paper and studied it thoughtfully. She scratched her eyebrow with a fingernail while she read. "Well, this appears to be in order," she said finally. To the rest of the room, she announced, "This is a Line Authority search-and-seizure warrant for the property of Max Dingillian. I'll spare you all the whereases. You're accused of transporting contraband."

Dad stood up, "Your honor, all I have are the clothes I'm wearing. If the court will provide me with something to wear, I'll be happy to give you these clothes."

"It's not that easy, Max. I'm authorized to detain you."

Dad shrugged. "Go ahead, Your Honor." He held out his wrists, as if awaiting handcuffs. "Take me away. I don't have anything—"

"Wait a minute," I said. I stood up, still holding the monkey. "Dad is telling the truth. He isn't carrying anything. I am. He gave it to me. I put it in the monkey."

Dad and Douglas both stared. "Charles—!"

I was already prying the back of the monkey opened. I pulled out the bottom-most memory bar and carried it over to Dad. "Here," I said. "Give this to the Judge."

Dad looked at the card, looked at me, looked at Olivia—she was carefully blank—then handed the card to Joyce, who handed it to Judge Griffith, who turned it over in her hands, examining it. "You were paid to transport this—?"

Dad looked to Olivia, looked back to the Judge. "Yes, Your Honor. I was paid to transport that."

"Well then, the warrant is satisfied." Judge Griffith passed the card to her assistant. "Joyce, seal that. It's not to be released to anyone." To Doctor Hidalgo, she said, "If it can be demonstrated that the intention of this warrant was to disrupt a lawful business enterprise, not only will I hold you in contempt, I will fine you for the full amount of damages. And you too, Howard. Let it be noted that this Court does not approve of the mischievous abuse of litigation."

"Your Honor," Howard-The-Illegitimate said, "We would like to re-quest that the...uh, monkey be confiscated as well. In case there are other memory cards—"

"Nope. The monkey doesn't belong to Max Dingillian. It belongs to Robert Dingillian. Sorry, Howard." She raised her hands in mock helplessness.

He sputtered. "But the warrant—!"

"The warrant says nothing about the property of *Robert* Dingillian. And as he is no longer under the custodial authority of Max Dingillian, we cannot even use that umbrella. Hm, I see you forgot to add an *a priori* clause that would have allowed me to grant your request. You should be more careful when you draft these things, Howard. You left a loophole big enough to drop an electric primate through. Given the wording of this document," she waved it at him, "this Court has no authority to seize the property of any other Dingillian. And I will not act beyond the authority of this document. If I did, the next judge up would have ample grounds to invalidate the warrant anyway. So consider that I'm doing you a favor. If you want the monkey, go get another warrant."

I couldn't help myself, I surreptitiously switched the monkey on—and whispered into its ear. It leapt down from my lap, ran over to Howard-The-Stupid and gave him a double-chocolate hot-fudge farkleberry with whipped cream and a cherry on top. Plus a noise like an elephant fart. Then it came scurrying back to me. Howard looked like he was going to explode.

Keeping her face carefully blank, Judge Griffith picked up her gavel and rapped it once. "We're adjourned." She looked at her watch. "And just in time. You have an elevator to catch, Mickey. Get your butt in gear. They're holding the gate for you—"

And then a lot of stuff happened all at once. Dr. Hidalgo waddled over and stood in front of Dad. "You have been very lucky, *Señor* Dingillian. Very very lucky. I hope for your sake and your children's sake that your luck holds out."

Dad shook his head and laughed. "And you've been very stupid, Dr. Hidalgo. Very very stupid. You never figured it out, did you?"

Dr. Hidalgo raised an eyebrow. "Enlighten me?"

"You and your people—I was never carrying anything. I was a *decoy*. Do you really think they'd trust that much money to my care? Even I'm not that stupid. Whoever it was, and even I don't know for sure, you probably know more than me, they wanted you looking in the wrong place. So they hired me. And I guess it worked. While you were busy chasing me up the Line, you weren't hassling a whole bunch of other folks—"

"That's an assumption on your part."

"Maybe so, maybe not. But I got my job done. Thanks again for dinner." Dad offered his hand.

Surprisingly, Dr. Hidalgo took it. He held Dad's hand in both of his. "You may yet need my help, *Señor*. I do not think you know what you are playing with. You keep my card. You call me if your new friends don't work out. *Adios. Vaya con dios*." And he turned and waddled over to confer with Howard-The-Unhappy.

Dad turned to look at me. And Douglas. We were whispering together. Dad must have seen the look on my face. And on Douglas' too. He said, "*What?*"

And I said to Douglas, "You tell him."

And Dad said, "Tell me what?"

So Douglas swallowed. Hard. "You sure, Charles?"

"Yes." I nodded.

Douglas turned to Dad. "We don't want you to come with us."

Dad looked confused. He looked from me to Douglas and back again. So I added, "Judge Griffith said we don't have to take you if we don't want to. Well...we don't want to."

Dad went pale. "Charles? Douglas? Are you sure—?"

"We have to go, Dad." Douglas hugged him quickly. "Maybe we'll see you on the moon. I hope so."

I went to Dad to hug him too, but I didn't say anything to him. He looked like he'd been stabbed—and was still waiting to fall down. He didn't hug me back, so I let go and followed Douglas over to where Mom was standing. She was holding Bobby, rocking him back and forth on her shoulder.

Douglas stopped before her, silently and sadly. Joyce, the bailiff, stood at a respectful distance, watching. Mom was holding Bobby as hard as she could. She glared over his shoulder at Douglas, and at Joyce too, and she held onto Bobby for the longest time, rocking him, stroking his hair, whispering into his ear, telling him over and over how much she loved him and how she was going to come and get him, not to worry—but at last, Douglas leaned over to take him, and she let him slip out of her arms. Tears were running down her cheeks and I was starting to feel real bad about this whole thing. Doug bent his head to kiss her, but she just turned away.

So Douglas turned away from her and she was standing there by herself, just looking at me—and I didn't know what to say or do. She walked over to where I was standing alone and when she spoke it was like being dragged naked over nails. She just shook her head and asked, "Why, Charles—why?"

I shook my head, helplessly. "I—I'm sorry, Mom. I didn't do it to hurt you."

"Was I really that bad a mother to you?"

"Mom, you're angry all the time—"

"Well, don't I have good reason to be? The way you treat me. The way your father treats me."

"Mom, this isn't about you—"

"Well, then *who* is it about—? Answer me that!"

"Mom, you don't listen! You don't *ever* listen—you're not listening now."

"Charles, I have a right to know. You're breaking up our family—"

"No, Mom. It was already broken. You and Dad broke it up a long time ago—"

"Is this really what you want—to hurt me like this?"

I wiped the tears from my cheeks. "Mom, what I want most—" It hurt to say it. My voice cracked—"What I want most is...to get away from you, right now. I can't stand it when you talk to me like this. It isn't *my* fault!"

"Go ahead then! You're just like your father, you little bastard! I hope you're happy!" And then—she slapped my face! For an instant, I saw stars.

I didn't know what to do or say. I was too shocked. She hadn't ever hit me before. I couldn't believe it—everybody was staring at me—so I just turned to go—and then she was grabbing at me, crying, "Oh, God, Charles—I'm so sorry, I didn't mean to do that! Charles, please—wait! Wait! Charles!"

There was one thing she could have said that might have made me stop, and I was listening as hard as I could to hear her say it, and maybe she *was* saying it in her own way, but I was listening for the words, and she never said them. She never said the words. So I kept going.

And then Doug put an arm around my shoulders and I started sobbing as we followed Mickey to the hatch of the transfer pod. Dad looked uncertain, then Olivia grabbed his arm and held him back so he couldn't follow us. I looked back to see Dr. Hidalgo and that Sykes woman rushing to Mom's side, and then Doug steered me into the waiting pod and then the door closed and they were gone—

"So what happens now?" I asked, still wiping tears from my eyes.

"I have an idea," Doug answered, shouldering Bobby with one arm, and hugging me with the other. "Let's go to the moon."

This one and the following story are proof that life in Los Angeles is inherently surreal.

CRYSTALLIZATION

It's the moment when liquid solidifies. The pressure rises. A critical threshold is achieved. The density of the particles forces them to form an impenetrable latticework. It crystallizes. Fluid stops flowing. Slush turns to sludge, mud dries and hardens. It petrifies.

For the first few hours after the Los Angeles freeway system hardened, most people believed the problem was temporary and that traffic would eventually start flowing again. Even for the first few days, they believed they would eventually chip their way out of the city's concretized arteries.

The slush of Los Angeles traffic had been slower than sluggish for years, churning through looping spaghetti channels of cement, in a lumpy torrent of metal and plastic peristalsis, everything in a persistent state of uncertain hesitation, punctuated only occasionally by forward jerking movements and uneven painful surges, a textbook demonstration of socio-technical constipation and definitely no place for a stick shift.

The city engineers had been aware of the potential for crystallization for nearly two decades, but few of them had taken their own warnings seriously, and eventually they took it for granted that the projections of crystallization were situational artifacts occurring whenever the simulators reached the limits of their ability to process the rapid flows of data.

Unfortunately, only the data was flowing rapidly. One desperate afternoon, even that stopped. The air conditioning broke down in the central monitoring station. The temperature rose uncomfortably. Fans didn't help. The computers began shutting down in self-defense. The screens went blank, or declared, "No signal." Blind and deaf, the traffic engineers could neither monitor nor prescribe.

The rest was inevitable.

Outside, in the place where facts don't care about simulation, events took on a terrifying momentum of their own. It was Friday, early afternoon on a three-day holiday weekend. Temperatures in the basin had peaked at 106 degrees shortly after 1:00 pm. Add to that, a localized gas shortage acerbated by higher than usual oil prices, a high degree of situational stress about the staggering economy, a disturbing series of terrorist bombings in the mideast, and three days of overheated shock jock nattering about a particularly scandalous high-profile murder trial, and crystallization was no longer a question of if or when, but *where*.

Surprisingly, it did not begin on the freeway. Not exactly. Although a freeway was involved. The first hardening in the traffic flow began in the San Fernando Valley where Burbank Blvd. intersected Sepulveda. Always a sluggish intersection, today it revealed its true capacity for horror. An overweight, overstressed soccer mom with two screaming children in the back seat of her SUV and a cell phone pressed to her ear, her attention everywhere but on the road in front of her, abruptly became aware of a motorcyclist coming up out of the blind spot on her right. Startled, she swerved left, forcing two teenagers in a dropped Honda Civic (don't ask) to brake suddenly. The empty tanker truck which shouldn't have been in the same lane behind them braked, swerved, and jackknifed sideways into a city bus, effectively blocking all three northbound lanes of Sepulveda and the middle two lanes of Burbank.

Almost immediately traffic stopped on both boulevards, backing up on Burbank as far east as Van Nuys blvd and as far west as Woodley. Sepulveda froze all the way north to Sherman Way and as far south as Ventura blvd. When the traffic at the intersection of Ventura and Sepulveda froze, the crystallization of the surface streets began to spread east and west on Ventura boulevard as well. In the horror about to happen, there would be no alternative routes.

The 405 freeway stretches north across the San Fernando Valley; the heaviest used access ramps are at Burbank blvd, just slightly east of the fatal intersection and up a slight incline. The northbound and southbound access ramps represent two additional intersections to interrupt Burbank's westward flow—it's a wasps' nest of lanes, contradictory traffic signals, and intermittent left-turn arrows. Even at three in the morning, it takes 90 seconds to negotiate this ganglionic nightmare in any direction. During crush hour, wise drivers bring a book or a magazine. Teenage boys change the radio station and readjust themselves in their jeans. Grown men pick their noses and think about business. Teenage girls turn their rearview mirrors and fix their makeup. Everyone else is on the phone, their attention two or ten or a thousand miles away. Watching the road is optional, something only sissies and old ladies do.

On any ordinary afternoon, traffic feeding into the northbound Burbank offramp would start backing up by two pm. By five, it would be backed up two miles south, all the way to the 405/101 interchange. This day, however, traffic was even more manic than usual. As soon as the critical intersection of Burbank and Sepulveda hardened, the crystallization of the 405 began spreading southward as fast as new cars arrived and joined the creeping boundaries of the linear parking lot.

Imagine the intersection of the 405 and the 101 as a cross. The entire northwest quadrant is the Sepulveda dam basin. For the next three miles west, there are only two surface routes that will take you north to the neighborhoods beyond, Balboa and Woodley, if you can get to Woodley. For two miles north, there is only one westward access—Burbank. But there are over a million residents northwest of the intersection and their *only* access from the south or east is through this interchange—or through the intersections of Ventura and Sepulveda, or Burbank and Sepulveda. As quickly as Sepulveda clogged, all of the intersections and all of the surrounding surface avenues began to solidify as well. Within forty minutes, an area ten miles square had crystallized.

The 405 and the 101 freeways only exacerbated the situation, feeding more cars into this black hole of traffic from all four compass points. With no place to go, the traffic ground to a halt both north and south on the 405 and very quickly after east and west on the 101 as well.

With the computers down, Cal-Trans was unable to post warning bulletins on the freeway alert signs. Instead, an Amber alert was posted to look out for a suspected kidnapper driving a black Ford Explorer, license number, etc. It was this particular (alleged) kidnapper's bad luck to be caught on the 101 westbound at Vineland. Traffic came to a halt with the SUV pocketed between a stretch limo on the left and a battered Plymouth pickup on the right, piled high with tree branches, and driven by three Mexican gardeners whose command of English was limited. Behind the pickup truck, however, was a distracted mother in a white Honda Civic, whose 11 year old son had read the Amber alert only a few moments before and who was now intently watching all of the traffic around the Civic on the promise of a ten-dollar bill if he spotted the suspect Explorer, but only if he kept absolutely quiet while he did, so his exhausted mother could listen to her deadbeat ex-husband (who apparently operated out of the bizarre belief that a good excuse is always an acceptable substitute for a tangible result) explain why his child-support check would be late again.

In the middle of this conversation, the 11-year old suddenly began shouting and pointing. Despite his mother's annoyed refusal to accept the obvious—that she now owed her son ten dollars that she did not have—she eventually accepted that indeed, the suspect's vehicle was only a few yards ahead in the next lane over. By then, owing to a repeat of the same Amber Alert news bulletin on static-riven KFWB, the inhabitants of two other vehicles had also spotted the Explorer. One driver was already calling 911. The other driver and his two passengers, (all of them new enlistees on leave from the marine base at El Toro and on their way to visit the Tarzana-based fiancé of the driver) exited their own SUV, two of them carrying baseball bats kept in the vehicle for occasional trips into West Hollywood for gay-bashing. With traffic temporarily halted—or so they believed (that it was temporary)—they approached the Explorer on foot. The suspected kidnapper panicked, tried to hit the gas, tried to force his way between a lime-green Volkswagen Beetle and a 1988 gray-blue Chrysler LeBaron convertible driven by a harried college student whose car insurance had just been cancelled, and the result was a three-way crunch, with three soon-to-be-ex-marines banging on the hood and fenders of locked Explorer with baseball bats. They had just escalated to smashing windows when the first officers arrived on scene and ordered them to stand down.

From there, the situation metamorphosed into a police standoff as even more motorcycle officers came racing up the still empty shoulders of the freeway, followed by the warbling and flashing cruisers of the California Highway Patrol and the Los Angeles Police Department. Very quickly, this nexus of confusion and rage was surrounded by armed officers, all of them crouching behind automobile fenders with guns drawn, while two police helicopters and three news choppers circled overhead and terrified drivers in all directions evacuated their vehicles, crawling quickly away through the lanes on their hands and knees—including the harried mother, still on her cell phone, and her 11-year old son who whined loudly that he wanted to stay and see the kidnapper get shot. The suspected kidnapper, his vehicle permanently jammed between the

Volkswagen and the Honda, was unable to extricate himself from the vehicle and sat there helplessly while police ordered him to get out with his hands up.

The irony of the situation was that the Amber Alert had been posted with the wrong license number. The driver was not a kidnapper, his only relationship to the kidnapping was that he drove a black Ford Explorer. He had only tried to flee, because he had seen three angry men coming toward his vehicle with baseball bats.

Nevertheless, innocent or guilty, this particular blood clot in the arterial flow of urban commerce effectively shut down the 101 in both directions, trapping even more drivers in their cars. Some of them turned off their engines and got out to smoke, leaning against their fenders or lifting themselves up to sit on the still-warm hoods of their rapidly-depreciating vehicles.

Meanwhile, the clotting of the freeway system spread south and east with pernicious speed. East along the 134 toward the 5, and southward down the 101, which was already terminal. It took less than an hour for the crystallization of the system to hit the nexus of the Pasadena, Harbor, and Hollywood freeways. The four-level interchange, one of the first in the nation, was in easy view of the mayor's office in the nearby city hall, a building that, contrary to popular belief, had *not* been destroyed in the 1953 attack of George Pal's Martians and their manta-ray shaped war machines.

With the news media now reporting that the 101 and 405 freeways were impassable and that drivers were advised to seek alternate routes— of which there were either few or none, the best thing to do was find a movie theater or a motel and wait for the weekend. Starting at city-center, the northward crush of traffic tried to force its way up the 5, an overstressed artery that crawled along the east side of Griffith park; the results were predictable and immediate—another nexus of crystallization. Nothing moved. The clotting of the Los Angeles freeway system was now irreversible. Within another hour, the 10, most of the 110, and a large part of the 210 were equally out of commission as were most of the surrounding surface streets. Too many cars, not enough road.

Unable to feed their traffic flows into the northward and westward traffic channels, the 710 and the 605 also began to solidify. Crystallization spread like ice across the surface of a lake, creeping steadily and inevitably toward a frozen stillness. As fast as new cars arrived at the outward edges of the solidification, that's how fast it spread.

And there were still four hours until sunset.

Most drivers, unaware of the scale of the growing catastrophe, unable to comprehend or believe that their trusted freeway system had finally, utterly, and completely failed them, remained in their cars, existing in a state of quiet desperation—or quiet domestication—because most of them still believed that it was just a matter of time until traffic began easing forward again.

The Zen master, Solomon Short, is quoted as saying, "No pebble ever takes responsibility for the whole avalanche." Nowhere was this so evident when the disaster escalated to its next stage.

Start with the sweltering sun. It's the fifth day of an impossible heat wave with no end in sight. There's no wind, the air is stagnant and brown. People are tired, uncomfortable, cranky, and selfish. Unwilling to be uncomfortable, every driver in a vehicle with air conditioning has rolled up his windows and has his air conditioner turned on full blast. To power his air conditioner, he's running his engine. Half a million vehicles. All those engines now create a furnace of additional heat at ground level, encouraging even more drivers to keep their engines running and their air conditioners blasting.

Frozen in time, as inert as the dead air above them, a million and a half cars and trucks and buses, idling impatiently, every second turning tens of thousands of gallons of gasoline into hot exhaust—as the sun's rays bake the day, various chemical transformations occur; the exhaust becomes a rising cloud of air pollution. All those restless waiting vehicles spew a cumulative soup of toxic fumes into the brown smoky air of the basin, aggravating an already deadly miasma that lay across the afternoon like a smothering blanket—and triggering the next stage of the catastrophe.

Sitting alone, stuck and frustrated, desperate and angry, people begin to demonstrate irrational behavior. Some people begin honking incessantly, triggering even more stress in the people around them. Some drivers turn up their music—too loud. The hyper-amplified subwoofers broadcast rhythmic pulses that feel like body punches to people in vehicles many lengths ahead and behind. Arguments begin. Fights break out. Windows get smashed with golf clubs. Ramming incidents occur. Even individuals who are uninvolved experience increased levels of stress. A few have panic attacks. Others suffer respiratory distress. Some go into full-blown asthma attacks. Then it gets worse. Kosh's corollary to Short's observation: The avalanche has already started, it is too late for the pebbles too vote.

Despite the efforts of social historians, an accurate account of the events of the day remains impossible; too many events, too many scattered and confused accounts. What is certain however is that once the cascade of failures began, each breakdown triggered the next; but the most catastrophic of all was the failure of the telephone system.

Stuck on the freeways, with relief from the sun still hours away, people began flipping open their cell phones and calling home, calling for help, calling ambulances and fire trucks and police, even calling Cal-Trans and the city councilmen and the Governor's office to complain. As the channels overloaded, the system began dumping calls to clear bandwidth; people began calling called their service providers to complain. In self-defense, the network went into emergency procedures and shut itself down. The result—increased feelings of alienation and isolation among those trapped in the crystallized traffic. The arteries became linear madhouses of desperate frustration. Increasing numbers of people lost control of their bladders and bowels, adding to their individual discomfort, both physical and emotional.

As the afternoon wore on, two pregnant women went into labor and a third miscarried. Two people enroute to hospitals died in the ambulances that could not get through. A burly farmworker, one of several crammed into the back of a pickup truck experienced debilitating food poisoning, a combination of projectile vomiting and near-projectile diarrhea that expelled more than two liters of fluid from his body in less than thirty minutes. A 56-year old type-A studio executive experienced crushing chest pains that left him gasping for breath and too weak to cry for help. No help was available anyway. Even where calls for help could still be made from emergency callboxes, impatient drivers had already filled both shoulders of the highway in their desperate attempts to escape. The rescue vehicles couldn't get in and the med-evac choppers had no place to land.

By mid-afternoon, a significant number of vehicles had run out of gas. Even under the best of circumstances, a single stalled automobile in a middle lane could back up traffic in all four lanes for miles. Under these circumstances, with hundreds of dead vehicles scattered throughout the system, and more dying every minute, the crystallization had become complete. The vehicular arteries were solid and terminally impassible. The patient was dead, although it would be several days before any of the specialists would admit it.

But on some unconscious level, some people were already getting a visceral sense of what had happened. Maybe their survival instincts were kicking in, or maybe they were simply overcome by frustration—but it was the final moment of breakdown, the recognition that the system had failed and could not repair itself. Drivers started getting out of their cars. They locked them up, out of some optimistic belief that they would eventually have the chance to come back and retrieve them—and then they left them where they were. They gathered what belongings they could carry and abandoned their metal sanctuaries. First one or two, then a few more, and finally a veritable flood of refugees, they hiked between the sweltering lanes toward the nearest off-ramp and their separate illusions of relief.

Not all drivers were that easily persuaded. They sat and waited in desperate hope, afraid to leave, afraid to let go of their attachment to their vehicles, afraid to disconnect from the pernicious false identity—*I am my car*—that pervades Los Angeles culture. Still believing that this was only temporary, they sat in their cars, their engines still running, their air conditioners still blasting. (Even today, all these years later, archaeologists are still finding mummified bodies in some vehicles, including many varieties of small animals.)

Some engineers argue that even up to this point, the Los Angeles freeway system might have been saved, if only the next phase of the disaster could have been prevented. Others argue that the next moments were inevitable from the first beginnings of the crystallization process. Computer simulations have given us no clear answer.

It was this simple. All of those automobiles, all of those desperate drivers too attached to their metal and plastic personalities, unwilling to leave the technological illusion of identity, security, and safety—they sat in their wombs of music, unaware that their engine temperatures were steadily, inexorably rising. The automobile engine is designed to cool itself while in motion; it needs a steady flow of air through its radiator so it can dissipate excess heat. But now, immobilized, all of those engines ran hotter and hotter without any chance of cooling, the temperatures around them rose, and overheating was inevitable. The first vehicle caught fire at 3:31. Like a good idea occurring to many people simultaneously, fires began breaking out everywhere. Within the next half hour, thirteen more vehicles began to smolder—some drivers had blankets and fire-extinguishers in their trunks, some didn't—so very soon, flames were licking out from under the hoods of seven of those vehicles.

But the fire trucks couldn't get to them. The shoulders were jammed. Cars with plastic gas tanks exploded with surprising fury, and the fires began to spread, leaping from vehicle to vehicle with alarming speed. Drivers who only moments before had been completely resistant to leaving the comfort of their sedans panicked and fled. Soon, there were firestorms. The biggest raged on the 405 where it intersected with the 101, at the heart of the first big clot in the system. Another firestorm flickered to life further south on the 405 where it intersected with the 10. A third fire exploded just west of where the 10 intersected with the 110 and also where it fed into the 5. In a very short time, the two fires met in the middle and expanded into a terrifying wall of flame that cut across the heart of the city.

Aerial tanker drops helped to slow down the flames, but it wasn't enough. Before the end of the 7:00 news broadcast, the governor had declared the city a disaster area. All across the world, people clustered around television screens, mesmerized by an event that was both incomprehensible and horrific. Los Angeles was choking to death on its own vomit. Like a great beast shuddering to a halt, the city of the angels was collapsing and shutting down.

Even after the fires were contained, even after the last smoldering embers were extinguished, most of the inhabitants of the city continued to believe that normalcy could be restored, that someday traffic would flow again. Maybe they believed this because there were still pockets of mobility scattered throughout the urban sprawl, quiet neighborhoods where housewives could still drive to the corner market for milk and bread and eggs; but by the fourth day, as the stores began to run out of perishables, the problem of resupply became critical. How could the city feed its stranded millions?

Despite promises from local, state, and federal authorities that the freeways could be restored and working again within a few days, well maybe two weeks at the most—all right, full recovery was probably at least a month or two away, but the city could function and survive, just a little more time, that's all we need—despite all the promises and reassurances, by the middle of the week many Angelenos were beginning to experience growing fear, frustration, and skepticism.

The city hadn't yet succumbed to panic, but the seeds were growing. Many of those who lived on the edges of the city, especially those who had access to uncongested avenues, began evacuating themselves voluntarily to other communities. In the first week alone, Orange County took in over 40,000 refugees, San Bernardino accepted 50,000; many went to the homes of friends and relatives, others went to hotels, the most desperate camped out in tent cities erected on the grounds of local high schools, colleges, and the parking lots of several major malls. But there were still over five million people within the affected areas of the city.

At least twenty thousand came out on motorcycles or motor scooters; while the trip through the surface streets was slow, it wasn't impossible. Many more rode out of the disaster area by train. Metro-Link borrowed trains from as far away as Seattle to ferry passengers from Union Station to refugee camps in Santa Barbara, San Diego, and Palmdale.

Even more came out of the frozen zone by subway and light rail. The Green Line and the Gold Line and the Blue Line were major arteries. The Red Line funneled people from the eastern edges of the San Fernando Valley down to Union Station, where they could transfer to the other colors of the rainbow, or to other trains which would take them even farther out.

A few people, not a significant number, escaped by helicopter. Van Nuys airport and LAX became hubs of activity for those who could reach them, with planes landing and taking off as fast as the overstressed controllers could open flight paths in the sky. The lack of aviation fuel deliveries to the airports meant that planes had to fly in carrying enough fuel for their outward journeys. All of the airports in the zone were given double-black stars, an unprecedented new classification which meant that travel to or from was at-your-own-risk. It meant limited-to-zero availability of rescue and emergency vehicles and facilities.

But the refugees from deeper inside the disaster zone, where there was no access to rail or air, had the most difficulty extricating themselves. Some refugees walked as far as ten miles to reach a subway station, or a Metro-Link access. Amtrak brought in emergency trains on freight lines, putting up awnings and tents and benches to create makeshift stations at convenient street-crossings and overpasses. The crowds gathered and waited. Many arrived with bicycles, overloaded with their belongings.

Red Cross helicopters lowered food and water to the waiting masses.

The disaster maps showed that almost every neighborhood within an area bounded by the 5 on the east, the 405 on the west, the 118 on the north, and the 105 on the south was pretty much immobilized to some degree or other, with tendrils of crystallization extending linearly outward from all of these routes.

While surface streets provided some relief, the spillover from the network of hardened freeways had choked most of the city's major thoroughfares. The streets were full of cars; the only reason the city had functioned before was that not every car was on the road at the same time. Now that the city was immobilized, a panic-stricken populace did they only thing they knew how to do—they rushed to their automobiles to make their escape. Evacuation didn't solve the problem, it exacerbated it. Broadcasting information on viable routes out of the city was self-defeating. As soon as a route was cleared and announced, it clogged up within minutes.

On Thursday, seven days after crystallization, as part of a larger disaster-relief package, the Republican-controlled Congress passed the Insurance Emergency Relief bill, declaring the disaster an act of God, thereby freeing automobile insurers from billions of dollars of exposure. This allowed the state to declare all abandoned vehicles a public nuisance and begin the wholesale removal of freeway blockages. The outrage that followed was not limited to the survivors of the disaster.

Leaders of the Democratic party were quick to point out that the Republicans had abandoned the protection of property rights in favor of the rights of big government. While not exactly a wedge issue, it did open the door for further political divisions. The Democrats portrayed themselves as the Party of Opportunity and painted the Republicans as the Party of Opportunists. The destruction of a million automobiles was seen as a gift to an automobile industry that would clearly benefit from the need to replace those lost vehicles. The bottom line, the Democrats insisted, was that the Greedy Old Party had no heart, they had abandoned the people of Southern California in favor of protecting the interests of their corporate sponsors. The Republican Congress tried to backpedal, but the damage had already been done.

Meanwhile, estimates of the time to full recovery now varied from six months to three years. The cranes and tow trucks necessary to clear the streets would have to work their way slowly to the center of the disaster and there were no computer simulations capable of the necessary extrapolations. Where to put the extracted vehicles and how to get them there complicated the issue.

The cars couldn't be removed from the freeways, because there was no place to put them. Trying to save all these autos for their owners' eventual return meant finding storage space for them and logging their locations in a master database. Perhaps, the surviving cars could be transported out to some wide-empty space out in the desert, from which owners could reclaim them. For a fee. Maybe. But did anyone really want to risk putting all these vehicles back into circulation where they could just clog the system again? The arguments were just beginning. (Some people advocated that this disaster represented an opportunity to remodel Los Angeles' dependency on automobiles and replace or augment the freeways with more light rail systems. But that particularly expensive alternative was not only an expensive proposition, it was not an immediate solution to anything.)

Even though the Vehicle Reclamation teams were now authorized to pile up cars in great towering pyramids of metal and glass and plastic wherever they found a big enough parking lot, there was enormous reluctance to do so. All those automobiles represented billions of dollars that nobody wanted to discard casually, especially not the far-removed owners. On the other hand, at the present rate of progress, by the time the reclamation teams reached the innermost majority of affected vehicles most of them would have rusted into near-total uselessness.

On the brighter side, the Los Angeles County Air Pollution Control District announced that air pollution levels for the basin had dropped dramatically. The air was cleaner than it had been since 1955 when the county finally outlawed backyard incinerators. An awkward spokesman embarrassedly announced that this was the direct result of taking a million and a half vehicles off the road, except that of course, those million and a half vehicles were still *on* the road. Just not moving anymore. But this was the *good* news. It was now safe to breathe in Los Angeles again.

Despite that incentive, the flood of refugees streaming out of the city continued, straining the resources of surrounding counties beyond the breaking point. By now, the first waves of escapees from the zone were spreading out across the continent, bringing with them sordid tales of non-vehicular terror and enough digital camera photos, phone-camera photos, and handycam videos to keep the news agencies happy for weeks.

Even after the continuing live coverage abated and regular programming resumed, the networks still scheduled ongoing special reports. This was as much an opportunity as a necessity. Universal, Warner Bros., Fox, Disney, and Paramount all had their lots within the frozen zone. The production of sixteen major television series had come to a halt, including (ironically) several that were set in locations as far removed as Orange County, Las Vegas, Manhattan, Miami, and Boston. Although there were finished episodes of all prime-time series in the pipeline, once those were aired, new episodes would not be available until new production facilities were established, or until transportation to existing facilities could be resumed.

Every news and current events show from *60 Minutes* to *Nova* began multi-part examinations of the collapse of an entire city, with alarming speculations about the possibility of similar crystallizations occurring elsewhere. Real estate values in small towns and rural areas began to climb.

The days stretched into weeks as refugees continued to stream out of the zone, sometimes as many as a hundred thousand a day. The nightly news kept a running tally on the numbers; the flood showed no signs of abating; but each succeeding day, those who had successfully escaped from L.A. seemed more and more despairing and desperate. While not quite ragged, they looked hungry and haggard, thin and wan. Many had gone for a week or more without fresh fruits and vegetables, fresh milk and other perishables. They had exchanged their tan healthy presence for more sallow dispirited complexions. The surrounding counties continued to absorb as many as they could, exporting the overflow to the rest of the nation as fast as transportation could be arranged. Amtrak borrowed Pullman cars from Canada and Mexico, and converted over a hundred freight cars into makeshift passenger units. A number of Jewish families refused to board anything that looked like a box car.

Entering the fourth week of the disaster, as it became apparent that this was the new normal, disaster recovery teams entering the frozen zone discovered a startling fact—some people had created ways to survive their transformed circumstances. The most amazing finding was that some Angelenos had given up their dependency on their cars and learned how to *walk*. (No, that is not a misprint. The word is *walk*.) Computer analysis of urban residential zones revealed that more than 35% of all residential dwellings in Los Angeles had access to supermarkets, pharmacies, banks, and other essential services within a radius of ten blocks or less. For most of these residents, walking might be an inconvenience, but it was easier than giving up their homes. Reports from the zone suggested that in some places, neighborhoods were reinventing themselves as actual communities.

Satellite maps revealed that fully 10% of those who were refusing to leave their homes were planting gardens in their back yards or on their front lawns. Others were creating a new economy using bicycles and motorcycles to transship goods from subway and light rail stations into the otherwise unreachable interior of the zone. Simulations projected that 20% of the city's population could survive without automobile access, possibly more if enough streets could be cleared so that trucks could deliver goods to local communities—but if enough streets could be cleared, the automobiles would return.

Surprisingly—or maye not so surprisingly—a small but growing number of people liked the new normal, and were starting to voice the opinion that they did *not* want the automobiles to return. They actually liked being able to see the Hollywood Hills clearly. They liked the way the air smelled in the morning. They liked working in the garden, walking to the corner store, actually talking to their neighbors, and living at a less frenetic pace.

Teams of sociologists who studied the phenomenon—now called disvehiclization—observed that it was not simply a rejection of the automobile, but of the entire technological cocoon that had enveloped daily life. The disvehiclized person was also more likely to leave his or her cell phone off, turning it on only for limited periods each day; the disvehiclized person rarely watched television; he or she also cut back on computer time, accessing the Internet only for essential news or shopping services.

But not everybody could afford disvehiclization; it was a luxury of the retired, and of those who could work from their homes. Those who still depended on day jobs could not survive without transportation. While the subway, light-rail, and emergency bus lines were able to provide some measure of service, they were simply not designed to handle the traffic load, nor did they provide the degree of coverage necessary to the entire basin. In the first month alone, over a million people emigrated from Los Angeles to surrounding counties.

In Orange County, rents soared first. Demand far exceeded supply.

Real estate values followed quickly. Automobile sales took off as well, both new and used; individuals who felt their lives were dependent on their mobility were quick to replace their lost cars. For the first few weeks, car dealers all across the nation were shipping as many vehicles as they could into Ventura, San Bernardino, Santa Clarita, and Orange counties.

Commentators have called this influx of additional vehicles onto the avenues and highways of the counties surrounding Los Angeles the "squeezed mud" effect. Squeeze a handful of mud, it oozes out between your fingers; squeeze Los Angeles, and the traffic oozes out in all directions across the state. Cal-Trans now projects that in the post-crystallization era, California will see at least an additional million vehicles on the highways of the four counties surrounding Los Angeles.

Cal-Trans officials are also quick to point out that the recent stoppages on the 22, the 55, and the 91 are only localized anomalies, and not representative of any larger process. There is absolutely no reason to fear crystallization in Orange County. Absolutely no reason at all.

If the previous story wasn't surreal enough, try this one.

THE TROUBLE WITH HAIRY

Afterward, they all agreed it had been a bad idea.

After all the allegations, all the excuses and explanations, all the accusations and apologies, all the recriminations, back and forth—there was enough blame for everyone—and especially after all the indictments, after all of that and more, everyone agreed it had been a very, very bad idea.

But it had seemed like a good idea at the time.

It had begun innocently enough at the 33rd Annual Convention of Convention-Committees. While the panel on Dealing with Difficult People was headed for overtime, because several people on the panel were being difficult, the husband of one of the panelists joined the wife of one of the other panelists in the hotel bar for a circumstance that was as far removed from hanky-panky as is possible for two human beings to achieve.

He was Doctor Verne ("Vernie" for short) Vellum, of the Newport Vellums (third cousin, twice removed), a graduate of the Pepperdine Programming Initiative, sponsored by the Pepperdine Business School.

She was Doctor Janine Pershing, a graduate of the UCLA Department of Medicine, specializing in cardio-pulmonary research and the clotting abilities of blood.

He was presently consulting for Cal-Trans, the California Transit Authority, on ways to manage traffic flow along the city's main arteries.

She was creating a model of the blood flow throughout the human body as a way to predict blood clots, aneurisms, strokes, and other hemolytic disasters.

What happened next was inevitable.

By the time they had finished their third round of Hairy Nilssons—

A Hairy Nilsson is rum and Coke, except it's made with Malibu coconut rum and a twist of lime. You put the lime in the coconut, you drink it all up. If you use diet Coke, it's a half-Nilsson.

—by the time they had finished their third round of Hairy Nilssons, they were both giddy enough to recognize that they were working on the same problem—how do you keep a fluid flowing?

Sometime after the fourth or fifth round of Hairy Nilssons, the light bulb didn't just light up—it exploded in a dazzling shower of sparks. The impossible idea flashed into being like Athena springing full-blown from the forehead of Zeus, and switching metaphors in the middle of the sentence, Pandora's box fell open with an ear-piercing clang. While their respective spouses were vehemently arguing with each other about ways to create peace, Vellum and Pershing were suddenly and drunkenly committing to a collaboration that would have left the average mad scientist weeping with envy. A Bond super-villain could not have dreamt up a better plan.

Now, ordinarily nothing much would have happened after that alcohol-infused conversation—normally, they would have exchanged business cards and forgotten they'd even discussed anything at all until a few days later, when they each got home and unpacked and—upon discovering the business card, would have frowned, trying to remember whose it was and why it had been proffered, might have vaguely remembered, "oh, that"—and then tossing the card aside, would have turned to a much more important question: "What's for dinner?"

Except this time, no.

Before they had gotten to the mandatory exchange of business cards and the necessary false promises—"We should get together soon"—they were joined by a fellow named Gonder O'Conner, an elemental of greed, a seducer of the unwary, an unfrocked Irishman who had made a career out of drinking various naïve American celebrities under the table and then convincing them to endorse whatever enterprise he was currently peddling to the unwary—whether it was a failed reboot of a cancelled TV series or an internet portal for dot-com investors. He was not so much a businessman as a wannabe-entrepreneur with either a terrible toupee or a very bad touch-up of his comb-over, no one was ever certain which.

Gonder said the magic words. "This could be worth a lot of money."

And with that single phrase, the genie was popped out of the bottle and what followed after was inevitable. Gonder took both their business cards, formed an LLC in Nevada the following Monday, created a logo and printed stationery on Tuesday, and issued a press release on Thursday. (Wednesday he went painting in the Louvre?)

Well, it seemed like a good idea at the time. That's the trouble with Hairy Nilssons. Everything seems like a good idea at the time.

Sometimes the ideas are good.

Like, for instance—

Why don't you put some of your peanut butter in my chocolate? Why don't you put some of your chocolate in my peanut butter? That worked out okay.

But sometimes the ideas aren't good. New Coke. Windows Vista. Jar Jar Binks.

Gonder O'Conner went to the Los Angeles City Hall with his proposal. He stood up before the City Council and explained that there was a scientific answer to the city's traffic problems and that—

Okay, to be fair—there were a few people who were skeptical of the proposal.

But Gonder, to his credit, was a skilled talker, if nothing else. Rumor had it that he was the illegitimate grandson of the man who sold refrigerators to Eskimos—as a way to keep their food warm against subzero Arctic temperatures.

After his proposal to the City Council, Gonder O'Conner held a press conference on the steps of the Los Angeles City Hall. "Imagine that the city of Los Angeles is a vast living organism. Her highways are her arteries, bringing nourishment from the farthest reaches of the globe. Her streets and avenues are the capillaries that feed the tissues of the city. Her institutions are organs providing services, water, electricity, police, and fire. All the stores, all the services, every park and museum and library, every bank and barber shop—every business, every dwelling, all of the separate entities—each and every one is a living cell that needs access to the nourishment that flows on the city's roads."

The few reporters who showed up stifled their yawns, collected the official press releases, and returned to their various newspapers, weeklies, magazines, television and radio stations, filed their stories and promptly forgot about Los Angeles as a living organism.

Yes. In theory, it sounded good.

In theory, there is no difference between theory and practice. In practice, there is.

The Mayor of Los Angeles, a tall black woman named Violet Kopanski, wasn't just smart, she was politically astute enough to know how to bury a good idea before it became a dangerous one. She convinced the city council to form a study group, a commission, a scientific advisory board. Call it what you will—the quickest way to kill any idea is to turn it over to a committee. The smarter the members of the committee, the more certain it is that the idea will be picked apart in a feeding frenzy of intellectual vultures, leaving only a few scattered bones for the conspiracy theorists to sniff and gnaw.

Sidebar: conspiracy theorists are like paleontologists who find a fossilized tooth and construct a whole dinosaur skeleton based on that tooth—never pausing to consider that it might very well have come from a creature that would have benefited from a skilled application of Jurassic orthodonture. (Never mind, the metaphor has gotten way out of control and is now stomping through the downtown paragraph, terrifying all the various nouns to go screaming like little verbs into panicky flight, one fraught with dangerous adjectives.)

But getting back to the primary narrative, Mayor Kopanski was right—unfortunately, her timing was awful. Three days later, just enough time for the news cycle to turn its attention to the latest ill-considered remark from a politician who had never realized that her fifteen minutes had ended several years previously, the thing happened.

Carmageddon.

Crystallization.

Gridblock.

A terrorist attack—a pattern of deliberate disruptions, specifically designed to create such unprecedented interruptions in the flow of traffic that the entire city was brought to an absolute standstill. More than six million cars idling in place, from the grapevine to the Orange crush, with additional backups stretching all the way to the border-crossing south of San Diego, each and every one of them farting ever more noxious pollutants into an already overloaded atmosphere.

LA residents reading that sentence will not shudder—that's a normal business day in the region. (Readers unfamiliar with the terrain will have to google a map.) But this was worse than they imagined. Indeed—it was worse than they could imagine.

Because it wasn't accidental.

A group of anti-socialist, libertarian free-marketers, who refused to recognize the federal government's authority to build an interstate highway system had decided to shut it down. Actually, that was their Plan B.

Plan A had been to seize control of the 405 and liberate it in the name of the people.

The leader of the group was Hammond Brody, a USC dropout who began by idolizing Che Guevara and ended up arguing that Charles Manson had been denied his civil rights and railroaded by a kangaroo court. Brody styled himself a modern cowboy—he had the hat and the boots to match and a pearl-handled pistol stuck into his belt in such a way that if he hadn't kept the safety on, the hair-trigger would have removed that part of his body he liked almost as much as his gun.

But after he and his two sons, and a couple of his hench-thugs, were caught in a six-hour traffic jam between LAX and the Getty Center off-ramp, it occurred to him that a massive traffic jam was a far more potent weapon for shutting down the viability of the federal infrastructure. And also a lot easier to maintain than a seizure of forty miles of superslab.

Brody's group had originally been called the Conscientious Revolution of Angry Patriots—and under that name they had gathered nearly three hundred followers, but when it came time to design a logo, someone reluctantly pointed out that the resulting acronym was probably not the best. After several weeks of arguing about the goals and direction of their cause (a process that would have made a great case study for the panel on Dealing With Difficult People, if they could have had access to the process), Brody's followers reformed as a network of study groups and changed their name to Revolutionary American Patriots, the Institute of Social Theory and Structure.

Well, not really study groups.

Independent cells.

You know, like the Communist Party, the John Birch Society, and the Science Fiction (and Fantasy) Writers of America—the primary purpose of a cellular institutional structure is to keep every member of the conspiracy from knowing who else was in the conspiracy or what they were up to, thus making it impossible for any authority to roll up the entire organization.

Brody's group operated in almost total secrecy—well, except for the three undercover FBI agents who had infiltrated the group, a reporter from the LA Weekly, several Scientologists looking for suppressives, and two recovering alcoholics who'd wandered into the wrong meeting and stayed for the doughnuts, not to mention the gay stalker who had fixated on one of Brody's sons—

Anyway, somehow they developed a plan.

Or maybe they were enticed into a plan.

Leaping ahead to a point several years after the event, the rest of the story came out when a government report was leaked to the internet by a dissident group of disgruntled hackers who'd been expelled from Anonymous. This group, known as Pseudonymous, dumped a cascade of classified documents onto the World Wide Web. Most of the documents were so boring as to barely cause a flicker in the needle of public outrage—but the reports dealing with the Gridblock Event suggested that two of the FBI agents had been involved not only in the brainstorming process, but had actively aided in the design, the development, the preparation, and the scheduling of the entire operation.

That leak resulted in a series of publicly embarrassing congressional investigations and the resignations of several high-ranking government officials. Fortunately, this focused all of their attentions so tightly they had no time left for creating larger and more substantial problems for the nation.

The documents also revealed exactly how the Gridblock Event occurred.

The plan was simple. It required only a few dozen disposable secondhand vehicles, capable of just enough mobility to get up a carefully selected on-ramp—and a few dozen naïfs to pilot them.

Think about it.

A single accident is enough to cause a five mile backup on any Los Angeles freeway. If you could arrange thirty or forty or fifty well-placed accidents at key bottlenecks and chokepoints, all of them occurring simultaneously, you could shut down the entire traffic system. You could block 527 miles of freeway in Los Angeles County and another 382 miles of conventional highway—not to mention most of the alternate routes and surface streets. You would paralyze the entire region.

Thirty million gallons of gasoline would be burned by six million idling cars, SUVs, vans, buses, trucks, and Priuses that had exhausted their batteries. Ten million tons of pollutants would be pumped into the atmosphere.

Millions of people would be late for work, late for meetings, late for dinner. Millions of people would soil themselves because they couldn't get to a bathroom. Fistfights would break out. Some people would have heart attacks. Other people would have babies. Even more would have panic attacks, seizures, and a few would even go into diabetic comas. People would die.

Genius. Sheer genius.

Start a car fire in the Orange Crush. Get a flat tire and block the transition lanes from the 405 to the 101. Do the same at the downtown interchange. Blow up an engine at the top of the Sepulveda pass. Crash two SUVs together at the Century Boulevard off-ramp, blocking access to LAX. Do the same where the 5 branches off to the Glendale Freeway. Paralyze the 134 where it feeds into the 170 and the 101. Paralyze the other end of the 134 where it feeds into the 5. Add a few accidents to the Hollywood Freeway, a couple more to the 10, the 110, the 710, and the 605—and don't forget the 60 and the 105 either. The 90...? Piece of apple strudel.

What fun.

Hammond Brody, one of his sons, the gay stalker, and one of the FBI agents spent a week and a half driving the highways and byways of Los Angeles County, everything from Long Beach to Chatsworth, from Azusa to Agoura, marking choke points and bottlenecks on the pages of an old Rand McNally roadmap. (Exhibit 42 in the government's case.)

They almost blew it.

They were pulled over three times by the California Highway Patrol. Once for a busted left tail light, once because the FBI agent tossed a Taco Bell wrapper out the passenger side window, and the third time for an expired registration. The first time they got a fix-it ticket and assorted failure to wear seatbelt tickets, the second time they got a littering ticket and assorted failure to wear seatbelt tickets, and the third time they nearly had the car impounded—except that Hammond Brody had the paperwork for the renewed registration in the glove compartment, he'd just forgotten to install the colored registration tab on the upper right corner of the license plate, so they had to settle for a third set of failure to wear seatbelt tickets. (And those are expensive, too.)

If any of the three ticketing officers had aspired to become detectives, they would have paid closer attention to the hurried shuffling of papers in the back seat of the vehicle. But one was three weeks short of retirement (in any other story, that would have been a death sentence), a second was thinking about his upcoming wedding, and the third was thinking about his upcoming divorce.

After that, the rest of the implementation of the grand plan proceeded without interruption. Each study group—each cell—was presented with a specific task. Procure a vehicle. When you are given the go-ahead signal, you will crash it or set it on fire, or otherwise disable it at this precise location at this specific time on the given day.

No cell was aware that any other cell had been given the same instructions, albeit a different target location. Each operative was led to believe that their accident was a targeted bit of revenge against a local jurisdiction. Or maybe a loyalty test. Or something. Stop asking questions, just do what you're told. You don't need to know what you don't need to know.

Brilliant.

And it worked.

Now, to be fair—the FBI had planned to apprehend Hammond Brody and his sons, and the various cells they had identified (which was most of them) on the day before the go-ahead signal was to be sent out.

Unfortunately . . .

Due to a scheduling conflict with a major sporting event, CBS had moved Hammond Brody's favorite television show, The Golden Girls: The Next Generation, to a different night—and because Hammond Brody wanted to be home in time to catch the season finale, he moved the plan up two days without telling anyone and sent out the go-ahead signal at two in the morning while almost everybody was tucked away safe in their beds.

At 3:37 p.m., Pacific Daylight Time . . . Gridblock began.

It went off better than Hammond Brody could have wished for—not just because of his somewhat inelegant planning, but also because there were so many volunteers who joined in the fun, inadvertently adding their own stalled, disabled, and crashed vehicles to the resultant urbanicide.

Among the volunteers were several motorcyclists who made the mistake of believing that they were immune to the gridlock, because of the ease with which their lanesplitting allowed them to zip through lines of stopped automobiles. They discovered the hard way that they were not as immune as they believed, when stalled motorists inadvertently opened their driver-side doors at the wrong moment, bringing those motorcyclists to very unfortunate sudden stops.

The Fire and Emergency Medivac helicopters were kept busy for the first several hours—at least until most of the cell phone batteries among the affected drivers stopped producing a flow of usable electrons. After that, passengers and drivers began abandoning their vehicles where they were and hiked to the nearest off-ramp. Local restaurants and motels appreciated the influx of new business, at least while there were still rooms to rent and burgers to fry. Without resupply, they quickly ran out of perishables.

Local grocery stores fared somewhat better. Their supplies of perishables lasted for two or three days before the shelves began to look thin.

Some of the worst problems occurred at Los Angeles International Airport. That had been targeted with six separate chokepoint incidents. With no way for departing passengers to arrive and arriving passengers to depart, very quickly the terminals began to look like a crowded refugee camp. The smarter arrivals booked themselves onto departing planes for San Diego, Santa Barbara, Ontario, and other nearby venues in the hopes of finding ground transportation to their desired destinations. Or they just collected their baggage—if possible—and flew home.

The worst of the traffic jams lasted six days—partly because emergency vehicles could not reach the affected areas. Military helicopters had to lift out many of the crashed and burned vehicles.

Normalcy never returned. Ridership on buses, trains, and the—really? LA has a subway?—increased by nearly four hundred percent, overloading the capacity of those systems almost to the breaking point.

And in the uproar that followed, the City Council had to demonstrate it was on top of the situation—they had to come up with a plan to prevent future shutdowns of the city's arteries.

Unfortunately, they had what looked like a plan.

And yes, it did seem like a good idea at the time.

Even though the Vellum-Pershing algorithms had not yet been fully tested, the surviving drivers of Los Angeles were impatient enough to demand immediate action. The City Council, never known for either its courage or its speed, in the face of such pressure, managed to demonstrate at least one of these attributes—unfortunately, the wrong one.

The city's traffic control computers were shortly reprogrammed with Doctors Vellum and Pershing's algorithms to regulate traffic flow as an organic process. The system went live at midnight of August 13th—a Friday.

The first test of the system occurred almost immediately—at 12:13 a.m., two street racers, a souped-up 2012 Honda CRX and a 1994 Chevy Corvette collided with a large truck at the Balboa off-ramp of the 101 in Encino. Despite the late hour, or perhaps because of it—various local events were just concluding—traffic began backing up almost immediately. By the time cars were slowing down on the 405 north and south connector ramps, as well as on the 101 as far east as Van Nuys Boulevard, the traffic control system flagged the event as equivalent to a blood clot in a major artery and sent in the white blood cells to repair the damage.

Oops.

That was the part of the algorithm that hadn't been . . . um, what's a polite euphemism . . . fully vetted.

See, on the second day of the Gridblock, United States Army General Daisy Cutler transferred control of four dozen military drones to the Los Angeles Traffic Control system for monitoring purposes. It had seemed like a good idea at the time, really, but General Cutler did not even have the mitigating circumstance of four Hairy Nilssons to motivate her decision.

Control of those drones had not been returned to the army.

The Vellum-Pershing algorithm saw those drones as white blood cells.

The white blood cells rushed to the site of the blood clot.

And—well, you see . . . in the rush to get eyes in the sky, only a few of those drones had been disarmed—they promptly targeted the offending vehicles and with the precision only a finely tuned military drone can achieve, initiated a surgical strike and blew the offending vehicles off the road, drivers and all.

In the aftermath, there was some official tongue-clucking about the death of the truck driver as unfortunate collateral damage, but most observers felt that the two young street racers had received what they rightfully deserved.

However . . .

Two things happened:

First . . .

Because subsequent traffic jams were treated as blood clots and as public concern began to grow, traffic suddenly became a lot safer. The incidence of reckless driving decreased significantly, enough so that the city of Los Angeles actually experienced two consecutive rush hours without a single fender bender or bumper jumper. The possibility of flaming death from the sky, without the interference of judge, jury, or predatory lawyers, had so terrified tailgaters, speeders, weavers, racers, chasers, and assorted drunks, that driving in Los Angeles actually became occasionally—well, not pleasant, but tolerable.

Second . . .

Local auto repair shops reported a sudden spike in maintenance requests. Several tire stores ran out of stock. Auto dealers had to schedule service appointments to manage the increased demand. New car sales upticked.

The Los Angeles economy boomed.

When accidents did happen, as soon as it became obvious that passing automobiles were slowing, as soon as it became apparent that traffic was going to back up—which was an inevitable phenomenon in Los Angeles, due to the high percentage of drivers who'd never seen an accident before and had to slow down to get a better look—the drivers of the affected cars would grab their belongings, their purses, bags of groceries, cell phones, dogs, and children, and start running, hoping to put as much distance as possible between themselves and the accident before the drones arrived.

Some were lucky, others not.

Collateral damage.

Too bad.

They shouldn't have had that accident in the first place.

At first, there were some grumblings. There are always people who are resistant to change, but most Angelenos adapted very quickly to the new normal—for one very simple reason: the number of traffic deaths had fallen dramatically. From an actuarial point of view, the system worked.

The insurance companies loved the new reality. Fewer accidents meant fewer claims—the infrequent claim for the total destruction of a vehicle was less than a few dozen claims for the minor damage of the average collision.

There were side effects, of course. There are always side effects. The families of the deceased were quick to file lawsuits against the city, but the Gordian tangle of nested paperwork and filings, all the various forms of red tape, the concentric layers of impacted bureaucracy, not to mention all the interconnected holding companies and shell corporations constructed by Gonder O'Conner and two of his purchased allies on the City Council's newly created board to manage the Regulated Autonomous Traffic System, meant that very few of the lawsuits would ever be resolved within the lifespan of the plaintiffs. Besides, the lawyers loved the sinecure of a steady income.

So, all in all—unless you were one of those unfortunates who got removed from the gene pool, and in that case you were in no position to offer an opinion anyway—what had seemed like a good idea in theory had actually worked out to be a good idea in practice. Unless, of course, well . . . you know. But collateral damage and all that.

Until . . .

Two events.

The first was a stalled school bus. Not one of those big yellow ones that carry fifty or sixty students at a time—this was one of those short yellow ones that carry less than a dozen children. The special ones.

Afterward, a large crowd of enraged parents descended on City Hall demanding the resignations of the Mayor, the entire City Council, Doctors Vellum and Pershing, Gonder O'Conner, and everyone else they blamed for the tragedy. Speakers representing the Asian community, the Latino community, and the African-American community all demanded a federal investigation—and indictments.

It was ugly.

It got even uglier when one of the defenders of the Regulated Autonomous Traffic System said, "If we weren't going to outlaw guns after the Sandy Hook shooting—and that was the deaths of twenty children— then why the hell do you think we're going to do anything after the deaths of only eleven?"

That's when the first chair was thrown.

Additional protests were scheduled against the weekend's presidential fund-raiser. An even larger group of enraged parents, many from more affluent areas of the city, suddenly concerned about the safety of their own children, were now demanding federal intervention.

That was when the second incident occurred.

A presidential motorcade requires the hosting city to create a bubble in the traffic flow. There's the presidential limousine. Then there are the limos of all the various attendants and aides and others invited to ride along. Then there are the secret service vehicles ahead and behind. And then there are the police escorts ahead and behind. And no other traffic is allowed anywhere near.

The system, the program, the bloody algorithm saw this as an air bubble in an artery.

Air bubbles are potentially fatal.

At the center of the air bubble was the presidential limo.

Not having an option for dealing with air bubbles, the traffic algorithm decided instead that it was observing a moving blood clot, one that seemed to be heading for the heart of the city.

Three drones, patrolling the eastbound 10 between the 405 and downtown, headed directly for the motorcade, triggering alarms everywhere. Two of them were shot down by the stealth helicopters that patrolled the airspace above the presidential motorcade. The third was able to launch two Hellfire missiles, which—due to significant tracking errors, as the Hellfire algorithms had not been written for moving targets—missed the presidential motorcade and hit a Pepsi-Cola truck instead on the westbound side of the freeway, just past the Crenshaw Boulevard off-ramp.

That the Los Angeles traffic control system was not shut down immediately was another comedy of errors. (Comedy of errors is the polite way of saying "clusterfuck.")

Several technicians charged with monitoring the drones had been watching the whole incident unfold in real time. As soon as they realized that an attack on the presidential motorcade was impending, they tried to override the drones' controls and abort the strike—but the drones had limited autonomy, just enough to reject unauthorized overrides.

As soon as the horrorstruck monitors of the system realized what had happened, they panicked. Several fled the building. One even fled the country, fearing reprisals and the inevitable accusation of terrorism because of his Muslim faith.

The fire department had to shut down power to the entire building and then disable two emergency generators before the system went down and the drones obediently returned to base.

Threatening the President of the United States is a Class E felony, punishable by up to 5 years in prison, a $250,000 maximum fine, a $100 special assessment, and 3 years of supervised release. Actually shooting a president is a capital offense—unless you miss. Then it's just a really, really, really bad felony. The kind that gets you put away for life. Unless the judge is lenient. Then you only get sentenced to a few hundred years in prison.

The Attorney General of the United States filed over a hundred and fifty-three separate indictments, citing the entire City Council as defendants for "creating a conspiracy of collective stupidity."

In particular, Doctors Vellum and Pershing, Gonder O'Conner, Mayor Violet Kopanski, all of the programmers, and everyone else who had collected a RATS paycheck, were brought up on charges. Additionally, just to be thorough, anyone who'd come anywhere near the project was indicted as an involuntary accomplice, although charges were eventually dropped for most of the lower-level technicians—except for the monitors on duty at the time.

"But I was only following orders," was not accepted as a defense plea.

The primary architects of the debacle were tried and convicted and sentenced to the maximum the law would allow.

Hammond Brody and family were charged as senior conspirators, in league with Doctors Vellum and Pershing—despite the total lack of evidence proving that any such link existed. Life sentences without parole.

Doctors Vellum and Pershing were likewise sentenced, with the additional restriction that neither of them were ever to be allowed access to any electronic device more complicated than a light switch.

Gonder O'Conner disappeared mysteriously, and although rumor had it he had been spotted living in Argentina, a more credible theory had him buried somewhere beneath the recently repaved parking lot of the new sports stadium in Inglewood.

Mayor Kopanski died of a heart attack while awaiting trial. Due to a paperwork error, her body was cremated before an autopsy could be performed.

General Daisy Cutler was not indicted—although she was court-martialed for unauthorized transfer of army property for civilian use. She was allowed to resign at rank. Elsewhere, certain military engineers and programmers were quietly assigned to study the failure of the missiles to hit their targets. One hundred and thirty-seven million dollars were allocated to find and fix the cause of the errors, so that next time, if there was a next time, the accuracy of the nation's defense technology would not become a public embarrassment.

The Bloody Algorithm, as it came to be known, was wiped from the Los Angeles Traffic Control Computers and the Regulated Autonomous Traffic System was consigned to the trash heap of history, along with

8-track tapes, floppy disks, Instamatic cameras, and folding maps.

Within a week, traffic in Los Angeles returned to normal—that is, the previous normal.

A trip from the northwest end of the San Fernando Valley to anywhere south of Anaheim was once again a four hour drive. Regardless of which freeway you took. And that was on a good day.

One more thing—bartenders throughout the state were quietly advised to discourage customers from ordering Hairy Nilssons.

And that was a very good idea.

THE GREAT PAN AMERICAN AIRSHIP MYSTERY
or
WHY I MURDERED ROBERT BENCHLEY

After all is said and done, I blame Nikola Tesla.

It's his fault.

Because—if we're going to talk about cause and effect, then we have to go all way the back to the original cause.

No, Nikola Tesla did not set out to invent an efficient method of low-cost helium extraction, it was a side-effect of his coal-fusion research, but if he hadn't discovered it, no one else would have. At least not in our lifetimes.

Tesla often gave away many of his discoveries, but not this one—he patented the helium extraction process. The technology that followed created so many new industries and opportunities for profit that it pushed Tesla's own company into the Fortune 500 within 18 months.

Knowing that Tesla was unlikely to invest in lawyers and lawsuits, patent violations started cropping up everywhere. The Third Reich, for instance, began extracting their own helium from the Ruhr, the large coal fields located in the west of Germany in North Rhine-Westphalia—they used the helium to lift over a dozen huge vessels, all modeled after the luxurious Hindenburg.

Not to be outdone, the United States Congress created the National Aeronautics Studies Administration—NASA for short—to fund research and development in aerial transport.

Three years later, in June of 1937, The Great Pan American Airship

Line began operations at their expansive new terminal on Welfare Island. Due to rising international tensions, as well as considerable domestic pressures against foreign competition, the trans-Atlantic German airships would be restricted to the airfield at Lakehurst, New Jersey.

To demonstrate America's commitment to a new age of aerial transportation, Pan Am announced the inaugural journey of their magnificent new flagship would be a coast-to-coast celebrity cruise. They held a nationwide contest to choose the name of the vessel they had nicknamed The Big Lady, and three lucky contestants would win berths on the first trip to prove that economical air travel for everyone was now a reality.

At 11:33 am on Thursday morning, June 3rd, 1937, First Lady, Eleanor Roosevelt officially christened the vessel in a grand ceremony and the Pan American flagship *Liberty* lifted majestically into the air while the United States Marine Band played *America, The Beautiful.* The Chorus of St. Patrick's Cathedral accompanied and WNBC broadcast the event on nationwide radio. RCA also broadcast an experimental television signal originating from the top of the Empire State Building. Receivers at Grand Central Terminal showed a grainy image of the *Liberty*'s liftoff, although most people could have simply stepped outside onto 42nd street or Fifth Avenue for a better view.

Three times larger than the Hindenburg, she was a gleaming silver illusion. She circled Manhattan island three times while tugboats below thumped their horns, fireboats howled their sirens and sprayed jets of water, and Mayor La Guardia read a poem of salute by Robert Frost on the WNBC radio station.

Most people assumed that circling Manhattan was a salute to the city. Actually, it was an opportunity for Captain Bradley to test all the systems of the airship, one after the other, and reassure himself that everything was operating up to spec. It was a second shakedown cruise, unofficial but necessary. Coming around Battery Park for the third time, finally satisfied that the ship was handling the way he wanted, he spun the wheel to the left and the "Big Lady"—her affectionate nickname—turned gracefully to port. She was now officially on her way. We passed over the Statue of Liberty and out across New Jersey.

Aboard the vessel, a host of Broadway and Hollywood celebrities waved to the crowds below. George Jessel, Al Jolson, George and Ira Gershwin, and George M. Cohan, waved from the portside windows. Dorothy Parker, F. Scott Fitzgerald, Robert Benchley, George S. Kaufman,

Heywood Broun, Alexander Woollcott, and several other members of the notorious Algonquin Round Table waved from the starboard side. Also aboard were Charles Lindbergh, Amelia Earhart, and William "Billy" Mitchell. 65-year-old Orville Wright had been invited as well, but had politely declined. He still believed the foolish idea that heavier-than-air vessels would become the primary vehicle of modern air travel and felt it would be hypocritical to lend his name or support to this journey. Tesla had also declined the invitation, saying there was nothing in San Francisco to interest him right now.

Less notable, several high-ranking members of the army and navy were also among the complement of passengers, but much less conspicuous. They seemed more concerned with the operational aspects of the *Liberty* than with the promotional aspects of the journey.

Pan Am's official statements asserted that the average air-speed of the Big Lady would be 85 miles per hour, and that the non-stop voyage would take no more than 36 hours. The Big Lady would be going around the south end of the Rocky Mountains rather than over. But some of the engineers were betting that Captain Bradley would push the engines hard, hoping to average more than 100mph—as well as crossing *over* the peaks to give the passengers a spectacular view of the mountaintops, ultimately arriving at San Francisco at 10:30 A.M. the next day, a journey of only 26 hours. If that did happen, then despite traveling more than 24 hours, we would still arrive an hour earlier than our departure time, an artifact of our westward passage through three time zones.

Heading west over New Jersey, many of the passengers still crowded the windows and speculated about the crowds below. Tiny people came running out of their houses and their businesses, shouting and pointing and staring skyward. They cheered and hollered and waved. When the shadow of the *Liberty* passed over, some of them panicked. We saw a few small children crying, they were carried inside by their reassuring mothers—where they promptly leaned out of the upstairs windows to stare again.

After a half-hour or so, after the second or third tray of drinks had been passed around, the Gershwins commandeered the piano in the salon and started playing. Later, Oscar Levant took over the piano, providing accompaniment for Cohan, Jessel, and Jolson as they worked their inebriated way through an impromptu medley of popular songs.

When they finally tired out, Jack Benny, and Fred Allen began trading quips—it started with Fred Allen asking Jack Benny why he hated the violin so much that he kept playing it. Benny responded with an observation that bags under Fred Allen's eyes were so big they required their own porters. Allen replied that Jack Benny couldn't ad-lib a belch after a plate of Hungarian goulash. Benny promptly turned to him and grumped, "You wouldn't say that if my writers were here."

I wished his writers were aboard as well. I would have loved to have met them. I assumed they would be very funny men.

I was—at that time—a guest relations steward aboard the *Liberty*. My job was to keep the customers happy for the nearly two days it would take to travel the 2600 miles from New York to San Francisco—actually a bit more, because our course would zig-zag a bit to fly over several important cities and landmarks. That meant maintaining the well-being of everyone onboard who assumed they were entitled to special treatment—and that was everyone onboard. In the case of my specific charges, that mostly involved keeping them drunk enough to be cheerful, but not so drunk as to be uncontrollable. Passed-out was not an option.

But holding a tray of martinis was not my career goal. I intended to bootstrap my career by writing a memoir of this adventure. I planned to sell articles wherever I could to establish a name for myself.

I was already making notes for a profile of the celebrity doings for *Life Magazine*, a revealing slice of salacious gossip for *The New Yorker*, a report on the amenities of a flying hotel for *Popular Science*, a complementary article about the maintenance of the onboard necessities for *Scientific American*, a description of how well the six electric propellors performed for *Popular Mechanics*, and possibly even—I'd have to do it under a pen name—a futuristic story for *Astounding* about a giant passenger vessel journeying through outer space to Venus or Mars—I just needed a plot.

I had to trade a few favors, including a couple of sexual ones (that was fun), but I did get myself assigned to take care of the Algonquin Round Table crowd—that might have happened anyway. It turned out they were a boisterous group, hard to deal with, and none of the other stewards wanted to acommodate them and all of their shenanigans. A couple of the Algonquin group were putting away enough booze that their breaths had become flammable. I expected—hoped—that after they settled in and became comfortable that they would start discussing important literary issues.

Lunch was delayed because of the unscheduled performances—none of the staff were brave enough to interrupt the entertainers, the rest of the passengers would have dropped us out the nearest window, so we didn't serve until we were well over eastern Pennsylvania and Oscar Levant remarked, "You can smell the cheese even from up here."

We weren't that high, he could have been right. The *Liberty* cruised below the clouds, usually only three or four hundred feet above the ground, mostly so passengers could have a great view of the landscape, but she was engineered to go much higher. Tanks of pressurized helium gas were stored along her keel to inflate additional lifting ballonets when more altitude was needed—such as flying over a mountain. To descend again, the extra helium would be released, or pumped back into the storage tanks. Large tanks of water were also used for ballast. This was the same water that passengers would use for washing. If the *Liberty* needed altitude quickly, it could be released in a massive shower. By the time it hit the ground, it would be little more than a mist. At worst, a momentary drizzle.

The *Liberty* carried 200 passengers and 85 crewmembers. By comparison, a Hindenburg-class ship could carry only 72 passengers and required 62 crewmembers to manage the journey. The *Liberty* had been designed to carry 400 souls, but Pan Am was using the inaugural journey to demonstrate the large cargo carrying capacity of the *Liberty* as well. A half-dozen new Fords were stored in her hold. None of the military officers would discuss it, but more than once I saw them scribbling numbers on yellow pads and arguing about balancing the weights of tanks, trucks, cannons, troops, and supplies.

Cross-country shipping by railroad could take anywhere from three days to two weeks, depending on how much you wanted to pay. For some industries, air transport would be both faster and cheaper—like fresh fruits and vegetables from the California fields to the New York markets. And then there were those lucrative mail contracts to consider.

After lunch, some of the passengers retired to their cabins to rest up for the rigors of dinner. The cabins were spacious and well-equipped, deliberately more luxurious than those found on any ocean-liner where space would be at a premium. The opposite was true aboard the *Liberty*. Here, weight was the limiting factor, not space.

Only the control gondola hung below the body of the craft, I'd delivered coffee and sandwiches to it on our training flight, it was a broad comfortable platform. All the other passenger and crew spaces were in-side the *Liberty's* envelope. Because a massive framework of aluminum girders and steel tension cables was needed to provide a stable structure for the huge array of giant lift bags, there was also considerable space beneath the ballonets for accommodations. There was almost too much space.

When Tallulah Bankhead boarded, she looked around the lobby and asked the nearest steward—me—"What time does this place reach San Francisco?" She had the most amazing voice, as deep and husky as a vel-vet martini. Then she stared into my eyes and asked, "Who do I have to fuck to get a drink?" You can bet that sent me scurrying.

The interior of the airship and all of her trim and accessories, were decorated in the latest Art Deco style—Streamline Moderne—very light and bright, all minimalist and futuristic, exactly the statement Pan Am wanted to make. Willliam F. Lamb, one of the principle designers of the Empire State Building, had supervised the design of the passenger spaces of the airship. He was also onboard, somewhere.

A broad salon stretched across the front of the aircraft, outlined by a terrifyingly open horseshoe of glass. This was the main gathering place for the passengers. It was almost too sprawling, too wide, too open, it felt cavernous. Huge windows stretched across the front of the deck and circled wide around both sides—that and the high ceiling gave the whole chamber a broad spacious feeling, much like Hollywood's conception of a blissful afterlife.

A second level of walkways circled the high windows so every passen-ger could have a grand view without ever having to crowd. All of them would be able to observe the ground easily through the large downward-angled panes. The sheer size of those glass walls made it feel as if we were not within a vessel, but simply drifting along on an airy platform, as removed from the mundane cares of the world as the gods of Olympus—well, we were—but the sense of a heavenly condition was deliberate. We floated gracefully across the sky, trailing a massive shadow across the ground below, a visible reminder of the *Liberty's* astonishing size.

Across the main floor of the salon, there were step-up levels for service areas and step-down levels of various sizes for gatherings of passengers to discuss common interests. The chairs and couches were upholstered in muted shades of red, silver, and blue—all very Pan American. The floor was carpeted in a lighter blue, a reflection of the sky. The walls were eggshell-white with gold trim. Silvery murals portrayed Lady Liberty in a variety of heroic poses.

Just aft of the salon was spacious dining hall. Behind that was a selection of smaller spaces, a cozier bar, a reading room, a smoking lounge for gentlemen, and a corresponding lounge reserved especially for the ladies. For overseas flights, the billiards room would be converted to a small casino. Further back, the airship contained a motion picture theater, a gymnasium, a quiet reading room stocked with many current magazines and a selection of popular books, even a bowling alley and a tennis court, and other lightweight amenities to alleviate the tedium of a long voyage. There was almost too much acreage on the main deck. The designers had run out of ideas before they had run out of space.

The original blueprints had included a swimming pool, with the water in it doubling as ballast. At the last moment, the airline had postponed the installation. It wasn't the weight of the water that concerned the engineers, it was the weight of the support structure of the pool and all the additional plumbing and pumps and filters needed to maintain it. The pool hadn't been completely ruled out, but the accountants at Pan Am had successfully argued that the loadweight could be more profitably used for cargo, and the company was still weighing the pros and cons.

After Pennsylvania, we headed across Lake Erie. Captain Bradley diverted course slightly south so that people all across the northern shore of Ohio—Cleveland, Lorain, Sandusky, and finally Toledo—could see the *Liberty* and cheer and wave. Beneath us, more boats tooted their horns and people waved flags and banners to catch our attention. Many of the passengers went to the windows to wave back.

But not the Round Table group. They had gathered themselves near the bar again and were proceeding to work their way through pitchers of martinis, as well as a heated discussion of something they called, "writer's block." That sounded promising. As a burgeoning author myself, I hoped to learn some of the wisdom of the sages, especially the hard part. How do you get the words onto the page?

Sometime after lunch, Dorothy Parker sent a radiogram to her editor: "I have not forgotten you. I have only forgotten to write the article."

Two hours later, her editor wired back. I brought the radiogram to her myself. She plucked it from the tray, took a puff off her cigarette, and opened it nonchalantly. I had never seen anyone open a radiogram so nonchalantly before. She must have received so many of them in her career that she took them for granted. She looked around at the rest of the group. "He says," she said, and read it aloud. "'Put down the damn martini and find a typewriter. Benchley has one. He never goes anywhere without it, even if he has no intention of using it.'" She frowned across the table. "Is that true, Robert?"

Benchley had the good grace to look embarrassed. "Well, yes. It's impossible to procrastinate properly without a typewriter."

Mrs. Parker looked up at me, still waiting with the tray held out. "Are you waiting for a tip?"

Yes, ma'am. But I didn't say it aloud. "Will there be a reply?"

"No. Yes. Send this back. 'Benchley and typewriter defenestrated over—" She frowned. "Where are we? Oh, it doesn't matter. Defenestrate him over someplace interesting. No, make that boring. Oh, never mind. He'll have to look up defenestrate and he hates looking things up. Begone now."

I bewent.

I bewent all the way back to my station next to the bar. As much as I would have liked to eavesdrop on their conversation, it would have been rude—and against the rules. I was only allowed to approach if summoned by a gesture, or if I was emptying ash trays.

Nevertheless, snatches of conversation still floated over to the bar, enough to suggest that the topic of writer's block was still circling the conversation like a maiden aunt.

Because lunch had been delayed for more than an hour, dinner was also delayed, but only thirty minutes. We were over the northern part of Indiana when the sun touched the horizon ahead of us. Oscar Levant advised against looking out the windows at the broad plains of Indiana. "It's only the people we fly over."

The entire meal service was scheduled for ninety minutes. Soup, salad, fish, three kinds of carvery meat, dessert, coffee, and after-dinner drinks. The Algonquin crew managed to stretch it out to two and a half hours. By the time they finally heaved themselves laboriously from their chairs, it was nine o'clock and we were approaching the Chicago flyover. The city was a bright sprawl of lights ahead, searchlights sweeping the sky.

As we approached, we could hear music coming from a band on the pier, but the distance kept it from being clear or identifiable. It sounded like a badly-tuned radio. According to Fred Allen it was "an excited crowd of bagpipers, accordion-players, and Jack Benny fans." Beside him, Benny replied, "I'm having trouble seeing your fans, Fred. Are there any?"

Over the city, we were blinded by searchlights hitting us from the ground, they blazed up at us from everywhere, especially along the shoreline and the major boulevards. "It looks like a dozen Hollywood premieres," said Bankhead. "Louis B. Mayer should see this. He'd crap his pants." She pronounced it "Louie."

"I wonder what it looks like from down there," said a tiny woman, one of the contest winners. The winners had been picked by their weight, a fact not made known to the general public.

I took the opportunity to answer. "Did you see the glow in the water as we passed over the lake? That was our lights. The entire airship is outlined with Nikola Tesla's new illuminators—the ones that give off almost no heat. He calls them light-emitting-diodes. They print them on some thin panels of glass. From the ground the *Liberty* looks like a great silver spoon, blazing across the sky. The airship's name is spelled out in lights like a Broadway star—only bigger than any marquee on broadway. Each letter is 24 feet high."

Beside her, a nondescript little man—the publisher of a pulp science fiction magazine, *Thrilling Wonder Stories*—spoke up. "Imagine if we could put a news-marquee on the side of the airship, like the one in Times Square. We could display messages to the people below." He thought a moment. "Or perhaps we could put projectors inside the skin of the dirigible and show motion pictures on her sides. Of course, the skin of the ship would have to be translucent enough for the movie to show through. Perhaps someday we'll have airships anchored above cities, projecting television programs to thousands of people at once."

He frowned, another thought crossing his mind. "That would use a lot of elecricity, wouldn't it?" Still frowning, he added, "I wonder if Professor Tesla's wonderful diodes could somehow be reversed to turn light into electricity? You could put rows of panels across the top of the airship and power its engines off sunlight all day long. Hmmm." He pulled out a notebook and hurriedly scribbled his thoughts into it. "Perhaps I'll write a sequel. Ralph 124C42+...." He wandered off, lost in thought.

The woman, the one who'd won her passage in a contest, said, "What a strange little man. Is he an inventor?"

"His name is Gernsback. He's a science fiction writer."

She frowned in confusion. "Science fiction? What's that?"

"Pulp fiction. The silly kind. The kind you don't want to let your little boy read. Rocket ships to the moon. Giant mechanical brains. Robots. Silly things like that."

She made a face. "Oh, that terrible stuff. No, we'd never let Jeffty read that trash."

By ten, the Algonquins had reclaimed their place in the salon and another pitcher of martinis was meeting its olive-strewn fate.

"Do they ever stop?" the evening bartender whispered to me.

"I don't know. I think Broun—or is that Woollcott?—got up to pee once. The rest of them must have iron kidneys."

Between emptying ashtrays, retrieving pitchers and replacing them with full ones, occasionally delivering and sending radiograms, and always being as unobtrusive as possible, I managed to glean a sense of their evolving conversation. Tallulah Bankhead's remark about Louis B. Mayer had sparked a conversation about writing for the movies, something that both Dorothy Parker and F. Scott Fitzgerald had dabbled with.

Before long, they were plotting a film of their own—or perhaps just plotting. The story involved, of course, a beautiful Broadway star traveling aboard a gleaming new airship when a terrible murder occurs. For the better part of an hour, the group argued about who to murder, perhaps someone in their own group? That ended abruptly when Bankhead declared, "Dah-ling, you can't murder a writer. Nobody will notice. It has to be someone important."

Oh, good grief. Didn't they realize? The writers are the *most important* people in Hollywood. If it isn't on the page, it isn't on the stage! You have to take it seriously!

But instead, they wasted another hour of discussion about who might be worth murdering. The comedians were quickly dismissed, so were Jolson, Jessel, and Cohan. The Algonquins finally settled on George Gershwin as a suitable victim, then moved on to speculating about the identity of the murderer and what possible motive he (or she?) might have for killing America's most gifted composer.

"Possibly his brother, Ira?"

"What motive?"

"Over a girl maybe…?"

"How tawdry. How boring. Besides…."

"No, dear. George isn't gay. He's been bedding all those women—"

"—yes, trying to prove he's a man."

"What a strange way to prove it." That was Oscar Levant, who'd been passing by, but stopped for the gossip.

I didn't hear the end of that discussion, there were several other late-night gatherings that needed my attention, but none as interesting. The next time I passed by, they were arguing about writer's block again. That was something I really wanted to hear about—how did the great ones get past it?

It was either Broun or Woollcott—I never could figure out which was which—who said, "Oh, there's a very easy trick to break a block."

Benchley was already glowing with inebriation, had been since lift-off, but he looked across the table with all the interest he could muster. "What?" he said.

"Quite simple. You put a sheet of paper in the typewriter and you type the word 'The.' The human mind abhors a vacuum. It is incapable of leaving the sentence unfinished. You will find yourself typing something to complete the sentence almost immediately."

"Yes, dear fellow," said Benchley, "but what about the sentence that follows it? And the next after that? And the next and the next?"

The other one—Woollcott or Broun, or maybe it was George S. Kaufman—spoke up then. "Pablo Picasso says that all art is recovery from the first line. He was talking about drawing, of course, but I believe that's true of writing as well. Once you have that first sentence on the page, the rest will follow."

Benchley had already written quite a bit about his ability to procrastinate—that only the pressure of a deadline inspired true creativity—but in this group of trusted colleagues, he could admit that sometimes writing was difficult. Not the typing itself, but getting the right words in the right order. Others agreed. "There's an elegance that we aspire to achieve, but the limitations of our own selves remains our greatest challenge."

Benchley put his martini glass down. It was already empty anyway. "The…" he said. "The…." And then, "The the the the the." He nodded. "Yes. The…." And then he leapt up from his chair. "It's an admirable idea. I shall now proceed to test it." And he staggered off in search of his cabin.

The others went back to discussing murder, now arguing whether Jack Warner or Louis B. Mayer might be a better victim. There would be no shortage of suspects or motives. I did catch one line in passing. "No, not Walt Disney. If he doesn't like an actor, he tears him up."

By midnight, we were crossing Kansas—a dry state, it had the most restrictive alcohol laws in the nation. Legally, once we were in the state's airspace we were forbidden to serve liquor. When the company announced the flight itinerary of the *Liberty*, the Attorney General of the state had sent a letter of inquiry to Pan American's lawyers asking if the state's liquor laws would be observed while the *Liberty* was flying over the state. Pan Am's lawyers had promptly sent back a note assuring the Attorney General that state officials, including county sheriffs, were free to board, inspect, and serve any necessary warrants on any Pan Am aircraft flying over the state of Kansas. So far, none had done so.

Captain Bradley had altered the course a few degrees south to avoid a rumbling storm system spreading across the Dakotas and down toward Nebraska where it would probably turn into tornado weather. The big chart in the salon was automatically updated every fifteen minutes. It showed our location and also demonstrated that we were averaging 93 miles per hour, so we were ahead of schedule, but nowhere near the 100 miles per hour that some had predicted. The figures were also available in knots for the aviators aboard. Of which, I was not one.

Along about 1:30 in the morning, the Algonquins finally started making noises that suggested they might be through for the evening. Two other stewards and I had to escort several of them to their cabins. When the last one had finally been tucked in, we looked at each other in exhaustion. "When do any of those people actually find time to do any of the things they're supposed to be famous for?"

We secured all the windows, checking to make sure that none were left open to the night, we couldn't risk a drunken passenger falling out, then adjourned to our separate bunks. Crew's quarters were nowhere near as luxurious as the passengers', but we each had a private space, a sink, and a shower—and a window! It was an uncommon luxury. Eventually, on a full flight with 400 passengers, we'd be doubling up, two crewmembers to a cabin.

The cabins on the *Liberty* had what they called "picture windows." The windows in the salon were even larger, as broad as those in front of Macy's department store. By contrast, the windows on a passenger plane were little more than portholes—even on the newest aircraft under construction that Boeing was building in Washington state.

Pan Am had ordered six of those airplanes—the Boeing 314 Clipper long-range flying boat—for trans-oceanic flights. But with the success of the *Liberty*'s maiden voyage almost certainly assured, those planes might end up going to the army instead. Britain's Royal Air Force had also expressed an interest in picking up those contracts if Pan Am cancelled—as expected.

Unlike an airplane, it's easy to sleep aboard the *Liberty*. Her electrical propellors are so silent, and so distant from the passenger cabins, you can barely feel any vibration, just a gentle susuruss. Unlike the clattering internal combustion engines that keep airplanes aloft, the *Liberty*'s engines run on the same electricity that powers the lights and runs the radios. Everything aboard the airship runs off Professor Tesla's marvelous new graphite-and-lithium batteries. The batteries were kept charged by three diesel generators.

Although technically I was on a 24-hour shift, in practice I would not be needed until at least 10am, maybe later, if the Algonquins slept in—as expected—but I was already up and ready to go at 8:30am.

We were already over the northwest corner of New Mexico, and on course to pass over the Grand Canyon, then Boulder Dam, only two years old and already providing electricity for much of the southwest, then past Las Vegas, a small desert resort town, up over the Sierras, and eventually north up the coast toward an early evening arrival in San Francisco. Passengers could expect a glorious California sunset as we landed.

The course of the airship was primarily determined by weather, but the airline wanted everyone in the country talking about the airship. That meant flying over as many cities as possible so the people on the ground could see the *Liberty*. It also meant flying over the most spectacular scenery below so that passengers could take photographs to show their friends and families.

Of course, *Life Magazine* had photographers aboard the aircraft as well, two of them, and more stationed on the ground all along the route as well. We'd lifted off on Thursday, June 3rd. The next issue of the magazine would appear on Monday, June 7th. We were guaranteed the cover, of course, and would likely have at least four pages of departure pictures, showing liftoff from the field as well as more photos of the airship over New York, then probably six pages of enroute photos, especially aerial views of various landmarks, and another four pages for the arrival and landing.

According to the flight plan, we would head up the California coast, then sail in over the brand-new Golden Gate Bridge for even more spectacular photo opportunities. The bridge had opened on Thursday, May 27th, exactly a week before our liftoff, so it was a grand occasion to demonstrate America's growing industrial future, the strength and know-how that was bringing us back from the Great Depression.

After crossing over the bridge, the *Liberty* would circle the entire bay so people in Sausalito, Berkeley, and Oakland could also get a good look at the *Liberty*, then back across the bay to the Pan Am terminal at San Francisco Municipal Airport. We expected to see large crowds everywhere, but especially at the airfield where a motorcade awaited.

Governor Frank Merriam would be there to welcome us. He'd dedicated the bridge the week before, kissing every baby he could find. This week, he'd certainly make sure that the photographers would get pictures of him with George Gershwin and Al Jolson and Jack Benny—but not Tallulah Bankhead, she was developing an unsavory reputation among Republican voters, and Merriam needed all the good press he could get—he had a tough election coming up next year.

Not all of our celebrity passengers were placing themselves where photographers might find them, some actually found the photographers a nuisance, but the photographers themselves were having no shortage of photo opportunities. Even if they couldn't find Gershwin at the piano or Cohan and Jessel and Jolson mugging together, there were always the huge, downward-angled windows. They had already taken enough aerial photos for a dozen special issues and were now arguing which side of the Salon would be best for photos when we crossed the Golden Gate Bridge. The two *Life Magazine* photographers had the best plan, they would station themselves one on each side.

Most of the Algonquins slept through breakfast. Not surprising. But they missed a great view of the Grand Canyon from the air. That Gernsback fellow, the one who published *Thrilling Wonder Stories*, speculated aloud, "I suppose that's what the canals on Mars must look like, only larger, to be visible from Earth. What a grand civilization the Martians must have. We must make friends with them somehow."

Amazing, what some people thought about. I couldn't imagine anyone taking that science fiction stuff seriously.

The Algonquins did show up for lunch, one by one staggering bleary-eyed into the dining hall. Not the best argument for the life of a writer. These people were famous. They were role-models. Why weren't they acting like it? I was beginning to hate them.

They had the best job in the world—they were the caretakers of culture, the shapers of opinion—and they were behaving like common drunks. But if writing is one of the best jobs in the world, it's also one of the hardest—it's all decision-making, all day long. This word or that one, over and over and over again, all the way to the end of the sentence. And even if you get to the end of a sentence, you still have to start again at the beginning of the next. It's exhausting.

Maybe that's why writers drink—to escape having to make any more decisions, except perhaps how many olives in the martini. Or maybe a twist of onion instead.

And maybe what I was seeing was only an aberration. I couldn't expect these people to be brilliant and noteworthy everywhere, all the time, could I? This was a vacation for them, a break from the stress. Maybe they just needed to recharge their creative batteries? Who was I to judge?

They took their coffee in the salon, along with a pile of fresh pastries that quickly disappeared. I circled regularly, alternating between brewing fresh pots of coffee and refilling their cups. They were now arguing about the best way to murder Louis B. Mayer. Throwing him out the window of the airship was quickly discarded. If there's no body to discover, you lose the scene where the French maid screams in horror.

That led to a discussion of why the maid had to be French. Woollcott—by now, I was pretty sure it was Woollcott—noted that a young French maid was always going to be more fun to look at than a dumpy English maid. Bankhead responded that the dumpy English maid was a great part for a good character actress, and good contrast. "What she means," Dorothy Parker pointedly observed, "is that the star should be the prettiest one. Not upstaged by the ingenue."

Woollcott was undeterred. "Ah, but I have the perfect young actress—"

"Of course, you think she's perfect. She's sleeping with you and you're vain."

Bankhead leaned in. "Not perfect. Desperate." Then she added, "On the other hand, if you actually believe her orgasm, we should cast her, that proves she's a real actress." Turning to the rest, she said, "What if the producer's body is found inside one of the—what do you call them—

the big balloons that hold all that nice helium?" She turned to me and stroked my arm suggestively.

"Lift bags," I said. "Or ballonets."

"Oh, ballonets. I like that. How very French. There's a bit of French sophistication for you, dear. Without all that messy business of having to buy a maid's costume. We shall find Louis B. Mayer's body in a ballonet. Suffocated because there's no oxygen. All blue in the face. Perhaps he has even been screaming. But no one could hear him."

"Umm, if I may—" I politely lifted a hand.

The actress looked at me, her hand still on my arm. "Yes, dear boy?"

"If he were in the ballonet screaming, the helium would affect his voice, make it higher pitched. It's the density of the gas." She frowned in puzzlement. I demonstrated. "He'd sound like this. *Help me! Help me!*"

The entire group fell out laughing. "Oh my god, that's priceless. Can you imagine Louis B. Mayer sounding like Mickey Mouse?"

"More like Betty Boop."

"Makes me think—maybe we should do this as a comedy."

"Somebody go find Jack Benny. He's got the best writers—"

"We'd have to put him in the picture—"

"Oh, right. Never mind."

"But if it's a comedy—"

"Who says it has to be a comedy—?"

"If we're murdering Louis B., it will be—"

"No, not a comedy, but certainly a feel-good movie. We could get Capra to direct—"

"No, we should get whatsisname, that little round English fellow, the one who does all those suspense movies—"

"I've met him." Bankhead shuddered. "I have no intention of working for him. He's..." She searched for the word, finally found it. "He's creepy."

She squeezed my arm, "Not you, dear boy," and finally let go, but not before giving me the kind of delicious look that made me wish the dirigible was a lot slower so we'd have one more night in the air.

"I have a question..." I was pretty sure that was Heywood Broun now. Maybe. "How do we get him into the lift bag? If we slice it open, doesn't the gas escape? Wouldn't that create a risk of explosion?"

"No, that's hydrogen. Helium doesn't explode. Isn't that right, steward?" They all turned to me as if I was the expert.

"Yes, that's correct, sir. Hydrogen is too dangerous. But helium is perfectly safe."

"But the gas would still escape, wouldn't it?"

"Well, yes. But the lift bags are very big. You could cut a slice near the bottom, shove a person in, then seal it again with duct tape. We use it to repair small rips. They do happen sometimes, so there are rolls of tape everywhere—in all of the tool kits and there are tool kits everywhere in the frame, for the convenience of the engineers. So that wouldn't be a problem. Unless the victim struggled. You'd have to knock him out."

"Or get him so drunk he passes out—" Parker pointed to Benchley who was quietly snoring in his chair.

"No, we can't murder Benchley. He still owes me money."

"Well, we can't murder Louis B. either then. He owes me a picture."

"Yes, but now that we have a plan, we'll have to murder the steward too, because he knows too much. We could practice on him. Would you like a martini, lad?"

"I don't drink, sir," I said, and excused myself to refill the coffee pot again. When I returned, they had decided that murdering a steward had no inherent drama. A murder mystery is only riveting if the victim is important. "So, you're safe, dear boy," Bankhead reassured me. "You're not important enough to kill. Don't take it too hard."

"Thank you," I said, noncommittally.

"Somebody wake up Benchley—"

"Why? He'll just start talking—"

"He's snoring!"

"You'd rather have him talking?"

And so it went. Somebody looked at me and asked why I was carrying a coffee pot instead of a martini pitcher, and they were off again. But they still weren't talking about writing. Or anything relating to the literary world. I didn't understand it. Every other profession, the people in it talk shop. These people, they just drank. They did wake up Benchley in time to see the huge white slab of Boulder Dam. "Impressive! You could project movies on it!"

"It's a long drive from Los Angeles. It'd better be one hell of a flick."

Then they retired back to their chairs in the salon. "Las Vegas? Nothing there to see. Just a wide spot in the road. It'll never amount to anything."

Somebody remembered that Benchley had been procrastinating his way through a writer's block—until somebody told him to go type the word 'The' on a blank sheet of paper. Dorothy Parker puffed on her cigarette and asked, "So how did that work, Robert?"

Benchley frowned. "How did what work?"

"The great 'The' experiment, remember?"

"Oh, that. Yes. Thank you." He frowned again. "Well…" He cleared his throat, preparing himself for an extended explanation. "One has to be well-prepared for the task, you know. Procrastination is not for the faint-hearted. It takes genuine commitment. You cannot just sit and do nothing. You must make it appear as if you are preparing to do something. A pipe is very useful in that regard. It requires a great deal of attention. It's an excellent way to look like you are preparing to get busy. Lighting a pipe demands a specific ritual, an elaborate ritual, a very time-consuming ritual. There is the selection of tobacco, followed by the process of delicately filling the bowl, pinch by pinch, then the tamping. One cannot tamp the tobacco too firmly or it will be hard to light. Likewise, one cannot leave the leaves too loose or they will simply burn up. Then there is the application of the fire. As soon as the match has been applied to the tobacco, the smoke is over. This necessitates refilling, relighting, and oh, yes—reknocking. The knocking out of a pipe is as important as the smoking. You have to have the appropriate surface to knock the pipe on. Not just any table will do. No, knocking the pipe is a whole other ritual, you see, all part of the process, and if you leave any part of it out, you're simply not serious about procrastinating."

"Yes, you've bored us with this story before." Kaufman yawned. "You really must write it and sell it someday so we won't have to listen to it again. But we didn't ask you how to procrastinate. Most of us already know how to do that, we've each developed our own specific set of skills. What we want to know is how well the experiment worked?"

"What experiment?"

"The one where you typed the word 'The' on a blank sheet of paper—remember?"

"Oh, that experiment. It worked very well. You were right. I typed the word 'The' and almost immediately, the rest of the words came flowing out as easily as if poured from a pitcher of martinis. Of which, I will have one, if you please, steward." To the rest, he said, "It's still sitting in my typewriter. Feel free to look."

Unable to resist the invitation, the rest of them scrambled to their feet and headed for the corridor, leaving Benchley behind with a martini glass held high in his hand. He saluted me with it, knocked it back, then held it up again for a refill.

When the group returned from Benchley's cabin, filing back in like children after recess, they were smiling and nodding to each other, but they were already talking about something else. Benchley waited expectantly for their reactions. Parker glowered at him as she seated herself. "Too clever by half." A couple of others shook their heads as if Benchley had punned in public—a good pun, but still a pun, the literary equivalent of a fart. Bankhead gave him a scowl of approval. The one I'd identified as Kaufman parked himself, nodded and admitted, "Nice."

I was curious too, but I couldn't leave my station. By then we were coming out over the California coast, and following U.S. Route 101 north. It ran all the way from Mexico to Canada, with portions of the route known as El Camino Real—"The Royal Road."

The Spanish had built their 21 missions in California each one a single day's travel from the next, so journeying missionaries would always have a safe place to rest each evening. Many of the state's coastal towns and cities still retained the names of the original missions: San Diego, San Juan Capistrano, San Gabriel, Santa Catalina, Santa Ysabel, San Pedro, San Fernando, Santa Clarita, Santa Barbara, Santa Clara, San Luis Obispo, Santa Inez, Santa Cruz, San Jose, San Francisco, and a few more that always fell out of my head. How did I know all of this? Because it was part of Pan Am's training for stewards. Passengers would always have questions about the scenery below. It was the stewards' job to provide accurate answers. Any question we couldn't answer was added to the training guide.

The rest of the journey was pretty much without incident. The Algonquins, exhausted from all their drinking, had given up their plans to murder Louis B. Mayer. For some reason, they were now muttering imprecations against several New York critics—individuals who were not aboard. "Murdering a critic would only be poetic justice—" Bankhead said, "They've murdered so many shows."

Benchley cleared his throat loudly. "I am a critic too, you know."

"When you're writing, yes. But most people know you as a humorist."

"I resent that," he replied, but without much emotion. He was giving more of his attention to his martini.

"Besides, you're too nice to murder."

"I resent that even more."

"We can't murder a critic. There would be too many suspects to make the plot workable."

"There would be even more suspects if you killed Louis B. Mayer."

"True, that. Maybe we *should* kill Benchley. Some people like him. That makes it even more of a mystery. Why would someone want to kill Robert Benchley."

"I can think of—" Kaufman quickly counted off on his fingers. "—four reasons."

"Besides that—"

"I think the question isn't *why*, but *who*." Bankhead looked to me. "Oh, hello, dah-ling, bring those martinis over here. Tell me—would you like to murder Robert Benchley?"

Before I could answer, Dorothy Parker said, "Oh, no, no, no. He's not important enough—"

"But he's adorable enough. No one would ever suspect him. I know—" She waved her martini glass for effect, but to give her credit she didn't spill a drop. The woman could hold her liquor. "I'll tell you exactly why he wants to kill Robert Benchley. He's a frustrated young writer and he's jealous—that's it! Jealous of all of us! Robert is just the first. Before the journey is over, he'll kill every one of us. It'll be just like Agatha Christie. *Ten Little Indians*. Only on an airship." She turned to me. "Would you like that, dah-ling?"

As deadpan as I could manage, "It's against airline policy to kill passengers. It might be bad for business."

Bankhead guffawed like a choking foghorn. Quickly recovering herself, she turned to the rest, "You see, darlings. He's perfect! Nobody would ever suspect him."

Kaufman shook his head. "No, no, no. It won't work. He's scenery. The murderer has to be a lead, not a second banana. But I do like the idea of killing Benchley. There's a sadistic kind of elegance to it. Although once he's dead, you lose some of your best opportunities for comic relief."

Woollcott added, "Having the steward be the killer is too much like 'the butler did it.'"

"Has the butler *ever* done it?" Parker asked. "I mean, how can it be a cliché if nobody's ever written it? Maybe that's how we make it work. If Benchley is the victim, then the other suspects have to be us. And here we are saying, 'Oh, it couldn't be the butler, that's too obvious—and it's the butler all along.' But we never considered it because we don't like clichés."

Silence, while they all considered it. I waited patiently to find out if I was going to be a murderer or not.

"Well…" said Kaufman, "We'd have to build up his part a bit. I do like the line about it being against airline policy to kill passengers. Notice he didn't say he wouldn't do it—only that it's against airline policy. Nice bit of misdirection there."

"That little lecture about the Spanish missions—and all those other bits of triva too. Electrical engines and lift bags and why helium makes your voice squeaky. We can use all of that—we'll play him up as stiff and boring. He'll be a dry comic presence for the first two acts. In act three, we reveal his seething core of resentment against those with real talent."

Bankhead slid her hand up my arm. "What do you think, dah-ling?"

I couldn't say what I was thinking. Fortunately, I was rescued by the chime announcing afternoon tea. Having missed breakfast, having drunk most of their lunch, the Algonquins agreed among themselves almost immediately that food was as good an excuse as any to relocate. They rose almost as one and headed for the dining hall, where trays of sandwiches and salads were being set out.

F. Scott Fitzgerald was the last to follow, still holding a glass of whiskey. He stopped and frowned at me, as if trying to figure something out. "Why would you want to murder Benchley?" he asked, very seriously. "I think I'd be a much better victim, don't you?"

"A very good point, sir. Shall I help you to your table?"

A southerly headwind slowed the *Liberty*, so we observed sunset while still passing over Santa Cruz. On the starboard side, we could see The Giant Dipper roller coaster, the highlight of the Beach Boardwalk amusement park. There were colored lights flashing, people shouting and pointing, and carousel music. After that, the hills darkened quickly, a color somewhere between emerald and blackened indigo.

On the port side, the sun went fireburst orange, then sullen crimson as it dipped into the horizon. For a few magic moments, the ocean glimmered with golden highlights across the surface of the waves. Several of the photographers got into a heated discussion about the limitations of monochrome and whether or not Kodak's new color film—called Kodachrome, of course—would ever be able to capture the dynamic range of such a view.

The Algonquin group's tea stretched on so long, they decided to remain in the dining hall and wait for dinner, now planned as a gracious evening affair over the San Francisco Bay, followed by a joyous welcome at San Francisco Municipal Airport—and apparently, I was no longer an accessory to their murder plot, which might have been just as well, because I had already begun considering several better mechanisms of violence, including a way to frame Hugo Gernsback for the entire affair.

No, these people were not a good influence. Any last thoughts I had still been nurturing about the glamor of writing had begun to evaporate somewhere after their second pitcher of martinis. What was left was a sodden residue, about as appetizing as the last forgotten olive in Dorothy Parker's glass.

But while they were at dinner…when no one was around, I took advantage of the opportunity to let myself into Benchley's cabin, ostensibly to make sure he had clean towels and a last full bottle of gin.

His typewriter sat on the desk, a tidy stack of paper next to it. In the machine, a single sheet. I had to look.

There, at the top of the page, a single sentence.

The hell with it.

Now I did have a reason to kill him.
It was too late for this voyage.
I got him on the return trip.

You're entitled to a warning.

This story may be the most horrifying nightmare I have ever written.

It has graphic sex, it has emotional violence, it has a dangerous amoral center.

If you don't want to deal with any of that, skip this one.

JACOB
IN MANHATTAN

BONUS STORY

Lying naked on the bed, next to Jacob's porcelain body, the blankets tangled at our feet, I listen to the sound of my own breathing. Sweat tingles on my skin. My heart still pounds.

"That's it?"

"That's it," he confirms.

"I thought I was supposed to drink your blood."

"Body fluids. It's all the same. This was a lot more fun, wasn't it?"

I have to smile. I can still taste him.

Morning growls at the window, the curtains are drawn to keep it at bay. There's a stain on the ceiling shaped like a dog's head. I feel a strange hollowness within myself. I touch my heart.

"Is this it? Has it started?"

"No. Not yet." Jacob rolls onto his side, facing me. He puts a cold hand over mine, listening to the frantic beat inside. "You're scared—?"

"Yes, I am. I don't know what I've done and it's too late to change my mind, isn't it?"

"Way too late. You're committed." Jacob laughs gently. "It's like the first time you get into bed, naked, with another man. It's scary and delicious, both at once. This is the same thing, only more so." He leans toward me, I turn halfway to meet his embrace and he kisses me. He pulls me close, wrapping me in his arms. "It'll be all right. I promise."

He holds me for a long time, long enough for me to feel his heart beating against mine. We synchronize emotionally and physically, a strange sensation. Finally, when we are both complete in the moment and ready for the next, he releases me back to the rumpled sheets. The dog's head stain has an open mouth. He's panting too...? Or is he smiling, laughing? He saw the whole thing, the frantic scrambling of two naked bodies rocking together, the coupling and uncoupling and recoupling. What does the dog head think?

Do I care? It's just a stain on the ceiling. Water? How did it get there? It looks old. Is it a reminder of some long-passed storm that ripped away part of the roof and pissed its wrath into the structure below? Do I care? No.

I glance back to Jacob. He studies me with shining eyes.

"So ... when will it happen?"

"It's already happening. You're just not going to feel it for a while."

"How long?"

"Hard to say. Depends on your metabolism." He smiles and his eyes gleam with a strange kind of inner light. Desire? Insight? Knowledge? Amusement? How does he do that? I can't look away. The silence grows with a dark intensity, a sense of something impending.

I have to speak—not to speak, but to break the moment. It's too intense. Whatever is rushing down on us, I need to postpone it a moment longer. "Um—"

"What?"

"Um—nothing." Anything. "You were right. The sex was fantastic."

He laughs softly, a quiet sound, barely audible. He traces his fingers down the center of my chest, down through the few brave strands of masculine identity—as if he's tasting them with his touch.

"That's just the beginning. It gets better."

"I can't imagine it."

"That's right. You can't. Not yet."

I listen to the sound of my breathing. I listen to his inhalations and exhalations as well, trying to decipher meaning. What is he thinking right now?

I'm impatient. I want to see the rest of the spectrum. I want to hear the higher sounds, the lower ones. I want to smell the things I'm missing and feel all the sensations I've never known. Everything he promised.

Jacob still studies me, reading me, watching the way my feelings flicker across my face, revealing all the internal processes, both physical and emotional. He seems fascinated.

"What are you doing?"

"Watching you change."

"I thought you said—"

"Not the physical. The emotional. There are steps—all the way from fear to anger to curiosity, eventually acceptance and ownership. You're still at fear."

I look inside. It's a trick I learned at the keyboard—all that writing, all that typing. The only soul you have to examine is your own. Jacob is right. I am afraid.

"I never asked—will it hurt?"

"Does being born hurt? Does sex hurt? It all hurts—it upsets your equilibrium. But if you choose to enjoy the hurt, then it doesn't hurt at all. It's...it's something else. Something beyond pleasure."

"Okay."

"Here..." He lets his hand—his pale porcelain fingers—explore my chest, my belly, then back up again to gently tweak a nipple. "First you're going to feel cold. Very cold. So cold you'll l think you're dying. And that's when the fear will kick in. The panic. The first terrifying reactions of horror—it's really happening. The adrenaline will flow and you'll start sweating. Cold first, then hot. Hotter. Very hot. Hotter than that. Feverish. You'll feel like you're on fire. You'll smell your flesh burning, you'll hear the crackling sounds of transformation inside, you'll see red and orange flames scouring your body, inside and out—because all your nerve endings will be tingling at once.

"You'll get into a cold tub and it won't be cold enough. You'll see steam rising off your skin. Real? Or another hallucination? You won't know. That's why I'm here. To ease you through it. You'll hold onto me, screaming, crying, raging. You'll probably try to beat me—you'll be furious that I've put you through this. You'll be delirious. You'll see me as a monster—and then you'll see me as your lover again—and then you'll want to abandon yourself to delicious sex with the monster. Your body will be racked with ferocious energies—

"Yes, Joseph—it'll hurt, it'll be the worst hurt you ever felt—but it'll be a good hurt—like stretching, like waking up, but it'll still hurt. And you'll cry. You'll weep, you'll sob, you'll howl in anguish. And because all your nerve cells are firing, you're going to hallucinate—like the worst and greatest drug trip ever. Dazzling fluorescent colors, all shifting and twisting. Amazing sounds, a symphony of contradictions. And the smells, the cacophony of odors. All of that. And the physical feelings too. Everything. You'll feel your skin from the inside—you'll taste the way your organs slide against each other, how they work, the ferocious balance of this against that—all the flavors of hormones and enzymes, sugars and aminos and everything else. Oh—and you'll feel dizzy, like you're flying, falling, turning every which way, tumbling into a bottomless well of fear and despair, curiosity and wonder, amazement and regret—"

"Until—?"

"Until you're exhausted. Until you have expended every last particle of energy you have to draw upon. You'll collapse. Your heart will slow. Slower than normal. And your breathing will get shallower, very shallow. You'll get cold. Cold as death. You might panic, thinking you're going to die. But there won't be any energy left. You'll be so empty you won't even have the strength to die. So you'll just go ... call it dormant. But it's not that either. You'll be conscious, just conscious enough to know that you're not dead yet—not yet. You'll be hovering just above death—"

"But I'm not going to die...?"

"No. Not while I'm here."

"Some people do?"

"Yes. Some bodies don't have the strength to survive the transition. You do. You will. Now listen to me—when it starts, when you're going through all these feelings, it's going to be scary, delicious, confusing all at once. Just keep remembering, just keep saying, 'This is what Jacob told me would happen. This is part of it.' Keep reminding yourself of that. It's all part of the process. You don't have to be scared. Just experience it. Enjoy it. Be it. Own it. I know these words don't make sense—try it this way. Whatever you're feeling, look into the heart of the feeling, look as deep into it as you can, dive into it, be the feeling. The whole feeling, ferociously, passionately, completely. Okay? And whenever you need to reach out for me, I'll be there holding your hand, talking you through it. Can you do that—?"

His eyes are intense. I nod. "I'll do it for you, yes."

"No!" He's suddenly angry. "Do it for yourself. Be everything you can see and hear and touch and feel—everything. That way, when you come out on the far side, all of that will belong to you."

He squeezes my hand too hard, his strength is incredible. "You're hurting me—"

"Yes, I am—" How much fury burns behind his eyes?

"Jacob, you're starting to scare me—"

"Good—" For a moment, the pain is impossible—and then the intensity finally breaks. He lets go and pulls back. "You need to know this, Joseph. I'm not doing this to you. You chose this. You are doing this yourself. You're going to be all alone in there. You can die—or you can come back. It's up to you."

"So you're saying I could die…?"

"You could. If you choose it. If you give up. If you let the panic overwhelm you. If you choose to control it, if you remember that you're the owner of everything that happens to you—you'll endure it long enough for your body to start rebuilding itself. You'll be dormant for a long time, but I'll be here watching you, keeping you safe. And if you can remember that—" He takes my hand again, this time not so hard.

Something clicks.

"You've done this before, haven't you?"

Jacob doesn't answer. Not right away. But his expression shifts, darkens—I've caused him to remember.

"Yes," he finally admits. "You're not the first."

"So there were others before me?"

"Yes, there were."

"Where are they? What happened to them?"

"They died."

"They died—?"

"Yes. We can die. Sometimes we get caught, not very often though. Usually, if a Nightsider dies … it's because another Nightsider killed him."

"And yours? The ones you created—?"

"Ahh. That's a different story—"

"Tell me?"

"You really want to hear this—?"

"Yes, I do."

"You won't like it."

"All the more reason to tell me."

Jacob laughs. "You might be right." He rolls over onto his back, stares at the ceiling. "Okay—"

I was living in New York. This was long after Monsieur had died. I had an apartment in the village. Greenwich Village. It was just outside of the boundaries of polite society. Bohemians and artists and sexual perverts lived in the village, so it was the perfect cover.

I was almost 90 years old, 88—I looked maybe 32, a good age. And I had considerable resources, not just the initial inheritance I had received from Monsieur, but quite a bit of my own as well. It turned out that the original amount I had received when I first was led to believe that Monsieur had perished in a fire was only a small fraction of his holdings. It was the amount that he had given lawyer Durant to manage. But there were other lawyers, other holdings, other identities. A dozen, maybe two. Monsieur was over two hundred years old. You don't get that old by accident. You learn a lot of ways to protect yourself.

Nightsiders cannot maintain any identity much longer than a decade. People start to wonder why you're not aging. And after the umpteenth joke about a painting in the attic, it's time to move on. So a Nightsider maintains multiple identities and multiple properties in as many cities as he can afford. Most of the time, he's an absentee landlord, but every few years, he sends his "son" to live in a new city, and the lawyers who manage those holdings are instructed to manage his accounts. From time to time, the absentee landlord passes away and the "son" inherits the properties, and rearranges the management to suit himself until it's time for the next progression and the Nightsider moves on to a third city and a fourth.

To any investigating agency, I was merely a renter in one of the more elegant and respected buildings in the neighborhood. The building was owned by a small property-management firm, which also managed properties in the Bronx, Queens, Harlem, Brooklyn, and several spacious brownstones on the upper east side, just off Park Avenue. I paid my rent directly to them.

Every quarter, the company sent a profit-and-loss statement, plus a sizable check to a downtown corporation, which distributed the earnings to its various shareholders. Several of those shareholders were companies based in other states. They distributed their earnings monthly, quarterly, or annually to other companies and other shareholders. Eventually, after passing through at least a dozen shell companies, some of the funds would arrive at my current lawyer's office, and the rest to the offices of other lawyers in other cities. Most of the time, the lawyers and the executives managing the various properties were scrupulously honest. Several times they were not.

I wish I could report that lawyers are an acquired taste. They are not. They taste of dust and dogma. They are oatmeal.

But that's a different discussion, which we will have another time. I was speaking of my apartment in the village. It was small and comfortable, a retreat from the responsibilities of a larger domain. Much of the furnishings were leftovers from an earlier time, dating as far back as the turn of the century. The nineteenth had become the twentieth and twentieth had become a century of escalating horrors. It was a delicious era. The first half, anyway.

The war in Europe had ended, but the war in the Pacific was dragging on. War weary combat troops were arriving from England and France and Italy by the shipload, almost every day—and just as fast, they were loaded onto westbound trains, where they would be loaded onto other ships—headed for some unknown island base from which the invasion of Japan would ultimately be launched. Everyone expected it to be a hard brutal campaign. Perhaps a million casualties. No one knew.

So, even this far away—even at this remove, the city was a pressure cooker of uncertainty, a mixture of giddiness and fear. There were good times ahead—but maybe there weren't. The Japanese weren't like the Germans. The Germans had momentarily succumbed to the insane fantasies of a madman, but the Japanese had invested centuries into the conviction that their emperor was the living son of heaven. The Imperial Sovereign was much more than a political delusion. He was the nation. Americans were having trouble understanding this—it was too alien.

So down in the streets, the mood was alternately grave and manic, depending on the hour.

Daytime, people went about their business, rushing to work, rushing home, rushing to the store, rushing to spend their ration coupons on butter and eggs.

Nighttime, however, as the storefronts shuttered, as the office buildings locked up, a different world began. The later it got, the more interesting the night became. Darker buildings beckoned. Shadowy doorways flickered open, briefly revealing red-lit spaces within. Silhouettes moved together. It was heaven—

This particular June night, I wasn't hungry, I wasn't anything—I was restless. The night was hot and humid, the city stank of sweat and garbage—there was no magic anywhere. But it wasn't the city, it was me. I recognized the feeling, it was a different kind of hunger. When you're that old, even novelty isn't novelty anymore, it's just a different way of recycling the past. But when you're that old, you don't look for newness, you look for nuance.

Eventually, I gravitated to a midtown bar—not one I'd visited often, I didn't like the flavors of humanity here. They swirled around me as if I didn't exist. I understood why. Mostly servicemen—they were still unfolding themselves from the rigors of the war. They didn't know how to talk to anyone who hadn't been over there. So I chatted with the bartender.

He had a friendly smile, not just a professional one—he actually enjoyed his work. He flashed a flirtatious grin and slid a beer in front of me without my even asking.

Maybe his name was Bud. Everybody called him that, but I got the feeling it was only a nickname. He wore a black silk shirt and a red bow tie—and a gold ring in his right earlobe. Did he know the meaning of that? I'd grown up in Seattle in the 1860s. A fisherman wore a gold earring in case he died—the earring would pay the undertaker for his burial.

I doubted that Bud knew that particular history. Apparently, in this world—this place where men sought intimacy with other men—apparently, it meant something else, I wasn't sure. I hadn't kept up with the nuances of this subculture, but I was charmed by it. Bud was proud of his difference. That should have been a warning, but I wasn't paying attention to my own senses. Or maybe I was enchanted by his silk shirt—it suggested he had a sensual side.

I admit, I was preoccupied, not just that evening, but for several weeks preceding. Although the tumultuous circumstances of my own recent past had been resolved, albeit not as smoothly as I had intended, my designs for the future remained uncharted. I was unfocused and still circling through my thoughts, rehearsing all the mistakes I'd made, as well as my fumbled recovery, wondering how I had stumbled into that situation and if there had been any possibility of extricating myself more effectively than the clumsy way I had finally resorted to. Only the urgencies of the moment, the influx and transshipment of massive numbers of troops and all the mishaps and miseries that inevitably accompanied such a circumstance, had spared me a closer examination by the local authorities.

This internal conversation had been continuing long enough to become an annoying loop, a broken record of repetition. Finally, with an anguished shout of frustration, I fled from the cage of my apartment, bursting into the night like a restless spectre, seeking something—anything—to distract me from another evening of relentless self-absorption. As chance would have it—

Bud's casual flirtations were essentially meaningless, but for the moment I played the innocent again. I was doing post-graduate work at NYU, or I was here on business from St. Loo, or maybe I was just another lonely husband, out on his own for the night and looking for an illicit thrill—a dalliance, a bit of sexual adventure to prove that I was still young and virile and attractive. Or perhaps I was once again just another college boy from Boston, all alone in the big city.

Whatever. I let Bud flirt with me and I smiled in appreciation. I was flattered at the attention. Men of our nature do not flirt in the same manner that men of another nature flirt with women. It is a dance of meanings, both deliberate and casual, it is a testing of intention—playful banter disguising a very real negotiation. It is the construction of a different kind of relationship than exists in the more common world.

In the larger domain of humanity, when two men meet, there's a brief flicker of hesitation. They size each other up. The unspoken question is "Can I take him?" Sometimes they test each other—the relationship remains unresolved for as long as it takes to determine which of the two will be the stronger, which will lead and which will follow. If the question never gets resolved, the men become rivals, enemies in a constant state of opposition.

But when men of a different nature meet, the unspoken question is not one of opposition, but intimacy. "Can I take him?" exists in a vastly different context. It becomes, "Do I want to be naked with him?" Not just physically naked, but emotionally as well.

And yes, it is that same emotional nakedness that Nightsiders still crave—even after a century or more of life. Everything else is just cardboard dancers moving against a flattened panorama—as unconvincing as a theatrical backdrop. It does not have to include a sexual intimacy, but when it's possible—

And in that moment, I allowed myself to be charmed by Bud's easy flirtations. When he said, "Stick around. I get off at midnight," I was charmed. I said, "I'd like that."

No, I was not hungry—not for that. That's another assumption that daysiders make—that Nightsiders are only interested in feeding. We are not. Well, at least, I am not. I'm not a glutton. There are too many other pleasures in life—and with the enhanced senses of my condition, even the simplest of flavors can be a joyous delight. Vanilla ice cream? Most people just eat it—never truly tasting the complex ballet of flavor and texture and temperature. If you take the time to savor its delicacy, it can be as filled with discovery as a seven course banquet.

The same is true of the other senses, particularly that frenzied grappling for position that passes for sexual connection. The way that sexual relations are portrayed in cinema—it's a pernicious lie, a fable for the impoverished souls who hunger for intimacy and accept physicality as a poor substitute. What is portrayed is not even the palest intimation of what is possible.

Did I believe that true connection might be possible with Bud? No, I did not. And I wasn't hoping for it either. As I said earlier, I was exhausted from the recent past, I was allowing myself this convenient bit of exercise. But then again, I have been surprised more than once by what can occur when I let go of expectations. This evening, I expected little more than some enthusiastic pistoning leading to an easy climax. It would be enough—a sufficient diversion to hold back the onset of ennui.

When the hour arrived, Bud and I left quickly. He asked if I had a place nearby. I nodded. I had a midtown apartment I maintained for one of my out-of-town identities, a convenient and disposable safe-house. We walked the few blocks without talking. We both knew what we were up to, there was no need to negotiate. Once inside, we wasted little time peeling off our clothes.

The bow tie was a clip on, the silk shirt unbuttoned smoothly—revealing an attractive, rugged body. His chest hair, dark and curly, formed a classic tree-of-life. He stretched his arms, his upper torso was muscular, his shoulders and arms well-corded, but he moved with an easy grace, comfortable in his body. Levis dropped to the floor, revealing well-shaped legs and calves. His black silk boxers bulged with anticipation.

He pushed me backward onto the bed. I allowed it to happen. Normally, I am not the submissive partner, but tonight I was coasting, allowing events to proceed as they would. In contemporary terms, I am pansexual, I am whatever my partner wants me to be, so it was easy for me to lie back in anticipation of what this man intended.

He tugged off my briefs, studied me for barely an instant—I have always been slim, never truly muscular, and after my transformation, I have maintained an unusually youthful appearance. Young blood helps with that, the younger the better. I admit it is uncharacteristic, but I'm not yet ready to age. Older blood has more character, but younger blood has greater vitality and I prefer the bounce it gives me.

But I wasn't looking at Bud that way. As I have said more than once, I am not a glutton, and I do not need to feed as often as portrayed in the movies. Once or twice a month is sufficient. And it isn't necessarily a fatal encounter for my selected partner. Only when—but I'm still getting to that.

Bud studied me for a moment. Compared to him, I was skinny, undeveloped. And because I was so slight and pale, perhaps he saw me as effeminate. That had always been part of my attraction to some of my patrons. And certainly, Bud had chosen me for some reason. He had flirted with me deliberately, and he had asked me to wait and meet him at midnight. He would not have done so had he not desired me—

So I expected Bud to be as affectionate in bed as he had been at the bar. I expected a slow sincere seduction. Instead—

He flung himself at me, straddling me like a cowboy on a steer and began slapping at my face and arms, the whole time shouting a stream of invective so startling, I didn't know whether to laugh or cry—

I cried.

What? You think Vampires have no souls, no feelings? We do. And so much more intensely than even the most passionate of daysiders—

Bud had caught me when I was vulnerable. When I was still feeling the pain and hurt of what I had previously lost. I had not yet expressed my grief, I was still carrying it around inside, like an oyster clutching the sandy irritant that would someday become a pearl, but for the moment was still a source of anguish. He'd caught me by surprise and my emotions burst from me in an explosion of despair.

My tears must have excited him, because he only increased his efforts. Enraged, he kept slapping at my face, shrieking now—

"This is what you deserve, you ugly little piece of puke. This is what a real man does to a faggot like you—" And more. Much more, much worse. He used words I would not repeat anywhere. And the whole time, he pumped furiously at his organ. The greater his abuse, the greater his arousal.

I let him pummel me—I wasn't afraid, I welcomed it. The stimulation of this beating was a purge, a scouring, a scourging of the horrible detritus of the despair that had crippled me for so many long weeks. So yes, I welcomed it. I encouraged it. I shrieked with pain—and yes, it hurt, but it was a delicious hurt—

And the whole time, part of my mind was wondering how this charming bartender had become the author of this monstrous assault. Was this his normal release? And if so, where did he find partners? And why hadn't anyone else at that bar warned me—? Surely, someone else must have—

It was only when he started punching me that I realized the intensity, the depth of his fury. This wasn't just a sexual release for Bud—he intended to hurt me. His expression was distorted with rage, his mouth twisted, his eyes burning. This crazed man was strong enough to injure me, and he was furious enough to do so—despite my enhanced ability to heal, I began to fear the level of damage he could inflict. He might even need to kill me to achieve the emotional release he so desperately craved.

It was when he raised his fist too high—high enough to deliver a punishing blow—that my alarm finally exploded. With a burst of internal fire flooding outward from my heart, I flashed into Q-time, that acceleration of the flesh that turned the rest of the world into a slowed-down panorama. His fist came down slowly—slow enough for me to watch it in amusement—and sank deeply into the mattress beside me. I had already twisted away. Missing me, not meeting the expected resistance of my terrified face, put him off balance, he fell slowly sideways just enough that I could roll backward, bringing up my knee, my foot, to sink it into his solar plexus, pushing into it, pushing and pushing and pushing into it until he rose up and away, flying slowly gracefully backward off the bed, arms spreading outward in surprise, astonishment creeping across his face, until he slammed against the ceiling—hard! Even in Q-time, I could feel the impact. He held there for a long slow-motion moment, and then began descending as gently as a deflating balloon—by which time I had already rolled off the bed, sticking the landing like a champion gymnast.

I only look harmless. That's my power.

Bud splatted into the bed, face-planting into the mattress, sprawling in shock, gasping, unable to breathe, barely able to curl himself into a ball around the horrible knot of pain in his gut. I had aimed my kick deliberately.

There's this about violence—as much as the movies lie about sex, they lie about fighting even more. In the real world, most fights are over quickly. In the movies, the opponents are always equally matched and equally indestructible, enduring assaults that would cripple a normal person. In real life, the one with the power disables the target as quickly as possible, usually with a single well-placed application of force to the most vulnerable part of his opponent's body. One good kick to the solar plexus—actually one exceptional kick—and it was enough to slam Bud into the ceiling above the bed. Hard. Hard enough to crack his spine—and the ceiling plaster. After that, gravity did the rest.

By the time he was mostly through vomiting, Q-Time had eased, not completely, but enough that I could start to recover my own strength. I had my head low, my hands on my knees. I was gasping for breath as well—that sudden swift exertion of energy was going to cost me. I was good for another hour or two—after that, I'd need a few hours of dormancy. Four, maybe six.

I awoke to sunlight streaming in through a crack in the curtains. I was sprawled across the living room sofa. Judging by the angle of the sunbeams, it was late afternoon. I'd slept longer than I intended. And I still felt weak and groggy.

Coffee first. While it was brewing I took a long hot shower. I ignored the muffled noises coming from the bedroom. Time enough for that later.

When I finally entered the bedroom, Bud's frantic eyes followed my every movement. He made some noises from behind the gag, but I ignored them. I did check the bindings on his arms and legs, they were secure. My father had taught me well—I still remembered how to tie a secure knot. It was the only legacy he'd left me, but I'd made good use of it more than once. This time, I had cut Bud's black silk shirt into narrow strips, braided them for strength, and tied him spread-eagled to the four bedposts.

I dressed in silence, there was no need to talk to Bud. Not anymore. He'd waived all rights the moment he curled his hand into a fist—the moment he'd decided to hurt me. First, I had some shopping to do.

It was late enough in the day that most of the streets were already shadowed. That's one of the advantages of living in a city of canyons. It's easy to avoid direct sunlight. I spread my purchases up the east side of Manhattan and down the west. There wasn't a lot I needed, but I didn't need to look suspicious either.

By the time I got back, the sun had already set. I unpacked the shopping cart methodically, laying things out in neat rows on the table in the dining nook. Decisions, decisions. I started with the baby bottle. I filled it with milk and put it in a pan of water on the stove. A very low heat. While it warmed, I unwrapped the rest of the packages.

First I lit the incense. Patchouli. A particularly noxious scent, but while it wouldn't blanket the most offensive odors, it would mask them enough to be tolerable.

Then I filled a bowl with warm soapy water and dropped the bathing sponge into it. As I expected, when I entered the bedroom, Bud was a mess. He lay there in a puddle of his own urine and feces. He looked haggard. His eyes were wild. And even without asking, I could tell that his muscles were cramped with the effort of trying to break free. Sorry—not from my daddy's knots. His distress was palpable.

Without acknowledging his predicament, I began to quietly and methodically wash him. I lost count of how many times I had to empty the bowl into the toilet and refill it with clean water. But I didn't stop until the stink of shit and sweat and urine was no longer a visible haze in the air and the apartment reeked of patchouli.

At some point, I stripped the sheets and mattress pad from the bed and dropped them into the bathtub. I left them to soak in detergent overnight. I'd probably have to rinse and soak them several times. Eventually, I'd let them dry so I could send them out with the rest of the laundry. It wasn't the first time I'd done this drill. Fortunately, there was a rubber sheet on the bed, so the mattress would remain unsoiled.

Finally satisfied, I returned to the kitchen and washed my hands for several long minutes in water almost hot enough to scald. I had a lot on my mind. Had I forgotten anything?

I returned to the bedroom with the package of adult diapers. I didn't bother to explain to Bud the necessity. I could tell from his frantic expression that he understood—he was going to be here for a while. To his credit, he didn't struggle much—but then again, I hadn't left him much wiggle room when I'd tied him down.

By now the milk was warm enough, I held up the bottle so he could see what I had. "This is it. This is all you're going to get. Nothing else." I sat down next to him on the bed.

"Now, before we start, I want you to understand something. From this moment on, you have only two choices. You can die painfully—or you can take a long time to die and you will die very painfully. It's up to you. If you understand, blink twice."

Blink. Blink.

"Next. You are not to talk to me. You are not to say anything at all. We are not ready to have a conversation. You have not earned the right to a conversation. You are entitled to silence, nothing else. If you understand, blink twice."

Blink. Blink.

"Good. Now, in a minute, I will remove the duct tape from your mouth. If you scream, if you speak, if you say anything at all, I'll put the tape back on and you will not get your dinner. If you understand, blink twice."

Blink. Blink.

"Good. Very good."

I held up the bottle so he could focus on it. "It's just milk. Warm milk. Just what every little baby boy wants. Do you want your bottle now?"

Blink. Blink.

I removed the duct tape slowly. The quick rip is more sudden and more painful, but the slow peel back is easier to replace if the client breaks his promise not to talk.

To his credit, Bud was very good at following instructions. He sucked at the nipple hungrily, gulping at the milk as fast as he could manage. When he finally finished, his eyes were wet with tears—either shame or gratitude, I couldn't tell and didn't care. I wiped his face with a clean towel, then applied a fresh piece of duct tape across his mouth.

Yes, we could have had a conversation. We could have had many conversations. But I didn't feel like it. I didn't see the point. You don't talk to your hamburger, do you? And besides, I knew all the variations already: "Why are you doing this to me?" "What do you want?" "I have money!" "Please, please, for the love of God, have some mercy!" "What kind of a monster are you?!" And all the other things they say—all the things that never work.

I picked up the blue blanket from the foot of the bed and pulled it over him, tucking him in carefully. I even laid my hand on his forehead and gave him a gentle kiss. The expression in his eyes was terrified. "Sleep tight, baby. Tomorrow is another day."

Yes, it would be. I hadn't put my hand on his forehead out of gentleness, I was checking his temperature. It was already dropping. He was right on schedule. By morning he'd be feverish and I'd have to connect the IV. He'd need a lot of nutrients to keep his strength up. I didn't want him to die. Not yet, anyway.

I wasn't happy that he was in my bed. I didn't like sleeping on the sofa. I could have gone back to my apartment in the village, but I didn't want to leave him alone and untended either.

This whole project had been a spur of the moment decision, motivated more by anger than anything else. I had chosen it, so I had to live with the consequences. The sofa it was.

And I didn't like having my sleeping hours reversed either—he had me keeping the same hours as a daysider. I'd have to do something about that as quickly as possible too.

I won't go into the details of Bud's transformation. It's really rather mundane. But I did finally remove the tape from his mouth so we could talk.

No, I didn't owe it to him. I didn't owe him anything, but I had grown bored waiting for him to ripen. His physical strength was sufficient to give him some resistance to the process, so I needed him to tell me what he was feeling, what physical sensations he was experiencing.

"That was a lucky kick," he said.

"If that's what you want to believe, okay." I continued placing ice packs on his chest and belly. "This should help with the burning. A little, anyway."

"I feel weird. What did you do to me?"

"Just a little—oh, let's call it seasoning—to improve the flavor."

"You drugged me."

"That's one way of saying it. Not very accurate, but—"

"Whatever you think you're doing, you won't get away with it—"

"Mm hm. Someday, one of you fellows will be right about that."

That shut him up for a moment. The realization that he wasn't the first—and that I knew what I was doing.

"I'm sorry—" he said.

That stopped me. I put the last ice pack on his chest and didn't move for a long moment. I left my hand on his sternum, feeling the nervous beat of his heart beneath. Finally, I looked at his face. It was the first time I'd met his eyes since tying him to the bed.

No one had ever said that to me before. And by the twisted and distressed look of his features, he'd never said it to anyone either.

His voice cracked. "Please, I'm so sorry. I really am—"

"This is the first time you've ever apologized…?"

He hesitated, then finally admitted, "Yes…it is." His eyes were getting shiny, welling up with tears.

"So then, I'm not the first man you've ever beaten up, am I?"

"No."

"Can't you just have sex with a man—?"

"It's not enough—"

His response repelled me. I had no choice but to ask the next question. "How many…?"

He shook his head. "I don't know. I don't remember."

"How badly did you hurt them?"

He didn't answer. He couldn't.

"Did you kill anyone?"

Again, he shook his head—a denial, a refusal, a retreat.

"Did you kill anyone?" I demanded.

"I don't know. I don't think so. Maybe once. I don't know. I didn't wait to see. I never heard—"

"None of them ever went to the police—?"

His voice broke, but he managed to get the words out anyway. "The cops don't care. They laugh. They say he deserved it for being a fag."

"But you're not—?"

"Naw, man. I'm not. I mean—I'm not."

"But you invite men to have sex with you—"

"But it's not sex—"

"If it's not sex, then what is it—?"

"It's—it's what I do."

"Uh-huh. It's what you do. And yes, what you do is definitely not sex. It's something else. Something sick. Too bad you never learned how to have sex. Real sex. You wouldn't be here now—in this situation." I paused, studying him. He did have an attractive body. Spread-eagled like that, he was an open invitation. I allowed myself a delicious smile—enough to terrify him. "But maybe…just maybe, I'll show you what real sex is. Maybe—if the circumstances are right—I'll give you the chance to find out what real pleasure is."

A flicker of hope crossed his face—and fear as well.

"But not yet. You're not ready yet. Nowhere near—" I took my hand from his chest. "Are you hungry? I'll get you another bottle?"

"Please? Could I have something else instead? Real food?"

"No, you can't. You're still a baby. My baby. My sweet little baby boy. And we have a long way to go before I trust you enough to put anything solid in your mouth."

"I'm sorry." He tried again. "I'm really really sorry."

"I know you are. And I forgive you. Now open your mouth, baby boy. If you want your ba-ba."

"Do I shock you, Joseph?"

"Uh-uh. I'm not tied down to the bed."

"Would you like to be?"

"No, thank you. I'm quite comfortable this way."

He laughs and my head bobbles with his amusement.

I'm resting my head on Jacob's cool chest, he has one arm around my shoulder. Occasionally, he strokes my back. The tingling has become fire, the burning flashes out in waves, but it's a good feeling now. I'm floating in the center of a starburst of sensation. Strange colors flicker at the edges, and everywhere a crackling sense of something—I don't have words for it yet.

"But you have questions."

"You've done this before…?"

"Not as often as you want to assume. It's a lot of work."

"There are two of us now. I can help—"

Jacob laughs and my head bobs again. "I didn't imagine you would be impatient."

"I'm not impatient. It's just that there's so much to learn—"

"More than you know."

"Enough for another book?"

"Enough for a trilogy. Maybe a septology."

"I'll have time."

"You might not want to write it, my dear. It could be a very dangerous set of revelations—"

"If I was afraid of danger, I wouldn't be here—"

"That's true," Jacob says. His voice softens, his hand rests firmly on my spine, listening, tasting. "How are you feeling?"

"How am I feeling—?" I look inside, all the strangeness, the experience of stretching, expanding. Where are the words for this? Finally: "I'm flying—I'm flying on a magic carpet—a delicious man-ride, a silver slither in the sky. The stars are flowering all around us. Such beautiful colors"

Jacob strokes my hair. "Are you hallucinating or just showing off your skill with linguistic allusions?"

"Yes...."

"I see."

"Am I there yet?"

"Not yet. But soon."

We rest in silence for a while. Starflakes of desire and apprehension surround me, all in shades of white and gold and rose. And a darker apprehension of hunger as well.

Bud was strong, even stronger than he looked. His transition took the better part of a week. When the burning ebbed, he slipped deep into a dormant state, the cells of his flesh slowly regenerating into a different state of existence.

By then I was no longer feeding him milk. He was taking a bottle of rich beef blood every two hours. It's not that hard to obtain, not if you have a Companion working in a slaughterhouse. I could have gotten him human blood as well—but that was a luxury he didn't deserve.

Even before he resurrected—that's the Community's term for the first awakening, our own little ironic joke—even before he resurrected, I had already tapped the artery in his right arm. I'd taken a few sips, but like any vintage worth savoring, he needed time to mature.

When he finally awoke, the first thing he did was test his bonds. He struggled on the bed for a while, twisting and writhing until he realized it was useless. Finally, he looked up at me. "You changed them—?"

"I did. The silk was strong, but not strong enough. These are stronger."

"You're a son of a bitch—"

"You've already called me worse."

"I apologized."

"And I forgave you."

"Then why didn't you let me go—"

"Because I might have forgiven you, but all those others—they didn't. They trusted you, they took you to their beds, and you betrayed them. You beat them up. You might have crippled and maimed them. You hurt them—not just physically. You made them afraid. You made them afraid to love. I can forgive you because I'm not them. But they can't forgive you—because you took something away from them that can never be recovered. You took away their willingness to trust. I don't think that part can be forgiven."

"You bastard—"

"Accident of birth," I said calmly. "But you—you had a choice. And this is what you chose."

He fell silent then, his expression said it all. If I had not strengthened his bonds, we could have had hours of glorious combat, a deliciously brutal mutual pummeling. But as arousing as some might find that, I do not. I have spent a century and a half avoiding serious discomfort. I have no taste for it. Perhaps if I had been possessed of a larger, more rugged physique, I would feel differently about the extremes of athleticism, but I am comfortable in my body—indeed, I'm actually quite fond of my appearance. I have even—when it has been convenient—been able to pass for a young woman, if one does not study me too closely. That is not one of my desires either. But I like the ability to be a wraith. It's a survival skill.

At last, he spoke again. This time, his voice was quieter. His fury subsided, he had sunk into resignation and resentment. "What did you do to me?"

I sat down next to him on the bed. I touched his chest, put my hand on his heart to listen, to taste. "I seasoned you—"

"What the hell does that mean?"

"It means you didn't have enough flavor before. Now you do."

He hesitated, uncertain. I have to admit, my answer was designed to terrify him.

His eyes were wide now. "So…which is this?" he asked.

"Which is what?"

"You said I had a choice."

"Oh. Yes, I did."

"You said I could die painfully…or very painfully."

"No, I said you could take a long time to die—and die very painfully."

"I cooperated with you—"

"Yes, you did. That's why you get to take the long time to die—and very painfully. Very very painfully. Because that was what you chose."

"No, I didn't—I didn't choose that."

"Yes, you did. And this is it. But if you're as smart as you pretend to be, which I like to think you are, you will enjoy dying very painfully a lot more than you would have enjoyed just dying."

"You're crazy."

"Yes, maybe. Certainly by your definition of sanity. Not by mine. Now, the real fun begins."

"This isn't fun for me—"

"No, it isn't. But you already had your fun, dear. Now it's my turn." I made as if to rise, then turned back to him. "We could have had some fun together. If you had been that kind of man. And if you had been, you'd be back at work tonight. But I brought you up here to have some fun—and if I'm not going to have fun one way, then I'm going to have it another way. This is it. And if you're starting to feel just a little bit like some of the men you abused—well, consider that a bonus. You get to have fun their way now."

I got up and went to the kitchen, filled a bowl with warm soapy water, procured a towel and a sponge, and returned to the bedroom. "It's time for your bath, little boy—"

Yes, I was humiliating him. I was doing it deliberately. I wanted him angry and I wanted him afraid. But I also wanted him in tears as well. I wanted to reduce him to a completely infantile state—so that his fear and rage were complete and total and ferociously beyond his ability to control. I didn't need to hurry this—I needed to break him, shatter him into fragments, and leave what was left resigned to the reality that *this* was his existence. Nothing else.

After I cleaned him, I gave him a gentle dusting of baby powder so he'd smell good. I sat down next to him on the bed again. "I want you to notice something—you've been strapped down to this bed for the better part of a week. But you're not cramping up, you're not hurting, you're not getting weaker, and if anything, your muscles are tighter than ever. You are, in one sense, in the best shape of your entire life.

"I want you to notice something else as well. Your senses have been heightened. You can hear the rats scrabbling through the woodwork three floors below. You can see every speck of dust in the air illuminated by nothing more than distant starlight. You can smell the flavors coming from the restaurants two blocks away. And your sense of touch—? The nerves beneath your skin are flickering with impatience. You can taste the dancing moments of the breeze, all the seasons of life. You hunger for sensation—

"Close your eyes and look inside. You can feel the waves of blood pulsing outward from your heart, across your chest and belly, out through your arms, down through your legs, echoing off the extremities of fingers and toes, and bouncing back again to be recycled through your lungs. Feel your lungs expanding, tasting and savoring the air. Notice how your organs fit together, slide against each other. Feel the peristaltic churning of your intestines. Everything—notice all the different processes of the flesh, that's you—all of that is you, I want you to feel it intensely—

"No, don't resist. Resistance is pain. Experience it. Experience is sensation. When you let it in, you become it, it becomes you—"

No, I wasn't hypnotizing him, I was meditating him—and he interrupted it to ask, "Is this it? Is this when you give me my very painful death?"

If I had laughed, it would have terrified him. I did not, but yes—I found his reaction amusing. "No, I am not going to hurt you tonight. I'm going to do something worse. I'm going to give you pleasure—the most intense pleasure you have ever experienced in your short pathetic life. Bud, my little baby, I am going to take you so far beyond the limits of ecstasy, so far past anything you could ever have imagined, that you will never again be satisfied with anything less."

That was the most terrifying thing I could have said. He didn't realize the full horror of it—if he had, he would have screamed for the mercy of instantaneous oblivion, but he recognized enough of it that his eyes widened in apprehension. And his heartbeat quickened—with both fear and eagerness.

"Are you ready to begin? Never mind, it doesn't matter. I'm ready— "Let me tell you about the human body. Did you know I'm a doctor? I've been studying medicine for...oh, it must be seventy years now. We've made a lot of advances. And with tools like the new electron microscope, who knows what we'll discover about how human biology works. It's an exciting time to be alive. Another seventy years, we might even know how to assemble the fundamental chemicals of life, who knows what miracles we'll accomplish then? But you don't need to concern yourself with that question, you won't be around for that. I will, but you won't.

"Oh, but I was talking about the body today, wasn't I? And what we know about it right now, how it grows and develops, how it works. You see, dear little baby boy—we all start out as girls. Every single one of us. Still with me? It's about to get exciting—"

Bud's attention was on my face, on my voice. He was so caught up in the word pictures I'd been painting, he hadn't noticed that my fingers had been circling out from his heart, tracing patterns around the left side of his chest, and now—only now, slowly narrowing in on the target.

I leaned forward then, putting myself directly in his line of sight, just close enough for him to focus on my eyes. "Let me tell you how you got here, baby boy. It's an amazing journey. Your daddy—he put his penis inside your mommy, back and forth, back and forth, in and out, in and out—he probably thought he was having fun, maybe even the most fun a man can have— well, what passes for fun for men like that. Two or three minutes, maybe five—and then bam! A few quick spurts and it's all over—it probably felt like a big thing to him, but if he was like most men, doing it the way most men do, it wasn't anywhere near what it could have been. But that spurt had a few million little swimmers and one of those swimmers—the fastest one or the strongest one—well that little swimmer got to the egg, and well—despite all the odds against it, you got started. There were a million other little swimmers, a million other little people who could have gotten started, but you got here. Isn't that amazing?

"Now...for the first eight weeks, just floating inside mommy's safe little space, you were just a funny-looking little pink salamander, as sexless as a jellybean. Not much to look at, really. But as I said, after a couple months, if you've got boy chromosomes, something inside the jellybean lets loose a little squirt of boy-juice, and that causes the tiny little button at the bottom end of your notochord, what will eventually be your spinal cord, to become a pee-pee. Isn't that interesting—?

"Never mind, we're not interested in your little pee-pee yet. See, until that little squirt of boy-juice, you're still a girl. Well, developing like one. And that's why, when you finally pop out of mommy's warm oven, you have these two little reminders that you were once a little girl—these cute little nipples right here. This one and this one. Because they started developing before that little squirt of boy-juice gave you a pee-pee. And yes, it's such a cute little pee-pee—and because it's the bottom end of your spinal cord, you think it means something. As soon as you can get your fat little hand into your diaper, wrapping your pudgy little fingers around it, you decide it's important. Silly you. But these other two things, right here, where you can see them every time you take off your shirt, every time you look in the mirror, little rosy peaks—you think they're useless? Oh, no. They're there to remind you that inside, you've got some girl stuff. A lot of girl stuff. I'll let you in on a secret. These two little peaks, they're really little volcanoes just waiting to erupt—"

I pinched his left nipple hard enough to make him flinch. "See? Just like a girl—a very girly-girl—you've got a lot of very active nerve-endings inside there. Most men don't realize it, you probably didn't think much about it—but your nipples are very very sensitive. And yours—more so now than ever before. You can feel everything." I squeezed again. "See? And this is the part where it finally gets really really exciting—"

By now I'd been tracing circles around the left areola long enough that it must have been getting very sensitive—almost raw. And every so often, I'd give it a pinch or a tweak—or I'd roll the roseate flesh between my fingers. I needed to keep all the nerves firing.

When I finally felt enough heat beneath my fingers, I leaned in and slowly licked his nipple, flicking it with my tongue.

He gasped—

That's when I began to suck it. Not ferociously, but sweetly, like an infant, like a lover, like an exquisite torturer, all of those at once.

Among the books I had in my library—in the locked part of my library—I had a shelf of rare and valuable volumes that had been imported at great expense from India, Japan, and China. The illustrations were marvelous. All of the books were accompanied by painstakingly accurate English translations. Apparently, our far eastern cousins had been studying the intricacies of the human body for millennia, much longer than any western practitioners.

Some of the books were about the methodologies of torture. Others were about the physics of sexual congress. The two subjects were not that far apart—both were about the repertoire of stimuli available to the human body and ways to evoke specific suites of sensation. Over the years, I'd had opportunities to practice many of these techniques. Tonight, however—I had a specific goal in mind.

It is not commonly known—indeed, I would not have known it had I not experienced it myself—but you can bring even the most rugged of men to orgasm merely by sucking his nipple. It takes time and intention, it requires patience and cooperation, and it is not a male orgasm, that sudden explosion of sexual energy—it is a female response, a gradual ascension of pleasure, culminating in waves of delight and joy. I had time. I had patience. There was no need to hurry. I intended to enjoy myself.

Poor Bud had no choice but to lie back and let me have my way with his baby-smooth chest and his singularly exposed anatomy.

Oh, did I forget to mention? While he had been dormant, unable to move but still feeling everything in exquisite detail, I had shaved him clean and hairless. He had a magnificent body, even more so without those curly black mats everywhere. With his skin glistening all pink and shiny, he looked like he was sculpted out of exquisitely radiant porcelain. He almost looked like the innocent and beautiful teenager who might once have had a future. I think that may have been one of the reasons I intended to take such care with him. After everything he must have been through to turn him into what he became, he deserved the opportunity to be something else for a while.

By the time I had him moaning, even writhing in ecstasy, I knew that he had gone to that place where pain and pleasure were no longer identifiable as separate sensations. I could feel the physicality of sweetness flashing through his body, racing outward in waves of delight that ebbed only when I pulled back to survey the landscape of his rapture. I bent again to coax him to even greater peaks of emotion and the intensity of his experience had him gasping, crying, even screaming in wordless grunts. I'd simultaneously raised him to the peak of sexual energy and reduced him to the basest level of animal existence.

After that, the rest was ... well, even more fun. For both of us. I made sure of that. If even a single nipple can be an avenue to nirvanic bliss, it is almost beyond imagination what ecstasies are possible elsewhere in the human physiology. You think it's all about some specific erogenous zone? What foolishness. The entire human body is an erogenous zone.

Never mind. If you haven't been there, you haven't been there.

Within days, I had poor Bud begging for my attentions. I took him every way it is possible for one man to take another, and each time, I took him farther than the time before—until I had him passing out in delirious joy, and then coming back to consciousness with only a single desperate plea on his lips. "More…more…Please, more. God yes."

The physical bindings were long gone, unnecessary. He came crawling across the bed, naked, unashamed, begging for even the slightest touch of my hand. His body enflamed by the strange new blood coursing through his veins, he existed in a state of insatiable desire. He was consumed by it.

I had addicted him. Not hard to do, given his transformed physical state and the hallucinogenic mental processes that followed. I'd vampirized him, I'd stripped him of his humanity, and I'd overpowered his ability to experience his own body. I'd overwhelmed his soul.

From time to time, I tasted him, just the slightest sip. He didn't mind—he enjoyed it. For him, it was another way to experience pleasure. For me, however, it was the tasting of the dish as it simmered on the stove.

Bud's flavor was developing nicely. He was young and powerful, brutal and delicious. The aspects of desire were already creating in him a most savory vintage. He was going to be delicious. But it was still too soon. He wasn't ready yet. There was more to do. A great deal more.

It's all about the seasonings.

———————◆———————

I come awake, blinking. Jacob is watching, an impish smile in his eyes. "How are you feeling?"

"Amazed. I think that's the word for it."

"It's as good as any."

I turn on the bed to face him. "I thought that being dormant was supposed to be like death—"

He touches my cheek. His hand is cool and reassuring. "It can be. But it doesn't have to be. Sometimes you keep yourself awake and aware while you regenerate your strength. It takes longer, sometimes a lot longer, but when you're dormant, you're vulnerable. So sometimes, you go only part way down."

"It was weird. Even with my eyes closed, I was aware of everything around me. Like a dream—"

"It's called dreamtime. You'll learn to manage it. It takes practice. The first few times, when you're still learning how deep you can go, it can be kind of scary. It scared me. I thought I was dying. That's what it feels like. I came out of it screaming. But Monsieur was there to reassure me. No matter how deep you think you're going, you can't die in dreamtime. It doesn't work like that. Once you get some sense of your control, you'll see that you can go as deep as you want. One day you'll get curious how far down the bottom is—you'll find out there is no bottom. You'll see.

"Monsieur once showed me he could go dormant for weeks at a time. I expect that's one way to survive during times of famine. And that's probably how the whole undead-thing started, way back in the times of superstition and ignorance. And if you were a Nightsider back then, if all a man knew were the horror stories, that—and the hallucinogenic quality of the whole thing—that could have been enough to drive him mad. He might believe he really was some kind of undead thing—and at the same time, he'd be relishing his new afterlife. I think that's how a lot of the whole mythology started. It would certainly be worth some serious study."

"If there were any records, yes—"

"Oh, there are. Church records, especially. But most of them are inaccessible. Locked up in the Vatican or buried in vaults somewhere. It wasn't exactly a popular subject. Monsieur knew quite a bit about it—"

"He was that old?"

"No. But his...his creator was. Or his creator's creator. I was never quite sure."

"Is that what you are? My creator?"

"That's one term for it. Patron or mentor are good words too. It's whatever you want the relationship to be."

I rolled over and stared at the dog head on the ceiling. "I was kinda thinking ... partner. Or lover."

"Too soon for that, sweetheart. Let's go with companion for now. Associate."

"Friend?"

"Mmm. Vampires don't have friends."

"We don't?"

"I haven't told you the rest of it. Then maybe you'll understand."

It did not take long. Within two weeks of that first seduction, Bud was completely enslaved by his own hallucinogenic desires. When he complained about having nothing to wear but diapers, I gave him a boon. We discarded the diapers in favor of frilly pink panties and a matching top, what they called a Baby Doll nightie. But Bud was delighted at the silky sensation of the soft nylon against his skin. He barely noticed the intentional humiliation of the circumstance—he was too consumed with the privilege of being a sissy-boy.

I'd done my job well. I'd managed his hallucinations from the beginning, regularly working his skin to keep it as sensitive as a newborn's. I now had him so terrified of the world beyond the bedroom that I could release him from his bonds and let him roam freely from one corner of the bed to the other. He was so whipped by his condition that he wouldn't use the bathroom unless I accompanied him to confirm that he was behaving like a good boy.

Eventually, he did overcome that reluctance when I showed him how much fun we could have in the shower and the bathtub. That became his second playroom, and he'd ask me every day if we could take a shower together, and if he was really really a good boy, would I let him do this one thing he had learned to enjoy—or perhaps that other thing that he liked even more—or perhaps first one and then the other…?

And then, finally, on the day that even a slab of raw beef and a tumbler of beef blood were no longer enough to satisfy his physical hunger—on that day, it was time.

"I'm going to have to punish you, Bud—"

He leapt onto the bed eagerly, squirming in anticipation. He went down on his hands and knees and pushed his panty-clad butt up for the desired spanking. He wiggled his ass excitedly, an enthusiastic invitation—a hopeful provocation to the expected pleasures of epidermal assault and intestinal penetration.

Tempting, but no.

But we'd come so far in so few days. I had to smile.

Bud's disappearance from the bar had created a small stir among the patrons. I had slipped in quietly to see if he had been missed. Apparently, he had been a popular host and several of the patrons had expressed a flicker of regret before waving their glass for a refill. But the turnover in that community was fast-paced and Bud had been quickly forgotten, his successor even more popular—and probably less dangerous to the clientele.

But if they could have seen what he had turned into, scrambling around like a big clumsy puppy, a naked boy in crimson lingerie—they would have been shocked and embarrassed and disturbed. That was then—today, it would be an internet event, a viral sensation. The human race, always inventive, has always found ways to turn its fetishes into commodities.

But it's unsurprising to a Nightsider. It would be unsurprising to anyone who has journeyed through enough decades to see that the only thing that changes is the rationalization. The species that birthed us is a species of pretentious justification. Civilization has never been much more than a thin veneer hiding the squalid truth of a much darker nature. We are gluttons for sensation.

The difference between Nightsiders and daysiders is not our appetites—we share the same compulsions. No, the difference is that Nightsiders don't pretend to be good. We don't pretend to be sane. With the clarity of sense that comes with transformation, we know exactly what we are.

We are monsters, yes—but we know we are monsters. It has been our choice to become monsters. We move among the daysiders, mostly undetected because we choose to remain undetected—and when we behave monstrously, it is also because we have chosen to do so.

Daysiders—the pathetic and unformed, the desperate and defeated—daysiders act as if they have no choice in the matter. And that is why they are always so shocked when one or another of them is caught in monstrous behavior.

The difference? Nightsiders don't get caught.

I turned my attention back to Bud, still waggling his ass suggestively. "Please, sir. May I be punished?"

"Yes, you may—but not like that."

"How then, master—?"

"I'm going to tie you up again."

"With the ropes? Oh, yes. Please. Tie them tightly. Stretch me hard.

I like that."

"You like everything now—"

"Because I can feel everything. Everything feels so good now. You taught me well. Please teach me some more."

Did the thought cross my mind that I might have gone too far with poor Bud, transforming him into such a pathetic figure, a sexual mendicant, a caricature of lust? Yes, the thought did occur to me—a pale echo of the moral sense my distant father had once tried to instill in my youthful soul. But I had only to remember Bud's own brutal behavior— his intention to punish me—to remind myself that what I intended next was an appropriate response. Appropriate for a Nightsider, that is.

"You're going to have to stand up for this one, Bud."

He looked puzzled, but complied.

"Now, you're going to have to take off your panties. And your bra."

I waited while he quickly scrambled out of them.

"Now, cross your arms over your chest—like this. That's it."

From the play chest at the foot of the bed, the chest I always kept locked, I took out several long rolls of gauze bandages and began wrapping them around his torso, pinning his arms to his chest. I wound the strips from his neck to his hips, then back up to his neck again, around and around, turning him slowly as I wrapped, until the upper half of his body was thoroughly mummified. A second set of rolls and I bound his thighs and calves as well. I left his ass and uncovered, his penis as well.

When I was done, I pushed him down onto the bed, centering him in the sheets, and tied him again so he couldn't roll away, not to the right, not to the left.

The whole time, he giggled in delicious anticipation, occasionally asking what I intended. I shook my head as I worked. "It's going to be the biggest surprise of all." Another few rolls for his head and his neck. I left his eyes and his mouth uncovered—as well as an access to his carotid.

When I was satisfied that he would not be able to free himself, I stepped back to survey what I had accomplished. I had reduced a dayside monster to a creature of nightside obsession. His obsession, not mine.

Nightsiders do not experience passion as an uncontrollable force, but as a store of energy to be appropriately channeled and focused as the need arises. Passion is a choice. Myself—I am passionate about my intentions, but I rarely dramatize them. Drama betrays the soul to others. Unchecked rage reveals where you hurt and where you can be hurt even worse.

Survival requires a veneer of impassivity, a seemingly dispassionate demeanor. From there, everything is deliberate, everything is a performance suited to the moment. That's a lesson that takes time to learn, even more time to put into practice—but everything I had done to Bud was the cumulative result of that education. And the end result—it was an expression of the highest art a Nightsider might aspire to, a symphony of emotional experience, a palette of exquisite sensations to be savored like wine.

From Bud's position, however—

Well, the trap had closed around him the moment he drew his arm back and curled his fist. From that moment, this was inevitable. But this is the part that neither Bud nor any other daysider could understand—nothing of what I had done was for the purpose of either his elevation or his embarrassment. None of it was about his experience at all. No—the entire process was merely a means to an end.

I sat down on the bed next to him. I put my hand on his heart. It was beating rapidly. He was delirious with anticipation. A multitude of sensations were piling up inside him—the feeling of the gauze against his skin, the tightness of his bindings, his inability to move, the complete loss of physical mobility, and the concomitant surrender to circumstance—his willing submission to my absolute control over his existence, all because of his addiction to the pleasures attendant to transformation. All of it was the deliberate and methodical progress toward this specific moment.

As I tightened the ball-gag so he could not speak, I patted him gently on the head, stroking him to ease his excitement and prepare him for what would come next.

"Do you remember when I said you could choose how to die? Painfully? Or very painfully? For a long time? Remember that? And you chose the long time and very painfully?"

He tried to nod. He couldn't. So he blinked twice.

"Well, this is that. This is where it begins. I taught you how to enjoy yourself. I want you to enjoy the exquisite pain that begins now."

His heart began beating faster with anticipation.

"One last thing. I'm going to leave you now. Will I be back? Maybe. Maybe not. You have no way of knowing, do you? So there is only one thing you can do—the only thing you are capable of now. You can go dormant. You can go deep. Just how long you survive will depend on how deep you go. I recommend going all the way down. There is no bottom, but go all the way anyway."

I started to rise, then stopped myself. I sat back down. "Nobody knows how long it's possible to stay down. The longest I've ever heard of anyone surviving was just a little over a century. But you're not really asleep. You're still kind of conscious the whole time. So the one who stayed down for a century—when he came back up, he was insane. Of course, he'd been in a coffin that whole time, so that might have had something to do with it too.

"I considered that for you—but it seemed like an awful lot of trouble, more effort than you really deserve. I think this will be more interesting for you—and more interesting for me in the long run. If I get curious, I might come back. But then again, maybe not. You weren't as interesting as I had hoped. And your flavor is—well, it's enthusiastic, but I doubt you'll ever be a treasured vintage, one worth aging in the cask, so to speak. But I could be wrong. Winemaking is a skill I haven't really mastered yet. I'm not sure anyone has—not this kind of liqueur, anyway."

I patted him on the head one more time, a gentle farewell. I locked the door on my way out.

"And you never went back?"

"On the contrary. Do you think I'm some kind of monster?" Jacob strokes my cheek, laughing gently. "Well, I am, yes—but I'm not that kind of monster."

"Huh?"

He leans over and kisses me. "You are so sweet. This is the part I love best. Shocking the newborn out of their naiveté."

"You're mocking me, aren't you?"

"Only a little."

"I know I'm not the first, but—"

"But you're the first in a long time who's gotten this far."

"You do realize, none of this is reassuring me—?"

"Joseph, my dear little sweetmeat. If I wanted you that way, I would have taken you that way a long time ago. And if you had wanted to escape this possibility, you would have been gone a long time ago. You can still walk out any time you want—but you won't, because you want to know the rest. You want it all. That's been clear from the beginning. No, my little morsel, I never had to stalk you. From the beginning, you set yourself out as bait for me."

I have no response to that. He's right.

"You pretended to be horrified, but you were fascinated. You pretended to be repelled, but you never realized how deeply I could read your reactions—you weren't casually attracted, you weren't enthusiastically interested—you were compelled to follow this journey to this end. You made yourself into something that you believed I would desire."

I can only nod in submission.

"I'm right, aren't I? Admit it."

"You're using *the voice* on me, aren't you?"

"No, I'm not. Admit it, Joseph. This is what you wanted from the beginning."

Hesitation. I understand the feeling. If I say yes, if I admit the truth— then I am finally, completely, totally, one with him. I will never be able to say he forced me into this, that I was unwilling, that I was captured and unwilling....

If I say it, if I say the words, then I will be crossing the final line.

"Is this what's different—between me and him? Me and the others?"

"If you say so, yes. If you choose it, yes." His eyes meet mine, his gaze is piercing. "Say it. Say the truth, Joseph."

"The truth...is...that yes, I did choose you. I chose this."

"Yes, you did." He puts a finger under my chin and lifts my face to his. "The truth about seduction—the truth about the submissive partner—it's the submissive who's in control. Nothing happens without the submissive's consent. He can say stop at any time—and it stops. Otherwise, it's rape. So he's really saying go, but go slow. Make it a delicate game of pretend-conquest, one nipple at a time."

Hm.

"Think about it, Joseph. The submissive chooses it, one step at a time. I didn't seduce you, Joseph. You seduced me—it was all a dance of desire from the very beginning. You wanted me to seduce you, but it was you who opened the door and invited me in. Look inside—at your own feelings. Do you recognize that now?"

I blink hard. The truth is inescapable. Painful tears start to well up in my eyes.

"You see it now, don't you?"

I give him my humblest agreement. "That first night—when we went out in the dark, just to talk—whatever it was, yes, I felt something. And I wanted to know what it was I was feeling. I wanted—I didn't know what I wanted, I just knew I wanted it. Otherwise, I wouldn't have gone. Call it curiosity, attraction, even desire—but you must have sensed it, how could you not?"

"I saw what you were feeling...."

"So now you have to admit something too, Jacob—there was something about me that you wanted. Otherwise, I'd have never seen you again—"

"Yes, there was something. There still is."

"So I guess I got something right—?"

"More than something."

"Okay. Tell me. Why me? Why did you choose me? Or whatever—why did you let me choose you?"

"It was your curiosity as much as anything. No—that's not it. You wanted to learn, but more than that, it's that other thing you do—research. That was me when I started. Joseph, you're a scholar. And a reporter—"

"Oh, I'm a reporter? I reported your stories. Does that make me Dr. Watson?"

"My stories are true—"

"So, I'm Boswell—"

"But you're telling your story too."

"Ahh, I'm Proust."

"Oh, please no. You smell one silly cookie and it unleashes a whole torrent of memory, seven volumes and more, your whole tedious life story. What a ghastly bore—no, that's not you. You have enough skill to get to the punch line before I die of boredom."

"And what's the punch line here, my beautiful naked vampire man-boy...?"

"Ahh." Jacob sat up in bed, crossing his legs and facing me. "The punch line...?"

Bud wasn't very smart, he still thought he was playing his part in an intricate sex game—just another exquisite expression of his sexual enslavement to a compelling and delicious master, he had never realized just how wrong he was—but he was smart enough to go dormant.

In fact, he went so dormant he didn't even wake up when I came back for my first taste—three weeks later, or maybe it was five or six weeks, I don't remember, and it doesn't matter.

I sat down on the bed next to him. I stroked his neck for a while. Finally I nipped at his neck, not a huge bite, just a little sip. He was developing well, enough that I could wait a while longer to see what other flavors might express themselves.

It is in my nature to talk a subject to death. It is perhaps something I learned from Monsieur—first you learn, you explore and you discover, you ask the first question and then you ask all the questions that are unlocked by that first one. And then, as you proceed deeper and deeper into that inquiry, you share what you are discovering so that it does not die with you. Sharing your journeys make them real—to yourself and to the people you share them with.

Sitting there next to him, listening to the darkness, the quiet grumbling of the sleeping city, watching the moonlight slowly cross the floor, I realized I was finally slipping back into my own contemplative state—that place of awareness without action, thought without intention—that sublime condition which defines the Nightsider existence. It is the ability to stand on the mountaintop of—oh, call it enlightenment, though it is anything but—and survey the entire landscape of existence spread out below as a feast to be enjoyed at leisure.

The thought did occur to me then that Bud and I did have a relationship, even though his perception of it was vastly different than my own, but because that relationship did exist—well, the performance of it anyway—I was duty bound to give him some explanation for what I had done to him—and why. If I did not explain it to him, then his side of the relationship would remain unresolved. And while another Nightsider might have taken a certain sociopathic delight in leaving Bud confused and alone, uncertain and hurting, silently traumatized by the apparent abandonment of his master—that was not me. I would have felt equally unresolved.

Let me clarify something here.

Two months had passed since that first night in June, Japan had surrendered and the nation had succumbed to its own delirium. No one knew what would happen next, but everyone was certain it would be wonderful. It probably would not be wonderful—the problems of cleaning up afterward are always much more complex than anyone considers while making the mess, and this is exponentially true of war—or any kind of violence.

But for a Nightsider, any dramatic shift in the national mood represents a wealth of opportunities—not just a marvelously enhanced menu at the buffet of humanity, but more than that—the chance to create new identities as insurance for long-term survival. As I have said before, a Nightsider must move at least once a decade, and usually more often than that.

Given all that, my obligation to the completion of Bud was significantly reduced. Indeed, I had no emotional investment in punishing him. He was just another piece of meat.

I could have taken him on that first night—but as I admitted at the beginning, I was bored. Worse than bored. I had been sinking into a languorous ennui.

Bud had been an opportunity to break that continuing decline in my spirits. Now that I had returned to the far more meditative state of Nightsider existence, my interest in Bud was significantly reduced. The exercise was in its final stages and my concerns would shortly be turning to the larger opportunities of the post-war situation.

Ultimately, I decided that it could be a useful opportunity to give Bud the truth of his situation—would this new set of realizations and consequent emotions do to his flavor? Would it add delicious undertones of resignation and despair? Or, was he so enraptured by his submission to the inevitable that new flavors of joy and sweetness might develop? Or would he develop a rich blend of both at once? It was an interesting conundrum to consider. What could I say or do here that would achieve that combination of tastes?

By the time that train of thought had arrived at its terminus, I had been sitting with Bud, my hand resting on his chest, for more than an hour.

He was down deep, too deep to wake up easy, and I doubted he could learn how to come back up from that deep—not without a mentor. If I chose to leave him dormant, it might very well turn out to be a permanent slumber for him.

"So, Bud—here we are again. I know you can hear me. And I know you are wondering if you should wake up, but I don't think you know how and I'm not going to teach you, not tonight anyway. I think you should stay where you are. So just relax—well, you can't do anything else but relax—so that's all right. Just relax and listen.

"I suppose you're wondering when the fun begins. Well, this is it. This is the fun. Not yours. Mine. And for no reason at all that concerns you, I shall explain exactly why it is fun—for me. And maybe for you as well. If that's what you want.

"You see...this condition you're in now, way down there in the dark place of dream-time, this slowed-down time of geological awareness, it's not an unpleasant place to be—well, not unless you start to resist it. Then it gets very unpleasant, very fast, and stays that way for a very long time. You can scare yourself to death that way. A long excruciating descent into madness—maybe followed by death, but probably not. I don't recommend it. So...because you really don't have a choice in anything that's going to happen for the rest of your life, your only option is to just let it happen. Relax. Submit. Surrender. And enjoy your long slow painful decline, into madness or death, your choice. There are many who would envy you. They never got that choice.

"Anyway—whatever you choose, this is the part where you die very painfully and take a long time doing it—whether you enjoy it or not. And now I'm going to tell you the rest of it—so you can understand exactly why you have been given this particular ecstasy. Consider it a—oh, let's call it a boon, a favor, a gift. Because normally, I wouldn't bother. I mean, do you ever apologize to a pig for liking bacon...?

"You see, my little brute-sissy. There was something you asked once—way back when we started. You asked me why I was doing this and I told you why. You had your fun. Now it was my turn. It's still my turn. In fact, it has always been my turn.

"But don't take it personally. It was just—are you familiar with the word *karma*? It's an eastern concept. It's about how your actions make ripples in the world and those ripples come back to you—a fancy way of saying 'what goes around comes around.' What happened was you got what you created. I was just the...um, what's a good word...the instrument of delivery.

"You see, when we got into this bed—remember that? I thought we were going to have some fun together. But we didn't. I mean, you had fun—but it wasn't fun for me. Remember? You hit me. You slapped me. You called me names. You raised your fist to me. You treated me like an object for your selfish gratification—do you remember that? It seems like such a long time ago, doesn't it? But that was when you chose this. Because that was the moment that I chose you as an object for my selfish gratification. Fair is fair, correct? Of course, my gratification takes a lot more effort than yours...."

I stroked his chest lightly. Even through his bandages, all those layers of gauze wrapping, the sensation must have been marvelous and excruciating. His eyes flickered, but didn't open. He was so deep he was cold. Room temperature. When they found him—well, it would probably be an interesting autopsy—especially when the first knife went in and he came screaming awake. Pity the poor pathologist.

"Y'know, Bud—this is only vaguely relevant, but maybe it isn't. It seems to me sometimes that people like you tend to channel yourselves into specific patterns of conduct. The obvious example of course is the dominant-submissive structure of sexual gratification. It's a binary construct, Bud—apparently limited only to black and white, with no real shades of gray possible between. You are either one or the other, a top or a bottom—so when a person is limited to that way of thinking, he becomes self-limited to either one or the other of only two possible roles. Top or bottom. Dominant or submissive. That's not me, I find that boring—but apparently that was all you were capable of, wasn't it?

"Maybe you believed you were a dominant. And maybe you needed to express it as brutality. But I think there's more to it than that. I think you were ashamed of your own desires—and therefore you had to punish anyone who saw you as desirable that way. You would be an interesting chapter in any textbook on psychotherapy.

"Anyway, if that was your sexual identity—and based on the evidence of the past two months, I think I'm right about this—when that specific expression was taken away from you, completely and totally obliterated as an option, there was no place for your identity to go, was there? No escape, except to assume the reverse expression of that same role. You flipped over completely and became the most abject submissive. And, my dear sweet puppy, apparently, you have been enjoying it even more than your time as a dominant. This seems to have been what you wanted all along—someone to force you into your own desires, so you wouldn't have to be ashamed of enjoying them. You can still pretend it wasn't your choice. Except—well, in this case it was. Remember? I gave you the choice.

"Okay, I admit it—I wasn't completely honest. But then again, neither were you in your invitation, so let's not worry about which of us is the bigger monster or who was the most at fault. It doesn't matter. This collision was inevitable the moment you raised your fist to me.

"You do know what I am, don't you? You must have figured it out by now. And you must also have realized what I turned you into—oh, wait." I lifted my hand away from his chest, I held it up in mock denial—an unnecessary gesture to be sure, but I was beginning to feel melodramatic.

"Yes, I turned you. I created you. I transformed you—but despite that, you are nothing like me. Nothing at all. And you never will be. That was never a possibility. You are not my equal, you will never be my equal.

"You, my dear—you are a snack table. Maybe, with a bit of thyme and seasoning, you could become a whole meal—but right now, you're still a snack.

"But then, you should have realized that by now. All the sipping and tasting I've been doing—like an Italian grandmother fussing over the sauce—

"Let me explain. I get hungry. Approximately once a month. No, not the full moon. The dark of the moon. I don't need a whole meal, but I do need to slake my thirst—enough to satisfy the cravings that arise. And over time, I have become something of a connoisseur. It was inevitable. Doing the same thing over and over—first it's a habit, then it's a routine, finally it's a rut. And a rut is a grave with the ends knocked out. So…I look for variation. And over time, my tastes have become more than epicurean—they have become esoteric and exotic. You—don't flatter yourself—are nowhere near the pinnacle of taste. But you are—well, you are what you are—a demonstration that even a casual slab of flank steak can be tasty with the right preparation.

"The goal in any project of this type is to create a unique vintage. To an ordinary human being, one who has not been given this particular gift, blood is blood, it all tastes the same—a little salty, a little metallic, a little meaty. But to a Nightsider, blood is nectar and this is the important part, every person has a unique flavor—a distinctly identifiable blend.

"Pay attention now, Bud. This is important. Someone who has lived a reckless life, too much of this and too much of that, he's overspiced—he's a Texican burrito loaded with jalapenos and habaneros and God knows what else—not my style, very much an acquired taste. On the other hand, a teenager, young and naïve and mostly inexperienced—that's a nice healthy drink, youthful blood is invigorating, but too often it's as flavorless as veal, occasionally delicious but just as often as unsatisfying as oatmeal. Now, if you can find an innocent lover, blood laden with endorphins—he can be as sweet as peppermint ice cream, but cloying.

"When you've been around for a while—half a century or more—sampling here, sampling there, occasionally gorging, you begin to develop a sense of taste. The more you drink, the more that taste develops. What do they say? Taste is the product of a thousand distastes? That's even truer for a Nightsider. A quickie grabbed in a dark alley is little better than the grilled hockey puck they call a hamburger at the Woolworth lunch counter. Frankly, my dear—I do not want an industrial burger. I want prime rib.

"And…when I can have it, when I can make it myself, that's when it's the best. Are you getting it yet? The darkest blood is the richest. And the richest blood is vampire blood. I wish you could taste yourself.

"The blood of the Nightsider is the best. It has the most subtle of flavors, deep and rich, unfolding on the tongue like a symphony. What makes it so delicious and desirable is the symphony of flavor. It's the seasonings, the spices of emotion and experience, all of them together—as carefully blended as a fine whiskey, aged for decades in an oaken cask. That was why I turned you, Bud. For the flavor."

Was that a flutter of emotion? It was too faint even for me to tell. I could have taken a sip, but if the emotion had been that faint, the flavor would have been undetectable. Never mind.

I patted his chest and went on. "But even fresh vampire blood—like yours now—has a youthful and intoxicating quality. You see, the real flavor of the vintage develops in the fermenting—the process of transformation.

"A good transformation takes time—not just the physical process, but all the learning that must come afterward as well. That's the best vintage. But—if you're like me, occasionally impatient, and if you're hungry enough and if it's obvious that all you have is hamburger, not prime rib—then you settle for a well-prepared burger. It depends on the Nightsider. And, like everything else, it's a matter of taste. I'm not boring you, am I?"

I had my hand back on Bud's chest. His heartbeat remained glacial, counting out his dreamtime in a funereal beat. Not even a flutter.

"All right, Bud, I will admit—in the beginning, in that first moment of capture, yes, you had some flavor, a strong flavor, but a very simple flavor, lacking any real depth. And frankly, it had very little potential.

"But I was bored. Bored enough to be curious. Bored enough to experiment—what might be possible with a little seasoning, a little spice? You see, what you were missing was the full range of human emotion. I began to wonder what you might taste like with a modicum of Nightsider flavor added. That would require some effort on my part, but at the time, like I said, I was bored and I was curious and I had nothing else to do.

"Oh, I won't pretend I didn't enjoy the exercise. I enjoyed it quite a bit. Humiliating you, Bud—humbling you, reducing you to the most abject of all submissive behaviors—there was a poetic satisfaction to it. You confirmed my belief about the binary character of your sexual identity—indeed, the shift in your behavior occurred so quickly you surprised me. Thank you for that. There is little that surprises me anymore.

"And yes, you seasoned up well—better than I expected, although not quite as flavorful as I had hoped. But that's not my fault. It's yours. You're really quite a shallow fellow.

"Nevertheless, it was worth the effort. I took you through as much of the emotional landscape as you were capable of expressing. Fear? That's where I started—fear is the fundamental ground of being for anything with a spinal cord. What's that lurking in the dark? What just made that noise? What's out there? And what's going to happen to me? Oh yes, Bud, I had you nervous, I had you queasy—but most of all, I had you panicked, terrified, pissing your diaper in fear. That frozen chill of terror—your sweat reeked of it. Your heart beat so fast you were in danger of a cardiac event. I loved it—

"And then anger—that's so easy to create. It's the flip side of fear. If you can't flee, you have to fight. But if you can't fight, if you're tied down, if you're being tormented and abused, all you can do is burn with unrequited rage. Oh yes, I did that too—I took you from resentment to range and back again, over and over. I humiliated you and taunted you—I played you like a violin. Diapers and panties—those were just the warmups. What I did to your body, everything—it was a methodical campaign to strip you of your last pretense of masculinity. I stripped you as raw as a flayed corpse—just to feel the heat of your fury. And yes, you burned—you burned like the wrath of hell.

"And then—when you finally burned out, when there was absolutely nothing left to burn—I left you to grieve, to despair. I let you sink to the innermost depths of anguish and hysteria. You hung there, on the brink of insanity for the longest time—what bizarre hallucinations did you experience? Tiny spiders crawling inside your veins? Harpies shrieking into your ears as they ate your flesh? Eyeballs exploding out of your melting skull? Skin decomposing and falling away from your rotting corpse? What fun you must have had!

"And after that—when you finally resigned yourself to the contemplative hell of your captivity—that this was the shape of your death—that was when I began to tease and tickle you and take you on your journey of exquisite discovery—all designed to demonstrate the qualities of physical sensation available to a transformed body. I let you experience it as pleasure, as delight, as joyous rapture—and yes, I gave you an access to an emotional repertoire that you had never known before. That should have sent you plunging even deeper into fear and anger and despair—the realization that you had wasted your life on brutality when this had always been available to you—

"But no, I wasn't going to send you there—that would have been cruel. And besides, it would have spoiled the flavor. No, I wanted you enthralled. I wanted you totally captivated by my power to control and manipulate you. I wanted that sweetness in your blood—and while it smacks of bragging, I think I accomplished it quite well. Despite my casual disparagement of your origins, you might very well become a worthwhile and respectable vintage. Time will tell. Please don't die on me now. Let your death take a long long time. Very long. I'm curious to see how well you'll age."

———————

Jacob puts his hands behind his head and leans back against the headboard. "I kept him alive for three years, sipping a bit here, a bit there—until I realized that as good as he was, he wasn't going to get any better. So I ended him."

What my lover is talking about is so far beyond my experience, I don't know what to say. The best I can offer is a question. "Why not?

"Depth."

"Depth?"

"That's what was missing. Depth. He was incomplete. There was too much that he'd never experienced—"

"But you—"

Jacob faces me, his expression is intense. "It was my fault. I never let him out of the room. So he'd never had the opportunity to feed, never knew what it was like to capture and kill and celebrate the achievement of creating your own feast. You can't be a healthy predator without that skill. That's what was missing from his blood. He'd never had the chance to test the limits of his enhanced physical abilities. His body was vampire, but it wasn't full vampire. It was atrophied."

I hadn't experienced any of that. Not yet. I wasn't sure what it would feel like. I could only imagine. I could only nod.

Jacob takes a deep breath and adds a final observation. "It was a useful experiment though."

"Useful?"

"Mm-hm. By learning what I was missing, I learned how to do it better the next time."

"Next time...?"

"Mm-hm..."

"But if you realized what was missing then, why didn't you let him out so he could be complete?"

"Because he was stupid." Jacob rolls to face me, pulls me into his arms, holds me close in a mutually cold embrace. "Being a successful vampire requires skill and training. It's not enough to be a sociopath, you also have to be intelligent and cunning and practical. Bud was none of these things. He was brutal and selfish and stupid. He would have become a monster. I don't want that kind of attention. None of us do."

I have nothing to say to that. His arms are cold, colder than mine. His heartbeat is slow and methodical—and eventually my heart synchronizes to his. I feel our blood, his and mine together, pulsing outward in mutually exciting waves. He's smells delicious.

"Jacob?"

"Yes?"

"Can I ask you something?"

"You can ask me anything. I might answer...."

"Did you ever think of me that way?"

"What way?"

"You know what I mean."

He hesitates, then, "Yes, I considered it—"

"But...?"

"But nothing." He begins tracing his fingers along the curve of my chest, circling inward around my left nipple.

Watson without Sherlock. The movies never showed us that story. And it's long overdue.

THE LAST CASE OF SHERLOCK HOLMES
As told by Doctor John Watson, MD

SECOND BONUS STORY

After all these many years, and facing the end of my time on this Earth, I will finally record the true circumstances surrounding the death of Sherlock Holmes.

I am well aware that some may voice the opinion that by writing this account I am dishonoring the memory of my dearest friend, but if I do not make my best effort to relate the facts of what I observed and experienced, then I would be dishonoring myself and that would have earned the strongest possible reproach from Holmes.

And yet, even as I record these events, I can still hear Holmes snorting in contempt because so much of this violates his own long-standing skepticism about certain supernatural events. Nevertheless, I shall report and you, dear reader, shall decide for yourself if these events actually happened, or if I am suffering from the delusions of age.

Until he retired from public life, Sherlock Holmes and I shared lodgings at 221 Baker Street, where we were well-tended by the unforgettable Mrs. Hudson. Faithful readers of these adventures know that Holmes had retired to the Sussex Downs, where he took up beekeeping, but that was not always a permanent situation. From time to time, he would grow restless, an unintended consequence of the solitude and return to the vast possibilities for diversion to be found in London.

Sometimes he came back at the request of Superintendent Lestrade, and sometimes simply to take on a particularly interesting challenge. Because I had stayed in our flat to maintain our various case files, it was convenient for Holmes to return and resume our partnership.

Although she never said it where Holmes might hear, Mrs. Hudson would occasionally observe that it was not always the challenge of the case that drew him back. She was of the opinion that Holmes missed my companionship as much as I missed his. Working with Holmes was a unique privilege, and as this narrative will soon demonstrate, our partnership succeeded not just because of our mutual commitment to justice, but because of our singular friendship as well.

I have always been reluctant to acknowledge gossip of any kind, even when there is a kernel of truth, because the existence of that kernel is so often used to justify the larger and often erroneous speculations. Nevertheless, at this late point in life, I will finally address this one rumor and erase all doubt in the matter.

The collaboration between Holmes and myself was based on profound trust and respect, nothing more. We shared a flat because it was beneficial to our work. Holmes did not keep business hours. Sometimes he would pace back and forth for hours, gnawing at a particularly challenging puzzle. That we developed an easy familiarity in our work was simply the result of our common interests. Nevertheless, there were some distracted souls who assumed that such familiarity was proof that the two of us might have been coupled in some unseemly way.

The first time I heard of such a speculation, my immediate first impulse was to publicly denounce that squalid gossip, but Holmes stopped me before I could act. In his wisdom, he pointed out that such an effort would only call attention to the matter. "Do not, dear Watson, invest yourself into any pursuit you do not wish to magnify. There is no way to stop these people from giggling their gossip over biscuits and tea. It is their only joy in life. Do not give them the credibility of your notice. Besides," he added, "it is well known that our dear Mrs. Hudson would never allow anything so unseemly in any rooms she rented." He was right, of course. By letting the matter drop, it was mostly forgotten.

It was a small thing, but it served once again to demonstrate that Holmes was possessed of a unique ability to observe and deduce. Despite his own brusque manner, he continually exhibited a rare insight into human behavior. I believe this unique skill was one of the reasons why he was unmatched as a consulting detective.

Often, while he pondered the circumstances, he would mutter to himself, his way of putting his thoughts out where he could examine them at some remove. Equally, he might repeat some philosophical distinction as a way of examining the underlying foundation of an event. Of course, I make no claim that I was ever Holmes's equal in intellect, but our close association gave me ample opportunity to observe and learn his methods. Eventually, I came to the realization that my own remarks were a necessary part of Holmes' conversations of analysis. Though Holmes never specifically acknowledged it, I am certain that was why he shared his thoughts aloud, so as to gauge my reactions. My participation was part of his deductive process.

Not commonly reported by myself or anyone else, Holmes would occasionally observe, "There are no causes, Watson. There are no effects. There is only process. Understand the processes and much becomes clear."

The first time he made that assertion, it confused me. In fact, I found it a source of puzzlement for quite some time. I had so rigorously trained my thinking in the field hospitals of The Great War that I saw every wound, every disease, every condition as the result of specific causes. Therefore Holmes' remark seemed at odds with his unusually precise deductive skills, but ultimately, as I shall soon demonstrate, this was a key understanding to unraveling the events that followed his murder.

Yes, Sherlock Holmes was murdered.

For many years, the actual circumstances of that most horrible crime have been known only to a few. When the last of us has gone to the grave, there will be none left to tell the tale. But as I said at the beginning, the truth must be told. Holmes would have demanded nothing less.

There may be those who will dispute what I am about to disclose. They will take refuge in the many published accounts that Holmes died peacefully in his sleep—but various political pressures made that falsehood necessary. Had any other account of his death been reported, the result would have been severe social turmoil and endless politically-motivated investigations, making the resolution of the actual mystery much more difficult to achieve.

Nevertheless, Holmes' death was neither natural nor accidental.

The day began in a most unsettling manner. Instead of the maid bringing our tray, it was Mrs. Hudson who came up the stairs. Holmes recognized her footsteps and remarked, "Mrs. Hudson is upset," even before she knocked and came in.

Mrs. Hudson wore an angry scowl and she was muttering her own litany of rage. Holmes steepled his hands in front of his face and observed. It was immediately obvious, even to my own limited powers of deduction, that something was terribly wrong. The final piece of evidence was the tea service—instead of our usual service, she carried a dubiously ornate teapot and cups, a flowery porcelain confection that had sat unused on the top shelf of her cupboard for as long as we had lived here.

She had prepared a greater than usual repast. Tea, milk, Bacon, poached eggs, toast, butter, those awful preserves that only Holmes liked, fresh scones and clotted cream. Holmes ignored the food; he took the ghastly set from Mrs. Hudson and laid it on the table, then guided her to his chair. "You are upset," he said. "And based on the evidence, it is because someone has stolen my tea service and you have prepared a sumptuous breakfast to make up for it."

Mrs. Hudson needed a moment to gather her words. Knowing that Holmes required precision, she did her best. "Yes, your tea set," she said. "How many years have I served you with that set? How many? All these years! It's gone!"

"Is it possible you might have misplaced it?" I asked.

A harmless question perhaps, but Mrs. Hudson looked at me as if I'd insulted her. "I know my kitchen, Doctor Watson!" She turned back to Holmes. "Someone—pardon my language, but some vile area sneak—broke into my kitchen last night. I can't believe the boldness, the impudence! Only an animal would invade a lady's home. That's why I check the locks every night, right after Mr. Holmes. That's how I know he came in by the roof and he left by the back door, right into the mews. And he left the door wide open, like he had no manners at all. Oh, I tell you. It's bad enough, him just coming in where he has no right, but that shameful scoundrel helped himself to—with all the other nice things in my kitchen—why would a thief steal a tea set? Especially that one. It was—I'm sorry, Mr. Holmes, but it really was rather plain and unremarkable. Not worth a tuppence, if you ask me. Well, you did ask me, didn't you? I meant only that it was really quite worthless. It wasn't important to anyone, except maybe you."

"Precisely," said Holmes. "That was why it was stolen."

"Beg pardon, Holmes," I interrupted. "Why would someone want to steal such a mediocre tea set? There's nothing special or unique about it. Not even a monogram." It was a fair question to ask. Holmes had brought the service with him when he'd moved in. The cups and teapot were plain white porcelain with only the slightest bit of Dutch-blue trim. Holmes had asked Mrs. Hudson to never inflict that fancy set on him again. He said that her tea service, all decorated with gaudy pink roses and gold piping, was simply too distracting.

Holmes said, "Value is not a constant, Watson. It is a subjective experience. The elaborate adornments of this service in front of us practically shrieks for attention. As such, it distracts the user from attending the true purpose of the cups. The user compliments the ornamentation instead of appreciating the tea. The purpose of this extreme embellishment is a vulgar and pretentious display. It's arrogance applied to the inanimate. Conversely, the austerity of the stolen service demands that the user consider only its function—the tea. The deliberate humility honors its purpose."

Embarrassed, I fell silent. I had never given much thought to the way tea was served or why. Holmes obviously had.

Holmes turned back to Mrs. Hudson. "Did they take anything else?"

She shook her head. "Not a thing, not that I can tell."

"Of course not. The tea service was the purpose of the theft."

"I hope you don't mind," Mrs. Hudson continued, "but the first thing I did, I told the Irregulars. There's always one or two hanging around in case you need their eyes and ears."

"Quite wise," said Holmes.

"There must be twenty of them prowling the streets now, doing whatever it is they do, I'm sure I don't want to know everything they get up to. But those boys are resourceful, they are. Whoever stole the service, it wasn't a random idler passing through, nor was it one of the hangers on always lurking about, looking for an opportunity for mischief. One of them said that this was a much more professional job. If you could call it a job. I call it a disgrace. Breaking into someone's home like that." She sniffed with disapproval. "Of course, I had to report it to you, Mr. Holmes. What use is it having a consulting detective in the house if I can't consult?"

"Perhaps it was a souvenir collector," I suggested, "one of those fellows who scuttles about, collecting the odds and ends of other people's fame or notoriety."

"A useful observation, Watson." Abruptly, Holmes went to my writing desk and pulled the cover off the Underwood typewriter that one of my American admirers had sent over in the vain hope that I might write faster. Myself, I saw the infernal machine as an insult to my penmanship, but Holmes had regarded it with fascination and quickly taught himself to type. He rolled a piece of stationery into it and quickly pecked out a note. Seeing Holmes in action, Mrs. Hudson watched the whole performance in a state of curious bemusement.

Holmes signed the paper, folded it over, slid it into an envelope and handed it to her. "If you would be so kind, Mrs. Hudson, please have one of the Irregulars deliver this note to Senior Superintendent Lestrade at Scotland Yard."

Glad to have purpose again, Mrs. Hudson retreated downstairs. As soon as she had left, I turned to Holmes. "But why would a souvenir collector take the whole set? Why not just a cup? Taking the entire service seems excessive to me."

"And to myself as well," said Holmes. "An unusual theft, Watson, yes—until you consider the underlying process. The thief ignored many other things of value in Mrs. Hudson's kitchen, but took the tea service. Why?"

"I have no idea, I'm sure."

"Oh, Watson, my dear friend—isn't it obvious? You are the one who made that service valuable. Because you have published so many romanticized versions of our work, you and I have taken on a degree of fame, even celebrity in certain circles. Think of the history you have created. For nearly thirty years, Mrs. Hudson has used that same service to bring up our tea every morning. Imagine someone who has deeply invested himself in your stories. To such a person that service is not mediocre. Those cups and that teapot represent a personal connection to the unrestrained narratives you have created about the world's greatest consulting detective. Imagine the obsession of one who relishes drinking tea from the same cups that we have used."

"I would prefer not to imagine it. It sounds foolish. And a bit disturbing."

"More than a bit," agreed Holmes. "But that very obsession may lead us to an easy resolution. We shall see soon enough."

"Your note to Lestrade?"

Holmes nodded. "Scotland Yard is familiar with the most avid collectors of crime memorabilia. Some of them have even approached us occasionally. Perhaps our thief intends to sell our tea set to one of those collectors. What would be more enticing to one of our followers? Owning our tea set—or helping us actually catch the thief?"

"But it's such a minor thing," I said. "Hardly worth the effort."

"Ah, no. Remember what I said, Watson? Value is not a constant. It is subjective. It is assigned by desire—and desire is a reflection of identity. The processes of the mind have their own unique logic, quite different from the logic of science or math. What a person values defines them."

He sat down in his chair facing Mrs. Hudson's appalling pink pottery and poured himself a cup of tea. "Now, Watson, please go and see to Mrs. Hudson. She'll want to find an appropriately uninteresting service to replace the stolen one. You should accompany her. It will resolve some of her upset over the morning's events. I shall pay for it, of course."

"Without my tea?" I asked. Mrs. Hudson had prepared some delicious looking scones, with strawberry jam and clotted cream, to make up for the pretension of the cups and saucers.

"You shall have your tea when you return. Mrs. Hudson's state of mind is far more important."

I did not argue. As always, Holmes was right—and while I did not say so at the time, I thought it might also be necessary to explore other avenues of investigation as well. Perhaps there were possibilities that Holmes might not have considered worth the effort. While I fully expected him to be proven right in such an assessment, I still felt compelled to address those details.

Holmes had remarked more than once, "When you have eliminated all which is impossible, then whatever remains, however improbable, must be the truth." Of course, that conclusion, by its very definition, must require eliminating all which is impossible. Or at least, impractical.

It was not unusual for Mrs. Hudson and I to accompany each other on certain local errands. She appreciated the company, I'm sure, and I appreciated her expertise on the more practical matters of the city, in particular her remarkable skill at negotiations in the marketplace. Over the years, she had saved me quite a penny.

On this day, however, finding the right tea service for Holmes was not an errand that Mrs. Hudson could enjoy. She was still fuming about the violation of her kitchen, therefore the necessary restoration of her household's equilibrium was a personal charge, a matter to be pursued with diligence. She was committed to finding as near a duplicate of the stolen service as could be managed.

Although there were a number reputable vendors in the neighbor-hood, at my suggestion we began by visiting several local pawnbrokers. It was unlikely that we would find the same service, but neither was it im-possible that we might find a suitably plain equivalent. More important, it gave me an opportunity to inquire of the shopkeepers if anyone had sought to sell a tea set this morning. Unfortunately, there had been no such offers. Nevertheless, I did not consider it a wasted effort. It would help to confirm Holmes' own thesis.

Despite her clucking disapproval of most of the wares offered, Mrs. Hudson finally found a tea service that didn't displease her and one we both agreed would not be too distracting for Holmes. The cups were plain white with silver piping around the rims, but no other decoration.

I did express a thought that Holmes might find the silver too elegant for his taste, but Mrs. Hudson disagreed. "You and Mr. Holmes have lived like paupers long enough. I can accept that my rose and gold flow-ers are too much, but it's time to allow yourself a bit of fancy when you have your tea. And you may tell Mister Sherlock Holmes I said so."

Except for the bit of silver trim, the tea service was utilitarian and plain. Even the accompanying utensils that Mrs. Hudson chose were of a simple design. This was again due to Holmes' insistence on the simplest expressions of function. He was adamant that that his attention not be diverted into irrelevancies. Deduction, he said, demanded precision of thought. Mrs. Hudson had learned long ago not to argue with Holmes about how to reason, just as he had also learned not to argue with her about how to run her house—and I had learned not to argue with either of them. I nodded to the clerk, "Wrap it carefully, please," and dug out my pocketbook.

As we had walked quite a distance to find the right tea service, I hailed a taxi, a somewhat unusual luxury for Mrs. Hudson. She felt taxis to be an unnecessary expense. She had never liked the hansoms that once crowded the ways with noise and clutter and smells; now she had an even greater distaste for the many automobiles churning the streets of London. To her, they were loud and ugly and filled the air with a foul miasma. Men and women were made to walk she insisted, but this morning she did not object to riding. She held the new tea service on her lap as a personal vindication that the world could be made right.

The traffic was worse than usual. It was getting worse every day as more and more automobiles filled the streets. Someday, perhaps, traffic in London might grind to an absolute standstill and it seemed like today might be that day. But eventually we arrived back at Baker Street. I paid the driver and Mrs. Hudson bustled inside intending to restore order, if not to the world then at least to her kitchen.

While Mrs. Hudson busied herself, unwrapping and washing all the separate pieces of the new service, I made my way upstairs, thinking of scones and jam.

Holmes was asleep in his chair, his hands neatly in his lap, still holding his violin and bow, as though he had momentarily paused to consider the next musical phrase and quietly nodded off. I had seen him in this exact position so many times I knew not to disturb him. Besides, there was that matter of the unfinished scones.

Knowing that Holmes and I tended to have long speculative conversations while working our way through the daily papers, Mrs. Hudson always put a small spirit lamp under the teapot to keep the tea hot all morning. I was grateful for that. I prepared my belated breakfast, keeping as quiet as I could so as not to wake Holmes. But when I reached for a spoon, I felt a sharp jab at my elbow, sharp enough to knock the spoon out of my hand where it clattered across the tea tray.

I reached for the spoon again, and this time it leapt away from me, across the floor and somewhere into the shadows. Holmes gave a dreadful cry. "Don't touch it, Watson!" The intensity of his yell gave me a cold chill.

"But it's only a spoon—" Then I realized that Holmes had not moved at all. He still sat silent. "Holmes?" When I touched his arm, it fell limply to the floor, but still clutching the neck of the violin. "Holmes?!"

His skin was cold to the touch.

I am a doctor. I knew what I was seeing, but I did not believe it.

Sherlock Holmes was dead, had been dead long enough to lose all body warmth. He must have died at least an hour previously, while Mrs. Hudson and I were selecting a new tea service.

I'd seen my share of death on the battlefields, I was not horrified by the fact as much as I was dismayed at my own failure to see what should have been obvious. I had been so consumed with anticipation for tea and scones that I had assumed Holmes was quietly napping.

I said, "Oh, Holmes, what have you done now?"

As I said this, the violin slipped out of Holmes' hand. As it slipped to the floor, its strings caught briefly on his fingers, just enough for the instrument to give up one last heartbreaking note. It was at that moment the dreadful blow of realization overwhelmed me. I would never hear Holmes play the violin again. The icy chill in the pit of my stomach became a wave of overpowering emotion that flooded through my soul as a wave of crushing despair. I sank to my knees, too limp to stand, too weak to speak.

The full force of it overwhelmed me. I had never thought ahead to this possibility, had never considered that one day our adventures and our friendship would come to its inevitable mortal end. I could not accept the dreadful reality, yet here it was.

Perhaps I only imagined it, but Holmes was standing behind me, speaking his annoyance. "Oh, get up, Watson. There's much to do and I need you to do it."

"Yes, yes," I said. "I understand. You're indisposed. Being dead, as it were. So I have to take care of matters. Sorry, Holmes. I was distracted by my own grief. Very thoughtless of me." I stood up, brushing myself off, realizing how foolish I must have looked, talking to a dead man as if he were still able to communicate. Nevertheless, it felt appropriate.

When enough of my rationality returned that I could function again, I went downstairs to the front door. Occasionally, a young and inexperienced reporter might be waiting there, hoping for some bit of news, some hint of an important story that would catapult him into the higher ranks of his profession. Today was no different. A brash little fellow shouted at me, "What's up, gov? Is the game afoot?"

I ignored the question and gestured instead to Billy the page, a young relative of Mrs. Hudson, and one of the Baker Street Irregulars. Even though Holmes hadn't needed the services of the Irregulars for some time, he maintained the organization, just in case. Billy was lanky and kept himself just enough unkempt in his appearance that he would be ignored by most passers-by, the influence of Holmes perhaps. I pressed a shilling into his hand, a larger than usual amount, but necessary to stress the importance of the message. "Mr. Holmes is out of pipe tobacco," I said loud enough for the reporters to hear, but the real meaning was, "*Get Lestrade, now!*"

Lestrade had long since been promoted to Superintendent. Despite the shift in his duties, he had maintained his connection with Holmes and myself. This was not just an acknowledgment that Holmes' assistance had been valuable to the Yard on more than one occasion, it was a measure of his considerable respect, even friendship.

Billy shrugged as though I'd asked him why he was not in school somewhere, then wandered away with an insolent posture. As soon as he saw that the reporter was no longer watching him, he took off running.

"There's a case, isn't there?" shouted the reporter.

"No, there is not." I replied. "Fellows like you are the reason why Holmes has retired. A detective needs discretion. If Holmes cannot go anywhere without an entourage, he can no longer be effective. Now go away and leave us be." I'd given that speech before, it was a familiar one, but it had little effect, he just laughed as though it was all a great game.

I shut the door behind me. Taking a deep breath, I went back up the stairs. As difficult as the tasks that lay ahead, I had learned well from Holmes—do nothing physical, but take careful notes until official support arrives.

Perhaps it was my long history with Holmes that gave me pause, but no—I had distinctly heard Holmes' dreadful shout. It was Holmes who had knocked the spoon out of my hand. I hadn't imagined it. Therefore, something was quite wrong.

If this were a murder investigation, I would suspect poisoning and would examine the contents of the teapot and the sugar bowl and the scones as well. That was the obvious evidence and the first items to investigate. But Mrs. Hudson, despite her occasional irascibility could not possibly be a suspect. So what else should I consider? Holmes had been sitting alone in a locked room all morning. No, it didn't make sense.

I sat down opposite Holmes and stared at him. "You have picked the wrong day to die," I told him. "It's very thoughtless of you, more thoughtless than usual. You have put me at quite a loss. And I have no idea how to tell Mrs. Hudson. This is going to break her heart. And I still haven't had my tea."

And then I closed my eyes and began to weep uncontrollably. This was more than I could bear—but once again, I distinctly heard Holmes's voice, "Oh, stop that foolishness, Watson. Get up and investigate my murder."

"Eh?" I said. "Murder? Of course not, Holmes." I explained about the locked room and the complete lack of suspects. "Let's be logical. Sometimes people die of natural causes, you know."

But even as I said it, I could feel his disagreement. Sometimes people die of unnatural causes too.

"You're the detective," I said. "Not I." Of course, I did have considerable experience assisting him, and occasionally even Scotland Yard as well, certainly more experience than most people, but I still didn't consider myself an expert.

He didn't have to say it. I already knew how he would answer. "Process, Watson! Process."

"You're being quite stubborn, Holmes." But he was right.

In his later years, in his studies of something called forensic science, Holmes had spoken well of processing the scene, processing the evidence. He had a wooden case he sometimes carried to crime scenes. If this was a scene to be investigated, he would gather samples of the tea, the sugar in the bowl, the jam, even the spoon that stirred the tea. But no. If this really was a crime scene, then I had to leave everything in place because a police photographer would be called in by Lestrade to photograph everything—but I could make notes and I did that meticulously.

I was just preparing myself to venture downstairs to inform Mrs. Hudson of Holmes's passing, when she came fussing upstairs to announce that Superintendent Lestrade was here. "Mr. Holmes, did you call Scotland Yard about the stolen tea set? Isn't that a little much? Really now. Oh, he's asleep—"

Lestrade followed her up, pounding with his cane, and huffing and puffing with the effort. Lestrade had gotten quite thick in his later years and now preferred to work from his desk in a supervisory position, instead of venturing out into the city as much as he had in the past. I had told him more than once that this was not good for his health, but in his own way Lestrade was as stubborn as Holmes. Nevertheless, he always made himself available.

"He's asleep?" Lestrade asked, coming into the room, then stopped himself abruptly. He understood immediately. "How?" he asked. "When?"

Mrs. Hudson realized at the same moment. She put her hands to her mouth. "Oh, no," she said, sinking into my chair. "Dear lord, no!" She buried her face in her hands and began to pant uncontrollably in great wracking gasps of shock. I rushed to give her my own handkerchief, which she clutched immediately. She kept repeating a single word over and over. "No, no, no."

Meanwhile, Superintendent Lestrade knelt in front of Holmes' body, squinting in close examination. "It appears he fell asleep," Lestrade decided. "He passed peacefully." He straightened again, his tone somber. "Did he leave any instructions how he wished—how he wished us to proceed? Or would you like The Yard to handle this? I can make the arrangements."

I held up my hand to stop Lestrade from saying anything more. "Please, allow us a minute." I did not want to speak my concerns in front of Mrs. Hudson and give her additional cause for dismay. I went to the door and called downstairs for the maid. Then I took her by the hand and led her to the stairs. "Perhaps you should stay with Mrs. Turner for a few days," I said. I repeated this suggestion to the maid. "Take her someplace quiet and give us a chance to…take care of things here."

It was not a casual suggestion. If as I suspected, Holmes might have been poisoned, then whatever killed him might still be there, lurking in the tea box, the sugar, the milk, the jam. I prayed I was mistaken, but I would not take any chances with anyone else's safety.

"Now, listen—" I instructed the maid. "This is a terrible thing that has happened. The reporters will be all over it like vultures. Even the best of them behave like carrion feeders, chewing through the lives of the dead. They can't help it, it's their profession." That was the explanation. Now I snapped out orders as I once did in the field hospitals. "I don't want Mrs. Hudson to be at the mercy of such devils. Take all the help, take Billy too, use the back doors. Don't speak to anyone. Stay there until you hear from me."

Mrs. Hudson turned to gather the tea service, but I stopped her. "No, leave that for now. Don't bother about the kitchen. Just go as quickly as you can. Superintendent Lestrade will take care of things here."

Still sobbing, tears still running down her cheeks, still dabbing at them with my handkerchief, Mrs. Hudson somehow managed a nod of agreement and followed her maid downstairs.

I turned back to Lestrade, but now it was his turn to collapse into my chair. Lestrade had known Holmes even longer than I had. He owed much of the success of his career to Holmes. He was unprepared for this. Despite his normally brusque manner, he was shaken. He looked up at me, his eyes red and puffy, then he stared off into his memory. "A long life is about saying goodbye, over and over. I have said goodbye to too many already, I have learned to expect it—but this one, this farewell is unbearable. In all of these churning times, Holmes has remained the singular rock of certainty. Forgive me, Doctor Watson, I am at a loss."

"As am I," I said. "As am I."

Lestrade took a moment to recover his composure. Now he stood up and faced me. He put his hand on my shoulder. "But you were closer to him than anyone. Are you all right?"

"No, I am not all right," I replied testily. "My best friend has been murdered."

Lestrade shook his head. "How can you say that? There's no evidence here of foul play."

"That's because you see, but you do not observe."

"Hm, yes. That's what Holmes would say."

"Yes, and he was right. There's more to this." I pointed to the gaudy tea service. "There. That's the evidence."

Lestrade looked at me, puzzled. "Is that what this is about? Mrs. Hudson said something about a tea service?"

"Not this one," I said. I had to take a moment, I was hovering between grief and anger and horror. I detailed this morning's events precisely as I could. "Holmes' tea service was stolen because there has to be something about *this* tea service that would introduce an extremely fast and toxic poison to the intended victim. It could have been both of us, Lestrade. It was only Mrs. Hudson's upset and Holmes' concern for her that saved my life."

Lestrade started to protest, then stopped himself, possibly out of respect, but more likely because he had learned to listen to Holmes, and now myself as well. "What would you have me do?"

"Test this entire service, everything on this tray. And test everything in Mrs. Hudson's kitchen that she would have had reason to use this morning."

"You're not suggesting that Mrs. Hudson had anything to do with Holmes' death?"

"Of course not. Nevertheless, you must test the service to be certain that it was not tampered with, because that's what Holmes would require."

Lestrade nodded. "Yes, Holmes would certainly demand it—and it's probably well that we eliminate any doubt as to the cause of his death, otherwise there will be unsavory speculations in the press. But tell me, Watson, why do you think Holmes was murdered?"

"Because he told me himself."

"I beg your pardon?"

I stopped myself. Lestrade was not a man given to belief in the supernatural. Neither was I, but I could not deny my own experience. Finally, I said, "Call it a feeling, if you will."

Lestrade looked puzzled, even annoyed, but he accepted my answer. "All right, Doctor Watson, I am skeptical, but if it will put your mind at ease, I will treat this as a murder investigation. I'll send a photographer immediately, one who knows how to be respectful and discreet. And then a forensic pathologist. A whole team, if you wish."

"Thank you, Superintendent. I do appreciate your assistance here."

Lestrade shook his head, "I am not doing this as a favor. You do understand, don't you, that Holmes' death is a world event. I cannot trust anyone else with this investigation, especially if there's any hint of foul play."

"You must pursue your investigations in secrecy," I said. "Complete secrecy. If you determine that Holmes was murdered, then we must have absolutely no publicity, not until the murderer is apprehended. Think of it. What an awful legacy it would be if this crime were never solved. It would be a terrible blot on Holmes' memory, it would overwhelm all of his brilliant triumphs. I beg you, Lestrade—"

The Superintendent stopped me. "Let me assure you, Doctor Watson. I share your concern. We have men at The Yard who understand the necessity of discretion. And I will personally oversee their efforts. There will be no publicity." He looked to me. "You know, you'll have to inform the Crown. And then you must make a statement to the press as well."

"I have been dreading the task."

Lestrade cleared his throat politely, his way of signaling that he had something else to say and was asking permission to say it.

"Yes, Superintendent?"

"You must be discreet as well in your public statements. Sherlock Holmes represented the inevitability of justice in London. His death might embolden certain criminal elements." He put his hand on my arm and looked at me firmly. "And if you'll permit me a personal concern, it might also compromise the reputation of The Yard if it was believed we had failed to protect Holmes. That might also embolden certain political elements."

"Quite," I said. The Superintendent's concerns were understandable. "Yes, I see your point. I will say only that Holmes has passed away in his sleep and leave it at that."

"Good man," said Lestrade. "Are you up to the tasks ahead? You have notes to write. Buckingham Palace, Number 10 Downing Street, and also *The Times*. Send them directly to me and I'll see them quietly delivered. If you don't mind, I will inform Mycroft Holmes of his brother's passing."

Lestrade let himself out and I set to work composing the notes.

It was not an easy task, and I labored for some time before I found the right words. There is no easy way to convey this kind of news, and in this moment, in this circumstance, it was especially difficult.

It has never been a secret that I despise the telephone. I find it an unwelcome intrusion on private life. Anyone anywhere with access to a telephone of their own can ring a bell in my sitting room, without regard to courtesy of any kind, and interrupt the thought processes necessary to my writing.

I said then and still maintain today that a telephone conversation can never be a reliable substitute for actual human contact. Human beings need to see the posture of the other person's body, their facial expressions, all the many nuances of behavior, to understand the full intention of any conversation.

But Holmes had insisted on having one of those infernal devices installed in our sitting room. He disliked leaving home unless he had to. More than once I suggested that the phone appealed to his essential laziness. He never disagreed. Eventually, and reluctantly, I assented to the installation of the device, but only if we could disconnect the foul thing outside of business hours. That had been a continuing source of contention between Holmes and myself, because as he correctly observed, most criminals do not keep business hours, not even those in politics.

This morning, however, despite my convictions, I reconnected the damnable thing and called for a reliable messenger service. The lad arrived on a bicycle only a few minutes later. Drawn by the rumor of Superintendent Lestrade's presence, a small group of reporters had gathered. I brought the boy inside and handed him a thick packet to deliver to Lestrade. I gave him a few shillings to secure his cooperation. "You must deliver them directly to the Superintendent. No one else. Do not, under any circumstances, say anything to anyone about this." Before I could warn him of the possible consequences to his employment, he straightened like a soldier. "Sir, I thanks you kindly, but don't you fear none, I take me job serious. It's a sacred duty."

He tipped his hat and peddled off. There were seven reporters gathered now, all of them sensing that something was up. It was getting harder to ignore them. Passersby were starting to notice and comment as well.

I went upstairs to draft a formal statement for the general press. Even the best of them had an uneven relationship with accuracy, but they couldn't misquote a written statement. I felt no need to hurry, but the composition was something to occupy my mind while I waited for the photographer. To be sure, I had no plans to release any statement to them it for at least a day, not until after *The Times* had published.

By the time I got downstairs, the crowd of reporters and photographers had grown to more than a dozen, another unintended consequence of the telephone. Reporters could be alerted immediately and crowds of them could gather faster than ever. Three photographers held up their cameras and snapped photos with bright annoying flashes. The reporters were already shouting questions. I had purple spots in my vision, and I couldn't see any of them clearly.

"We heard there's something up," said one. "Lestrade visiting and all. A new case, perhaps?"

"I will not lie to you," I said, and closed the door in their faces. I retreated upstairs where I sat down opposite Holmes for what would probably be the last time.

He must have approved my actions. I couldn't say how I felt his presence, but somehow I did not feel alone.

I felt his presence again at the funeral. It was intended as a very private service at Mycroft Holmes' estate, but as it happened Superintendent Lestrade had to bring in a small army of constables to hold reporters and the general public far back so as to keep the whole ghastly business decently private.

I hadn't seen Mycroft in many years so it was a shock to see him so enfeebled and in a wheelchair, but for once his dour and disapproving manner was perfectly suited to the occasion. Other than the Prime Minister and his aides, only Mrs. Hudson, Superintendent Lestrade, and several officers from Scotland Yard attended. With my permission a small contingent of the Baker Street Irregulars were allowed to attend. They chose to watch from a respectful distance.

The service was short and simple. Holmes would have approved. "Farewell is enough," he had once opined. "Extravagant displays are pretentious and designed to distract from the lack of real emotion." The casket was lowered slowly into the ground. We said our goodbyes and went our separate ways. Mrs. Hudson and I returned to Baker Street together. I retired upstairs to putter through random papers and pretend I was working. Mostly, I sat in my chair feeling bereft and without any sense of purpose. I had not realized how much of my life was about Holmes.

Evening crept in through the windows, I barely noticed, not until Mrs. Hudson came puffing up the stairs with a tray. She set it down on the table, I barely glanced at it. I wasn't hungry.

"What a mess," she said.

"I'm sorry," I started to say.

"No, not you, Doctor Watson. All those busybodies from Scotland Yard. They made a mess of my kitchen. Oh, I know they tried to put things back the right way after they were through with all their sampling and testing, but I could tell. I have my things organized just so. I could tell they were there. The same way I could tell the tea service was gone. The same way I could tell nobody had fiddled with the service neither you nor Mr. Holmes liked. But you tell them anyway, I appreciate that they made the effort." She looked at me. "They were testing for poison, weren't they?"

I nodded. "They just wanted to be certain."

"No," she corrected. "It was you who wanted to be certain. You and Mr. Holmes, you never believed anything you saw. Always looking under the doilies, you were. So to speak."

"Mrs. Hudson," I said. "You would have made a great detective. You not only see, you observe."

"Achh." She shook her head. "If I could have had the schooling, and if there was a place for a woman in that work, and if pigs could fly, maybe so. Maybe so. But in the meantime, there's a kitchen to clean." She headed back down the stairs.

Two days after the funeral, Lestrade returned Mrs. Hudson's tea service to her, all carefully wrapped up. She did not look happy to have the accursed things back in her kitchen, but she thanked him appropriately.

Upstairs, Lestrade filled me in on the details. "We tested everything," he said. "And as I expected, we found no evidence of poison, no evidence of anything untoward."

"You tested everything?" I echoed.

"Everything on the tray and everything in the kitchen. The cups, the spoons, the teapot, the tea, the sugar, the milk, the butter, the preserves in the bowl, everything. I assure you, Watson, The Yard is thorough. Will this settle your mind at last?"

I nodded politely. I didn't know whether to feel relieved or disappointed. I felt confused and puzzled. Holmes had been murdered. I was sure of it, but I had no evidence. I couldn't prove it. I had to be missing something. Holmes would have figured it out, but I was at a loss. Superintendent Lestrade had done all that he could. There was no point in belaboring the issue.

"Thank you, Superintendent. To be sure, I never wanted to believe in the possibility of foul play, but I have spent so many years pursuing so many sordid investigations with Holmes that it has become a habit with me to distrust the obvious."

Lestrade nodded. "It's the policeman's curse as well. Nobody is innocent. We just don't know what they're guilty of." He looked at me oddly, then. "Doctor Watson, I don't have to tell you how difficult these next few months will be. You have suffered a great loss and you will need time to take care of yourself, but you still have much of life ahead of you. Someday there will be new challenges and when you are ready, you will embrace them."

"I understand what you're saying, Superintendent. But accompanying Holmes, writing about our adventures, that was my greatest ambition. I cannot imagine a life without him." I took a deep breath. "But you may rest assured I will not fall into despair. Holmes wouldn't hear of it."

"That's reassuring, but grief is a strange beast and there may be darker days ahead. Please call me if you need anything." He pressed a card into my hand. "Or if you just want to spend an evening sometime. Here is my personal number."

"I will do that," I reassured him.

After he left, Mrs. Hudson came upstairs, looking sad. "I didn't want to say anything, Superintendent Lestrade has been so good to us these past few days, but—"

"Yes?"

"It's the tea service. The Superintendent brought it back short one spoon. Perhaps in their investigations they misplaced it somewhere? Do you think you might ask him to look for it?"

I reassured her that I would definitely do that, but her question left me wondering. I could hear Holmes muttering his annoyance. "Watson, the answer has been in front of you the whole time."

"Stop being so impatient with me, Holmes. My mind is not as fast as yours. And my body is slowing down too. Just getting up the stairs some days can be a challenge."

I sank down in my chair, exhausted. I had no strength in either my mind or my body. And now, Holmes was nagging me about something I should have noticed at the beginning.

Even though it wasn't tea time, not yet, Mrs. Hudson was thoughtful enough to bring up a tray, the same service we had purchased that terrible morning. "I hope it's all right," she said. "It'd be a shame to not use it. And maybe it's a way to honor his memory. What do you think, Doctor Watson?"

"I think it's a splendid idea, Mrs. Hudson. Very thoughtful, indeed."

"I shall miss his adventures. It will be very dull around here without him. All the comings and goings. I'll have to learn how to appreciate the quiet." She paused. "Sometimes I think I can still hear him puttering around. Last night even—"

"Yes?"

"I thought I heard him playing his violin. Silly old me, I'm hearing things."

"I heard it too," I said. "It must have been one of the neighbors. Aren't there students living up the road?"

"Yes, of course. But I prefer to think it was him, don't you?"

She went back downstairs then, leaving me alone with my tea—staring at the service he never got to use.

"Watson, what are you forgetting?"

"I'm not forgetting anything," I said, stirring my tea angrily. "I still haven't forgiven you for knocking the spoon out of my hand. That was very rude of you, Holmes—"

I stared at my teacup, the spoon in my hand.

That's what I had missed!

The spoon—the one he'd knocked out of my hand! It was somewhere under his chair. Or behind the music stand. Or maybe behind the drape? There it was! Under the footstool. Gaudy and ornate.

It was evidence. I scooped it up with the morning's newspaper, folding it into a careful square. I placed it on the shelf and stepped away from it, thinking hard. "Holmes, if this is what I fear it is, I shall be very unhappy. I do wish to be wrong—or maybe I don't, I don't know.

Oh, Holmes, you damnable spirit, what thoughts have you put into my head?"

Against my better judgment, I picked up the phone and called Lestrade. "There's been a...a development," I told him. "I found something—a missing spoon."

Lestrade replied, "Doctor Watson, I realize this is a very difficult time for you—so I shall humor you this one time. But when we find nothing suspicious at all, you must let go of this conviction."

"Superintendent," I said stiffly, I used his title deliberately. "This is a question of evidence. We must have certainty. Holmes would have demanded nothing less."

Lestrade sighed. Despite my deep dislike of the informality of the telephone, I could still hear his exasperation. "I shall be around in the morning to pick it up," he said and rang off.

I did my best to distract myself. I sorted through the piles of books and documents, organizing and sorting and filing. The British Museum Library had expressed an interest in creating a private collection of Holmes's work, but Holmes had politely demurred. He felt he had a responsibility to protect the people involved from any public examination of their circumstances. It was one of the few instances where Holmes had demonstrated real anger. "Vultures and jackals feed on carrion because they have to," Holmes said. "Human beings do not have to, yet there are those who insist on picking over the corpses of the past as if there is still meat to be found on those bones."

"I feel the same way about reporters," I said. "They pick over the bones of the present."

Holmes had nodded agreement. "Not everybody needs to know everything. A person's privacy must be sacred." Nevertheless, he felt that he had a moral responsibility to the science of detection. "It's still in its infancy," he once remarked. "Imagine what we might accomplish if we had a more advanced discipline for investigation."

"I wish we did," I replied. "Perhaps then there would be answers to the questions that are still rattling around in my mind."

Yes, I was still talking to Holmes, still trying to maintain my side of the conversation. His words were like hammers of thought, so loud in my head I couldn't tell if I was imagining it or if he really was standing beside me.

When Lestrade came around, I shared my convictions. "Perhaps the stolen tea service was a deliberate distraction. Perhaps the real intention was to force Mrs. Hudson to use her own tea set to serve Holmes. Perhaps this spoon is the missing clue? If it has been dipped in some kind of poison—"

Lestrade held up a hand to stop me. "Doctor Watson, please. I will certainly have the spoon tested. But think about it. How would your presumed poisoner know which exact spoon to target? It would have needed very precise planning, and there are too many ways it could have gone wrong. How could the killer know which of you would get the poisoned spoon? And even if this spoon contains some kind of toxic potion, we found nothing in Holmes' tea or on his spoon, so there is no evidence that his death was anything but natural causes."

"Perhaps the poison was undetectable in the tea, I don't know. I just know that this spoon must be tested." I did not say that this was the spoon that Holmes had knocked out of my hand.

Lestrade's expression was strained. He sighed. I knew he felt he was humoring me now, but he had learned from long experience with Holmes that the evidence tells its own story.

At last, on the afternoon of the third day, Lestrade came around, bearing the spoon. "It was clean. Nothing on it at all. You can give it back to Mrs. Hudson." Then he said, "You don't look well, Watson."

"I have not been sleeping well," I said.

"Understandable," Lestrade said. "I've been having the same problem."

He cleared his throat. "I do have one other bit of news. It might ease your mind. We have recovered the stolen tea service."

"I say—?"

"We caught the thief. Just last night. Not a very smart fellow. And not a poisoner at all. Just a petty criminal looking for an opportunity. He offered to sell the set to a private collector. Unfortunately, for him, the collector was one we had contacted. He informed Scotland Yard and we had him arrange a meeting. We nabbed the fellow at the promised exchange."

"So he's not the killer we're looking for."

"No," said Lestrade. "Perhaps there is no killer. Perhaps Holmes died of natural causes."

I did not argue. I had only my own conviction and Holmes had said it many times, conviction is not evidence. Neither of us had much else to say and we parted on uncertain terms, not knowing if either of us would ever see the other again. Without Holmes, there might be no reason.

After Lestrade left, I sat alone in our rooms, my rooms now.

Perhaps Lestrade was right. Perhaps there was no case. Perhaps it was all a delusion, a comfortable pretense that there was still one more mystery to resolve. And yet, I still couldn't shake the feeling that Holmes had spoken to me, that there was still more to consider.

Eventually, the afternoon darkened and Mrs. Hudson brought up tea. "You have to eat," she said. "You're no good to anyone, least of all yourself, if you don't eat." She set the tray down on the table, I barely glanced at it. I wasn't hungry.

"I'm not leaving," she said. "Not until you have a bite and a cuppa." She began bustling around the room, pretending to straighten things up. She must have been feeling lonely. Or perhaps she didn't want me to feel so alone. I didn't have the heart to tell her that I wanted no company.

"It's so dark in here," she said, throwing back the curtains. The orange glow from the street lamps did little to help my mood. It only made the room seem emptier. "You shouldn't be sitting like this, you know. It's bad for the liver. You have to stay active." She looked to me with her most serious expression. "And you'll have to sort through his things soon," she said. "You can't leave everything piled up like this."

"I will, I will," I said.

"Are you going to eat?" she said, pointing to the tray. "Or are you going to leave everything untouched again? You know, I don't like wasting."

"It's all right, Mrs. Hudson, I'll eat something."

"Oh. That reminds me," she said. "What should I do with the jelly?"

"What jelly?"

"Mr. Holmes' jelly. The preserves. That awful stuff he likes. Liked," she corrected herself. "I know you didn't like it. I never touched it myself. It didn't seem right. Is it all right if I throw out the rest of it? Not much left in the jar anyway."

"Yes. Mrs. Hudson. I don't care." I felt a sudden chill of realization. "No, wait—" A thought was forming. "Let me have it. Bring it up to me."

She looked confused. "Did you want some bread with that?"

"No, no, just the jelly, please—"

She disappeared down the stairs, mumbling to herself that she hoped

I wasn't going funny in the head with Holmes to mitigate my foolishness. I paid her no attention. I was thinking about the jar of preserves.

Mrs. Hudson was right. I never developed much of a taste for it, it being an unusual and slightly unpleasant flavor. The label on the jar identified it as Stoneless Greengage—some kind of plum, pale green with golden flesh.

There was an odd little shop up the street, a place called Elrod's. Mrs. Elrod had taken it over after Mr. Mandy died and she favored Holmes in no small part for his continuing patronage. By his custom, he had debunked the rumors that she was a witch. She preserved odd combinations of fruits and vegetables, things like rhubarb chutney and cinnamon-persimmon preserves. So there was jealousy and gossip among those who felt threatened by her experiments with different recipes. Holmes had sampled most of them at one time or another. It was part of his research he said, though I suspected he just enjoyed the different tastes. Eventually he developed an affinity for one or two specific flavors and Mrs. Hudson would pick up a jar or two almost every shopping day, so there was always a small bowl of jelly on the tea tray.

There was none in the tray tonight. The empty bowl was an accusation. I had missed the obvious.

"How could I have been so stupid?" I exclaimed. "It was right there in front of me the whole time."

Mrs. Hudson stopped what she was doing and stared at me. "Whatever are you going on about?"

"Nothing, nothing at all." I hastened to reassure her. "I just had a thought."

She shook her head. "Sometimes, Doctor Watson. Sometimes—"

"Never you mind, Mrs. Hudson. I shall have my tea now. You can stop worrying about my appetite. I have suddenly rediscovered it."

She sniffed her general disapproval and left.

Yes, now I had a case to ponder. We had a case.

It wasn't the spoon or the tea or the sugar. It was the Stoneless Greengage jelly! Holmes liked it, I didn't. And Mrs. Hudson wouldn't have touched it. So that was how the killer had targeted Holmes without any danger to anyone else! Oh, I can be so damnably stupid! I should have seen this sooner! I had been so wrapped up in my own grief that I hadn't seen what was in front of me the whole time.

No, wait—I stopped myself. I had to think this out.

Lestrade said the jelly had been tested. It was just fruit and sugar and a bit of spice. But it had to be the jelly. That was the only thing that made sense.

I paced around the room, much like Holmes whenever he pondered a difficult problem. I muttered aloud like Holmes as well. "But what if someone could have substituted a tainted jar? Consider that problem. How would one get the tainted jar into the kitchen without Mrs. Hudson knowing? Perhaps they substituted it before it got into the kitchen? Perhaps when Mrs. Hudson was shopping, could the killer have replaced the jar in her basket? A skilled dip perhaps? Not impossible at all."

That had to be why Holmes had knocked the spoon out of my hand. He knew that something was wrong. He didn't know what, but he had to alert me. He needed me to be suspicious.

I stopped and looked at the telephone. I thought about picking it up and calling Lestrade. I even put my hand on the handset. But no. All I had was a theory. I had no evidence. It would be wrong to bother the Superintendent with a wild and unprovable theory. And I still had to figure how the killer could have substituted an innocent jar again before Scotland Yard gathered it up for testing.

I returned to my chair and sank down into its reassuring comfort. It was the Stoneless Greengage, I knew it. I just had no way to prove it.

I did not sleep well that night.

In the morning, Mrs. Hudson came up to ask me if I wanted her to pick up anything specific when she did her morning rounds. I shook my head. "Can't think of anything."

"I'll have to tell Mrs. Elrod we won't be wanting any of her special jellies anymore."

"No, I'll tell her," I said. "I think it would be better if she heard it from me." A thought was forming in my mind.

"She probably already knows. There's no shortage of gossip in the market, and the papers were quick to report the bad news."

"Yes, they're very good at that. Just the same, I should go round and thank her. She was a good friend to Holmes. He did like her jellies."

"Yes, he did. Very much. Well, I'll be off now."

Mrs. Elrod mostly kept to her pots and pans, her cutting board and her stove. She puttered about with jars and mixing bowls and only came to the front when someone came into the shop. At first glance, she seemed of a quiet manner. A casual passerby might have thought her plain, not much to look at, but if asked about her latest combinations of tastes and textures, her face would light up and she would become as animated as a sprite. Her enthusiasm made her radiant. It was no wonder some people thought she possessed a supernatural attribute.

"Doctor Watson," she said, taking my hands in hers. "I'm so very sorry. Sherlock Holmes was such a good man. I can see you're too proud to show it, but your pain must be overwhelming."

"Thank you, Mrs. Elrod. Thank you for understanding. And thank you for all the delicious flavors you shared with Holmes. He enjoyed them all."

She laughed. "You don't have to be polite, Doctor Watson. I know you pulled up your nose more than once. You don't have to pretend around me, I know my recipes are not to everyone's taste. The Greengage, for instance. Holmes liked it, most people did not. I only made it for him. Now he's gone, I doubt I'll ever make another batch."

"So nobody else ever bought it?"

"Well, there was one, a an odd little woman, middling of age." Mrs. Elrod frowned. "Two weeks ago, maybe three. Like I said, very odd." She scratched her temple, pushing back the white scarf she wore around her hair. "She wanted three jars, that was unusual. Not something I'd forget easily. But I didn't have any, I told her she'd have to come back later. I was planning to make some up for Mr. Holmes. I'd just make a little more than usual. She didn't like that. She didn't hide her annoyance. Very impatient, she was. Not very nice, I remember."

"You said she wanted three jars of the Greengage? Three?" I felt a sudden pounding in my chest, as if my heart were about to burst.

Mrs. Elrod squinted at me. She cocked her head. "You are investigating, aren't you? You and Holmes, always peeking under the covers. You can't help yourself, can you?"

"Ah, Mrs. Elrod, you're a sharp woman. There's no fooling you, is there?"

"A woman has to be sharp to survive in this world," she said. "You have to notice things. Like you and Holmes do—did. But the woman? She paid in advance, she did. Told me to send it around as soon as it was done. Wait, I'll look it up." She bustled into the back, returning with a well-worn ledger, already paging through it. "Yes, here it is, Miss Ardie. She told me to send it to a lodging house. That was another odd thing. She didn't look the type. Not a working woman, not at all. Her hands were too soft, and her clothes were too fine. Maybe she'd fallen on hard times, but three jars? That's a pretty penny. It makes no sense."

No, it did not make sense—except in the most ominous way.

Mrs. Elrod wasn't finished. "I wouldn't have given it much thought, sometimes even the poorest among us like a bit of a treat, except there's not much custom for the Greengage, it is an odd flavor, after all, and she wasn't from around here, but a penny is a penny and a shilling is a shilling. Do you want the address?" She turned the book for me to see Miss Ardie's full name and address. I waved for a cab immediately.

The lodging house was not in the best of neighborhoods, mostly shabby and rundown old buildings, all crowded together like hungry miners lined up at the employment office. No longer homes, these dark edifices were remnants of a more illustrious past, now mostly inhabited by poor working women, the ones who were not inclined to seek a husband, or sadder still had given up all hope of finding one. They served as maids or cleaning women, whatever employment they could find.

It was not a safe place for someone like myself, even the cabby, as rough as he was, expressed reluctance to take me into that neighborhood, I had to double his usual fare, but as Holmes would have said, the game was afoot.

The proprietor was a thick woman, stiff and dour, dressed all in black, and with an expression of permanent disapproval. She met me at the door, but did not invite me in. She did not give her name or any other information. "I do not speak about my ladies," she said. "They are entitled to their privacy. Men like you—" she sniffed. "You're not welcome here."

"Yes, I understand. I apologize for the intrusion." I turned to go.

"Wait—" she said.

I turned back.

"You're not from around here." Not a question, an accusation.

"No, I am not."

"What is your intention?"

"One of your residents applied to a household I represent. We wanted to assure ourselves of her trustworthiness." It was a harmless but necessary invention.

"Hmpf," she said. "This house provides services only for a select institution, one that I will not speak of, but the engagement is secure. All of my ladies are trustworthy, and I doubt that they would seek employment elsewhere. Good day, Doctor Watson."

"Yes, of course. Thank you." It was telling that the woman had seen through my misrepresentation, and by that I knew that she would provide no further information, but she had already given me something useful to consider. Indeed, even the location of the lodging house could be relevant. I returned to the waiting cab.

Back at Baker Street, I sat alone again, my mind churning with a dozen disconnected notions. I barely noticed when Mrs. Hudson brought up the tea. I was so lost in thought, I mumbled only the most perfunctory acknowledgment. It didn't help that Holmes was standing behind me, muttering, "You see, Watson, but do you observe?"

"Oh, please shut up, Holmes. I am already at my wits' end."

"Have your tea then," he said.

"Yes, I will have my tea. Everything is about tea, isn't it. Have your tea, Watson. Can't live without your tea. But if it hadn't been for your damnable tea, we wouldn't be having this conversation." I started to pour a cup anyway.

And stopped. The realization was immediate. And complete. All the pieces assumed their place as precisely as the jars on Mrs. Hudson's spice shelf.

"Thank you, Holmes," I said, and went to the phone to call Superintendent Lestrade. He did not have the same dislike of the phone that I had, he picked up immediately.

"I know how Holmes was murdered," I said. "And I know who did it. And it is imperative that we act immediately."

Lestrade started to protest, but I insisted. I would not be deferred. "You must hear me out.—"

"Watson," he said patiently. "We have been through this. You are becoming obsessed with this—"

"I am not obsessed with anything—" I said. "Except justice."

He didn't answer. I knew he was trying to think of a polite way to stop me—but there was no polite way, not now.

"You would have listened to Holmes," I said. "Will you listen to me?"

Lestrade sighed in exasperation. I was getting better at interpreting other people's reactions over the telephone. Finally, he said. "What is it you want?"

"Safe tea!"

"Safety?"

"Yes!"

I didn't wait for Lestrade. I went directly to Scotland Yard and found my way down to the lab where various assistants were working at a long row of tables, many of them women. The rooms were well-lit with bright incandescent lamps. The many shelves were filled with brown bottles, all carefully labeled. Several of the tables held Bunsen burners and beakers of fluid in metal stands. There were microscopes and slides as well.

The head of the department was Dr. William Greene, a long-faced man, he looked scholarly and preoccupied and vaguely unkempt. He peered at me through thick glasses. "Watson, is it? That fellow who writes about Sherlock Holmes? I was told to expect you. As you can see, we're very busy around here. Not a lot of time for flapdoodle and lollygagging. Let's just get to it. What is it you want to know?"

"Your tea ladies, when do they come in?"

"At tea time, of course. Is that what this is about? You're interrupting our work to ask about tea?"

"Please, Doctor Greene, humor me. It could be important. I need to know about one of your tea ladies, Miss Ardie. Is there anything unusual about her behavior?"

He frowned. He pushed his glasses higher up onto the bridge of his nose. "She tries very hard to be helpful. She doesn't get in the way. Well, there was that one incident a week or so ago. She dropped a cup of hot tea into poor Doctor Charles' lap. He had to run to the lavatory. She was very apologetic. She cleaned up his entire desk. Spent a good bit time on it, a thorough job. And she wouldn't let Charles pay for his tea, not for the day. Not for the rest of the week, I think."

"Doctor Charles? Was he testing the items from Mrs. Hudson's kitchen?"

"We all were. Superintendent Lestrade put the whole department to work on that task. Interrupted a week's worth of investigations. What is this all about anyway?"

I looked away across the room, at all the assistants working, then back to Dr. Greene. "It's a formality. Something Holmes taught me. About tying up loose ends for the final report. Do you think I might speak to Doctor Charles?"

"He's out sick. Took ill quite suddenly. We don't know when he'll be back." He fixed me with a fierce expression. "If this is going to be another one of your lurid stories—?"

"I don't write lurid stories, Doctor Greene." I thanked him for his time and went looking for the little kitchen where the tea carts were stored. That's where I found her.

She had her back to me. She was wiping down the teapot with a damp cloth. She finished what she was doing. She put down her cloth, and carefully replaced the teapot on the cart. Then finally, she turned around to face me. "Doctor Watson, how good of you to come."

Plainly dressed, in the uniform of a loyal servant, she would have been unnoticeable to anyone too busy to look. She was a thin woman, almost skeletal, with features narrow and unpleasant, and while I will not say that she smiled, her expression was one of quiet satisfaction.

"Would you like some tea? I was just going to put on my own pot."

"Thank you, no. I believe I've had enough tea for one life. I am planning to resume my affection for coffee."

"If only Holmes had done so, don't you think? But then we wouldn't be having this conversation, would we?" She went to the stove and busied herself with the kettle. "But because Holmes can't be here, let me see what I can deduce." She turned to face me, her expression alive, almost glowing in the orange light of the room. "Even though you had no evidence, you have determined that Holmes was murdered, and even though you had no evidence, you have determined that the jelly was poisoned. Stonegage Greenglass, yes?"

"You know damn well."

"Yes. Why should I pretend. You are not the dolt you pretend to be. Now, where was I? Oh, yes. Deducing. But when you realized that Holmes was the only one who would have touched the preserves, you knew that had to be the murder device. But then—I'm still deducing here—you had to figure out how the poisoned jar could have gotten into Mrs. Hudson's kitchen and then replaced again before it could be tested. Am I correct, so far?"

I kept my emotions in check. I said simply, "You flatter yourself. It was obvious."

"Afterward, yes. Let me help you out. Mrs. Hudson sometimes pays too much attention to the sausages or the apples or whatever it is she's brooding over. It would be easy for a skilled pickpocket—like myself— to switch the jars in her basket, but even an unskilled girl could do it. Bump!" She affected a younger manner, "'Oh, I'm sorry dear, I'm so clumsy. Are you all right? Here, let me help you pick things up.'"

I shook my head. "So simple. My mistake was thinking that you would have attempted something more elegant."

"Too many moving parts, Doctor. I favor simplicity. It gets the job done."

"Or perhaps you are not be as clever as you would like me to believe."

"Or perhaps that's what I want you to think. We can play this game all day, if you wish. In one thing, you and I are very much alike. We are most effective when other people underestimate our abilities. So here you are, which means you must have deduced how I switched out the jar to be tested."

"Not all the details," I said, "but yes. So here we are, and who has outsmarted who?"

"That is the question, isn't it?"

"Holmes said you had a remarkable intelligence. He also remarked, more than once, what a shame it is that such a mind should be wasted on criminal enterprises."

She looked at me oddly, so I explained. "Holmes was not unaware of your existence. He followed your career as a chemist. He thought you were brilliant. Misguided, but brilliant. Myself, I must also admit some admiration. From the beginning, I suspected a fast working poison that could be mistaken for heart failure. Perhaps a highly concentrated barbiturate. It would have required a great deal of experimentation to adjust the chemistry so that the toxin would break down within a few hours. It would be the perfect murder weapon. No test would detect a poison like that. Holmes would have suspected you from the beginning. I just took a little longer."

She turned her back on me. She went to the stove for the kettle. "The tea is almost ready. Have you changed your mind about having some?"

"No, I have not. What I also wanted to say—it is fortunate for the rest of us that your criminal career has now come to an end."

"Oh, yes," she said. "That was always part of the plan."

"Ending your criminal career?"

"Ending on my triumph." She allowed herself the hint of a smile. "I spent quite a few years planning this effort. I had to give every part of it a lot of thought—because every action has a reaction, isn't that what the science says? Do you know what else they say? Better late than never." Now finally, she smiled—an evil expression. "Especially when it's the late Sherlock Holmes."

She held up her tea cup in my direction. "This is really quite good.

See, I've tasted it. You have nothing to fear. No? Well, then I shall continue. Consider a chess game. Every piece has to be in the right place to achieve a victory. To make this work, Sherlock Holmes first had to return to London, so there had to be a case here that would interest him. That took some time to set up, because it had to be a worthwhile puzzle, but still solvable by Dear Old Uncle Sherlock. Of course, we're not really related, but he's been part of my family history for so long, it's like he's a dear old uncle, even from a distance. So sometimes, he's Uncle Sherlock to me."

She sipped at her tea, "Oh, I do like this flavor, very much," then turned her attention back to me. "This was the part that made the challenge so exciting. I had to determine the specific habits of Mr. Sherlock Holmes, but I couldn't just ring him up and ask, could I? No. I couldn't. I started by reading your stories, Doctor Watson. They're not really very good. I always get the feeling you're leaving the important parts out, just so you can pretend to surprise us later on, but that might be just my own intelligence at work, never mind. Despite the low quality of your tales, you very often and very unwisely revealed a great deal about your own habits and the habits of Sherlock Holmes. And then there's the gossip around the neighborhood—as well as the gossip and speculations of those who think your work is worth following. But—" She sighed. "In the end, it was too easy. Mrs. Hudson and Mrs. Elrod love to chatter. Well, they all do. It can be a sad life for a woman, not as many good opportunities. So most women don't talk about opportunities. Mostly, what they talk about are irrelevancies of the worst sort. It's impossible not to hear. Mrs. Hudson and Mrs. Elrod, they can get loud sometimes. Oh, your dear Mrs. Hudson she does wonder aloud why Sherlock was so particular in his tastes. Maybe she felt she had to apologize for having to buy the Stonegage Greenglass preserves. Everybody else is happy with strawberry jam or lemon marmalade. Why does Sherlock Holmes like this awful stuff? That was interesting, yes, but when she allowed that even Doctor Watson doesn't like it very much, I had what I was looking for—a mechanism that would work on Uncle Sherlock, but would still spare you." Miss Ardie nodded. "Oh, yes, Doctor Watson. You are part of the plan, too."

"I did wonder about your name. Your pseudonym. Mary Ardie. But I assumed you chose it to honor your father. The physical resemblance is obvious."

"I did not choose the name to honor my father," Mary Ardie said. "I chose it to catch your attention. And it worked. All the pieces, even the last little pawns on the chessboard. They all serve a purpose, each in their own way. You are a pawn. I am a chess master, and I am playing for a specific endgame."

"I think you're forgetting something," I said. "Chess has two players, and the winner is the one who best understands the other's endgame. So yes, I did wonder why someone would go to such trouble to murder Sherlock Holmes but spare Doctor Watson? Why not eliminate both? It would be the crime of the century. But once I knew it was you, I understood that whatever you had planned, it would have only the darkest of motives. I might be the only person that you could hate more than Sherlock Holmes, because I repeatedly detailed your father's failures in public, so clearly you have something else in mind for me."

"That's an unusually arrogant assertion for one who likes to play the dolt. I can see why Dear Old Uncle Sherlock kept you around. But yes, just to put your mind at ease, I do hold you in a very low regard, even more so because your repeated attempts at literacy have been so dreadful. You should be charged with assaulting the English language. But regardless of your own crimes against the world of letters, Holmes was always the target, the only target. Never you."

Now she lowered her voice and spoke with an almost desperate intensity. "You might have made Holmes, Doctor Watson, but I destroyed him. Your despair is a minor satisfaction, but it was never the endgame."

"Just killing Holmes? That's all? Long after he was retired?"

"He was never retired. You and I and Superintendent Lestrade all know it. And yes, I know that you are not here alone. Lestrade has surrounded this room with his officers. They have heard everything. They are about to come in here and arrest me. I know my future. I will go on trial for Uncle Sherlock's murder and I will be convicted and sentenced and the Crown will send me to the gallows. But that will not erase my triumph."

"I fail to see how being hanged is a victory."

"Watson," she mocked. "You see, but you do not observe. London is a city of frenzied reporters, all of whom will be eager to explore every facet of my victory, every detail of how I accomplished the unthinkable. When I stand before the court, when I am convicted, and when I am hanged, that will be my legacy, because from that moment forward, my fame will be indelible. Do you not see it? I will be the one criminal that Sherlock Holmes, The World's Greatest Detective couldn't outsmart, couldn't defeat. History will forever know me as the woman who killed Sherlock Holmes."

At last, emotion overcame me. I couldn't help myself. "What madness!" I cried. "Have you lost all sense? Have you no shame?"

"The word is meaningless, Doctor Watson." She finished her tea and put down the empty cup. She raised her voice. "I am ready to go. You may arrest me now, Superintendent Lestrade."

Almost immediately, the doors sprang open and the room filled with grim-faced officers, Lestrade in the lead. She stood up to face them calmly, holding out her hands for the inevitable manacles.

Lestrade nodded to me. "This was well done, Watson. Holmes would have been proud."

A thought occurred to me. "Miss Ardie," I said, "I will concede the elegance of your plan. But there is this. Your imagined triumph depends on the cooperation of others. I wonder if perhaps you are never charged with murder, if there is no case, then your crime can never be known. You have committed more than enough assaults upon human decency for the Crown to keep you locked away for a long time. It may very well be that yours is a fragile victory, easily erased. Perhaps the world will know only that Sherlock Holmes died of natural causes."

"It is no matter. I will still have won. You and Lestrade will know it. If that is all there is, then that will be enough. If that is all that there is." The damnable woman smiled, and this time it was obvious—an expression of insanity, a personal intoxication, even as she held out her hands for Superintendent Lestrade's waiting handcuffs.

"Wait," I said, before Lestrade could usher her out. "There is one more matter."

Lestrade and the other officers paused. "Every piece of crockery in this room, every tea cart, every pot, every kettle, every cup and spoon, every jar, everything in this room must be handled with extreme care. It must be taken away, broken, and burnt."

"Eh?" said Lestrade. "But she made herself a pot of tea."

"Yes, she did. I saw. And I observed. She was very careful in her actions, the kettle, the teapot, and the cup she used. She would have given me a safe cup too—all to create the illusion that everything else in the room is safe. It is not. This woman is an expert in poison and everything in this room is suspect. The room itself must be totally cleaned, completely decontaminated. Yes, I have observed. Eliminating Holmes—that was only the first part of Mary Ardie's plan, but it was the necessary part, because Holmes would surely have deduced what she was up to and he would have stopped her. So she needed to get Holmes out of the way first—because this was no small plan. She couldn't resist boasting about that. When Doctor Charles became suspicious, she had to poison him too."

Lestrade said, "I believe she underestimated your abilities, Doctor Watson."

"It is useful to be underestimated," I said. "Mary Ardie's real goal has always been much larger than a single murder. Today was her next step. She has been in here all morning, preparing to poison the entirety of Scotland Yard. And then, with The Yard in disarray, she could proceed to her next goal."

"Which was?" Lestrade asked.

"That? I honestly don't know. Holmes could have deduced it, but I'm not Holmes. I couldn't even try to guess. Perhaps in the next part of Mary Ardie's plan she intended to rob the Bank of England or steal the Crown Jewels. But she definitely needed to start by destroying Scotland Yard and its ability to respond. And of course, she would also have destroyed any reputation for infallibility that The Yard currently enjoys."

I turned to Mary Ardie now. "You did not destroy Holmes. That was always impossible. You killed a man, yes—but you could never destroy Sherlock Holmes. Despite any inadequacies of my ability to tell his story, Holmes has still become a legend. But your legacy? Your father's legacy? That will always be a small piece of borrowed fame—a piece that will never be more than a history of failure."

With that, I turned and left. She may have said something to my back, but I didn't hear it. There was more, but I needed to leave that damnable space as quickly as possible. It had been a long difficult day and I was at the end of my strength. The effort of this last most difficult confrontation had left me exhausted.

And there is this:

In most of my stories of Holmes, I usually concluded the narrative at the point the criminal is apprehended. In truth, few cases were ever resolved that neatly, and this one was particularly complicated. I had to spend much of the rest of the day and well into the evening explaining to

Lestrade and his assistants, in as much detail as I could manage, how I had put all the separate pieces together. I did not tell them that the voice of Holmes had been a constant irritant in my head. But at last, Lestrade finally drove me back to Baker Street.

The Superintendent made an effort to comfort me. "You mustn't let her words disturb you, sir. The woman had long since abandoned rationality. You cannot let her madness infect you."

"I appreciate your words, Lestrade. I do appreciate the effort. But there is still this—my best friend is dead."

He put his hand on my arm. "Doctor Watson, you must know how important you were to Holmes. He wouldn't want you to feel this way, and neither do I."

I had no answer to that and we rode the rest of the way in silence.

I retired upstairs to the flat I had shared for so long with Holmes. Despite the emptiness of the rooms, I could still feel his presence, as though he were still watching over me, as though his spirit could not be free while I was still sunk in the depths of despair. If that were truly the case, Holmes' spirit could only look forward to a long and dreadful wait.

Two days later, Mrs. Hudson announced a visitor, a senior minister from some unspecified government office. As I was sunk deep inside my own feelings, I took no note of his name. Nor did I rise from my chair.

The man stood just inside the door, holding both his hat and his portfolio before him. "Thank you for seeing me, Doctor Watson. I am here on behalf of Mycroft Holmes. Mr. Holmes apologizes for not coming himself, but as you saw at the funeral, he no longer enjoys the good health of the past and is unable to travel, but he sent me specifically to convey his deepest and most sincere condolences. He feels that no one was closer to his brother than yourself, sir. He admired you for your partnership with him."

"You may tell Mr. Holmes that I am grateful for his thoughts, thank you."

"I shall do that." The man cleared his throat apologetically. "The other purpose of my visit is to deliver this letter to you." He undid the ribbons on his portfolio and pulled out a sealed document. "Mr. Holmes does not know what it says, therefore felt it inappropriate to hand it to you at the funeral."

When I still did not rise from my chair, he laid the letter down on the table—the same table on which the fatal tea service had rested. "There is another matter, as well. But I must be assured of your complete discretion."

I held up my hands in protest. "There is nothing that I need to say to anyone, least of all write it. I doubt there is anything anyone could say that would compel me to take pen to paper again."

"Nevertheless...?" he asked.

"Nevertheless, yes. You may be assured of my discretion."

"Thank you" He cleared his throat and continued. "The Crown owes the Holmes family many debts, obligations that can never be fully repaid. At the request of Mycroft Holmes, the Home Office has authorized me to grant you access to certain information."

I waved my hand at him, a gesture of impatience. "Just say it already."

He cleared his throat again. Either he was coming down with a cold or he was uncomfortable having to speak. I assumed it was the latter. The man looked to the left, then to the right, as if to reassure himself that we were alone. Finally, he spoke, "From time to time, the Home Office has found it expedient to remove the most dangerous individuals from society without public notice. The Home Office wishes to avoid the kind of attention that creates gossip, scandal, and embarrassment—so where conviction is required and where the outcome is certain, trials may be conducted in a sealed court. If the court determines that the accused suffers from criminal derangement, the most dangerous form of insanity, there is an appropriate avenue of action. The Crown has established a very private custodial residence to provide a safe containment for such individuals."

"Yes, I know."

He stopped, surprised. "I beg your pardon?"

I looked at the man directly. "Holmes became aware of this when he examined the mysterious circumstances surrounding the case of Jack the Ripper—and the way those investigations always ended in a chaotic web of deliberate misinformation."

"He never said anything to his brother about it."

"Of course not. He had no reason to. May I assume that you are about to tell me that Mary Ardie will be removed to this—what was your word—containment?"

The deputy coughed nervously. "That name no longer exists. It has been erased from all public records. There remains no evidence that such a person ever lived." He cleared his throat and continued. "But I can tell you that among the poor souls who have been sequestered, the most recent is an unfortunate woman possessed of the most bizarre derangements. Sadly, this poor deluded soul will have to live out her days in severe isolation, lest she infect someone else with her dangerous fantasies."

"I suppose I should be grateful. The woman I'm thinking of deserves only obscurity."

"Then we are in agreement, yes."

"As much as possible, I suppose so."

"Thank you," he said.

After the man from the Home Office left, I picked up the letter, already fearing to read what was written there.

It was Holmes' own handwriting, as familiar as my own. "In the event of my death, deliver this letter to Doctor John H. Watson. (signed) Sherlock Holmes."

My hands trembled. I broke the wax seal and fumbled the note out of the envelope.

"My dear Watson,

"Our work shall never be completed, not by either of us. There is too much to be done in the science of deduction. Future generations will now inherit the responsibility. How I envy them, the tools they will have and the discoveries they will make.

"Toward that end, you are authorized to organize all of my files, notes, and papers with the intention of preserving anything that may advance the study of forensic investigation. Whatever you think appropriate, you may pass on to Scotland Yard. You may do so as the sole custodian of our partnership.

"But finally, Watson, there is one additional matter I must address. As much as I have cherished and appreciated all of our time together, I have equally disapproved of the manner in which you have portrayed our work together. Despite the clear and direct purposefulness of your narratives, there was one unforgivable error that you continued to make throughout your entire literary career. Your presentation of yourself and your collaboration in our investigations was woefully inaccurate.

"In your many accounts of our cases, you frequently accentuated my gifts, and downplayed your own considerable skills, thereby diminishing your many significant contributions. The logical error that this introduces in your narratives is the assumption that the man portrayed as me would find any use in the man you portrayed as yourself.

My dearest Watson, you must take this into your heart. The most valuable aspect of my entire career was our alliance, and the most valuable part of my personal life was our friendship. Be assured, Watson, that I have greatly treasured you in all of our days together.

Very sincerely yours,

Sherlock Holmes

I read the letter twice more. These were his final words to me and I could hear his voice in every sentence.

As carefully as I could, I folded the letter and put it back into its envelope. I sat for a moment, holding it. In that moment, I distinctly felt his presence behind me as though he were standing there in the flesh. "Holmes," I said. "I shall ever regard you as the best and the wisest man I have ever known."

"And you, Watson," I heard him reply. "And you as well."

ABOUT THE AUTHOR

David Gerrold has been writing professionally for half a century. He created the tribbles for STAR TREK and the Sleestaks for LAND OF THE LOST. His most famous novel is THE MAN WHO FOLDED HIMSELF.

His semi-autobiographical tale of his son's adoption, THE MARTIAN CHILD won both the Hugo and the Nebula awards, and was the basis for the 2007 movie starring John Cusack and Amanda Peet.

His latest novel is **HELLA**, available on Amazon.

If you enjoyed this story and would like to see more, you can find more at

www.facebook.com/DavidGerrold

and

www.patreon.com/DavidGerrold